THE SHADOW CROSSER

Also by J. C. Cervantes

The Storm Runner
The Fire Keeper

THE
SHADOW CROSSER

J. C. CERVANTES

RICK RIORDAN PRESENTS

Disney • HYPERION   LOS ANGELES   NEW YORK

First Edition, September 2020
1 3 5 7 9 10 8 6 4 2
Printed in the United States of America
FAC-021131-20199

This book is set in Aldus Nova Pro/Monotype;
Cocotte, Genplan Pro, Vonn Handwriting/Fontspring
Designed by Phil Buchanan

Library of Congress Cataloging-in-Publication Data
Names: Cervantes, Jennifer, author.
Title: The Shadow Crosser : a Storm Runner novel / by J.C. Cervantes.
Description: First edition. • Los Angeles : Disney-Hyperion, 2020. • "Rick Riordan presents." • Audience: Ages 8–12. • Audience: Grades 4–6. • Summary: "When a few Mexica gods try to put their Maya counterparts out of commission, it's up to Zane and some godborns-in-training to save the universe"— Provided by publisher.
Identifiers: LCCN 2019037905 (print) • LCCN 2019037906 (ebook) • ISBN 9781368052771 (hardcover) • ISBN 9781368055482 (ebook)
Subjects: CYAC: Maya mythology—Fiction. • People with disabilities—Fiction. • Friendship—Fiction. • Maya gods—Fiction.
Classification: LCC PZ7.C3198 Sh 2020 (print) • LCC PZ7.C3198 (ebook) • DDC [Fic]—dc23
LC record available at https://lccn.loc.gov/2019037905
LC ebook record available at https://lccn.loc.gov/2019037906

Reinforced binding
Follow @ReadRiordan
Visit www.DisneyBooks.com

For Alex, because the world needs another Batman

Dear Reader,

You were probably expecting this letter to be from Zane Obispo, our young hero. But this book is different from the other two. Zane, a worthy scribe, could not write the introduction this time. There is a reason—one you may or may not like, depending on the type of narrative you prefer.

I, for one, did not enjoy parts of this account—neither the tragedy and sorrow, nor the terror and darkness. Like the other Maya gods, I was ripped from my life and thrown into the middle of this twisted, sordid tale. Sadly, none of us saw the end coming. I doubt you will, either.

Nevertheless, like all stories, this one must be recorded and preserved. By reading it, you are giving energy to the words on the page and feeding a much greater magic for all storytellers everywhere. Thank you for doing your part. Truly, I am sorry for what you are about to experience.

Yours in story,

Itzamna

1

•

My life pretty much tanked the night I left home with a two-thousand-year-old demon.

Wait. *Tanked* isn't the right word. It was more of a slow unraveling, like a thread that comes loose in an old sweater and can never be fixed, no matter how hard you try. All you can do is wait for the dumb hole to get bigger one centimeter at a time.

I should have seen the signs, but in my defense, I was distracted. You would have been, too, if you had spent the last three months, two days, and sixteen hours sleeping in fleabag motels, eating cardboard hamburgers and soggy tater tots, and catching nasty whiffs of Iktan's demon breath. For the record, demons don't brush their fangs. And two thousand years is a long time to go without Colgate!

As if that weren't bad enough, my mom had told me that, regardless of the fact that I was godborn-hunting, I had to do all my distance education homework, which meant hours hunched over my iPad. I had also spent way more time than I wanted to admit looking over my shoulder, expecting Camazotz (Mr. Bat God) to appear out of a trail of black fog so he could rip off my head with his iron claws. I was pretty sure he had dreamed of nothing else since our battle in the junkyard.

So, yeah, I was ready to go home. Back to Isla Holbox, where everything was sun and sea and safety. I was *so* close, I felt like I could practically fall over the finish line. Because, tonight, Iktan had tracked down the very last godborn I was trying to find: lucky number sixty-four.

The night had started like this:

I tumbled headfirst out of a gateway into a dark alley littered with aluminum cans, Chinese-food take-out boxes, and a sofa hemorrhaging its stuffing. The air was thick and muggy. "Just this once," I groaned to Ik, "could you make a gateway that doesn't spin me on extra high and smell like leftover death?"

Tonight, the demon had taken the form of an eleven-year-old human girl with a gap-toothed smile and braided reddish hair. She wore denim overalls and a shirt patterned with little red hearts. But I knew what lay underneath all that.

A green neon sign on the wall above us gave her a sickly glow. If I looked super close, I could see her natural blue pallor underneath the fake human one. Iktan altered her appearance as quickly as someone might change a mask, constantly seeking a disguise that wouldn't make her itch all over, which was never going to happen, because she was allergic to human flesh. The best part of her allergy? She couldn't eat humans.

"Death is an acquired smell, Zane," Ik said, scratching her dimpled chin. "Urgh. Human skin is like poison ivy. What a stupid invention."

"Skin, or poison ivy?" And, technically, neither is an invention, but I wasn't about to have *that* convo right then.

She growled. "Both!"

Whatever. Nothing was going to put me in a bad mood. If all went as planned, in a couple of hours I would be rid of Itchy Ik and her reeking, churning gateways. I grunted, getting to my feet with the help of Fuego, my cane/spear. I was born with a limp—one leg is shorter than the other—and my cane helps me bolt when I need to, like if I'm about to be sliced open by some bloodthirsty monster. Fuego also conveniently turns into a spear when I have to defend myself against said monster. It was a present from my dad, the Maya god Hurakan.

"So, where are we?" I asked.

"Hell's Kitchen. *Hardly* hellish, if you ask me." Ik gave a hard grunt. "To be more specific, New York City."

"*This* is New York?" I stabbed a wedge of discarded Styrofoam with my cane, thinking that this dark, seedy alley looked like none of the pictures I'd ever seen of the shining city.

Iktan kicked an empty soda can under the sofa with a huff. "I know. How could a place this nice be Murderers' Row? What a big fat disappointment."

"At least we won't be here long," I said.

Tugging on a braid, Ik said, "Anything to eat in this place? I'm starving."

"We ate, like, ten minutes ago."

"Yeah, well, you don't have a demon's appetite, do you? And I'd hardly call chicken fingers eating. No blood, no bones . . ." She scrunched up her face in disgust. "And why do they call them chicken fingers, anyway? Chickens don't even *have* fingers! Only tasty, crunchy feet . . ."

"I think it's because we eat them with our fingers?"

Just then, Ik's head snapped up, her eyes burning red, a snarl curling her lips. Crap! I knew that look—she was getting ready to hunt. My stomach squeezed tight.

A white cat leaped off a rusty dumpster and zipped down the alley. My arm shot out to prevent the demon from following, but I wasn't fast enough.

Ik streaked toward the cat like a tornado.

"No!" I shouted.

A few seconds later, I reached the demon at the dead end of the alley. She was hunched over with her back to me. Breathless groans erupted from her throat, and I swallowed hard. I did *not* want to see matted cat fur stuck between her teeth. I'd seen it before, and believe me, it was muy disgusting. But when she turned around, she was empty-handed.

My very first thought was: *Yay! No blood anywhere.*

"It disappeared." She panted, and her pupils expanded so big her eyes looked black. I wished hard that she wouldn't dress up like a kid. It was seriously disturbing.

I looked around. How had the cat escaped?

She pushed her bangs off her big forehead. "It must have fallen into a gateway."

"Cats don't just fall into gateways," I argued. Heck, *nothing* accidentally tumbles into the magical portals that gods and sobrenaturals use.

"It's happened once or twice," she said with a huff.

I had a hard time believing her. She was probably trying to save face for failing to catch a skinny gatito.

"I don't make the gateways. They're all around us." She

let out a forced laugh. "Oh, that's right—you can't see them, because you're not as powerful as I am."

I ignored her 183rd insult and, since I'd never met a demon who knew how to kid around, asked, "Really? People and animals can just, like, disappear into them?"

"It's rare." She glanced up like she was trying to recall something. "Everything has to align just right. Something about angles, rising planets, unflossed teeth, and other stuff. I never paid attention, because I don't really care what happens to humans. It's depressing enough that I have to hang out with you."

"So that's how you've been getting us everywhere so fast." I'd always wondered how come Iktan never needed a gateway map like the one my friend Brooks and I once had to use.

"How many times do I have to tell you?" Ik growled. "Demons are superior to godborns."

Sure, okay. Like I said, nothing was going to ruin my almost-home good mood. Not even an egotistical itchy demon. But there was something different about Iktan tonight—something I couldn't name. "Come on," I said. "Let's go find this godborn."

"I still don't understand why we've had to go to all this trouble for a few pathetic half-breeds," she grumbled, falling into step with me. "And please do not bore me again by telling me about your vow to Ixtab."

I'd promised the queen of the underworld that I would find all the remaining godborn children who were still out there. They deserved to know the truth about who they really were.

"Let's hurry up and get this over with," Ik went on. She

might have looked like a little kid, but she sounded like a mean army sergeant. "You know the drill. We establish visual contact, assess the situation, then—"

"I make my move."

"I was going to say 'go in for the kill.'"

"Enough with the kill stuff, okay?"

"Such a killjoy," she muttered before asking, "So, do you feel anything?"

"Yeah," I said. "Nausea from your death gateway."

"Focus harder! You never see me taking this long to do *my* job," she whined. "Like I said, superior."

Her only job was to track the godborns. The rest was up to me.

And my blood.

That's right. I'd had to make a deposit (half a pint, to be exact) into the craptastic Blood Bank of Ik, so she could learn the "stink" we godborns share. Ever since she'd sniffed my blood from a cup, she could pick up a godborn's odor from miles away. Demons don't have very sensitive noses (unless their prey is right in front of them, like the cat); instead, they have these little scent receptors that pop out of their necks (it's way beyond gross) like tentacles. Iktan could follow a single godborn trail, laid down more than forty-eight hours before, even in a crowd as big as ten thousand.

But Ixtab, being a meticulous goddess, had added an extra layer of security. Ik could only get me within half a mile of the godborn before the demon would lose the trace. I had to do the rest, using what I call my GPS—godborn positioning system. Whenever I got close to a godborn, I'd feel this kind of cold pull in my gut. I experienced it for the first time when my bruja friend, Ren, washed up on the shore of Holbox. Since then, all my time on the road had only made my skill stronger. Or, as Ixtab said, *fine-tuned*.

"It's this way," I said, leading Ik out of the alley and around the corner. The neighborhood was pretty sketchy at this time of night, with drunks staggering around, lost-looking tourists rolling their suitcases behind them, and a few homeless people hunkering down in shuttered doorways.

Ik looked around. "So where is the little beast?"

I turned in a slow circle, waiting for the connection to grow, to tell me which direction to take, but it was like something was jamming the frequency.

Or some*one*.

2

••

"Well?" Ik barked.

"Could you be quiet? I'm concentrating." The signal was weak, but I cut right and headed down West Forty-Sixth Street. Stopping midway down the block, I turned around. "You're sure this is the right area?"

Ik pressed her lips together like a curse word was wedged in the corner of her mouth. "Listen, Fire Boy, demons have the most sophisticated tracking ability in the universe, and all you godborns have the same stinky blood." Dozens of three-inch blue spikes popped out of her neck, wiggling like worms on a hook. "We must be getting real close now, 'cause I'm comin' up empty."

"Could you *not* do that whole creepy tentacle thing in public?" Chills ran up my spine.

"Someone sounds *jealousss*," she hissed, stretching the last *s* for way too long.

"Uh-huh. I've already done this sixty-three times," I reminded her, scanning the street.

Ik rubbed her forehead impatiently. "Then be the pro you think you are and find the mutt."

Long, lean shadows stretched across the asphalt. A cab rolled by slowly. Lights blinked off in the apartments above.

A slow-burn fire began to rise in my blood. "Something isn't right."

"I have an idea," Ik said semi-brightly. "Let's go over what you're going to say. Loosen you up."

"No thanks." I kept moving.

"Do you just walk up to the godborns and say, 'Hey, you're part Maya god. Come with me or else'?"

"Not exactly."

Up until now, I hadn't let Ik stick around for any of the encounters. Lowering the godborn boom on the kids was enough of a shock—I didn't feel like also explaining that I was hanging with a demon in disguise. Plus, two to one always makes a person feel ganged up on.

I focused on the connection that was getting stronger with each step. "I also tell them about the World Tree, where they can learn about their abilities and get trained in how to use them."

"Okay. Then, after all that, do you tell them that Camazotz wants to feed their hearts to the Mexica gods?"

"Keep your voice down!" For half a second, I imagined burning off Ik's eyebrows with a single spark from my fingertip. Instead, I whispered, "If you have to know, yes. I tell them about Zotz's plan to use godborns to resurrect the Mexica gods and how it *failed*. They deserve to know the truth."

Ik's face turned bright red, and I thought smoke might start curling out of her ears. What was her problem? She took a couple of deep calming breaths. "How noble of you."

More often than not, the truth worked. Most of the kids were pretty psyched to find out they had a godly parent and might have inherited a power of some sort, especially after I showed them my fire-shooting skills. I was always careful to leave the enemies-ripping-out-their-hearts stuff for last. By then, they were usually too distracted by the word *power* to care about anything else.

But, if I'm being totally honest, not everyone had been pumped about the news. A few godborns had thrown up or passed out. The runners were the worst—I hated chasing them down. In the end, curiosity always won out. So far . . .

The godborns' human parents had a different reaction, but more about that later.

My blood ran hotter. Why couldn't I shake this feeling? I twisted my hands around Fuego and tried to push the sensation away, but it punched me in the chest anyway.

There was no doubt about it: we were being watched. Or maybe I was just being paranoid. I mean, no one could be following us. Ik always released her magical misty whatever to cover our tracks so completely that even if we were ambushed and thrown into an underground cave, no one, not even Xib'alb'a's best tracking demons or hellhounds, would find our leftovers.

"Uh . . ." I glanced over my shoulder at the dark and empty sidewalk. "Do you have a feeling something is way off?"

"You're *that* guy, huh?"

"That guy?"

"The one in the scary movie that everyone should have listened to before they got murdered." She rubbed her stomach. "Can you hurry it up so I can eat?"

Just then, my phone rang. Mom had bought it for me,

saying that if I was going to hunt with demons, she had to be able to reach me.

"A thousand bucks it isn't that girl." Ik leaned closer, nasty breath and all, to get a look at the phone's screen. "Ha! Told you. Don't answer it."

Ik had spent the last three months telling me all the reasons why Brooks hadn't called. *She doesn't care. She thinks you're boring. She's just not that into you.* But no way would my best friend, the awesome shape-shifter who had saved my hide more than once, ghost me. Even if Brooks *had* read all that sappy stuff I wrote about her in my first book, the one Ixtab had forced me to write. Stupid truth paper!

My best guess was that Brooks had joined some undercover network with her sister, Quinn, and couldn't talk to anyone.

I answered the FaceTime call. "Hey, Hondo."

My uncle's smiling face filled the screen. Ren's silvery-blue eye loomed in the corner. "You'll get a chance to talk to him," Hondo said to her with a grunt. "Move over."

"You don't need the whole screen," the godborn argued.

"Hey, guys?" I said. "I'm kinda busy right now."

My dog, Rosie, whined in the background as Ren grabbed the phone away from Hondo. "My phone tracker says you're in New York?" She had thought it was a good idea to share locations with each other. Just in case.

Ik tapped her foot. "Tell them you can't talk. Don't they know we're on an important mission?"

"Did you find number sixty-four?" Hondo shouted from the background.

"I'm working on it now."

"Oh, good." Ren smiled. "Then you'll be home tonight?" She flashed what looked like a notecard. "We got another invitation, with the same instructions as before: Don't pack anything. Don't bring your phone. Blah, blah, blah."

"I am *not* going to wear a SHIHOM uniform," Hondo chimed in.

He was talking about the Shaman Institute of Higher-Order Magic at the World Tree. All the godborns were supposed to report there next week for summer training. My uncle, a full-blooded human, was going to teach combat and meditation and stuff.

I pressed my face closer to the screen. "Why did we get a second invitation, do you think?"

Ik made a bored face and mouthed, *Who cares?*

Ren shrugged. "They want everyone to report sooner."

Iktan's tentacles popped out. "Sooner?" she whispered.

"As in the day after tomorrow, first thing in the morning," Hondo said. "And they better have all the equipment I ordered for the kick-butt drills I have planned."

"Why did they change the date?" I asked as Ik nodded vigorously. How come she was so interested in our schedule all of a sudden? It wasn't like *she* was heading to SHIHOM.

Ren said, "Guess we'll find out when we get there."

The gods had reasons for everything they did (mostly related to stuff that was best for them), so yeah, I had a bunch of red flags slapping me in the face about then.

Ik snatched the phone away, ended the call, and turned off my phone. Thin trails of black smoke floated from her eyes.

"Hey!" I shouted.

Tossing the phone back to me, she frowned. "You're letting outside stuff get in the way of this mission. Now get your brain in the game so we can get out of here. You're not the only one with a schedule to keep."

I widened the distance between us and took a deep breath, focusing all my energy on the last godborn. The signal grew stronger and stronger. I followed it . . . then froze in mid-step. "This can't be right."

Ik glanced around. "I don't see any mutts."

I pointed to a darkened store across the road. "The god-born is inside the antiques store."

"The one with the Closed sign in the window?"

Right. What was a kid doing in a closed antiques shop at ten thirty on a Wednesday night? Maybe it was a family business or something.

"Are you sure?" Ik asked, and I swear she started drooling.

"One hundred percent." I threw her a side-glance. "Need a napkin?"

I crossed the avenue, cut between some parked cars, and stalked toward the store window. Ik was right behind me.

"Did I ever tell you why the Statue of Liberty is blue?" she whispered.

"That's random, and she's actually green." I crouched at the edge of the window front, trying not to be seen as I peered into the shop. Two hooded figures lurked inside.

So which one was the godborn? My GPS should have been screaming at me by now, pointing its finger with total accuracy, but it was like . . .

Whoa!

Was that even possible? They were *both* godborns?

I wanted to ask Ik why her "superior tracking" had only picked up one, but she was still fixated on the Statue of Liberty.

"Its sculptor was a demon," Ik offered. "He wanted to pay homage to all demons everywhere."

My eyes were trained on the taller godborn with square shoulders. The one inspecting something in their palm while the other inched closer to get a better look. And then the something began to glow red. What the holy heck?

"Do you know why he wanted to pay homage?" Ik's voice turned gravelly.

Why was she still talking about this? I ignored her, pressing my forehead against the window. "I think . . . they're stealing something," I muttered. "It's glowing."

"Because the statue is a reminder that demons are the *real* lords, superior to *everyone.*"

The taller godborn's head jerked up. Our eyes met.

I was so focused on what was *beyond* the glass, I didn't notice the reflection *in* the glass until it was too late.

Shining black eyes, a twisted smile, and murderous claws raised and ready.

Just as I snapped back, Ik's talon slashed my cheek. I cried out. The pain was instant, the venom fast.

"Foolish, foolish boy," Iktan tutted. "Never trust a demon."

Fuego slipped from my grasp as my knees buckled. I collapsed and my head slammed into the concrete. The world slanted. Glass shattered. Agony ripped through me.

"Don't blink, Zane," Ik whispered in my ear. "The bat god is coming for you."

And the last thing I saw before my eyelids closed was a shimmer in the air and the rush of familiar dark wings.

3

•••

I heard a shuffle. Grunts, pounding footsteps.
A store security alarm pierced the air.

And then I was lifted up, up, up. With a mighty struggle,
I opened my eyes.

Brooks!

I would have pumped my fist if I could have felt my arms.
But I was as floppy as a half-full garbage bag, and when she
set me down on a rooftop, I crumpled in a heap of worthless
pain. Stupid demons. Stupid venom.

Brooks kneeled next to me. Her expression was focused,
intense. Scared.

Man, was I happy to see her. She's the one you want
by your side in life-or-death situations. She *squeeeezed* the
wound, trying to drain the poison. Okay, I never said she
was gentle.

I think I screamed. The venom raced through my blood
fast and furious, like hot acid. My chest seized as if an iron
fist were gripping my heart tighter and tighter.

"Zane!" she cried. "This isn't working. You have to burn
it out!"

My words came out in a slur. "Ik ... traitor ... godbor ..."
I tried to roll over, but my arms and legs weren't getting the

message, and to be honest, I was having trouble breathing. Little black dots danced in my vision.

Brooks grasped my head, forcing me to look into her fierce amber eyes as she shook me. "Are you listening?! Start a fire to burn it out of your system. It's the only way!"

Listen to the nawal.

I did a mental double take. That was the voice of Itzamna, the glittering god, in my head. Was he here?

Do it now, Zane!

I reached for the heat inside me, the flames that were as much a part of me as my beating heart. The poison sped up, shredding my insides.

Fire. Fire. Come on!

It's terrifying to sense your life slipping away. I'd felt something similar when I'd fought Ah-Puch, the god of death, but that moment had been big and loud and filled with do-or-die adrenaline. This was different. This time I was battling a silent, invisible monster racing through my blood. It wasn't quite as big-screen epic. Plus, who wants to die on a rooftop in Hell's Kitchen?

I concentrated with what little part of my brain was still working. Just when I thought the poison was about to pull me under for good, I heard Itzamna's voice again:

Listen, Storm Runner, unless you want this to be the end of the story, you really need to start a fire. Do I need to provide the match, too?

I reached for the power in my Storm Runner leg. I sensed a flicker and then . . .

"ZANE!" Brooks shouted.

"Get back!" I managed. The second Brooks inched away, heat blazed in my leg. Fire surged through my blood like lightning, hunting for the dirty, rotten, double-crossing demon's poison.

Blue flames erupted from my body and leaped high into the sky. The relief was instant. I waited a couple of seconds before I called the fire back. Then, breathless, I rolled to my feet and looked around.

Brooks held out Fuego, and the moment I grabbed him, she threw her arms around me and hugged me so tight, I stumbled back. It felt good. Make that *great*. She let go and shoved me in the chest. "You could have died!"

"Did you see Itzamna?"

She gave me a watery stare. "What? No! Did you hear me? You could have died."

"Are you going to cry?" I asked.

She was. She was totally going to cry, which could only mean one thing. She didn't *want* me to die. She *needed* me around. She'd missed me!

Brooks wiped her eyes and hugged me a second time. Then she shoved me again. "I think all that fire fried your brain." She studied me. "And you got taller."

I was definitely going to melt under the heat of her hawk eyes.

I took a few blinks to cool off my brain, to let everything resonate. "That poison," I said. "It was like some super-enhanced version."

"Super enhanced?"

"Yeah, I mean, it was *nothing* like the venom I felt back in the volcano last year." Before Brooks could start spouting off theories, I said, "Wait. Where's Ik, and . . . why are you here?"

"Quinn went after the demon." Her words spilled out in a rush. "I . . . I headed straight for you. I wasn't about to let you die on a dirty sidewalk!" Her eyes roamed my face. Police car sirens sounded from the street below.

"The godborns! We can't let them get arrested."

"Or Quinn!" Brooks turned her back to me and ordered, "Grab my shoulders."

I needed both hands, so with a single thought—*poof!*—my cane disappeared. The coolest feature of the new and improved Fuego (other than being stronger) is that instead of transforming into a puny letter opener (Ixtab's idea), it now changed into a quarter-size tattoo on the back of my hand: a black jaguar head in profile, with a golden eye (Dad's idea).

I took hold of Brooks's shoulders as she shifted into her ginormous hawk self. Having a shape-shifting best friend is cool, but having one that can fly with you on her back? Way cooler.

We soared over the roof's edge. Red and blue lights flashed on the scene below. The antiques store window was busted, its glass scattered all over the sidewalk, but there was no sign of Ik, Quinn, or the godborns. Brooks flew higher and out of view.

Whenever we were touching, Brooks and I could communicate via telepathy. Using it now, I said to her, *Up there at the corner. Go right.* My GPS told me the godborns were still in the area. If they got any farther away, I wouldn't be able to track them down. *My GPS sort of went down earlier. What do you think messed with it?*

Sorry about that, Brooks said. *Probably too many sobrenaturals around. All that magic can twist things sometimes.* She tilted left, her wings spread wide as she increased her speed. *I sense Quinn down there, too. Maybe she's with them.*

What if Iktan got to the godborns first? I asked. A ripple of panic crawled up my spine. *She's working for Zotz, but why? It doesn't make sense!*

You're right. Nothing about that demon makes sense, Brooks said. *We've been investigating her for a while, Zane.*

And you didn't feel like telling me?

It's called "undercover" for a reason. We had to be sure. Did you say "godborns" plural? Ik only reported one.

There's two, I said. *I'm sure of it. What do you mean "reported"?*

Iktan was calling in her progress to someone, but we don't know who. We didn't know she was going to attack you.

You set me up!

No! I swear. We had no idea any of this was going to happen, which is why we followed you so closely. Iktan hasn't called in a report for over a week. Something is off, Zane. Very, very off.

It made me feel better to think I wasn't Brooks and Quinn's guinea pig. "Down there," I said aloud, pointing to a dimly lit parking lot surrounded by a chain-link fence. "See that far corner? That's where the godborns are."

Brooks didn't follow my direction. Big surprise. Instead, she headed to the opposite end of the lot. "Brooks! I said the other corner."

Quinn is down there. I need to find her first, learn what happened before we just rush in.

Okay, so nothing had changed in the last three months. Brooks was still the ultimate planner.

A second later, we'd landed and found Brooks's sister. She was in the form of a very familiar white cat, perched on the hood of a gold Honda, licking her paws like she had nothing better to do. Ha! So that's why Ik had failed her feline-for-dinner mission—Quinn, another powerful shape-shifter, had probably changed into a flea at the last second.

Quinn and Brooks reassumed their human forms. Quinn wore white jeans with rips in the knees and a gray sleeveless sweater. Brooks was in her signature black leggings and plain tee with a white sweatshirt tied around her waist.

Pressing her finger to her lips, Quinn tugged me into a crouched position between a row of cars and telepathically informed me that Ik had disappeared when she went after her. *I followed the kids here,* she added. *They're hiding out in a car at the opposite end of the lot.*

They'd found an unlocked car? *We need to talk to them before they try to take off again,* I told her.

I rigged the gate so they can't get out. And don't forget, they just saw a demon, Quinn said. *Believe me, they're too scared to go anywhere. But we do need to hurry. No doubt Iktan will be coming back with an army.*

Reaching into her boot, Brooks tugged the gateway map free. She studied it with a frown.

I explained that Ik wouldn't be able to find the godborns without me, because she couldn't sniff them out within half a mile. For maybe the hundredth time, I was super glad for Ixtab's magic, born from her brilliant, cautious, overly skeptical mind.

"Nothing to stop her from tracking Quinn and me, though," Brooks whispered as she scanned the map. "Maybe you shouldn't be here."

"This is my mission," I argued. No way was I going to abandon the last two godborns or Brooks and Quinn. "Let's just be quick."

"Any gateways nearby to get us to Isla Holbox?" Quinn asked Brooks.

"We're taking the godborns to my house?"

Quinn quirked an eyebrow. "It's still surrounded by Ixtab's shadow magic. We'll be safe there until we can figure out next steps." Then she turned to Brooks. "Any luck?"

Brooks's frown got deeper. "Just give me a couple more minutes. I'll figure it out."

Quinn filled me in on some of the undercover work they'd been doing over the last few months. When it was my turn to talk, the sisters just kept nodding like I wasn't telling them anything they didn't already know. Then it hit me. "Were you . . . were you guys watching me the whole time?" No wonder Brooks hadn't called. She was too busy spying on me!

"Ik . . ." Brooks's cheeks flushed. "We were watching *Ik*."

Apparently, part of Quinn's assignment in Xib'alb'a (the stuff she couldn't tell me about when I'd last seen her down there) was related to a tip that Ixtab herself might be a conspirator with Camazotz. No way could that be true. There were so many other much more credible suspects. I mean, the bat god *had* once called the underworld home, so it made sense that he still had friends there. I was about to argue on behalf of Ixtab, when Quinn added that the intel had led nowhere. Relief spread through me.

Right. Ixtab was the queen of the underworld, probably the most duplicitous of all the gods, so why should I care?

Because she'd saved my life more than once. And Rosie's. Not to mention she reunited the god council and stopped my dad's public execution. All that counted for a lot in my book.

Quinn said, "The traitors ended up being some demons in Ixtab's army."

"But Ik wasn't one of them," Brooks chimed in, turning the map upside down.

"It's like Iktan came out of nowhere." Quinn twisted her mouth like she was considering a new idea. "That's why we were following your moves. To see if we could find out what she was after."

"I still don't get what Ik or the bat god wants with these godborns. We've already gone down that road. Our blood isn't powerful enough to resurrect a Mexica god."

"I don't know," Quinn said. "But whatever it is, these godborns are different and somehow necessary to Zotz's plans."

Brooks showed the map to Quinn, pointing to a spot. "There's a gateway in a laundromat ten blocks from here. We have twenty-six minutes before it closes, so let's do this." She folded up the map and stuck it back in her boot.

I thought about what Ik had said about gateways being all around, and I wondered how many invisible ones were looming right in front of us.

"Hang on," I said to Brooks. "Are you . . . are you working for the White Sparkstriker tribe now, too?" Quinn had joined the super-secret group of spies to get out of marrying Jordan, one of the obnoxious hero twins. Maybe she'd recruited Brooks.

A clanking sound caught our attention. The kids were climbing the fence about twenty yards away.

"Showtime," Quinn said, sweeping an arm in front of her body dramatically as if to say *You're up.*

I began to make my way over, when Brooks jerked me back.

"What's wrong?"

She tugged off her sweatshirt and started to reach for my face with it. Then she changed her mind and tossed it to me instead. "You're bleeding."

"Awww." Quinn fluttered her eyelashes melodramatically.

I blushed so hard my cheeks felt like they might melt right off my face.

Scowling at her sister, Brooks groaned. "He can't just walk up to them all bloody. Blood freaks some people out, okay?"

"Right," Quinn said with one corner of her mouth turned up. "I'll wait on the other side, just in case they succeed in climbing over the fence." She shifted back into the white cat and darted into the shadows.

I wiped my face, then tossed the dirty sweatshirt under a car, promising to replace it. But Brooks had already taken to the sky.

My mind shifted gears. Something was missing from the puzzle—something no one had thought of yet. Why did I have the feeling it had everything to do with that antiques shop and whatever the godborns had stolen?

I looked down at the jaguar tattoo on my hand and willed Fuego to reappear.

Then I headed toward the thieves.

4

••••

With Fuego's help, I cut across the lot in three
seconds. This new version of my cane made me a speed demon
when I needed to be. Okay, bad choice of words. It made me
fast. *Really* fast.

I stood directly beneath the kids, who were halfway up the
ten-foot-high fence. Here's the thing about my approach: It
had to be just right. Smooth but not fake. Calm but not tired.
Alert but not stalkerish. These two looked like the kind who
would appreciate the whole less-is-more thing. So I took a
deep breath and started with "Hey."

They stared down at me as they white-knuckled the chain
link. Their hoods kept most of their faces in shadow.

"Get away from us!" the taller one said. His voice was
gruff, but it teetered on panic.

"I just want to talk," I said. I felt like a cop handling a hos-
tage taker and every word had to be perfect or else.

Quinn emerged from the shadows on the other side of
the fence. But not as a white cat. Say hello to the massive
German shepherd with a growl that shook the warm air. Very
subtle. NOT.

The godborns were trapped.

"How about some chill, Quinn?" I said behind clenched

teeth. Then I called up to the godborns, "I bet you're wondering about the whole demon thing. Scary, I know. But I have answers, and I'm a lot nicer than that shepherd is."

Brooks circled overhead before landing on the top of the fence as a regular-size hawk. Okay, that was better than a ginormous hawk that might have plunged these guys even deeper into a sea of panic. But still, did she really have to do the whole glowy-eye thing?

This was so much easier when I did it alone.

"My name is Zane," I said to the godborns. "I'm like you."

All I got were vacant stares.

I kept going. "I remember the first time I saw a demon—it totally freaked me out. He was flying this twin-engine plane all borracho like, and it crashed into the volcano in my backyard and . . ." More blank expressions. "Look, I'm here to help you. I promise. Just come down so we can talk."

They peered up at Brooks, then down at Quinn before exchanging a glance. They must have decided I was the safer choice, because they hopped down like ninjas and faced me. I wasn't sure if I should be offended or happy.

We were only a few feet apart. My eyes cut through the shadows but couldn't see under their hoods.

The shorter one reached up and pulled theirs back. Dark curly hair with bright red tips spilled out past her shoulders. "We don't need your help," she said.

Quinn snarled, baring some seriously long fangs.

My gaze drifted to killer canine and back. "Uh, I kinda think you do."

The other one shook off their hood. His black hair was cropped close to his head. Like all the other godborns, they looked about my age. The guy was only a couple of inches shorter than me but definitely bulkier. As the pair stood side by side, I saw that they had the same brown eyes with gray flecks, the same dark skin, the same willful chin. They were twins.

Look, I don't have anything against twins in general. Just Jordan and Bird, the heinous magical mafia pair who want to gut me and hang my organs out to dry. So it's totally normal that my first thought was *PLEASE do not be like those guys*.

Lurking in the shadows wasn't going to earn their trust, so I risked a small step closer to give them a better view of my super-friendly face.

"Stay where you are," the guy warned. His eyes cut across the lot like he was looking for the best escape route.

I held up one hand in surrender. I couldn't blame them for being scared. First they encounter a full-on crazed demon, and then some stranger with animal friends shows up and tries to make nice. "Listen . . ." I said in a calming tone. "I know this is nuts, but I have a lot to tell you and not a lot of time to do it."

"We know why you're here," the girl said. Even though her voice quivered, she looked like the kind of person who would do everything to avoid a fight but *anything* to win one.

"And you aren't getting your hands on it." Her brother's face hardened in defiance.

It?

Then the boy said, "No matter what," as he shook his fist at me. Actually shook his fist! And not even in a tough-guy way. More like an *I-stayed-up-all-night-watching-YouTube-videos-on-how-to-look-threatening* way.

The godborns exchanged a glance, and if I didn't know better, I would have thought they were talking telepathically—a gift all godborns have, but only if there's physical contact. But the twins were standing at least three feet apart.

A sudden rush of wings and shimmering air turned the situation (which I had under total control, by the way) into a "Wow" (from the girl) and under-the-breath curses (that was the guy).

Brooks landed next to me in human form, wiped her hands, and flashed a painted-on smile. "I'm Brooks, your neighborhood nawal, also known as a shape-shifter. That dog on the other side of the fence is my sister, Quinn. This is Zane, son of Hurakan, Maya god of storms, wind, and fire. That nasty demon from earlier? She wants something you have—most likely your hearts. We're here to save you." She took a breath, smiled again. "Oh, and we're wasting time and risking everything by standing here talking about it. Can we go now?"

The twins' shocked gazes shifted from me to Brooks, then back to me like they were trying to decide who was in charge, or maybe who would be slower when they decided to bolt.

"Nawal," the girl muttered. "God. Demon." She ticked off each word with her fingers, side-glancing at her brother.

After a few seconds (or maybe telepathic words), he exhaled in relief. "It's not them, Alana."

Them? Were they expecting someone else? And did their eyes just flash blue? By the time I took a second look, their ojos were brown again.

Quinn shifted back to her human form and leaned against the fence. "Can you guys speed this up a little? By my calculations, we've got about twenty-two minutes before our gateway closes. And even less than that before Ik shows up to claim her prize."

The guy tugged his sister behind him, creating more distance between us before he said, "You think we're stupid?"

Was that a trick question? "How should I know? I just met you." *And you* did *just break into an antiques shop and trip the alarm....* But that could have just been sloppy thieving. "We really do have to get going."

"Yeah, well, we're not dumb." The girl lifted her chin toward Brooks, but it felt forced, like she was trying to look unafraid. "Everyone knows demons like blood and bones the best," she said. "Hearts are tough and chewy. Not their favorite."

Whoa! "Who told you that?" I asked. How could they possibly know about demon eating habits? Even *I* didn't even know much about their preferences, aside from the fact that they liked to hunt down anything on two or four legs.

"How do we know *you're* not a demon?" the guy said as he inched back. He started to raise his fist again, but his sister shot him a look that said *You already pulled that card.*

"That's fair," Brooks muttered.

I tightened my grip on Fuego's dragon-head handle as I tried to remain patient. "I'm not a demon. I'm a godborn, and so are you. Haven't you ever noticed you're different?"

Before they could respond, Quinn became an eagle and flew over the fence. She landed near Brooks, shifting into her human self the second her claws hit the ground. Totally impressive.

"Look, kids," she said in a strained voice that was bordering on full-throttle annoyance. "Here's the bottom line: your real mommy or daddy is a Maya god. That means you've got powers. There are others like you—like Zane. I know, not what you expected, but life's rough and unfair and oh well. You can't go back home. Not now, anyway. It's not safe. And our ticket out of here is going to be gone soon and I'd rather not be here when the demon comes back with her posse. So, you can come willingly, or I can drag you kicking and screaming. Either way, you're coming with us."

"I told you," the guy muttered to his sister.

"Told her what?" Which part? The Maya god stuff? Powers? Life is unfair?

Brooks made a face of disgust. "And how about a thank-you for saving your butts back at the antiques shop?"

"We didn't ask you to save us," the girl said just as her brother craned his neck with bugged-out eyes.

"Look!" He pointed to the sky.

The second we snapped our gazes upward, the twins bolted past me. Ugh! Runners are the worst.

"Hey!" I started after them, but Quinn held me back. "We'll grab them. Wait here."

She and Brooks shifted into their giant bird selves. The twins didn't get very far before Quinn swept up the girl by her shoulders.

"Adrik!" the godborn hollered, flailing her legs.

"Let her go!" Adrik screamed, chasing the eagle with his arms outstretched as if he could somehow reach her.

Quinn rose higher and higher. It didn't stop Adrik from racing through the rows of cars, successfully evading Brooks's talons. "Alana!" he shouted.

Okay, I know Quinn asked me to stay put, but I was so not going to stand around when this was *my* job. I went after Adrik.

Quinn screeched a warning, but I was already closing in, thanks to Fuego. Brooks was right above Adrik when he quickly dropped out of sight. Had he rolled under a car? Okay, the guy really was a ninja. I felt bad for him for all of three seconds. Then the fourth second ticked by, bringing with it a familiar smell: Iktan's signature scent of death.

She was here.

5

But where *was* the double-crossing demon?

I spun in circles, scanning every inch of the parking lot, every car hood and roof. Instantly, the security lights in the corners shattered, plunging us all into blackness.

Ik must not have remembered that I have perfect night vision and didn't need any light to battle her. I hurried over to the sedan where I'd last seen the boy twin.

"Adrik!" I whisper-shouted. "Where are you?"

Quinn, still clutching the girl, circled above in silence. Brooks hovered nearby. They sensed Ik, too. I was glad that Alana had wised up and was staying quiet now.

My eyes cut through the dark.

There.

A mere twenty feet away, five demons were perched on top of the chain-link fence, their yellow eyes glowing. Ik stood in the center, her silver braid whipping behind her like a scorpion tail. I quickly crouched between two cars, hoping they hadn't seen me.

Phipp. Phipp. Phipp.

I peeked over the car hood. Each of the demons had a long narrow tube pressed to their lips, aimed at the sky.

Crap!

Darts whizzed like white bullets toward Brooks. She zig-zagged to avoid them.

I launched Fuego at the demons, but my spear could only hit one at a time. It went right through the gut of the biggest beast, who vanished in a thin trail of black smoke.

Every demon eye shifted.

That's right. Keep your focus on me.

"I'm the one you want!" I shouted as I threw out my hands and blasted torrents of blue fire. The remaining four beasts leaped down, fangs bared. Fuego circled back to me as fireballs shot from my eyes, tagging two of the demons in their shoulders, arms, and legs. They howled, oozing sizzling yellow goop/blood onto the asphalt. Ik ignored the two demons writhing on the ground and stepped toward me, smiling evilly.

Brooks swept in like a rocket, talons extended. Her screech echoed across the lot. *Keeaar!*

"Brooks!" I shouted. "No!"

I watched in absolute horror as the other uninjured demon aimed its blowgun at her. As the hawk continued to dive, I flung Fuego at the demon, piercing its chest. It disintegrated with an agonizing shriek, and Brooks pulled up.

Iktan was nowhere to be seen.

I stood in the center of a wide lane, catching my breath, scanning the dark. Where had Ik gone? Where was Adrik?

"I know the godborn's here," Ik said. Her disembodied voice seemed to come at me from all directions. "Give the godborn to me if you want to live."

"Not happening," I said. At least she thought there was only one. Pish. And she claimed demons were superior!

"You can't beat me," Ik said. Then, in a huskier voice, she added, "How many will have to die tonight, Fire Boy?"

I clutched Fuego, ready to fight. "I'm thinking one more demon."

"Don't you mean four?" Ik and two more demons materialized fifteen feet in front of me. Their silver braids hung to their ankles and were pulled so tight, I thought their faces might crack open if they flared a single nostril.

I hurled Fuego, but my spear met only black mist. The demons were an illusion.

An identical trio appeared on the roof of a car. Then another on the fence. They were replicating themselves over and over, and I had no idea which ones were real.

I felt the rush of Brooks's wings nearby, but even with my night vision, I couldn't see her. At the same moment, an engine turned over. Tires peeled out with a hair-raising squeal as a red sports car barreled toward the demons standing in front of me.

The car smashed into the beasts—or I should say *through* them, since they evaporated into thin air. The vehicle screeched to a halt a few feet from me.

Adrik was in the driver's seat.

He jumped out of the car, wild-eyed and panting. "Where'd they go?"

A deadly growl emerged from the dark. Seconds ticked by. One. Two. Three.

I death-gripped Fuego.

Out of nowhere, a demon flew at me, tackling me to the ground. It buried its teeth in my neck, sending venom into my blood. But this time I was ready. Fire charged through me. I became a lethal inferno that had the demon screaming in agony as it vanished.

I whirled toward Adrik. He was wrapped in a demon's arms, thrashing and grunting uselessly.

"One move and I slash his neck," the monster croaked.

"Your *smell* could kill me!" Adrik shouted.

I froze just as Brooks appeared behind the demon. I blinked. She was still a hawk, but instead of brown and white, she was entirely black, blending into the inky night.

While I was distracted, Ik emerged from behind a car and leaped toward Adrik. But Brooks was faster. She slashed Adrik's captor across its spine with her talons, bringing the demon to its knees before Brooks hauled Adrik up and out of reach.

Ik raised her blowgun toward the hawk. I released a single stream of fire toward her, and the weapon burst into flame. Meanwhile, another demon flew at me. I quickly ducked out of claws' reach and scrambled onto the roof of a sedan. Two more demons rushed me, launching themselves onto the car. I fled, carefully jumping from roof to roof with Fuego's help. But the predators were agile and gaining.

Brooks circled back, invisible against the black sky except for Adrik dangling from one of her claws. "Grab the other leg!" he shouted.

Brooks hovered only a few feet ahead.

One more jump.

Using the last car roof as a launching pad, I leaped through the air, instantly vanishing Fuego to free my hands as I gripped Brooks's available claw.

Darts whizzed by, missing us by inches.

Crap! I threw up a wall of thick smoke to camouflage us.

The darts kept coming. Adrik looked at me wide-eyed. "Blast the filthy b—" I heard him shout before I released a stream of raging fire.

Brooks let out an earsplitting cry. I didn't need to look to know she had been hit. Her entire body tensed.

And we plummeted.

The ground rushed toward us at surprising speed.

"Brooks!" I yelled.

Her desperate voice reached me telepathically. *Zane, my wing!*

My heart punched my ribs with such ferocity I couldn't breathe.

She struggled, extending her one good wing, arching her back, and tensing her muscles as she tried to glide us to safety.

Adrik's expression was a contorted look of horror. "We're going to crash!"

We won't crash. We won't crash, Brooks chanted. *I can do this.* But there was no doubt she was losing the battle with gravity. And then all the fight left her. Her body went slack.

We tumbled through the air. In ten seconds, our heads were going to bust open like melons.

Down.

Down.

Down.

I felt a sudden jolt. My hands slipped a few inches. My stomach dropped. I looked up to see that Quinn had Brooks by the back of her neck.

"Adrik!" Alana shouted as she clung to the eagle's back.

"Quinn!" I hollered. "We have to get to the gateway!"

She struggled with the weight of the entire crew, her wings beating the air with tormenting slowness. Buildings passed beneath us at tortoise speed.

No way could we lose our window of opportunity. I had no idea how serious Brooks's injury was, but a demon dart had to be bad. I had to get her home quickly—Rosie's magic saliva could heal her.

Adrik readjusted his hold on Brooks's talons. "Can't the eagle change into a dragon or some other massively powerful creature?"

No, I thought. Hurakan had once told me that only Itzamna had the power to turn into a dragon. "We'll get there, okay?"

Quinn shrieked. She redoubled her efforts and flew across the night like everything depended on it. The second I looked down, my stomach clenched. Ik and another demon were racing on foot below us, keeping pace. Their necks lengthened and bent unnaturally so their beady eyes could watch our every move. A few cars cruised the street, but thankfully there were no pedestrians to get mowed down by the monsters.

"We've got company!" I shouted to Quinn.

"Are you joking me?" Adrik cried. "They're unkillable—like cockroaches."

I called on Fuego. A second later, my spear zipped toward Ik in a motion nearly untraceable to the human eye. Just as

Fuego was about to hit the traitor, Iktan transformed into a column of silvery-purple mist. The spear stabbed the demon she'd left behind, and a loud cry echoed through the night.

My eyes searched frantically for Ik. How much time had I bought us? There. The deceitful monster reappeared, racing across the tree-lined street.

We had a fifteen-second head start, tops.

When we finally set down outside the laundromat, Brooks shifted back to her human form, then fainted.

I caught her before she collapsed. "She's burning up!" All I could think was *Please don't let there be poison.*

"It's locked!" Quinn cried, banging on the door. "And the gate's disappearing!"

I looked through the window and, inside a giant commercial dryer, caught sight of the familiar shimmer of a closing gateway—a swirl of gold and silver with flecks of blue.

"We have to break down the door!" I shouted.

Quinn's eyes fell on Brooks, and I could tell she was torn, like she wanted to rush over and check out her sister's injury. But her warrior training wouldn't let her—she had to stay focused on the task at hand. Just when I predicted Quinn was about to shift into some massive ramming beast, Alana and Adrik shoved her aside and went to the door. They huddled so close I couldn't see what they were doing. And then . . .

Click.

They swung the door open. Okay, they really *were* professional burglars.

My heart launched into the stratosphere. We were going to make it!

Or that's what I thought until I saw Ik reflected in the window. She was only about thirty feet away, sprinting toward us with fangs and claws exposed.

Adrik screamed. Alana shoved him through the door as I threw Brooks over my shoulder, willed Fuego back into my grip, and hurried toward the flickering gateway at the rear of the laundromat. The demon's footsteps were so close. Too close.

For a split second, I considered throwing Fuego at Ik's ugly mug, but I couldn't slow down long enough and I didn't have a free hand to incinerate the monster, either. "HURRY!" I shouted.

The gateway glimmered weakly.

Ten feet.

Five.

Three.

Quinn threw open the dryer and jumped inside after Adrik and Alana. Just as it was about to disappear, I nose-dived into the portal, wishing I could watch as it slammed closed in Ik's double-crossing face.

6

Here's the thing about magical portals: They're a lot like cars. Some ride like a dream; others are hunks of junk that should be sent to a scrapyard. Yeah, well, we got the junk.

The world spun violently. Hot, turbulent winds sucked the breath from my lungs. I clutched Brooks tightly as white goose down and staticky socks showered us. Then a sudden drop in air pressure made my ears pop. As I was catapulted out of the gateway and rolled across packed sand, I lost my hold on Brooks.

I scrambled over to where she lay near a bent palm tree. She was unconscious and hot to the touch. My heart dropped into my stomach. "Brooks?"

Out of the corner of my eye, I saw Adrik and Alana get to their feet a few yards away. I quickly glanced over my shoulder to see waves rolling gently onto a small beach.

We had made it to Holbox. Thank the gods!

I jumped up, hurried toward the water, and from each hand shot a thick stream of fire fifty feet into the night sky. Rosie knew that red flames equaled SOS, as in *Get here pronto!*

When I got back to Brooks, Quinn was kneeling next to her and trying to keep Alana at bay.

"I've had first aid training," the girl twin said. "Maybe I can help."

"This will require something else," Quinn said. But she let Alana kneel next to Brooks anyway.

"How about a little light?" Alana asked me.

I squatted and ignited a small flame in my palm, allowing Alana to see Brooks's wound. "There's something in her arm," the godborn said. She was too calm, like she was used to escaping demons, falling through magical portals, and doctoring shape-shifters. "I need some tweezers or . . ." Her voice trailed off as she appraised our surroundings.

"If you guys had come with us sooner," I growled, "this wouldn't have happened."

From behind me, Adrik said, "We don't even know you! And I bulldozed some of those monsters, in case you forgot. It was totally cinema-worthy!"

"Blame won't heal her, Obispo."

Anger, frustration, and panic battled inside me, but I knew Quinn was right. We had to focus on Brooks. "Rosie's on her way."

Come on, Rosie. Where are you?

Quinn leaned closer. A small talon emerged from her index finger, and she used it to gently probe the wound. A stream of fresh blood ran down Brooks's arm as her sister dug out a silver dart tip.

I barely breathed. "Was it poisoned?"

"She wouldn't still be breathing if it was." Then Quinn released a stream of threats and promises of revenge.

"Why wouldn't it be?" I asked. "These are demons we're talking about."

Quinn shrugged. "How should I know? Maybe they ran out of poison. Maybe they weren't in a killing mood."

"They seemed like some pretty motivated murderers to me," Adrik said.

I followed Alana's gaze to her brother. The two shared a nod and a grimace. Then their irises changed to a deep blue-black, and I swear it was like their eyes were made of liquid. What the heck? They were definitely talking telepathically.

"It's good she's sleeping." Quinn stroked Brooks's hair. "That's how nawals heal." She stood and asked, "How far are we from your house, Obispo?"

"You *live* here?" Adrik asked. "Looks like a deserted island."

I knew every inch of Isla Holbox, including this stretch of isolated beach on the north end. "About three miles to the house," I said.

"She's awake!" Alana cried. "She . . . she moved."

I dropped to Brooks's side, grabbing her hand. Her fingers wiggled. A second later, her amber eyes opened and stared right into mine. Relief spread through me. "Are you okay?"

Barely above a whisper, she said, "I . . . Who—" She blinked. Her eyes darted from face to face before landing back on mine. "Why do you have goose feathers in your hair?"

Quinn let out a breath. "Can you sit up?"

"I think so." Brooks rubbed her head groggily as we propped her against the tree.

"How do you feel?" I asked.

"Woozy. The dart . . . Thankfully, it only clipped my wing. I'm sorry I couldn't fly." Brooks studied the wound on her arm, wiping the blood away. "I . . . I feel so weird. Like I'm in a dream. Am I dreaming?"

"You mean having a nightmare?" Adrik muttered as he glanced toward a rustling sound in the bushes. "Are there any alligators in this jungle?"

Just then, a wall of black mist rose up from the sand. Out stepped Rosie. She bounded toward me on her three legs, her tongue lolling out of the side of her mouth, her nub tail wagging.

"I missed you, too, girl." I embraced her, scrubbing her ribs.

"That's a huge . . . uh . . . Is that a bear?" Adrik asked while his sister just stared wide-eyed, studying Rosie's every move. Only a sobrenatural could see Rosie for what she was: a hellhound the size of two lions. To the human eye, she was just a regular black dog with three legs.

"Bear?" Quinn snorted. "Try the world's finest hellhound."

Rosie's soft brown eyes studied my face, landing on the cheek wound I'd already forgotten about. One slobbery lick and I could feel the healing properties of her saliva going to work immediately. "Brooks needs you, too," I whispered, wiping off some of her drool.

Rosie went to Brooks and, with a small whine, began to lick her arm. Brooks stroked her between the ears. "You're the best, you know that?"

Here's what I had finally figured out about my dog: She didn't need training; she didn't require orders to pull her weight. I could trust her to figure out what had to be done. That meant adiós to the commands Ixtab had taught her. We no longer had to yell *STEAK!* to get her to stop, and *DEAD!* to make her breathe fire. Those were just ordinary words to her now, which made conversations much easier.

Bright lights suddenly appeared in the jungle.

"What's that?" Alana stepped back, alarmed. She shielded her eyes as if the sun was blinding her.

Then came the familiar sound of wheels running over the earth. A second later, Hondo's tourist tram emerged from the trees, coming to a stop a few feet away from us. My uncle killed the engine but left the headlights running as he jumped off the vehicle and ran over. Ren was close behind, hollering my name.

I didn't realize how much I had missed them until I saw them in the flesh.

"Zane!" Ren squealed, hugging me and then Brooks, who had staggered to her feet.

Rosie threw back her head and let out a happy howl.

Hondo pulled me into a headlock and squeezed. "Good thing we have the location tracker, Diablo. What's up with the feathers? You been cleaning birdcages?"

He'd grown out his hair to just below his ears, and I guess Quinn must have liked it, because she smiled when she saw him. But the second he looked at her, her face returned to ice-queen mode. "I have to go see Ixtab. Give a full report," Quinn said before shifting into her giant eagle self and flying off.

Hondo's grin vanished. "Does she ever stay put?" Then he slung his arm over Brooks's shoulders. "Admit it," he said. "You missed me, Capitán."

A small smile crept over Brooks's face. "Not as much as you missed me."

"Could someone please kill those headlights?" Alana tugged a pair of silver sunglasses out of her pocket and planted them on her face. With her red-tipped hair, she looked like the kind of person who might be famous.

"What's with the shades?" I asked.

"I'm super sensitive to light," she said.

Was that the gateway to her godborn power? The weakness that was really a strength, like my limp or Ren's trances?

Hondo went over and turned off the headlights as I created a small bonfire in the sand. "Is that better?" I asked.

Alana nodded. "It comes and goes," she said, tugging off her glasses.

When Hondo returned, he pointed at Adrik and Alana. "I thought there was only one godborn left."

After Brooks and I filled in Hondo and Ren about everything that had happened, my uncle said, "Two-faced demon..." Okay, he said a lot more than that, but my mom would kill me if I wrote down all that cussing.

"We didn't do anything to those monsters," Alana complained. Then, as if the reality of it all was just now washing over her, she whispered, "They . . . they could have killed us. You saved our lives."

"Let's not get carried away," Adrik said. "How do we know the demons weren't after *them* and we just got stuck in the cross fire?"

"Because my sister and I have been tracking Ik," Brooks said, raising a single eyebrow. "She could have killed Zane at any moment over the last three months, but she waited until tonight to turn on him. Until Zane led her to *you*."

"Good point, Capitán." Hondo rubbed his chin thoughtfully. "Demonio estúpido. ¿Por qué join the losing team?"

Excellent point. Why would Ik choose to leave Ixtab's army, the most powerful in the universe, to join a bunch of loser gods who'd already had their butts whipped?

"And why would Ik want *these* godborns and none of the rest?" Ren asked.

Something told me Ik hadn't been after Adrik. And she hadn't even known about Alana. She wanted whatever it was they had lifted from that store. More specifically, Camazotz and Ixkik' wanted it.

"Look…" I began, addressing the twins. This part was never easy. And now that I also had my friends' eyes on me, I felt like I was taking a test I hadn't studied for. "Before we point fingers, I need to know who might be waiting for you back in New York. Ik could do something…." Iktan wouldn't hesitate to hurt someone the twins cared about. Not if it would get her closer to whatever her bosses wanted.

"What he means," Brooks explained, "is that we need to cover all our bases, make sure there are no loose ends."

"I know what he means," Adrik said stone-faced. "There's no one waiting for us."

Alana blurted, "Unless you count the Wicked Witch of the West."

Rosie collapsed onto her belly with a groan I translated as *This is going to take a while. Peace out.*

"You live with a witch?" Ren asked.

"A wicked witch," Alana repeated. "And believe me—"

Adrik cleared his throat, cutting her off.

Brooks drew closer, mirroring his scowl. "We can't help you or protect your family unless we know what's up."

Adrik clenched his fists. "Alana's right."

"That you live with a bruja?" I asked. Was that why Alana seemed so chill about all of tonight's supernatural weirdness?

"Whatever you want to call her," Alana said, "she for sure won't be looking for us."

"What if she calls the cops?" I asked. "Reports you missing?"

"She won't." Alana sighed.

"How do you know?" Ren asked. "Wicked people can't be trusted."

"Because if she does," Adrik said with a perfectly timed sneer, "she'll end up in jail."

Adrik said the words like he'd been practicing the lines forever.

Okay, so there was a lot more to these godborns than I'd thought. They were like those puzzle boxes that are impossible to open and after hours of failed attempts you just want to bust the things open with a sledgehammer.

"Jail?" Ren asked.

Alana lifted her chin. The firelight cast dark shadows under her eyes. "She's our aunt."

"What about your parents?" Brooks asked.

"There's only our dad," Alana said. "He's in the military. Got sent somewhere secret and—"

"Alana," Adrik warned, "why don't you just give them the four-one-one on everything!"

"They should know our dad won't be coming home for months, can't even call us, and our aunt is an evil, greedy hag who won't care if we never return. She'll probably throw a party." Alana folded her arms over her chest with an angry pout. "All she cares about is the money..." Her voice trailed off, but I'm pretty sure she said, "and the houses, cars, and servants."

No one else seemed to catch it, but I wanted to shout to everyone *except* the twins: *Are you thinking what I'm thinking? Why would a couple of rich kids break into a store and steal something?*

"So, where's the god in charge of all this?" Adrik asked.

Hondo smirked. "No gods—just us. Did you say 'servants'?"

I said, "So, you guys know...? I mean..."

"That our mom's some goddess?" Alana said. "Yeah, Dad told us that much."

"You knew?" Brooks repeated, sounding even more stunned than I felt.

"He also said someone really important would come for us someday, but..." Adrik stopped there, eyeing us like we were scrappy pirates.

"Then you'll come to the World Tree and learn how to defend yourselves," I said.

I reminded them about the ceremony where their godly parent would claim them and they would come into their god-born powers. Once I got started, everything spilled out of me like I just had to tell someone what being on the road with a traitorous demon for three months was really like.

Brooks brushed my arm with hers. *Good idea. Make them think they can trust you.*

They can *trust me.*

That's what I said.

Alana knit her eyebrows together. "So, the whole time you were sleeping next to a demon who was plotting to kill you?"

THERE WERE NO SIGNS! "Something like that," I mumbled.

Adrik played with his jacket zipper, pulling it up and down. "You think we're just going to go to some magical tree and what, meet our so-called godly mom and say, 'Hey, thanks for dumping us'?"

"You're not the only godborn who was dumped, kid," Hondo said.

Brooks sighed and lifted one shoulder. "I don't think they let thieves go to the World Tree."

I touched her arm. *Way to be subtle.*

Someone has to address the elephant in the room . . . uh, jungle. It's reverse psychology. Get it? Tell them they can't go and then they'll want to go.

"What she means is," I started, "um . . . what did you steal from the antiques shop? Is that what Ik is after? Because if it is, we have to know."

Adrik groaned. "No one *stole* anything."

"You were in a closed store," I said, "and there was something glowy in your hand. And believe me, demons don't go after nothing."

Ren said, "I bet it's just a misunderstanding. You guys don't look like thieves to me."

"They *are* kinda dressed like burglars," Hondo muttered.

"What do thieves *look* like?" Adrik asked.

"We want to talk to someone in charge," Alana said, tugging on a red hair tip. "Who would that be? Is there, like, some king of the gods?"

"All the gods think they're the boss," Hondo said. "So it depends who you ask. I bet that little round rain god thinks he's king. What's his name, Zane? Chaac?"

Adrik pulled his hood over his head, and it flopped over his eyes. That's when I noticed that the jacket was too big for him, like maybe it belonged to his dad. "So, about this World Tree," he said, "who's in charge *there*?"

See? Brooks said. *You're welcome.*

Technically, Itzamna, an all-powerful, all-seeing god, sits at the top of a sacred árbol. But he wasn't the boss of SHIHOM, which is what Adrik was really asking.

"Ixchel, the moon goddess, got the job," Ren said. "She's also known as the rainbow lady."

I was still desperate to find out what the twins were hiding. "If Ik is after whatever you have," I said, trying to cajole them, "that means Camazotz, the bat god, wants it, which means—"

"You two are on his hit list," Brooks finished. "And the only place you'll be safe is at the Tree."

Adrik and Alana shared a knowing glance. Silent words passed between them as their eyes flashed that electric blue. Then Adrik said, "Okay. We'll go."

"Bueno." I pulled my phone free.

Alana practically lunged for it. "Who are you calling?"

"1-555-MAYAGOD."

It was protocol. After I found a godborn and got them to

agree to go to the Tree, I always left a recording for one of Ixchel's assistants, usually an air spirit (they're into this kind of reunion/happy-ending sort of thing). It was their job to then explain to the godborn's human parent that their kid had been chosen for an exclusive art, music, math, engineering, et cetera summer camp complete with a scholarship to college afterward. No parent had refused yet.

As soon as I finished my message, including explicit directions *not* to call the twins' aunt, Alana leaned into my phone and added, "If you call the Witch, we bolt." Then she gave me half a grin and said, "Just making sure they get it."

Hondo stretched his arms over his head and turned to me. "Your mom doesn't know you're home. You should go see her. She's gonna flip."

As we drove through the moonlit jungle, I was relieved that Adrik and Alana had agreed to go to the World Tree, and not just because they could finally learn who they really were. Two things were certain:

1) They had stolen something tonight that our enemies were after.

2) They weren't like any of the other godborns, and I was going to find out why.

7

..

The past three months had been the longest of my life. They'd also been the más difíciles.

Before, I hadn't I realized how much I needed my family to feel strong. And I don't mean like fire-missiles strong—I mean the feeling that you belong somewhere, that someone has your back no matter what. Someone like my mom, who pretty much went crazy screaming and laughing and crying when she saw me, squeezing my guts out with a muy fuerte abrazo.

To be honest, I didn't mind. I'd missed her a lot. No amount of FaceTime can make up for *real* face time. Mom seemed just as happy to see Brooks—the hug she gave her was, like, a whole three seconds longer than mine. Not that I was counting or anything.

And when Mom met Adrik and Alana, she smiled, hugged them too (awkward!), and said, "Welcome to our home. Are you hungry? Do you want to get cleaned up?" Most moms would probably ask a million questions, like *Where are you from? How old are you? What's your favorite* (fill in the blank)? *How do you feel about being a godborn?* But my mom had a gift for knowing what to say (or not) and how to say it.

She was the queen of making people feel comfortable.

Mostly *other* people, because she kicked me out of my room to give Adrik and Alana a place to sleep. Brooks would stay with Ren and her grandfather in the casita. Me? I'd get the hammock on the beach patio. But I didn't mind. I mean, falling asleep under the stars while listening to ocean waves is hard to beat.

First, though, I enjoyed a light bedtime snack of Mom's homemade lasagna. Okay, so maybe it wasn't so light, but I hadn't tasted her cooking in so long. . . . As I chowed down, Mom filled me in on all the island gossip: Old Man Pedro had given up beer, a new mural was being painted on the side of a food market, and Ms. Cab and Mr. Ortiz had eloped and were on their honeymoon.

Honeymoon?! I couldn't believe it. I mean, Ms. Cab had been rejecting Mr. O's expressions of love for what seemed like forever, and now she was his wife? Had she been pretending the whole time, or had he finally worn her down? It was too weird to think about. And did old people actually go on honeymoons?

That night, Rosie slept right underneath me. It hadn't always been like that. After Ixtab turned her into a hellhound and moved us to the island along with my favorite dormant volcano, Rosie had preferred sleeping inside the mountain at first. Ixtab had made it a gateway to the underworld in case of emergency, and I figured Rosie liked being close to the goddess. But now her loyalty was in the right place again: with me.

So there I was, hammock happy, dreaming of surfing a

massive wave, when I heard, "This is no time to sleep in, Obispo!"

Quinn.

As she stood over me, the rising sun was at her back, and no, she did not look like a haloed angel. Not even close. More like a silhouette of Darth Vader with braids. She swept her black wrap behind her and huffed. "Does it look like I have all day?"

I turned over and saw Rosie open one eye, blink at Quinn, then go back to sleep. Typical.

Quinn grabbed the hammock and pushed, threatening to dump me out. Before she could, I rolled to my feet. "What . . . what time is it?"

"Time to go to the underworld."

I groaned. "Again?" I seriously hated that place. Last time I was there, I'd nearly frozen to death. Then I was thrown into a bath of bone dust and chased by flying demons. So, yeah, I didn't have a whole lot of warm and fuzzy memories of the trip.

A gunning engine caught my attention. I looked across the pale beach toward the surf. "Is that . . . What's that car doing here?"

"It's your ride to Xib'alb'a," Quinn said. "Why aren't you moving?"

"Hang on," I argued. "Why do I have to go to the underworld? What did Ixtab say about Ik and everything that happened? Does she have any intel?"

Quinn gave me a look that registered in her dark eyes as

I'm only going to say this once. "She said she wants to talk to you. Directly. She hates secondhand information, and if you keep her waiting, she'll probably make you swim laps in Pus River with a corpse tied to your back." She flashed a fake smile and added, "So, how about we get moving?"

I looked down at my plain gray T-shirt and faded sweatshorts. Ixtab would for sure hate my clothing choices. "I can't go to the underworld in my pajamas."

"No time to change."

I ran a hand through my bedhead hair and grabbed my flip-flops from underneath the hammock. It was bad enough I was going to have to stand in front of the queen of fashion looking like a wrinkled beach bum, but having morning breath? That might earn me a lifetime of bone-crushing duty. "Do you have any mouthwash?"

With an exaggerated sigh, Quinn said, "Let's go, Obispo."

We jumped into the backseat of the black Mercedes sedan. But there was one problema.

"Where . . . where's the driver?" I practically choked on the words, because no way was I going to trust some invisible ghost to get us to the underworld.

"Haven't you ever heard of a driverless car?" Quinn rolled her eyes. "Really, Obispo. I just don't see why Brooks likes you so much."

My face got all buzzy and hot. *Likes?* I figured Quinn meant like a brother, or a friend, or a favorite pair of slippers.

The tint on the windows was so dark I couldn't see beyond it, not when we splashed through the breakers, not when we cruised under the ocean with a few bumps and thumps that rattled me, and not when we came to an abrupt stop in Xib'alb'a.

We stepped out of the car into what looked like an airplane hangar, except it held dozens of super-cool exotic cars that Hondo would be able to name in ten seconds flat.

"Hang on," I said nervously. "You aren't taking me back to Clementino for a bone-dust bath, are you?"

Quinn tilted her head like she was thinking about all the evil ways she could torment me. "Well, that *would* keep the demons from sniffing you out and eating you, but we don't have loads of time, so I'm taking a shortcut."

She led me to a marbled hallway with six red doors on each side. The last one on the right read: ENTER AT YOUR OWN RISK. Then in smaller print: RISK OF DECAPITATION, DISEMBOWELMENT, OR FLAYING OVER AN OPEN FIRE.

So, of course that was the one we went through.

We landed in a big room with a window overlooking some kind of massive stadium. All the seats outside were filled, but I couldn't hear the crowd at all. "Where are we?"

"Hellhound races," Quinn said. "This is Ixtab's skybox, and that's a one-way mirror, so no one can see you. Oh, and it's also soundproof, so no one can hear you scream."

"Great," I muttered as I looked around. The room was decorated like the goddess's private chamber, where she had once revealed to me that she'd tricked the Maya gods into thinking I was dead. There were black leather wingback chairs and gray velvet sofas with fluffy pillows. The walls were covered in gold wallpaper, but unlike in her chamber, there were half a dozen painted portraits of hellhounds. I held my breath, looking for Rosie's face. Thankfully, she wasn't among them.

"Okay, my job is done," Quinn said. "See ya."

"Wait!" I clutched Fuego. "Why are you leaving?"

She glared at me. "Because I am a warrior of the White Sparkstriker tribe. I am too valuable to serve as your escort to the underworld. And I don't want to be here when you tell Ixtab all the clues you missed on your little godborn tour."

Here's the thing about Quinn. She's like a pot of water. She can be cool and still, or hot and bubbling. I got the feeling that if I pressed her further, she would boil over and scald me.

After she left, I stood there alone. You have no idea how awful it is to hang out in Ixtab's underworld chambers waiting for her to arrive. It's a gazillion times worse than sitting in the principal's office, knowing she's going to waltz in any second with an exasperated attitude and a million detention slips.

The hairs on the back of my neck stood at attention.

Slowly, I turned to find Ixtab standing a couple of feet behind me. She looked taller, probably because she had on white platform sneakers—like fresh-out-of-the-box white. She wore red skinny leather pants and a white silk blouse with tiny skulls embroidered on the collar. Her gold earrings dangled low enough to touch the skulls.

"Hey," I managed.

She stared at me, unblinking.

Was I supposed to say something else? *How's the weather in the underworld this time of year? How have you been? How do you keep your sneakers so clean?*

She eyed me up and down so hard I swear my skin was going to burn off any second. My hands started to sweat.

"You're taller," she finally said with a glower that could shrink a dinosaur to the size of an ant. "And extremely unkempt."

I wanted to say, *And you look supremely angry/bitter/ hostile, which means you're probably going to skin me alive for something I don't even know I did, and couldn't you have come to talk to me on the beach, because I'd much rather die in the sun than in hell.* Instead, I word-vomited all over the plush rug.

"I didn't know Ik was a rat. I don't know when she was turned or who turned her. She never let on—I mean, there weren't any signs or clues, other than the whole thing about the Statue of Liberty being made by a demon, but by then it was too late, and she just turned on me, almost killed me." I was hoping that last bit would get me an ounce of sympathy.

To my right, a big TV screen dropped from the ceiling and blinked awake with an image of the racetrack below.

"Welcome to the two thousandth anniversary of Xib'alb'a's hellhound races," an announcer boomed. "Plague, Misery, and Scab Face are the front-runners, so place your bets, beg fortune to smile on you, and—"

With the wave of her hand, Ixtab muted the voice. The goddess waltzed over to the sofa, plunked down, and began flipping through a home design magazine. "Tell me about the godborns."

"Uh, well, we found them all, and they all agreed to go to the World Tree." I forced a smile, thinking that must count for something. "Sixty-five in total, and—"

"I am completely uninterested in one through sixty-three."
She looked up. "Tell me about the last two."

"Oh, Adrik and Alana?"

"Really, Zane. Do you always have to state the obvious?"
Ixtab stood and, with a perfectly manicured hand, motioned
for me to continue.

I felt myself start to loosen up a little as I told her every
detail, including how the twins had stolen something from
the antiques shop. I kept my eyes on the screen as half a
dozen red-eyed hellhounds took their places at the starting
gate. Man, they looked gigantic and fierce and out for blood.

Ixtab came closer, so close I could smell her perfume,
which was clean and spicy and made me think of oranges.
"Did they exhibit any godborn gifts?"

I thought about the answer before I spoke, just to make
sure I didn't give her even a speck of false information. "Uh . . ."
My brain froze up. "It was dark."

"And you see perfectly well in the dark."

"Oh yeah, they unlocked a door that they didn't have a key
for. And they can talk telepathically without even touching,
but when they do, their eyes melt. I mean, not melt. They go
from brown to, like, electric blue." I heard myself babbling and
I really wanted to shut up, but my brain kept firing the words
minus the punctuation. "Like a bluish molten color it's kinda
cool actually and Alana wears shades because she's sensitive
to light and don't you want to know what they stole?"

Ixtab turned away and poured some tea from a brass tea-
pot that hadn't been there before. A rope of steam rose from

the cup, looking like it was waiting for a neck to wrap around. I retreated and swallowed the expanding bulge in my throat.

Ixtab took a careful sip, then turned back to me. "They don't sound terribly gifted," she said.

And as she did, her eyes flashed a familiar glowing blue.

8
•••

Okay, so I was a little slow on the uptake, but being in the underworld can really turn your brain to mush.

Ixtab's molten eyes made it clear.

"Oh my gods!" I practically shouted. "WTX!"

"WTX?"

"What the Xib'alb'a."

"Get ahold of yourself, Zane." She sighed. "And please refrain from using the sacred name of the underworld in your dramatics. A curse like that could bring all kinds of trouble down on your head."

WTX is officially struck from my vocab, I thought.

"The twins . . . they're your kids, right?" I knew it! Okay, I didn't exactly *know*, but I had definitely sensed that there was something different about them. So, *this* was why Ixtab had summoned me. She didn't want to hear a firsthand report about Ik—she wanted to hear about her kids!

"Do you like the races?" she asked, motioning to the TV screen.

She turned up the volume so I could hear the announcer: "We're only minutes away, and the hellhounds look restless. Who will be this year's champion? Who will be chosen to serve our queen?"

Was Ixtab seriously going to ignore my question?

"Do you?" she asked again.

"Uh—never seen them," I said. "The winner becomes your servant?" How was *that* a victory?

"None will ever be as grand as your Rosie," she said quietly, and I could tell she missed her. "Don't you agree?"

"Yeah, but, um..." HELLO! ARE THEY YOUR KIDS?!

The announcer droned on while the camera panned the track. It looked just like a horse racetrack except that the fence was made of bones and steam rose from the dirt.

"Do you think Rosie misses it here at all?" Ixtab asked.

My cheeks flushed with anger. "Why would she? She has a great life, and we're the perfect pair." To emphasize my point, in case the goddess hadn't been listening, I added, "She belongs with me."

"But you'd give her up if that was in her best interest."

How could living in the underworld ever be good for Rosie? And why did that matter now?

Oh. OH!

I finally got it. Ixtab was talking about Adrik and Alana.

"I'd do anything if it was best for Rosie," I said, and I meant it.

Ixtab nodded thoughtfully. "You are not to mention me to Adrik and Alana." Her voice was empty of any emotion, which was weird, but maybe only by human standards. I mean, gods don't feel things the same way we do.

"Oh, okay, but..." I inhaled, deeply worried that what I said next might land me in Rattle House, or worse, corpse-diving in Pus River. "You never said you had *two* kids."

"In what world would you think that is any of your business?"

"Look…" Yeah, I know. I was pressing my luck. But I'm famous for being stubborn. And though we weren't exactly friends, Ixtab and I we were definitely allies in a shared history way. "I know you wanted me to find the godborns," I said. "You baited me that first day in your chambers, when I was playing dead for the gods. You wouldn't have told me about the godborns if you didn't want me to be curious, if you didn't want me to find your kids." There. I'd said it. And my head was still attached to my body.

"Ah, Zane. The son of fire." She stretched the word *fire*. "How strong and bold you've become. Is that good or bad? Only time will tell. For now, my offspring are none of your business beyond your personal guarantee that they get to the World Tree safely. Because if even a hair on their heads is touched…"

"Let me guess: you'll throw me into Blood River."

She's the goddess! I thought. Couldn't she protect them much better than I ever could? And how was this *my* problem? I had fulfilled my end of the bargain. I'd spent three months in demon purgatory, found all the godborns, and blown their minds with the truth. Wasn't that enough to earn me a free cruise or something?

"I see you still have no imagination," she said. "I can think of exponentially worse punishments."

Crap! I could barely keep my own butt out of trouble. Now I had to be responsible for two godborn thieves who carried secrets in their pockets?

"But you'll come to the claiming ceremony, right?" My eyes flicked to the television, where black streaks zoomed around the track, and all I could think was *Rosie would smoke them all.*

"Of course. Do you really believe I would leave my heirs without their full powers just when they might need them the most? Really, Zane. What do you think I am, a monster?"

Sort of? "What do you mean, 'might need them the most'?"

The goddess's eyes ignited into blue flames. "My reputation has been sullied, which puts them in danger. Imagine anyone thinking I would assist the enemy! As if I would *ever* team up with that ghastly Camazotz or Ixkik'."

A girl's voice sounded in the room: "Escorts to Pus River's pier thirty-six. It's backed up with clueless souls who keep asking if they can have fries with that."

Ixtab pressed a button on her bracelet and spoke into it. "And you're bothering me with this because . . . ?"

"Oh . . . uh . . . many pardons, my queen." The girl's voice trembled. "Wrong extension. Oops. 'Kay. Bye."

"I'm surrounded by imbeciles," Ixtab muttered, rubbing her brow. It made me think briefly of Scar from *The Lion King*, but I was pretty sure he'd said *idiots.*

"Can't you just tell the other Maya gods that you're innocent?" I asked.

"If only it were that simple. The Council of Gods is looking at all the details."

Knowing Ixtab, she had her own spy crew working on it, too.

"Good," I said. "Make sure they know Zotz and Ixkik' want whatever it is the twins stole."

Ixtab flashed a terrifying scowl. "Are you calling my children thieves?"

Well, it was a closed antiques shop, and they were dressed like burglars, and I'm sure they lifted something. "Er . . . no, not thieves," I said nervously, followed by an even more nervous chuckle. "I'm sure they were just browsing."

She went on. "Right now, we need to be observant, diligent, intentional, and, above all, you need to report any and all odd incidents to me directly."

"Sure, but, uh . . . why would Ik join the baddies? She must think that Zotz will win, but how?" The demon's confidence had me a little freaked. It told me we didn't know everything, and whatever pieces were missing, they were big. I didn't want to be around when the truth exploded in the gods' faces.

"Iktan will be dealt with, as will the bat god and his pathetic sidekicks."

Right. Jordan, Bird, and their mom, Ixkik', aka Blood Moon. Yeah, if that nickname doesn't spike fear in you, I don't know what would. "But when?" I asked. "How? Like, who's going to do it, and can they do it soon?"

Ixtab clenched her jaw and looked like she might incinerate the entire room. Okay, bad question. Bad silence. Bad moment that I really wanted to exit pronto.

But I've never been good at keeping my mouth zipped. I stepped closer. "What aren't you telling me?"

She studied me carefully, like she wasn't sure she could

trust me to handle her answer. "Let's just say that the day we were hoping wouldn't come might be near."

"You mean the war that Zotz and his *pathetic sidekicks* want."

Her expression was deadpan.

"But no one fights a war without an army," I added. "And they already failed at raising the Mexica gods."

"There are other types of war, Zane. Wars that bring about worse things than dying."

"You . . . you think they've found a way to beat the Maya gods?"

Frowning, she said, "This is a game of war, and no one is better at that than the Maya gods. We will *not* be defeated."

Game?

"And whatever our enemies are after, it isn't going to be obvious. It is going to be cunning, shrewd, and so unexpected it will have your head spinning. Remember that."

Blood Moon's last words to me on that day at the Pyramid of the Magician rushed into my already panicky brain: *Someday, when you least expect it, you'll pay with your blood for this. My sons will show no mercy. Nor will I.*

That didn't sound like a game to me—more like a real live threat. I knew Ixkik' would try to make good on her promise, which made me want to throw up in the nearest trash can.

"Go home," Ixtab said. "Get ready for SHIHOM tomorrow." Her eyes glazed over like she was somewhere else, then they flicked back to me. "And, Zane?"

"Yeah?"

"Do not mention *any* of this conversation to anyone. No one is to know you were here. I have eyes everywhere and will know if even a syllable is breathed. Do you understand?"

I hesitated, wondering why everything always had to be a secret where Ixtab was concerned. But then I realized I wouldn't leave here with my head unless I gave my word. "I promise."

I was glad to get out of the underworld alive and grateful that Ixtab hadn't taken me back to Blood River for our private chat.

But as I headed home in the driverless Mercedes, all I kept thinking was what Ixtab's words had really meant: *Get ready for the games.*

9

By the time I got home, I was fuming. Like literally, my head was smoking worse than a tortilla burning on the comal.

If the gods thought they were going to make me (or any godborn) a pawn again, they had another think coming. I was tired of being played and used. Tired of being given morsels of madness that added up to nada. And even though Ixtab never said that the godborns would be used in this twisted war games scheme, she didn't have to. I knew we had a role—I just didn't know what it was yet.

That day, I couldn't help but watch Adrik and Alana closely, looking for similarities to the goddess of death or a clue as to their godborn gifts. It was pretty mind-blowing to think about all their possible powers. Like maybe one glance and—*bam!*—instant death for their victim. Or one fist bump and—*pow!*—total mind control. I mean, their mom *is* the queen of manipulation.

Whenever they'd catch me staring, Adrik would give me *what's-your-deal-stalker?* looks while Alana hid behind her shades, smirking. Then they would start talking telepathically, which was super annoying and only reminded me of their mom and all her secrets.

They liked *my* mom, though. She gave them some light

blue MAYA JOURNEYS tees from our isla tour business, since Adrik and Alana had arrived with only the clothes on their backs (Brooks had previously left a few of her things at my house for future use). But when Mom offered to wash their jeans, Adrik said, "No thanks," like a grizzly bear guarding the last of his food.

Right. He had something in the pocket he wasn't about to let go of.

Unfortunately, my over-the-top-generous mom also gave them a copy of my first book, the one the gods had forced me to write as a cautionary tale for anyone who might defy them.

When I asked my mom why, she just said, "They deserve the whole story, Zane. How can they make buenas choices without it?"

Ugh! I should totally burn all the truth paper in existence!

"Besides," she added, "you're such a good writer. I've read the story at least ten times. I really like that part about me driving like a pro stunt driver." She smiled and wrinkled her nose. "Do you really think so?"

I laughed. "Heck yeah, Mom."

"And Brooks?"

I stiffened. "What about her?" My face felt like it had been tossed into boiling water. Where was a rock when you really needed one to crawl under?

"Does she know how you feel?"

"Geesh, Mom . . . It's not like—"

"I know exactly what it's like," she said, grinning all goofy like. "And if you ever want to talk about it, I'm here."

She could be *here* all she wanted—no way was I ever, *ever* having that convo with her.

The next morning, we all stood on the beach waiting for some air spirit to arrive to take us to SHIHOM. That's what our invites had said, anyways. Mom stood at the edge of the patio and waved. I knew she was crying, which made me feel really awful. I mean, I'd just gotten home, and here I was, already leaving again.

I'd already hugged her good-bye. Just as I'd pulled out of her arms, she'd whispered, "Your father promised to keep an eye on you."

"When did you talk to him?"

Ignoring the question, she'd said, "Remind him that I will come for him if anything happens to you."

Yup. My pro-stunt-driving mom was probably the one person whose threat would strike fear into a creator-*and*-destroyer god like Hurakan.

Ren looked at her gold watch and frowned. "The air spirit's late." She would know, since the watch had come from her mom, Pacific, the goddess of time. According to Ren, it kept perfect Maya time, but it hadn't done any other magical stuff yet. I had told her not to worry—that could change tomorrow night, at the claiming ceremony.

"Maya creatures are hardly ever punctual." Brooks took a bite of her pineapple empanada. My mom had given them to us for our journey, and I'd already polished off three.

Hondo hoisted his pack onto his shoulder. I guess, as a

teacher, he didn't have to follow the same bring-nothing rules the rest of us did. Whatever.

"What's in the backpack?" I asked.

Hondo shrugged. "Just some stuff."

Alana pushed her shades up the bridge of her nose. My mom had given her a blue neoprene MAYA JOURNEYS strap so Alana wouldn't lose her glasses in case things got "adventuresome."

I was totally rooting for an unadventurous trip to SHIHOM.

Just then, a thick wall of greenish fog swirled around us. So thick I couldn't see my hand in front of my face. Rosie whined and nudged me with her wet muzzle.

"What the heck?" Brooks said.

"I can't see!" That was Adrik.

Hondo gripped my shoulder. "Someone really should tell the gods to ixnay all the creep-factor stuff."

The fog lifted like a veil, revealing a pre-dawn sky that was pink with wisps of silver and blue. Then, like flipping a set of blinds, the sky changed to pale orange with streaks of lavender. The sand glittered with gold and red and green, as if bits of rubies and emeralds had been scattered everywhere. And the sea? It was a brilliant turquoise with not a single wave.

"It's like a kaleidoscope," Ren whispered.

"Whoa!" Adrik blinked furiously, like he had a sea gnat in his eye.

Brooks's mouth fell open.

"Is this SHIHOM?" Alana asked, tugging off her shades.

I spun to find my house gone. We were definitely no longer on Isla Holbox. There were no palm trees, no hammocks, no gulls. It was just us, the glittering beach, and the kaleidoscope sky. Or at least I thought so, until three massive tortugas with dark shells lumbered out of the sea. Their eyes were deep blue, like pools of iridescent ink. And let me tell you, they were muy slow.

"Those ... uh ... don't look like air spirits," Hondo said.

"*That's* our ride to SHIHOM?" Brooks groaned. "Like, can't we fly or take a gateway?"

"How do we know they're friendly?" Alana chewed on a pinkie nail.

Her brother inched back and asked, "Aren't turtles carnivores? Do you see any teeth?"

"Definite flesh-eaters," Hondo said, popping the rest of his empanada into his mouth.

Ren smiled. "They look nice to me."

Rosie danced on her three paws. Her eyes glowed vibrant gold with flecks of green. And then she bowed, lowering her head to the sparkling sand as if to say *I worship you, O mighty turtles.*

"Are they some kind of royalty?" Alana asked.

I tugged on my dog's collar, but she didn't budge.

"This could be a trick," Adrik said, shaking his head.

Alana rolled her eyes. It was the first time I'd seen her brother get under her skin. "For real, Adrik? You think these turtles are just some decoys to get us into the water so they can drown us and watch our bones drift to the ocean floor?" She looked at Ren. "That's not a thing, right?"

Adrik scowled at his sister. "You read too many books."

"You watch too many acting videos."

"Well, when I get famous, I won't be thanking you!"

The turtles continued toward us, their domed shells shimmering in the morning sunlight. As they drew closer, I noticed that the scutes on their shells were a repeating pattern of obsidian and jade. Their heads and necks were dotted with black and white spots.

"That one in the middle has something in its mouth," Ren said.

Alana elbowed me. "Go get it, Zane."

"They're tortugas," Hondo sneered, "not demons." He closed the sevenish-foot gap and we all followed. Well, Ren, Brooks, and I did. Adrik and Alana hung back a few feet.

The center turtle blinked slowly and dropped a large clamshell onto the sand. I scooped it up and cracked it open with Fuego. Inside, instead of gooey flesh, there was a folded letter.

"Who's it from?" Ren said, ducking under my arm to get a better look. "What's it say?"

I read the words aloud: "'For Zane. Air spirits are on strike.'"

Brooks whispered, "Spirits go on strike?"

I continued reading, "'The aaks'"—I pronounced it *awk* as in *awkward*—"'will take you safely to SHIHOM. Only they can get you past the magical borders, so don't fall off or try any funny detours. Oh, and *do not* attempt to mount until the turtle chooses you. They can be quite moody, but don't worry, I fed them before they left. Got it?'" I looked up at the group's curious expressions. The last words came out in a whoosh. "It's signed A.P."

"A.P.?" Ren squealed. "Hooray!"

It had to be Ah-Puch. Ren and the god of death, darkness, and destruction had become BFFs during our last quest.

Ren stroked the messenger turtle's long, wrinkly neck. The creature closed its eyes in pleasure and stretched its head higher. "He doesn't seem like he would bite off anyone's head."

"The turtle, or the god of death?" Hondo asked with a smirk.

"God of death?" Alana raised her eyebrows.

"The same dude you trapped in fire?" Adrik said to me.

So they'd already read my book? Every time someone mentioned it, my skin got all prickly and annoyance reared up like a zombie. Maybe because it reminded me of the gods' greed and exploitation.

Hondo said to Adrik and Alana, "Different guy. Lots of gods and lords and demons of death. Can hardly keep up with all of them."

"Except the initials are the same as Ah-Puch's." Alana wasn't buying it.

"It's a long story," I said. "He's not evil anymore."

"He's *so* sweet," Ren chirped. "He risked his life to save us. Actually, he died and then Zane saved him."

I wondered if maybe I should let Adrik and Alana read my second story, which explains all that. They deserved to know everything, including why the Fire Keeper was so important, who the baddies were, and why the gods had finally decided to welcome their half-human kids. Knowing Itzamna, though, the book was already sitting on everyone's pillow at SHIHOM.

Alana and Adrik looked at each other, no doubt communicating telepathically.

Brooks harrumphed. "Shouldn't we all be more worried about turtles cruising us across a million-foot-deep ocean? Not doing it. Nope. I'll fly, thank you very much."

"You heard Ah-Puch," I said. "Only they can get us into SHIHOM."

Dark wings sprouted from Brooks's back and stretched toward the sky. "Then I'll fly until we get close."

The turtles started to scratch at the sand like bulls getting ready to charge.

"Great," Adrik said to Brooks as he backed away. "You've gone and made them mad."

The god of death was wrong. The turtles did not *choose* who they wanted to ride on their backs. They marked us! First, they closed their eyes and sucked in what seemed like a gallon of air.

We all held our breaths.

And then *Pshhhhkkrrrttt!*

We got hosed.

10

The thick pink substance was like Silly String.

And it had some serious distance, but worse was the smell: like vinegar mixed with Raid. I was super glad my mouth was closed. Hondo? He wasn't so lucky. And no, you do not want to know what curses flew back at the turtles. But the tortugas didn't seem to care. They just blinked slowly while my uncle turned red in the face.

"Couldn't they have just tapped us or something?" Adrik looked disgusted.

"Hondo," I said, trying not to laugh as I peeled the sticky goop off my T-shirt, "what happened to Mr. Chill?"

Hondo shot me a death glare that pretty much said *I will put you in a choke hold until you die.* "Do you know how long it's been since I've been in a good battle? Three months. *Three!*"

"Say your peace mantra," Ren insisted. "Don't even think about fighting. It's not good for you." She blinked. "I mean, unless you're defending yourself."

The messenger turtle placed its forehead against my dog's. Both sets of eyes shimmered the same coppery gold. Then the tortuga's shell began to glow in alternating blue and yellow like a cheap neon motel sign.

"Rosie speaks turtle?" Hondo muttered.

"They're glyphs," Brooks said, coming closer.

Rosie whined and walked backward toward me, wagging her body like a fish.

I looked at Brooks. "What do the glyphs say?"

"Forget about speaking," Adrik said. "The turtles can spell?"

Pressing her mouth together in concentration, Brooks said, "I'm not, like, a hundred percent sure, but I think it's saying, *These kids are smelly like . . . elephant breath.* Or maybe it's *lizard breath*?"

"Smelly?" Alana echoed. "They sprayed *us*!"

The turtle waded over and blinked up at Rosie again. This time my dog grunted twice, stomped her front paw once, and disappeared in a cloud of black mist.

Great! She got the shortcut to SHIHOM? Sometimes I think being a hellhound has way more benefits than being a godborn.

I changed Fuego into a tattoo as we all climbed onto our assigned turtles' backs. I rode with Alana, Ren was paired with Adrik, and my uncle went solo. A minute later, we were floating across the sea. A thin layer of mist rose in curls from the cool surface, chilling the quiet air. The tortugas stayed in their own lanes, evenly spaced about fifteen feet apart, and swam at a snail's pace.

Brooks soared high above. Hondo seemed to be meditating, or envisioning his next battle, and Adrik was completely focused on the ocean, as if preparing for a monstrous shark to chomp on his foot. Ren sat in front of Adrik and stroked her turtle's neck.

Alana sat behind me with her arms at her sides. She blew

out a long breath and traced her fingers through the cool water. "All this . . . it's so hard to believe. How is it even happening?"

"I remember when I first got introduced to the Maya world," I said. "It was pretty freaky, and I couldn't believe a lot of stuff, even when I was looking right at it. But you get used to it."

"I hope not," she said.

The tortugas paddled through the water as the sky continued to shift colors. Purple clouds floated above the iridescent ocean.

"By the way," Alana went on, "Adrik and I stayed up all night reading your story. Well, he read it super fast. I actually think he skipped a lot. Typical. But I read every line, like, twice. It explains a lot. Man, oh man. Those hero twins are pretty awful."

"You don't know the half of it." I explained how Jordan, Bird, and their mom, Ixkik', sided with Camazotz as part of a revenge scheme. The brothers had pretty much sold their souls and become part bat in the deal. I wondered with a shudder if they were all bat by now. Then I told her how Ah-Puch had sacrificed himself to save us and how I brought him back to life with the magic jade.

"The gods seem pretty unpredictable," she said. "My dad says unpredictable is the most dangerous."

"They keep a lot of secrets, too. Secrets that ruin everything."

"But some secrets are for good," she said. "My dad has to keep lots of them because of his job, and because"—she hesitated—"his secrets would be bad for me to know."

I knew from firsthand experience that secrets could be lethal for certain people—and gods. But that for sure wasn't the case with whatever Adrik was carrying in his pocket. And this was the perfect opportunity to find out more. Alana had one arm wrapped around my waist now, which meant I could open my mind to her.

Secrets like whatever you took from the antiques shop?

Alana stiffened. After a few moments, she said, *It belongs to our dad.*

What is IT?

It's just a stone, okay? Our wicked aunt sold it to that store. We just took it back. End of story.

It's not just a stone, I said, *or Zotz and Ixkik' wouldn't want it so bad. Which means it's part of some bigger, more evil scheme. So what does it do?*

I swear, Zane, I don't see how it could help Zotz and Ixkik'.

That's because you don't think up vile things like they do, I thought but didn't communicate.

Ixtab's words circled back to me: *Whatever absolute truth our enemies are after, it isn't going to be obvious. It is going to be cunning, shrewd, and so unexpected it will have your head spinning.*

I felt a sudden heat in my bones, similar to the night in Hell's Kitchen right before Ik betrayed me.

Maybe you just don't know its power, Alana. What if it matters more than you think?

She faltered. *If I tell you, you have to promise not to tell anyone else. Especially Adrik. Our dad made us swear to protect it. But if you for real think it could help—*

I swear!

All it does is—

Just then, Adrik shouted, "Ren! Hey! What's wrong with her?"

I snapped my gaze to the right and saw that Ren was in one of her trances, her back leaning against Adrik's chest. He threw his hands high in the air and shouted, "I didn't do anything!"

A long, dark shape glided beneath the water, right past my leg, like a giant stingray.

Please don't grow a face, I thought. I never knew what kind of shadows Ren was going to conjure, but man, I hoped this wasn't going to be a repeat of the skeleton in a top hat.

"What is *that*?" Alana whimpered, gripping my waist so tight I could hardly breathe.

"One of Ren's shadows." I didn't take my eyes off the spreading darkness. "They come from her dreams."

Brooks screeched, her claws drawn like she was ready to go in for the kill. But here's the thing about shadows: You can't kill them. You can't even touch them.

"Ren!" I shouted as dense fog rose from the water.

Hondo yelled, "Adrik! Wake Ren!"

"I'm trying!" Adrik splashed Ren, but no matter how much he soaked her, she stayed unconscious.

"ZANE!" Alana lifted her feet to avoid some black ooze in the sea, bubbling up like hot tar.

"Shadows don't bubble!" Hondo frowned. "Do they?"

"How should I know?" I stared at the dark churning *notwater* that was getting thicker by the second.

The turtles came to a halt, and before any of us could say another word, they swiftly joined themselves together, the sides of their shells connecting like Legos with a loud *click*.

"What are they doing?!"

"Maybe they're turning into turbo turtles," Alana said.

"Or ninja turtles," Hondo added, nodding frantically.

Or how about a speedboat to race us away from the creepy dark stuff circling us like toxic waste? I thought.

The tortugas' backs began to glow turquoise. One by one, glyphs emerged from their scutes and slid onto the surface of the sea, creating a trail of neon words I couldn't read. The images sped away as fast as shooting stars.

Were they reporting back to Ah-Puch? I wondered. Couldn't he have sent us a mode of transportation more effective than slowpoke unarmed turtles that knew how to spell?

I threw my gaze at Ren, who still looked lifeless as she slumped against Adrik. "Don't let her fall!" I warned. He gave me a *no-duh* look.

The dark waters gurgled.

"Go faster!" Alana cried as the fog tightened around us.

But even though our turtle's legs were kicking furiously, it wasn't moving an inch.

Hondo and I exchanged a look. "Ren isn't doing this," I said, terror settling into my bones.

"We are not going down like this!" My uncle swung his backpack onto his lap and rifled through it. Did he have a weapon for fighting evil sludge that I didn't know about?

I summoned Fuego and scrambled to my feet, balancing carefully, as if the turtle's shell were a surfboard. Not knowing what I was aiming for, I hurled my spear into the thickening ocean.

Alana began to cough violently, like she was hacking up a lung. I whipped around, crouching. Her nose was bleeding black.

"Alana!" Adrik screamed, reaching through the fog for his sister. His face was red with anger and fear. "Move it!" he shouted to his turtle, but it just kept paddling uselessly and churning out neon glyphs.

"I'm okay," Alana cried, wiping her nose, but she didn't mean it. It was just something to say, a hope that we would all survive this. She clutched my shoulders, her fingers digging into my skin. *Are we going to die?* she asked telepathically. Then, *Never mind. Don't answer that.*

Everything was chaos and shouting.

"What is it?"

"Kill it!"

"Blast it with fire!"

Oh yeah. Good idea. I launched three massive fireballs into the sea. They detonated on impact and did nothing to stop the bubbling ooze.

That's when I realized Fuego hadn't come back yet.

My eyes darted everywhere, desperately searching, waiting for my spear to zip out of the muck.

"The black stuff is spreading!" Adrik hollered, trying to keep Ren upright. "Alana, I . . . You're the best sister. I don't even mind you most of the time."

"Don't!" she screamed. "Don't you dare do that, Adrik!"

"I'm just saying . . ."

"Well, don't," she commanded, trembling so hard I started to tremble, too.

Brooks zoomed in, flying close enough to the water that the tip of her right wing touched the bubbling surface. She released a warning cry so loud I bet it was heard halfway across the world. I could tell she didn't know what to do, who to save, how to help all of us. She had to choose.

"Take Ren!" I shouted.

Brooks's eyes blazed copper. She shook her head, screeching as if to say *You're not the boss, Zane!* But I could tell she knew that sleeping Ren was the most vulnerable of us all at that moment.

She swept in, gripped Ren by the shoulders, and lifted her away. Brooks's right wing, the one that had touched the darkness, quivered, and bits of feather fell into the sea.

The water. THE WATER! "Don't touch—" I began to shout, when two slimy tentacles writhed out of the black ocean like they were looking for something. I launched a wave of fire, and they exploded with a horrific shriek.

Hondo was on his feet now on his turtle, gripping something in his hand, but before I could make out what it was, the fog thickened, instantly blocking all sight and sound. The world went still.

"Hondo!" I shouted. "Brooks!"

There was no answer.

The fog made my eyes burn and pressed on me so heavily I fell to my knees. Alana caught me. I clutched the turtle's shell with one hand while I tried desperately to swipe the mist away with the other.

My heart pounded. Think. *Think.* How do you fight a face-less monster that is everywhere?

To my horror, the edge of shell I was holding suddenly broke off in my hand. And just like that, the entire turtle beneath us began to fall apart.

NO!

In half a blink, it disintegrated like soggy paper.

Alana and I slipped into the black ooze.

11

I had to think fast.

No way was I going to let this sludge be the last thing my friends and I ever saw.

As I treaded the black gunk, wondering why it wasn't eating me alive, I shouted, "Alana! Adrik! Hondo!" Where were they?!

A terrible chill spread through me as some*thing* wrapped itself around my ankles and climbed slowly up my thighs. My storm runner leg vibrated with what felt like a million volts of electricity. Whatever was gripping it let go with a hiss.

YES!

I reached for more fire power, for any ounce of strength I had left, but there was nada, not even a spark. And the more I struggled, the farther the freezing muck pulled me under.

I was shivering uncontrollably. I sucked in huge gulps of air as I struggled to keep my head above the living darkness.

An image of my mom came into my head as the sludge crept up to my chin. She stood on the beach, throwing a stick for Rosie and smiling. The black liquid rose to my mouth. My eyes teared up as reality slammed against my heart and mind.

But right before I was about to take my last breath, a shape beneath my feet rose from the depths, lifting me out of the freezing sea. My legs trembled as I tried to find my balance on top of the moving form.

I drew in a lungful of air and looked around wildly.

"Hondo! Brooks!" I gasped for breath between each name. "Ren!"

The fog was still too thick to see through. Where was everyone? Were they okay?

A familiar heartless laugh filled the air.

I froze.

Ixkik'! Blood Moon. The wicked underworld mom to even wickeder twins.

I spun in a circle. My heart thrashed like it was on a mission to punch a hole in my chest. Then, slowly, the fog lifted like a stage curtain. Except I didn't want to see *this* stage. A sick feeling roiled through me.

"It was so tempting to just watch you drown," Ixkik' said with a sigh.

I was now standing on a fifteen-foot-long platform that was floating in the air at least five feet above the black sea. At the far end, a sludge-covered Alana was crab-walking toward her brother. Adrik sat up, shivering with a panicked look in his eyes as his sister pulled him to her, rubbing his arms to warm him up. Hondo stood over both of them, looking like he'd just taken a mud bath. His chest heaved as he gripped a stone ax that had to have come from the open pack near his feet. Around his neck, a plain jade face mask hung by a thin string.

What the heck? Where did he get *that*? And why was it perfectly clean? Had he just put it on?

The moment my uncle saw me, he let go of the ax, raced

over, and tugged me into a near-smothering hug. His voice came out in an exhale of relief. "Zane, you're okay. You're okay."

"How did *you* survive?" I held him tight, not wanting to let go. "Where are Brooks and Ren?" I searched the sky, but it was empty. Had Brooks gotten away? Had they . . . ? No! I refused to think about them falling into the dark sea.

"Ixkik'!" I shouted.

"What a sweet reunion," her voice echoed. "Now, how about we get down to business."

Before Hondo released me, he whispered in my ear, "Protect the stone!"

What?! I blinked back the shock of his words. How did he know about the stone? Was this an in-the-know teacher thing? *Forget about the stone!* I wanted to shout. *We need to keep our heads and get out of here alive.* Heck, I didn't even know where *here* was. Or how Blood Moon had found us. And how we were supposed to fight an invisible enemy.

"Enough with the theatrics!" Camazotz's gravelly Dark Knight voice soared toward us on a gust. Then, within a ring of ash and shadow, the bat god materialized. All ten feet of him—a semi-human body with huge, hairy wings, slimy claws, and slitted reptilian eyes that blazed yellowish-green.

My chest seized. How had they found us? I thought water was supposed to throw gods off. And then I realized—they must have tracked Brooks, the hawk flying *over* the water.

Alana and Adrik, still clinging to each other, gasped as he loomed over them, his wings spread wide.

I'd hoped (dumb, I know) that I'd never have to see the

bat god again. I stepped forward, slipping on the wet surface. "Let them go!" I yelled. "They have nothing to do with this!"

Hondo's gaze flicked down to the ax he had dropped, and to his pack, as if he was trying to send me a message.

"Where's your fire now?" Ixkik' laughed lightly. "Did the darkness steal it from you?"

So *that's* why I'd felt so cold inside and Fuego hadn't flown back to my hand.

Zotz turned to face me and smiled wickedly, showing all his fangs. The tiny bat mouths on the undersides of his leathery wings snapped hungrily. My stomach turned in on itself.

"It's been a while, Zane," he said, stroking his chin with curled claws.

Adrik kept his eyes on Zotz, never blinking. Okay, so if I managed to get out of this alive, Ixtab was going to gut me, because the hairs on Adrik's and Alana's heads had *definitely* been touched.

Ixkik' sighed, and I cocked my head, trying to figure out where the sound had come from. What was her deal with always hidey-holing? She'd done the same thing back at the Pyramid of the Magician. She could pass me on the street or bump into me at the mall and I would have zero idea it was her. And that made her more dangerous than Zotz.

"I'd like to be forthcoming, Zane," said the bat god. "Can we be forthcoming?"

I braced myself, knowing I wasn't going to like what he had to say. I waited, my senses on high alert for any weakness, any opening to escape this madness. "Okay," I said. As long as he was talking, he wasn't clawing out my heart.

"Good," he said. "Ixkik' is quite impatient. I agree it would have been so satisfying to watch the darkness devour you. Especially after you sidestepped Iktan and managed to thwart my plans for a second time." His eyes flashed as he clapped his wings. "Bravo. I really do applaud the effort. I had hoped our next meeting would be different. . . . No, not different—*excruciating*. But I must play the hand I have been dealt. So, without further ado, I am going to ask you a question. I want you to be very careful in how you answer. Do you understand?"

I nodded, swallowing the burning lump in my throat. I glanced up at the sky and saw a faint glimmer of silvery blue. Brooks?

"Good," the bat god said gleefully. "Let's begin. Where is the stone?"

No one said a word. It was like that moment in math class when your teacher asks for a volunteer to go up to the chalkboard to work out a problem. And even if you know the answer, no way are you going to raise your hand, because who wants to be a show-off and solve an equation in front of everyone?

Adrik stood shakily. "I have it."

Zotz jerked his attention back to Adrik. "Ah, finally someone with a speck of sense." He uncurled a claw slowly. "Hand it over."

Hondo stepped forward. "*I* have the stone."

"No!" I shouted, unsure of what Hondo and Adrik were up to. "*I* have it!"

Alana stood, tears making tracks down her black-streaked

face. Her sunglasses hung crookedly around her neck. "It's *my* stone. *I* have it."

Zotz dropped his head, shaking it. "I really wanted to save this for later, but you give me no choice."

I for sure thought he would spread his wings and let all those creepy mini bats scratch out our eyes for an afternoon snack, but instead, the sea boiled and bubbled, splashing over the sides of the platform and making the surface even slicker and shinier.

Zotz floated above the mess as if he was afraid to get dirty. A thick tentacle whipped out of the sea and lashed through the air. Before we could react, the thing seized Adrik, spun him off his feet, and turned him upside down, shaking him like a piggy bank.

Alana screamed, "Leave him alone!"

I had to give Adrik credit. He didn't flinch. He didn't even close his eyes. And no amount of acting videos can teach you *that* kind of control.

"I sense he doesn't have it, and I don't want to hear him speak another lie," Ixkik' said. The tentacle slid up to Adrik's mouth and covered it (gross!) so no words (or lies) could escape. "Let's get on with this!" she commanded.

"Patience," Zotz argued, eyeing Alana. Another tentacle whipped over the platform's edge, gripping her around the waist so quickly I barely registered the motion before the slimy thing began to drag her toward the sea nice and slow, like it wanted to make sure we didn't miss one heart-stopping second of her demise.

I sprang forward and tried to grab hold of her, but I slipped and crashed down on my knees. Hondo also made a lunge, only to slide across the platform's surface and collide with me. His mask was now tucked beneath his shirt. Was he hiding it from the gods?

Adrik kicked and squirmed against the giant tentacle's strength.

A hateful laugh came from deep within Zotz when Alana was tossed into the air like a coin. We all watched in horror as she fell toward the dark churning sea of sludge. Hondo and I scrambled and clawed our way across the platform like fish out of water.

Out of nowhere, Brooks swooped in. Ren, now awake, was on the hawk's back, her blue eyes fierce and angry.

Zotz's thick neck swiveled in Brooks's direction, but before he could raise a claw, Brooks snatched up Alana and rocketed her out of the bat god's reach. Then they were gone, as if the sky had swallowed them whole.

How was that possible?

Zotz stared at the silvery sky with a look of surprise that disconcerted me as he folded his wings. "Zane, Zane, Zane," he said. "I suppose I will have to kill you all one at a time until I get what I want. And I was so looking forward to the thrill of the hunt. Oh, well."

Hondo reached into his boot and pulled out something. *That must be the stone!* I thought. It was the size of a silver dollar and glowed red like a hot coal. "You want this?" he shouted. "Then come and get it!" He threw it high into the air.

The moment shrank down to a slo-mo tunnel view.

"Noooo!" Ixkik' and I screamed simultaneously.

Hondo, taking advantage of the distraction, hurled his ax at Zotz. A wing lashed it away. I'm pretty sure Zotz would have bitten off my uncle's head if he hadn't been so focused on the stone still spinning toward the sea.

Brooks reappeared, the edges of her wings silvery blue, matching the sky. That's when I realized she had never disappeared. She'd just used some sort of camouflage, like that night in New York. But how? Ren and Alana clung to her back.

Brooks dove toward the spinning red glow and nearly snatched it up.... But it slipped from her grasp and fell back toward the platform.

With a flick of his wrist, Zotz trapped the stone in a vortex, spinning it toward his outstretched talon. "Finally," he said with a sigh. "And now for the disrespectful little thugs. I'll start with the hawk." He sniffed the air. "A ha' nawal?" He traced a long claw across his jaw as he shook his gigantic head in amazement. "It's been more than a century since we've encountered one of those, right, Ixkik'? Which will make her a valuable addition to my legion."

"*Our* legion," said Blood Moon.

Ha' nawal?

I knew that Mayan word! *Ha'* meant *water.* But...what was a water shape-shifter? Brooks had always hated the stuff!

"We have the stone," Ixkik' said. "Now, let the suffering begin!"

I had mere seconds, and all of them mattered. I closed my eyes, searching deep for a flame, for any ounce of my godborn powers. Just one spark...And then I remembered: The sludge hadn't touched the top of my head. Or my eyes.

Fire. Fire. Fire.

"Zane!" Hondo shouted.

I opened my eyes. Zotz's gnarled claw was within inches of swiping Brooks. A stream of blue flame burst from my eyes, shooting directly at the god's neck. He clutched his burning throat in a silent scream as two bats raced out of it in a terrified frenzy.

The bat god fell to his knees, heaving. Steam rolled off his hairy back.

I lunged for the stone, but a frantic small bat got in the way, accidentally knocking it out of the vortex and over the edge of the platform, where it sank into the darkness.

"Oh, how those you love will pay, Zane Obissspo," Ixkik' hissed. "I promise you they will pay."

Suddenly, jagged stripes of lightning split the sky into a hundred pieces. Rain lashed down violently. Thunder crashed. The world felt like it was colliding with the sun.

Ixkik' shouted, "They're here!"

They?

A thin spiral of dark fog spun into the sludge as Zotz beat his hairy wings furiously. His eyes were burning with rage and pain and lust for revenge. In that moment, I swear the world stopped spinning under the weight of my enemies' threats.

Zotz flew closer to the black sea, desperately searching for the stone. Dark water splashed higher and higher like angry lava, driving back the bat god as tentacles lashed out.

The sky trembled, exploding in blasts of violent white.

"There is nowhere you can hide, son of fire!" Zotz screeched. "Nowhere you will be safe. I swear by the darkness, I will hunt you." Then he disintegrated into a million specks of dust.

The tentacle holding Adrik vanished, too, and the godborn crashed down onto the platform, which groaned, then tilted.

There was no doubt about it: we were going down.

I jerked my gaze to my uncle. He put on the jade mask.

"Hondo!"

"The stone!" he shouted as he jumped into the roiling darkness.

As the platform sank under our feet, the last thing I heard was Blood Moon's faint whisper:

"At last it is mine."

12

⠒

I expected freezing wet darkness, not miniature monkeys.

Wait. I need to back up. The scene was like some kind of dream sequence. You know, the kind you feel like you're looking at from outside your body?

We had fallen into the water/sludge/bubbling blackness. I squeezed my eyes closed and then—*bam!*—the next thing I knew, I was waking up drenched but clean on a fluffy white bed, staring up at a big ole opening in some thatched roof. Little greenish-gold eyes peered down at me from leafy branches above the hole. I blinked a few times, not sure I was seeing what I thought I was seeing. Blackish-brown critters that couldn't have been more than ten inches tall perched on the boughs, babbling away and smacking their lips.

My first thought was *I must be in Xib'alb'a and stuck in Monkey House.* Then I remembered that there is no Monkey House.

"Welcome to SHIHOM, Zane."

Hurakan?!

I turned my neck to see my dad standing on the other side of the room, which wasn't very far away, since we seemed to be squeezed into some kind of wooden dollhouse. Everything came back to me in a whoosh. I sat up, swinging my legs over the side of my bed. "What happened? Hondo and Brooks! Are they okay?"

Hurakan's dark eyes looked through me as if he could read my past, present, and future. He probably could. "Everyone is fine. But if the turtles hadn't sent those messages . . ." He drew in a deep, painful-sounding breath.

So that's what those glyphs were? Telegraphs to my dad?

Hurakan stepped out of the shadows and into the light. I hadn't seen him for three months, not since the Council of Gods had signed a new treaty making everyone promise to get along and quit killing each other. Seeing him felt really good, even under the circumstances. He adjusted the collar of his gray jacket. As usual, he was dressed casually, in dark jeans.

He held Fuego in his hands.

I jumped up so fast I got woozy, but not before I grabbed my cane/spear and fell back onto the bed. "How . . . ? Where did you find . . . ?" My mind was a jumble of memories, nightmares, and too many questions to count.

"Once the darkness fled with Zotz and Blood Moon," Hurakan said, "the sea reverted to its usual state and the cane was freed. I didn't find it—Fuego found *you*."

I clutched Fuego tight, like it was a living thing. To me, it sort of is. "How did they find us?"

Before Hurakan could answer, the truth slammed into my brain at a million miles an hour. If I was remembering right (and I'm pretty sure I was, even though I'd almost drowned in bubbling black ooze, and that's a real brain drain, believe me), Hurakan, god of fire, wind, and storms, had singed Zotz's sorry butt with some wicked lightning. "Wait—did you knock Zotz into tomorrow?"

My dad folded his arms across his chest. "Knock him into tomorrow?" he echoed, raising his eyebrows.

"Yeah," I said. "It sort of means to obliterate someone."

"No, I did not obliterate Camazotz. I was more interested in saving you."

Oh.

"Because my mom would kill you if you didn't?"

He half grinned. "Something like that."

I pushed back my wet hair and stood. Was I supposed to hug my dad? Shake his hand? Give him a high five? Tell him Ah-Puch is the worst travel planner ever?

"I opened an emergency gateway," he said. "It was rough. You've been unconscious for an hour. Maybe you don't have to tell your mom about this?"

"Ha! Okay."

Just then, a small creature dropped from the trees above, knocking a couple of miniature monkeys out of the way. She was about three feet tall, with enormous eyes and elongated fingers like a tarsier. Two membranous ears poked out of her short ocher hair, which looked more like fur, and she wore a red, blue, and green feather dress. The monkeys clicked their teeth and squealed with annoyance.

"Oh, be quiet," she said to them as she gripped a clipboard. "You don't own the place."

That only sent the primates into a chorus of shrieks and howls, and they began to throw toilet paper rolls at us.

"Hey!" I threw up my hands for cover as the rolls bounced off my head. The monkeys were smart enough to avoid hitting my dad, who I figured could *obliterate* them with one stare.

The little rascals snickered and retreated into the shadowy trees.

"Thieves," the creature muttered, shaking her head. Then, with a pained smile, she said, "Zane Obispo, how good of you to wake up. How do you like your tree house?" She glared up at the branches, which were shaking with monkey glee. "Make sure to keep all your belongings locked up."

"This is a tree house?" I was going to spend the summer here? Cool! Except for the toilet-paper-throwing monkeys.

"That's what I said." The creature wrinkled her nose and eyed me up and down. "You really smell."

My dad covered his mouth like he might laugh. I threw a glare his way as I sniffed a pit. "Really? I really smell?"

The creature rolled her eyes. "Why are you asking *him*? I'm an air spirit, the most trustworthy, honest creature in the cosmos. Much more so than earth spirits, or those sneaky mountain spirits."

"Hang on," I said, remembering Ah-Puch's note. "I thought you air spirits were on strike."

"Not all of us. Some of us need to earn a living. You think these imported feathers are cheap?" She glanced down at her clipboard. "Anyway, you don't have a lot of time. Ixchel's attendants will have to do their magic," she said, peering up at me with a scowl. "You certainly can't go to the claiming ceremony looking and smelling like that! Everyone is already there except you, and—"

"I thought the claiming ceremony was tomorrow night," I said to Hurakan.

"We moved it up," he said solemnly.

Oh man, I knew that expression. It meant *We moved it up and you aren't going to like the reason why.*

13

•••

"Zane can get cleaned up here," Hurakan said.

The air spirit started to argue until my dad twitched an eyebrow (a tiny little twitch!), which pretty much sent her into hyper adiós mode. Where could I learn to do *that* trick?

After she left, Hurakan turned to me. "We need to talk."

That was the understatement of the century. "Yeah, I have tons of questions. . . . But shouldn't we do it on the way to the ceremony?" I felt kind of responsible for all the godborns I had found, like maybe I should be there to cheer them on or something.

"I have something to show you first," he said. "And not until you clean up. You really do smell."

Whatever. Outside my tree house bedroom was a little sitting room. And I mean little, with a small desk and chair, and that was about it. No TV, no mini fridge . . . I guess godborns didn't have the luxury of lounging around.

The door in the sitting room led to a narrow hall with two other bedrooms, and an exit to the outside. Ugh! Housemates. I was kind of hoping I'd have my own pad. There was one bathroom, which I could barely squeeze into without hitting my head against the ceiling. I took a quick shower under a warm waterfall that sprang out of a wood-paneled wall and chirped like a million birds.

Back in my bedroom, the dinky dresser had only two drawers. One was labeled PAJAMAS, and the other CLOTHING. I opened the pajama drawer to find a pair of gray sweatpants and a matching T-shirt that read SHIHOM. In addition to some new underwear and socks, the clothing drawer offered three pairs of black drawstring pants, a pair of basketball shorts, and five black tees with SHIHOM on the front in white block letters. Did we really need so many reminders of where we were? There was also a black baseball cap that read HURAKAN. Seriously? We had to wear parent-branded stuff? No gracias.

I threw on a tee and the shorts. At the foot of my bed was a pair of black tennis shoes. I had to give credit to whoever had ordered all this stuff, because the right shoe was smaller than the left, to accommodate my different-size feet.

I met my dad in the sitting room. He was pacing around the cramped space like a restless jaguar. And I should know—I've seen him in that form.

Sometimes I forgot he was a god. And sometimes I forgot he was my dad. The whole thing was pretty confusing, but in this moment, I thought he looked like both.

"How did Zotz and Ixkik' track us down?" I asked again.

He turned, kind of startled, and said, "Your journey should have been top secret. No one knew you were traveling a day early." He rubbed his chin. "Come on. I want to show you something."

We walked down the hall to the exit, a screen door that opened to an outdoor platform. We were high up in a ceiba tree that had been strung with tiny lights. They flickered green and blue, casting a soft glow on the leaves. An intricate network of suspension bridges and ladders connected us to dozens of other shimmering tree houses. I noticed that some of the houses had full wraparound porches and floor-to-ceiling windows. Figures I would get the low-rent version. But where was everyone? The place was silent except for branches rustling, birds chirping, insects buzzing, and monkeys lip-smacking.

We descended a series of ladders and crossed a few bridges until we came to the edge of a stone arena. It was an obstacle course complete with flags, cones, wrestling mats, horizontal step equipment, and punching bags (painted with faces that looked a lot like Zotz, Jordan, and Bird). Stacked on an iron table were all kinds of weapons: spears, daggers, dart guns, throwing stars, and other stuff I couldn't even identify.

"This is all Hondo's design," Hurakan said as we looked around.

So that's what Hondo had been doing while I was away. Who knew? I felt a surge of pride. "It's awesome!"

"The godborns will do their training drills here," my dad went on as we made our way around to the other side.

The words sank in slowly. *Training drills.* All I heard in my mind was *war games.*

"*This* is what you wanted to show me?" I clutched Fuego, wondering why all the mystery. "It's cool, but . . ."

Hurakan stopped at a rugged stone wall at least fifty feet high. Six thick ropes hung from the top, and he tugged one of them.

"What I have to show you is at the top. Maybe it will answer some questions. Or maybe it will only create more."

He gestured to some steep zigzagging stairs. "We can take the steps, or..."

Our eyes met. My dad was the only sobrenatural I could communicate with telepathically when we weren't touching. Maybe it had something to do with our blood tie. The words formed in my mind and flew outward before I could stop them. *Is that a challenge?*

I blame my boldness on the near-death adrenaline still churning inside me.

I would never challenge a godborn, especially after what you've just been through.

My bones *did* feel like they had been pounded with a sledgehammer. Hurakan inched closer, igniting a flame on his right palm. I started to back up, but he closed the distance and placed the fire on my shoulder. The pain relief was instant.

Okay, I'll climb the rope, I said. *On one condition.*

Gods don't do conditions.

I vanished Fuego. *I wouldn't want to have to tell my mom about the whole sludge disaster....*

A small smirk tugged at his mouth. *What's the condition?*

No god powers.

He thought for a moment, then nodded. *No god powers.*

I grabbed hold of the rope with both hands, pulling myself up while anchoring my feet against the stone. Hand over hand, I walked up the wall, using both upper and lower body strength. I knew I should pace myself, but I was curious about what Hurakan wanted to show me up top, and I really wanted to get some questions answered.

Hurakan scaled the rock, matching my stride, but let me tell you, without his godly powers, he looked like a regular wall-climbing guy. I take that back. There was nothing "regular" about him, but he for sure didn't fly up the course like I know he could have. He actually seemed to be having a hard time! (Sorry, if you ever read this, Dad, but it's totally true.)

"Not easy being human, is it?" I huffed, trying to hide my toothy grin. There was something very satisfying about seeing Hurakan, the great creator god, struggling up a stone wall with nothing but a rope, his muscles, and his will.

He scowled. "You're cheating."

"Am not."

"You're using your storm runner leg."

"We said no god tricks," I reminded him. "No one said no godborn strength."

"You test my limits, kid," Hurakan said. But he was smiling a little.

Truth be told, I hadn't used much of the power that ran through my storm runner leg, thinking I'd wait until I really needed it, which was pretty much about now. I let the power surge through my blood faster than lightning as I raced up the wall.

I gotta give Hurakan credit. He wasn't going to go down easy. He redoubled his efforts and scrambled over the edge a respectable three seconds behind me.

My heart pounded. My muscles burned. My smile split my face in two. Had I really just beaten the great Hurakan?

I glanced over at my dad, who rolled to his feet. By the time he stood, his godly self had returned. "That was truly terrible." He wiped his hands together. "I actually feel sorry for humans. On second thought, not really."

When I stood, I saw that we were at the top of a bluff that overlooked a sea of green trees. Thin mist curled off the canopy, rising into the pale blue sky. On the horizon, there was an intricate column of lights. Wait. I blinked and looked closer. Those lights were on the trunk of a ginormous tree with crisscrossing branches that rose endlessly, as if reaching for the farthest corners of the Milky Way.

"Is that . . . the World Tree?" I knew the answer before Hurakan confirmed it. And after thinking, *That's so freaking cool*, I thought. *So THAT'S where Itzamna hangs out all day. No wonder the guy wears shades.*

"Welcome to SHIHOM."

"It's . . . it's amazing!" I turned to him. His grim expression wiped my smile away. "You didn't bring me up here for the view, did you?"

In the distance, I heard what sounded like rushing water-falls and a steady pounding of drums. The smell of summer rain floated over the trees.

"About the demon . . ." he began.

"Ik?" My neck got hot and my cheeks prickly. I wasn't sure what to say next. *I should have seen the signs? Sorry, but she's a duplicitous, underhanded traitor? Is the Statue of Liberty thing for real?*

My dad's face tightened. "You must always be prepared for the unexpected," he said sternly. "I will contend with Iktan, and we will unravel our enemies' plans, but for now," he went on with a beat of hesitation, "we might need you godborns."

And there it was. The real reason my dad wanted to get me alone, the real reason he had raced up the wall with me. It had been like a really bad classroom icebreaker. He was buttering me up!

Feeling Fuego's absence, I called my cane to me. "You guys are all-powerful gods," I said. "Why would you need a bunch of rookie godborns?"

Hurakan turned his gaze to the forest. I could tell he didn't want to be here. I don't mean at the World Tree—I mean in this position. He said, "Akan disappeared yesterday."

Okay, I for sure wasn't expecting *that*. "The god of wine?"

My dad took a slow and steady breath. "He's dead."

A tremble gripped me from the soles of my feet all the way up to my neck. "How do you know?"

"Each of the lights on the World Tree represents a god," he said. "His light is out."

I had never met Akan, but the news shook me. "Gone?" I swallowed.

"Camazotz and Ixkik' have sacrificed him to raise an enemy god." Hurakan twisted a black beaded bracelet on his wrist as he faced me.

"That's why you moved up the claiming ceremony," I said. "You need the godborns to have some chance, some ability . . . to fight."

"To protect themselves, and yes," he said slowly, "to fight if need be."

The air felt thick and dry. A fierce wind swirled around

us, and I knew my dad was causing it. "After the ceremony, all the gods will convene away from here, to make plans," he said, letting the gust die. "In the meantime, I need you to work with the godborns. You are the only one who knows *how* to be a godborn. How to connect with your power."

Hurakan had asked me months ago to help train the godborns, but I didn't think that meant all by myself! Panic struck my gut like a hot branding iron. "That took me months to learn." Being a godborn didn't just happen once you were claimed. Kukuulkaan's words came back to me: *You don't become a god automatically, with the snap of a finger, or because of your bloodline. Godhood has to be earned. Fought for.* I clenched my jaw, thinking how hard I'd struggled to become one with the fire. And then a worse thought occurred to me: "What if some of the godborns don't get any powers in the claiming ceremony?"

I remembered that day with the Sparkstriker. When she pounded lightning into my leg, she had said that I could possess nothing of true value and that I might be a terrible vessel with no ability to control any of my powers.

It seemed brutal and unfair. In all my conversations with the godborns over the last three months, I'd never even mentioned that having zero power was a possibility. How could I have overlooked that detail? I felt like the world's biggest jerk.

"Zane," Hurakan said calmly, "what are you talking about?"

"I'm the one who rounded them up, told them to trust me!" Why did it feel like the gods were (yet again) forcing others to pick up their mess? My eyes were burning and fire was blazing in my veins. A wave of flames burst from my free hand into the sky. "I told them to come here, and for what? To have zero power? To be used in a war that has nothing to do with them?"

"This has *everything* to do with them, with all of us!" He paused, took a breath. "And who said they would have zero power?"

"The Sparkstriker." I told him what I had recalled.

My dad held up his palm. "True value according to *her.* Just because someone can't wield fire or some other power doesn't mean they have nothing. Think, Zane. These godborns still have the blood of a god flowing through them!" My dad shook his head. Then he gestured to my hand and added, "Use a little more twist in your wrist next time."

Was he seriously trying to give me a fire lesson right now?

He took a deep breath with his eyes closed. When he opened them, they shone blacker than polished obsidian. "The other sobrenaturales will be here tomorrow, to help." Hurakan placed his hand on my shoulder and squeezed. "Remember, Zotz and Ixkik' still have to find a way to raise more than one god, to *try* to build an army great enough to challenge us. That takes time, and long before they succeed, we will crush them."

He said the words like he didn't want me to worry. Yeah, right. I remembered all too well what it was like to face the bat god. His hatred was so thick, it choked the air. He didn't seem like the kind of guy who would make threats when he didn't already have some kind of twisted plan. I mean, a few months ago, he had managed to trick me into coming to *him*, and he'd been shrewd enough to set up my dad's execution as a blood sacrifice.

"Zotz's mind is warped," I said, puzzling out my thoughts. "I don't think he wants to go to war. And I feel like...like there's something we're missing."

"Of course he wants war," Hurakan said. "Why else would he sacrifice Akan to raise an enemy god?"

"But if he *could* resurrect more than one Mexica-slash-Aztec god," I said, "wouldn't he have to worry about them turning on him someday, too?"

I know how this power stuff works. It's the same in middle school. One day, the quarterback of the football team is on top of the pack. The next day, some other kid has overthrown him and bounced his king status to the curb.

"I mean, what if the Mexica gods' allegiance to each other is stronger than their allegiance to Zotz or Ixkik'? Seems like a pretty big risk."

Hurakan rubbed his thumb across his chin, considering this. "You think the war is a distraction."

"Yeah, and their plan has to do with—" I stopped short, remembering my promise to Alana not to say anything about the stone. But that was before we were almost devoured by poisonous power-sucking sludge.

"With what?" he prompted.

I couldn't help myself. I told my dad everything. "And now Ixkik' has the stone," I said, recalling her words: *At last it is mine.*

My dad listened carefully, hanging on every word. "They've killed a god," he said. "They may have stolen a stone with a power we have yet to identify." He shook his head and added, "Our enemies have been hard at work."

"You're talking enemies without me?" came a familiar voice.

14

Here's a sentence I never thought I'd write: I was stoked to see the god of death.

Ah-Puch and I had been through muy scary stuff together. He'd risked his own life to save mine and Ren's.

Still, a part of me always worried that he might suddenly tackle me to the ground. I *had* defeated him once, after all.

But as he came toward us, wearing his signature black suit, he sported half a grin. "How do you like the place?" He swept his hand in front of him in a grand gesture, his expression loaded with self-satisfaction. "The tree houses were my idea, by the way."

Hurakan groaned. "Is there a reason you're sneaking around the jungle?"

"Who's sneaking? I'm right here. I heard Zane and crew arrived, and I wanted to welcome them." He conjured a bag of popcorn and tossed some into his mouth. "Mmm. Best corn invention in the universe. By the way, I greeted Ren before you, Zane. No offense, but she's my favorite."

"I'm shocked," I said.

"So, I heard Zotz and Creepy Lady found you, almost killed you," Ah-Puch said.

"Sounds about right," I said bitterly.

A slow smile spread across his face.

"How come you're smiling?" I asked. Now *that* was offensive.

His grin disappeared. "I'm just imagining what it will feel like when I rip out their hearts. With my teeth."

Hurakan filled Ah-Puch in on everything while the god of death munched on his popcorn. When my dad was done, Ah-Puch didn't really react. He just flung an unpopped seed over the cliff. "Kernels," he said with a shudder. "Bad memories."

He should have been grateful for kernels. I had restored his strength with a magical one.

"Zane," my dad said, "there are millions of stones in this universe. Could you tell us more about it?"

I frowned. "It was about the size of a silver dollar...."

The gods stared at me blankly. Too late, I remembered that the Maya didn't use coins. They traded in chocolate and other stuff.

"Never mind." Then I added, "Oh, and it glowed red."

"Well," Ah-Puch said, "that narrows it down to half a million." He handed me the bag of popcorn and wiped his hands together. "Think bigger. These godborns—"

"The twins," my dad clarified.

Smoke curled off Ah-Puch's shiny black hair. "I hate that word," he growled. Yeah, I didn't blame him. I had bad memories of Jordan and Bird, too. "These *godborns*," he said, "they had the stone, which begs the question: Where did they get it? And if you want the answer, you need to ask: Which god's blood is pumping through their veins?"

Hurakan studied me, waiting for a response.

I stepped back, ready to defend the secret, because who wants to be torn to pieces by the queen of the underworld? ¿Yo? ¡No!

Crap! I could tell by the gods' granite faces that I wasn't leaving here without telling them the truth. The whole truth, so help me gods.

"We're going to find out in a few minutes, whether you tell us or not," Ah-Puch said.

Just in case I was breaking some godly oath, I finagled a way to keep my promise to Ixtab about not breathing a word. I dragged Fuego's tip in the sand and spelled out IXTAB.

You could've heard a pinto bean drop.

I didn't think it was even possible for my dad to be stunned, but in that moment, he looked like someone who had just been told that cockroaches can live for weeks without their heads. Which is true, BTW.

And then it was as if the sky opened and the answer came whizzing toward me like a comet. "Do you think *she* made the stone?" I asked Hurakan. "Like you made the jade jaguar tooth?"

My dad had gifted me the jade, a conduit of pure magic. Its owner could bestow it with any power he wanted ... but only by giving it away. I know it was a stretch to assume that the twins' stone was the same kind of thing, but hey, there's more than one tooth in a jungle cat's mouth. ...

Hurakan and Ah-Puch shared a glance heavy with secrets that the other gods would kill for. And guess what? I was so over it.

"I just risked my life by spilling everything—now it's your turn. Tell me!"

Hurakan spoke first. "Ix-tub-tun spat the magic jade you used to give Ah-Puch his life back."

"Ix-tub-tun?" I'd never heard that name.

"She's a stone-spitting goddess," Ah-Puch explained.

"And?" I pushed. "You think she spat the stone Adrik had, too?" I can't believe I actually said that sentence.

Hurakan nodded.

My head was going to explode. I think the top of my hair actually sparked. "If it's as powerful as the jade, and Zotz and Ixkik' have it . . ." My mind reeled. "They could use it to do all sorts of damage."

"It isn't as powerful as the jade," Hurakan said. "Ix-tub-tun can never duplicate a stone."

And just like that, my big *I-figured-it-out* moment went up in smoke.

Ah-Puch shrugged. "Flawed design, if you ask me."

"No one's asking," Hurakan said, grabbing a fistful of popcorn from Ah-Puch's bag. Then he turned back to me. "If the stone is from Ix-tub-tun, Zotz and Ixkik' hold substantial power, yes, but nothing significant enough to enable them to raise an army of the dead."

"How do you know?"

"Because no single object has that kind of power."

"And there's no resurrection stone or wipe-out-all-your-enemies-in-one-breath stone?" I asked.

My dad laughed. *Laughed!* I didn't know whether to be

insulted or proud. Ah-Puch gawked at him like he had just morphed into a Keebler elf.

Hurakan said, "If there was, we would know about it."

I paced the edge of the cliff. "Can't we just ask Ix-tub-tun?"

"I'm afraid not," Hurakan said. "She turned herself into stardust and now follows the planet Chak Ek'. Otherwise known as Venus."

"Gods can do that?"

"Gods can do a lot of unimaginable things." Ah-Puch's gaze flew to the jungle below. "But why would anyone choose to be stardust when they could be all-powerful? *That's* the universal question."

I didn't think I would ever understand the motivations of a god. I mean, one day they can be pure evil, and the next day, your best friend.

A bell rang across the treetops.

"The ceremony's coming to a close," Hurakan said. "We need to head over there." He took me by the shoulders and looked me square in the face. And just for the record, I was almost as tall as him. "Zane, this is for the gods to worry about. Do you understand?"

"But the godborns are the ones in the cross fire, so I say we can be worried!"

"Not anymore," he said. "You'll be safe here. More magic surrounds this place than any other in the universe. When I return tomorrow, we'll have more answers about Zotz, Ixkik', *and* this stone, I promise—"

"Come on, Zane," Ah-Puch put in. "You shouldn't miss the end of the most boring ceremony of the century."

I accepted their words, but they did nothing to calm the fire still burning in my blood. A fire that told me that we hadn't seen the last of the darkness.

15

We emerged from the trees at the side of a
torch-lit ball court, a large T-shaped area with stone amphi-
theater seating on each side.

I scanned the stands for my friends but only spotted the
godborns I'd rounded up, including Marco, Louie, and Serena
from the junkyard battle. Those three were sitting together
in the front row, about fifteen yards away, like the tres mos-
queteros. I almost didn't recognize Serena, because her previously honey-colored hair was now black. Marco's chin scar
looked even bigger, if that was possible. And Louie? He was
chewing on a nail, looking just as nervous as he had the last
time I'd seen him.

Was that . . . ?

I swallowed hard. Blinked. Was that the Fire Keeper story
in some of the other godborns' hands?

"Itzamna gave them the second book, too?" I groaned.

"Well," Ah-Puch said, "you did write it for the godborns,
didn't you?"

"In the event I *died*!"

"Still a possibility," he muttered.

My dad shook his head, trying to stay focused on the
ceremony.

At the far end, the gods of the council were spread out on an elevated platform against a backdrop of eight-foot-high standing stones called stelae. The stones were carved with the gods' likenesses, except with more exaggerated noses and ears.

The Sparkstriker was there, too, with her back to us. She stood on a wooden stool next to a table at center court. Her electric pool of lightning fish shimmered nearby. Had she hauled that thing all the way from the Old World? Her hair looked as ratty as ever—maybe even rattier—with the same tiny bells tied to the ends.

The Sparkstriker's stone ax was poised high over her head, which told me that she was about to pound lightning into a godborn. My insides dissolved into mush at the memory of my own ceremony. I clenched my hands into fists, trying to hold myself together.

The crowd was hushed as everyone watched the ax come down with a blinding flash of white light.

Maybe it was instinct, maybe it was curiosity, but my legs started moving in her direction. Hurakan pulled me back. "Not yet," he said. "The dominant power must be located."

"This is twisted," Ah-Puch said, tossing more popcorn into his mouth. "And *I'm* the god of death, darkness, and destruction, so that's saying a lot!"

The torch flames crackled.

The warm air buzzed with raw energy.

The Sparkstriker stepped off her stool, and that's when I saw Ixtab and the twins. The goddess's eyes burned fiery blue as she watched Adrik and Alana shudder on the table. They were both dressed in SHIHOM uniforms: black tees and drawstring pants. Alana's shades lay at her side.

It was hard to watch their bodies convulse, their skin lit up like there was a fireworks show going on underneath. I knew their pain. Mine had been so awful I floated off to the Empty. But did Adrik and Alana know what was going on around them? Did they know Ixkik' had gotten her claws on the stone?

A minute later, Adrik and Alana sat up slowly. Adrik rubbed his head, and Alana put her shades back on. The crowd jumped to their feet and cheered.

The Sparkstriker said something to Ixtab, who scowled as she listened intently. Then the goddess turned and walked in the opposite direction without even a nod at her kids. She really was the queen of the cold shoulder.

"Where is she going?" My voice rushed out on a wave of anxiety. "Did she already claim them?"

"If this ceremony was anything like the others," Ah-Puch said, "the claiming happened before the ax came down on them." He pounded his fist into his hand to illustrate.

My dad's dark penetrating eyes never left Ixtab, who had made her way to the opposite side of the court. "It's time for us to depart."

I was getting pretty sick of the gods waltzing in and out of scenes like they owned everything and everyone. I mean, they sort of did, but whatever!

"See you tomorrow," Ah-Puch said with a forced glare. As soon as my dad's back was turned, he whispered, "I don't even want to go. The other gods are so boring!"

Then they both vanished in a circle of thick smoke.

When the air cleared, the Sparkstriker was standing right in front of me. I startled, clutching my chest. "You scared me to death!" I squeaked.

"Apparently not," she said, looking exhausted. "It's quite wearisome to work on so many. Quite wearisome. And where were you, Storm Runner? I expected you to be present."

A man's voice honked over a loudspeaker: "Report to your tree houses immediately. Lights out in fifteen minutes. The gods have graciously granted you a day of rest." He mumbled, "As if being pounded with lightning is hard. Mm-hmm."

"Why did you—" I started before the announcements continued.

"Training will begin as soon as the sobrenaturales arrive. In the meantime, no skulking, sneaking, loitering, yelling, complaining, or using any sort of unauthorized powers. I repeat: No using unauthorized powers."

The godborns began to file out slowly. I watched Alana and Adrik get shakily to their feet.

The Sparkstriker drew my attention back to her. "I'm going home to the Old World now. Tell the gods to lose my number."

"Hang on," I said. "What did you say to Ixtab? Why'd she just run off without even a good-bye to the twins?"

The Sparkstriker's eyes whirled and the bells jingled annoyingly when she shook her head. She leaned closer, and I got a whiff of mulch. "Seems that one of them has greater powers than the other. But you didn't hear that from me."

The ground opened at my feet, forcing me to jump back. In the hole, I saw a set of stairs going down. The Sparkstriker swept her red shawl behind her with a dramatic swoosh before she descended into the dusty dark. The electric pool on the court vanished instantly.

Then the ground closed up behind her, leaving just the words resonating in my skull. *One of them has greater powers.*

I had a sick feeling that Ixtab would soon be playing favorites.

16

I spotted Rosie at the far end of the court and
my heart did a little leap. "Rosie!" I shouted, but there must
have been too much commotion for her to hear me.

Ixtab stood at her side, stroking her neck like she was
her dog!

Yeah, I know I sound kind of possessive, but Ixtab is the
one who turned Rosie into a hellhound and trained her in
Xib'alb'a. That always made me worry that the queen thought
she had some kind of ownership papers or something.

"Hey!" I shouted, heading over with Fuego. Alana and
Adrik called out to me, but I gave them a *hold-up* sign, never
taking my eyes off my dog. With every step, I kept replaying
Ixtab's words in my head: *Do you think Rosie misses it here at
all?* "Here" being the underworld, and no way José was she
ever going to take Rosie back!

My dog bowed in front of Ixtab. A tiny orb of light floated
out of the goddess's mouth into Rosie's ear. If I had blinked, I
would have missed it.

"Ixtab!" I hollered.

She drew herself up, slowly lifting her cool eyes to meet
mine.

If there were an award for the most intimidating goddess,

with the most threatening *I-can-burn-off-your-face-with-one-look* gaze, she would for sure win it. And I don't care how fashion-y she was—she was muy scary!

In a blink, she vanished in a column of pale-blue smoke like all the other gods.

"It's Zane!" someone shouted. A few cheers erupted, but so did some curses. I didn't slow down enough to pay attention.

The announcer's voice boomed again. "I said no yelling! So pipe down or I will send for an earth spirit to bury you six feet under."

My entire focus was on Rosie, who bolted toward me with her lips spread in her signature smile. I was greeted with a giant slobbery kiss on the cheek. I loved it when she acted like her old desert dog self, which wasn't that often.

I hugged her tight, then pulled back to look inside her ear, but all I saw was a giant wad of wax. Whoops—she was overdue for a cleaning. "What did she do to you?" I muttered.

"Zane!"

I jerked to my left. Brooks was running toward me, followed by Ren and Hondo. The girls were in SHIHOM uniforms, but somehow Ren had gotten out of wearing the black sneakers and instead sported her trademark red cowboy boots.

Man, was I happy to see them.

Then others started calling to me—a few godborns headed our way.

Before I could respond, Ren waved her fingers in the air, creating a shadow circle around the three of us and Rosie.

Then she twisted the dial on her watch. Everyone outside the border froze.

I was almost afraid to ask. "Ren?"

Rosie let out a little whine. Her normally perky ears went flat.

Bouncing on her toes, Ren said, "My mom showed me how to stop time. So cool, right? But for now I can only do it for, like, five minutes." She pressed her lips into a thin, worried line. I got what she was feeling. As awesome as that gift sounded, it also seemed like a scary responsibility.

"Great. We don't need all those ears listening to us." Brooks gestured to the motionless crowd.

Folding his arms across his chest, Hondo said, "Something is off, Zane. The ceremony—"

"Everyone got pounded with lightning," Ren interrupted. "Even me. Sooo weird. I think I traveled to Saturn, but that's not the point."

I was about to ask *What* is *the point?* when Brooks said, "Akan's been killed." That opened the floodgates. The three of them started talking over each other, telling me all the stuff I already knew.

"Why don't you look shocked?" Brooks inched closer, eyeing me like she could see my secret before I even spilled it.

"Hurakan came to visit." I recounted everything that had happened, including my field trip to the underworld. I figured I could spill the beans now that Ixtab had claimed Alana and Adrik. Then I wondered, was that why she had walked away from them without saying good-bye? Because she gave one of her kids more power than the other? Could she really be that messed up? The terrible answer was YES!

Hondo leaned toward me and sniffed. "Why do you smell like popcorn?"

"Ah-Puch came, too—and brought a snack."

"Where is he now?" Ren asked.

"He'll be back tomorrow," I assured her as more questions ricocheted across my mind.

But my biggest question was practically burning a hole in my mouth. I turned back to my uncle. "How'd you end up with Adrik's stone in your boot?"

"He gave it to me," Hondo said matter-of-factly.

"What? Why? He was guarding it with his life," I protested. "Why would he just hand it over?"

"Adrik knew Zotz had come for the stone," Hondo said, "and the dude freaked, said he couldn't hand it over to the bat no matter what."

"I don't get it." I tapped Fuego on the ground, thinking. "Alana made it sound like the stone didn't have much power."

"Obviously not true," Brooks said with a dramatic eye roll.

Rosie sniffed Ren's watch and let out a stuttering grunt. I got the feeling she didn't like the whole stopping-time thing. Ren patted Rosie reassuringly.

Hondo threw up his hands. "Look, I didn't have time to ask Adrik why the rock matters so much. We were drowning in sludge, remember? If the dude hadn't been so desperate, I doubt he would have given it away."

"If it was so important, why did you *toss* it away?" I asked.

"Better for it to sink than end up in the wrong hands. And I thought maybe Brooks could—"

Brooks sighed. "Yeah, sorry about my fumble, Hondo. I almost had the stone. I mean, it was right in my claw-tips."

"No worries, Capitán. It was a total Hail Mary," Hondo said with a small shrug. "I'm just sorry I couldn't find the thing."

Frowning, Ren said, "I feel terrible that I zoned out and couldn't help you guys. Brooks told me that Adrik splashed me with that black water—it must have eaten up my powers, too. Even my Mexica ones!"

"If it could do that to your magic, it should have destroyed Hondo." Brooks twisted a curl around her finger and studied him suspiciously. "So why didn't it?"

I looked at my uncle, remembering how he had been covered in sludge, and how he had dived into the stuff like it was nothing, like he wasn't terrified of it sucking his bones through his nose. What was he hiding?

He scanned each of our faces, even Rosie, who was now sitting with her ears perked, like she wanted an answer, too. My uncle raised his hands defensively and with a guilty laugh said, "Maybe I'm just that tough."

Here's the thing about Hondo. He's the world's worst liar. Like, worse than me. And let me tell you, he was 100 percent lying through his teeth. But why?

Ren smiled gently. "You can tell us, Hondo. Really."

"Yeah, Hondo." Brooks crossed her arms. "Tell us. Really."

"It's a loooong story," he said, turning his face to me so I could see his barely raised eyebrow, which in bro-speak meant, *I can't tell you in front of them, but I will later. Promise. Help me!*

"Well, I want to hear it," Brooks said.

"Me too," Ren added. "But you have to tell it fast, because we're running out of time."

"Hang on!" I shouted a little too zealously as I changed the subject. "I forgot to tell you: Ixtab gave one of the twins greater powers than the other one."

"Oh man." Hondo groaned. "That bites."

Ren's face fell. "There's no justice in this world."

I shrugged, and Brooks gave me a knowing *I'm-onto-you* expression: twisted mouth and flashing amber eyes.

"And Hurakan still thinks war is coming," I threw out. "But I doubt Zotz and Ixkik' would be that obvious. I think there's a worse plan and we're being lured into some kind of trap." I told them about the stone-spitting goddess and the other stuff Ah-Puch and Hurakan had shared.

Brooks snapped her fingers. "Guys! There's an amazing library here. It's filled with thousands of ancient and sacred texts. I bet we could find some answers about the stone there."

"Forty-five seconds before time starts up again," Ren warned.

"It would be easier just to get the twins to tell us the truth," I said. Given who their mother was, however, they were probably champion secret-keepers and liars.

"You want to interrogate them now?" Brooks asked a little too excitedly.

Ren made a pitiful face and said, "They've been through a lot today. Besides, I already asked, and they got all tight-lipped. I think they're super bummed they lost the stone."

"Maybe they just need some time to get over it," Hondo suggested.

Brooks nodded like she was all too familiar with that kind of disappointment. "Let's meet at the library at dawn. See what we can find."

I understood Brooks's logic. If we could figure out the stone's power, we might be able to predict what Zotz and Ixkik' were planning to do with it.

Ren's fingers hovered over the watch's dial. "Zane, you shouldn't be here when I start time."

"Yeah, the crowd's likely to mob you." Hondo grinned.

Rosie nudged me with her nose.

Brooks gave me a look of sympathy, which scared me worse than when she gave me a murderous glare.

"What are you talking about?" I asked.

Hondo pulled a candy bar out of his pocket and held it up. A cartoon of my face was plastered on it. "Seems you're famous, Storm Runner."

17

I had bigger things to worry about than Ixkakaw, goddess of chocolate, putting my face on a candy bar. Like the fact that Hondo was keeping a secret from everyone.

My uncle and I took off before time started up again and I could be mobbed. Whatever. The second we were alone, heading to my tree house, I stopped under the shadows of a gran tree with a canopy so wide you couldn't see the sky.

"Spit it out," I said.

Rosie stood at my side, nodding her agreement.

"Spit what out?" he said innocently.

I threw him a *talk-or-else* expression. "And don't leave anything out, especially how you survived the sludge."

He told me I couldn't write about this, but it's pretty important to the story, so he's going to have to deal. Sorry, Hondo.

For the last three months, Hondo and Quinn had been "talking." As in, they *liked* each other. Yeah, let *that* sink in. But Quinn didn't want anyone to know because (1) Hondo's a human, and (2) Quinn was on a big undercover operation, aka Zane Obispo's Demon/Godborn Tour, and she wasn't supposed to be distracted. Seems that falling in love is a big distraction.

Anyhow, last month Quinn sent Hondo a warrior mask for his birthday. I mean, nothing says love like a warrior mask stolen from your ex's Casa Grito, right? Apparently, the mask gave the wearer the powers of the warrior who first owned it. And *that* was how Hondo had been able to dive thirty feet under black ooze to search for a stone barely bigger than a quarter.

Don't get me wrong—he wasn't like some newly minted Spider-Man or Aquaman or whatever. *But,* in extreme situations, the mask gave him a certain edge, and now that Hondo had worn the thing, it belonged to him and only him. And according to my uncle, the warrior had possessed some pretty sick powers, like heightened mind-body control. Apparently, when Hondo put the mask on, all he had to do was focus— "like deep meditation, mind over matter." There was only one glitch: every time my uncle wore the mask, its powers would be diminished a little. I guess that was the universe's way of keeping things in balance. Or the gods' way of keeping all the power for themselves, as usual.

The whole time my uncle was telling me this, I paced alongside Rosie. "So, you can survive, like, anything?"

"No sé. I only used the mask that one time," he said. "I wasn't even sure it would work, but I had no other option."

"That was a pretty big risk."

With a light shrug, he added, "You can see why I couldn't tell you in front of Brooks. Quinn doesn't want anyone to know she gave me the mask."

My head was spinning from all the information I'd had to process over the last few hours. Maybe that's why the next question just flew out of my mouth: "Quinn really likes you?"

Hondo let out a light laugh and stood taller. "*That's* the part you can't believe?"

Rosie yelped, then gave Hondo a big toothy grin telling him she totally approved. I guess I did, too.

Scratching my dog's neck, Hondo said, "Thanks, girl. I knew you'd have my back."

We continued down the path. "Dude, it's kinda hard to keep a mask a secret," I said. "I mean, we saw you wearing it."

"I know." Hondo wiped sweat off his brow. "And the mask only has power if a sobrenatural gives it to you. Which means Brooks will catch on, unless..."

I didn't like the look he was giving me. "Unless what?"

"You want to tell her *you* stole it."

"*Me?!* How did I become the thief in all this?"

"Just help me out, man. Throw your girlfriend off my trail."

I leaned against Fuego and felt heat rise in my cheeks. "She's not my girlfriend."

Hondo clapped my back. "Listen, Diablo. I'm here for you. To give you man-to-man advice, help you figure this out. It's complicated falling in love the first time."

I shrugged him off me. "You're the guy who's all lovesick. I...I don't want to talk about this." Who said anything about love? Geez.

When we got to the first ladder that led up to the tree houses, Rosie inched back, sniffed the air, and took off into the jungle. I guess it was dinnertime.

"Rosie can't climb ladders," I said. "Where's she supposed to sleep?"

"Uh—she's got some pretty killer accommodations."

My hellhound got a better bunk than I did?

As soon as I entered my tree house suite, a flurry of motion sent me tumbling back into Hondo. Six little monkeys dashed up the walls, carrying pillows and toilet paper rolls as they disappeared through the open roof.

"¡Los monitos!" Hondo flew into the house. "Give that back!" He shook his fists at the devious beasts that were now safely back in the trees, howling with laughter.

"With those thieves around," Hondo said, "you should probably keep everything locked up."

There wasn't much left for them to take. I saw an envelope with my name on it on the desk and tore it open. I read it silently as my uncle peered over my shoulder.

7:00 a.m. Breakfast (If you're late, you starve)

7:30 a.m. Physical Training with Hondo the Horrendous

I eyed my uncle. "Horrendous?"

He flashed a smile. "Gotta keep the kids on their toes. Easier to lighten up than tighten up."

I did a quick scan of the rest of the schedule (teachers to be determined), which would start the day after tomorrow:

1. *The Great Gods (Part 1 of 20)*
2. *The Art of Magic and Mayhem*
3. *Sinful Chocolate: From Bean to Bar*

I glanced up. "We have to learn about chocolate?"

Hondo's expression turned serious. "I guess there's a lot of history and magic in those little cocoa beans. Plus, Ixkakaw threatened to annihilate it all if the gods didn't offer the course."

"Man, that's the best threat I've ever heard," I said. "Don't do what I want? No chocolate for you for, like, ever."

I read the last couple of classes.

4. *Monsters, Beasts, and Demons*

5. *The Mystic Universe: Cosmology, Fate, and Time*

And two hours with Itzamna for writing classes, including how to read and write glyphs. *Two hours!*

"I bet the monsters class will be cool," Hondo said.

"I've already seen them up close and personal, so, uh, no thanks."

Hondo yawned and stretched. "Time to get some shut-eye. It's been a long day. See you at the biblioteca tomorrow morning." He went to the door, then turned back to me. "Brooks says it's the big red temple with a million steps. You can't miss it. And don't be late. I've gotta get ready for my big godborn training day."

After he left, I fell into bed and stared through the trees at the stars. My mom once told me that looking at the stars is looking into the past. If a star six hundred light-years away died a century ago, we still wouldn't know it. We'd be gazing at its previous form, clueless about all that death swarming beyond. The thought was muy depressing.

I settled into my pillow, and just as I was about to drift off, I heard footsteps in the hallway outside. It was probs one of my housemates finally getting here from the ceremony.

"You'd think the son of war would get a better house."

I groaned. I was stuck with bad-mood Marco?

"At least your dad isn't some minor god of thunder," a girl said sadly. "Like, couldn't I have gotten a little lightning, too?"

"So what's your talent?" Marco snorted. "Making a big boom sound?"

"You want to hear a boom?" the girl snapped. "Here you go." And then the outer door slammed hard enough to shake the walls.

I thought about getting up to greet Marco, but I was too wiped. I fell right into a dream. The air was thick and dry. Gray light pressed in on me. I heard the sound of fingers tapping on stone. My throat was so parched, it felt like I had swallowed sandpaper.

The world came into focus slowly, its edges worn like a soft blanket. I was back at my old elementary school, in Mr. Hawkins's classroom. Every single desk was occupied with a zombie-eyed student. They all just sat there frozen, staring straight ahead at the chalkboard where Mr. H stood like a mannequin, chalk in hand. Out the windows, orange leaves were suspended in mid-descent. I glanced at the wall clock: The hands were stopped at 2:32.

"Hello, Zane."

I startled, turning my attention to the voice at the back of the classroom. The Red Queen sat on top of Mr. H's desk, sipping a blue icy drink with a pink straw. She looked the same as the last time I'd seen her, which was right before I put on a death mask that was supposed to hide me from the gods. Okay, maybe she had a few more wrinkles. (Was that possible? Do the dead age?) She had the same black hair tied up in a tight bun and wore a band of jade stones around her head.

"You could have picked"—*slurp*—"a better"—*slurp*— "meeting place."

"Me? I didn't pick this place."

"This is *your* dream," she said. "If it were up to me, we'd be sailing across the Mediterranean, but here we are in a dreadful plastic world that smells like sawdust and child angst."

"I have no control of—"

She interrupted me with a sigh. "I have an ominous message for you. So, let's just get to it, shall we?"

18

No one in the history of the world has ever gotten excited by the words *I have an ominous message for you.*

Clenching my jaw, I thought, *This is just a dream and I'm going to wake up any second.* The Red Queen threw both hands into the air like she was shaking out a blanket. A wall of red smoke covered the windows, and with a satisfied exhale, she said, "That should give us some privacy."

I looked around at the motionless students and Mr. H. "What about them?"

"They are a creation of your own mind."

New SHIHOM class idea: *How to Improve Your Dreams.*

The Red Queen's dark eyes shone bright even in the gray light. "You know the rules," she said. "I cannot provide any information unless you ask the right question, and you cannot ask the same question twice or more than one question at a time. Now please be quick. We only have a few minutes before the smoke and I both disappear."

With Fuego in tow, I walked toward her between the desks, careful not to trip over any of the glassy-eyed students, who were kind of freaking me out. "What's the ominous message?"

"Did I say ominous? I meant calamitous, and it's a two-part message." She held up three fingers, confusing me further. "So make sure you're paying close attention."

"Who's the message from?"

"The Fire Keeper," she said.

"Antonio?" My eyes did a quick scan, like the guitar-strumming dude who protected the most magical fire in the universe might pop out from behind a desk. "Why didn't he come himself?"

"He moved to a distant isolated place to protect the flame, but he went to great lengths to communicate with me in secret. It really is a burden to be a former fire keeper! I received an honorable discharge when I died, and yet I'm still called to duty."

I ran my fingers over Fuego's dragon head. "What's the first part of the message?"

She took a long sip of her drink and gripped her forehead. "Ooh...brain freeze." After a few swallows, she continued, "Well, I am not sure how reliable this is. He *is* on the edge of the world, and the distance may have weakened his signal, but I do think I got it right."

Think?

She took a deep breath and licked her lips before she spoke. "'All is not as it seems.'"

Great! Glad we got that cleared up. "Can you be more specific?"

"Zotz and Ixkik' are five steps ahead of the gods. Or is it six?"

The walls felt like they were closing in on me. *Any* steps ahead spelled disaster. "How?"

The Red Queen adjusted her jade headband. "I think my head must be growing—this is so tight!" She stretched it over her thin eyebrows. "Your question was *how*? My answer is: How should I know?"

I held my motor mouth in check, knowing that one false move would set her off and I would get nada. "You're the messenger."

"I AM A QUEEN!" Her anger shook the room.

"Sorry... uh... You're right. I just meant..." Man, I was the worst backpedaler ever. "I meant the message isn't making sense to *me*." I gave a fake chuckle. "Human brain and all. Maybe you can explain it again?"

"Hmph." She gave me a stern look. "My job is not to explain. Now, do you want to hear the second part?"

Though I wasn't sure I was ready for it, I nodded.

"ASK THE QUESTION!"

I sighed, barely keeping it together. "What is the second part of the message?"

"Follow chapat..." She stared up at the ceiling, tapping her chin. "Or was it look for chapat and follow...? Being dead really messes with your memory."

I wished Antonio were here so I could tell him: *Next time you have an important ominous, calamitous message, send someone else!* I wanted to race to all the questions bubbling up inside me, but I remembered the rule: One at a time. "What's chapat?"

"Mayan for *centipede*." She extended her blue drink with a lipstick-stained straw. "Would you like a sip?"

"No thanks. Uh, this centipede... it's not, like, some giant monstrous thing, right?" Hey, I had to know what I was getting into. Being from the desert, I was used to scorpions, snakes, and tarantulas. But of all the creepy crawlers, centipedes were my absolute least fave. Ever try squashing one of the plump suckers? *Snap, crackle, pop!*

"Sometimes big isn't necessarily more dangerous," the Red Queen said. "A small bite from the tiniest of spiders can kill you. Especially magic ones."

That made me feel sooo much better. "Where do I find this chapat?"

"No idea."

"But you're a great queen fire keeper." I put lots of emphasis on *great*. "Surely you can see that, right?"

"Well . . . yes, I am great," she said. "And I am a queen."

She set her drink on a stack of ungraded worksheets and hopped onto the scuffed linoleum floor. With a single swipe of her arm, a faint ball of fire appeared between us. I was instantly drawn to the flame, expecting to see an image in it that would explain everything. But there was nothing.

Sighing, the Red Queen closed her small fist and the fire disappeared. "Not as good as the old days when I was alive. But the answer is: in the jungle where the earth spirit hides."

"Er . . . the jungle's kind of a big place." I needed more to go on than *Search for a centipede in the forest!*

"That isn't a question!" the Red Queen announced, shaking me from my thoughts. Her jade headband glittered for half a second. "Bah! Time's up."

"Wait! I need just a little more—"

She vanished, leaving me alone with the zombie students staring vacantly at Mr. H's hunched back. The wall clock began to tick, and I inched backward. A chair scraped across the floor. A student turned in his seat to face me.

"Adrik?"

He looked confused, his eyes wide and wandering. Then they zeroed in on me. "What am I doing here?" he said.

Scritch. Scratch.

I looked up.

The fluorescent lights flickered overhead. Mr. Hawkins's arm was moving.

A voice floated toward me. "The day is coming, Zane."

It was Ixkik'.

I wanted to scream, but nothing would come out.

Mr. Hawkins dragged the chalk across the board with a screech that set my teeth on edge, but what he wrote was even more disturbing.

Are your eyes wide open?

19

When I woke up, I felt like a cement truck had
backed over my head. Twice.

I squinted, trying to shake those awful words: *Are your eyes wide open?* What did *that* mean?

Brooks slipped into my room just then and whisper-shouted, "Why are you still asleep?"

"I'm not," I said, pointing to my face. "See?"

"It's dawn! Are you coming or not?"

"Okay, okay. Just let me get ready...."

After brushing my teeth and changing into the SHIHOM uniform of a black tee and drawstring pants, I met Brooks outside at the nearest bridge. The whole world was misty and grayish blue—even the trees took on a gloomy cast. Brooks was wearing clothes identical to mine and leaning against a rope, her arms folded like she was deep in thought.

When she saw me, she reached into the small straw bag hanging from her shoulder. "Hungry? I grabbed you a couple of burritos—extra chile and bacon, like always." She handed me a warm bundle wrapped in wax paper.

I hadn't realized how hungry I was until I got a whiff of the roasted peppers. "They make breakfast burritos here?" I took a bite of the spicy awesomeness.

"Come on," Brooks said. "You can eat and walk."

"You already know the way to the library?"

"I flew around, mapped it," she said casually. "In case we need an emergency exit."

We made our way across several bridges, passing a dozen or so darkened tree houses, until we reached a rope ladder that led us down into a thicket of silvery-green trees that were so ancient-looking it seemed like they had sprouted from some dead artist's canvas.

"Pretty awesome, isn't it?" Brooks said as we headed down a narrow path of shadows. "Did you know the temperature here is always a perfect seventy-three degrees? Oxygen levels are optimal, too. Oh, and it's all-you-can-eat—of anything you want! Well, mostly. Which is how I got the burritos. We can go to the café later so you can check it out."

I popped the last bite of breakfast into my mouth. So, the gods had made a paradise for us. That was super nice and all, but it did nothing to douse the fire that had been pulsing in my bones since the dream. Sometimes I wished the fire would just talk to me. You know, with direct messages like *Turn here, Don't go into that dark room*, etc.

"Hey." Brooks snapped her fingers in front of my face. "I know that look. What's the deal?"

It was weird. We'd been apart for three months, and it felt like it had only been three hours. All that worry about Brooks ghosting me or things being weird between us vanished. We were still friends, even though she'd read all those things I'd written about her in my book and I had, you know, maybe almost kissed her that night on the beach—emphasis on *almost*. I thought about what Hondo had said: *It's complicated falling in love the first time.* Is that what I felt for Brooks? Love? Or complicated? Or both?

I told Brooks every detail of the Red Queen's dream visit. Brooks stopped and faced me. "Centipede? Jungle? Earth spirit?" She sighed. "Does she ever give you, like, solid details?"

"Nope."

We walked a few more paces, and I thought Brooks was puzzling out the Red Queen's message, but she switched topics. "And did Hondo tell you how he managed to survive the sludge?"

I scratched my cheek, wishing she wasn't staring at me like that. "Just got lucky, I guess." I knew the lie was worse than pathetic the second I spilled it.

"Lucky. Uh-huh." Brooks stopped and stuck a hand on her hip. Uh-oh. She studied me hard, her eyes flashing copper. I was going to combust any second. Then she waved a *whatever* hand through the air and said, "Did you say that Ixkik' was your teacher?"

"Not my teacher. She was using him to write that message, *Are your eyes wide open?*"

"That doesn't sound good." She looked up at the sky, then back to me. "Maybe it was just a really bad nightmare."

"Nah," I said. "She was there for sure." Which made me never want to fall asleep again.

"And Adrik was there, too? Like *there* there, or like you just dreamed about him?"

I gave it half a thought and was shaking my head before the words came out. "He was there. Like, in the flesh." Adrik had looked different than the glassy-eyed students and Mr. H— they were more like paper cutouts, two-dimensional. He was fully there, in all three dimensions.

"Huh" was all Brooks said.

"Huh? Huh what?"

"Maybe his gift"—her eyes drifted to mine—"has to do with dream walking."

"Dream walking?" I remembered how my neighbor, Ms. Cab, had shown up in my dreams all those months ago, but I'd thought that was because I carried one of her magic eyeballs, making it possible for her to communicate with me.

"Dreams are sacred," Brooks said, continuing down the path. "They were once a way of communicating with ancestors. And I'm no expert, but Quinn has told me how, a long time ago, spies used dreams to send secret messages."

Brooks hooked a left down an even narrower, darker path littered with rocks and fallen leaves. Thick, knotted tree branches twisted in a creepy shadow web. I could feel the weight of the miniature monkey eyes on me even though I couldn't see the rascals. I braced myself for a toilet paper pounding.

"Then what happened?" I asked.

"The gods happened," Brooks said with a hint of sadness. "They banned the whole practice, because they didn't want anyone else to be able to communicate in secret. They're so mean."

"Well, if Adrik *is* a dream walker, then he should hang out in someone else's head. It was creepy, like being watched when you don't know you're being watched."

We came to a crossroads. Brooks looked left, then right, hesitating.

"Are you lost?"

She exhaled dramatically. "I mapped this when I was flying, and things always look so different when you're in the air."

I was about to ask if we should fly the rest of the way, when she glanced over her shoulder, then up to the canopy of trees. "This is right." We continued walking the tight path that began a sharp incline, and I thought how easy it would be to get lost here.

Fuego sank into the soft earth as I walked. "How am I supposed to find a centipede in the jungle, and which jungle?"

"Maybe it's not literal," Brooks said.

Brooks seemed different since she'd come back from her dad's. Don't get me wrong—she was still feisty and guarded, but she seemed more patient or more grown-up or more something I couldn't put my finger on.

"What do you mean, 'not literal'?" I asked.

"What if the centipede is a symbol, like an emblem on a ring, or a picture on a T-shirt or something?"

Brooks had a point. The Fire Keeper *was* a poet and songwriter, after all. His words could have a million meanings, which only added to my frustration. "Why do you think he sent me the message?" I was thinking out loud. "I mean, why not send it to Hurakan?"

"He likes you more?"

"I'm serious. Hurakan said this mess was for the gods to worry about."

"But the Fire Keeper said that Zotz and Ixkik' are way ahead of the gods," Brooks said. "So maybe he thinks *you* should handle it."

"Handle it?" I said, frustrated. "This isn't some chore like taking out the trash."

"It kinda is." Brooks patted me on the shoulder. "Relax. Hurakan and Ah-Puch will be back tonight. I'm sure they discovered all sorts of stuff at their meeting, and by the time they get here, I bet they're only two steps behind."

Was that supposed to make me feel better? "How about zero steps behind?" My gut twisted into a triple-knotted rope. I wanted to share Brooks's confidence, but the fire in my blood doesn't lie, and at that moment, it was hissing right below my bones.

And in all of the craziness of the last day, I had nearly forgotten one important thing the bat god had said. "Zotz called you a water nawal." I glanced at Brooks. She kept her gaze on her swiftly moving feet, acting as if I hadn't asked the question. "He said he hadn't seen one in over a century. What did he mean?"

We came to an enormous clearing.

Before us stood a bright red temple with multilevel platforms, massive steps that led to a pillared building on top, and corbeled roofing. The exterior walls were decorated with huge sculptures (probs of the gods) and glyph carvings. The temple had a single doorway on the bottom level and butted up against a lush hill blooming with red and yellow flowers.

Rosie sat at the foot of the stairs, licking her front paw like she had been waiting all day.

"Well?" I tried again.

Brooks continued to walk, and just when I thought she was going to clam up, or tell me to mind my own business, she said, "That's why I can blend in. . . . You know, camouflage myself."

"I don't get it," I said. "What exactly *is* a water nawal?"

Brooks stopped and turned to me. "It's just a shape-shifter that can blend in. I found out when I went to see my dad."

"What did he tell you?" Brooks didn't exactly have a great relationship with her dad. She'd only gone to see him because he was sick.

"He told me that when I was born, I wasn't breathing. It was only when they put me in water that I took a breath. I guess water nawals can always breathe in water, except I can't. Not anymore."

"Why?"

Her face fell. "My dad didn't want the gods to know about me, so he kept me away from water, made me afraid of it. He said he knew the day would come when my water nawal spirit would reveal itself and I'd learn the truth, but he wanted to put it off as long as he could." She shrugged. "It's no big deal."

"That he didn't tell you, or that you're a super-cool water-breathing shape-shifter chameleon?"

"I told you, I can't breathe in water, Zane. My dad stole that when he kept me away from it for so long."

How could he just control her future like that? It seemed

wrong, even though it was meant to protect her. "I'm really sorry."

Brooks croaked, "Yeah, me too," as she headed toward the temple.

Rosie greeted us with a big yawn at the entrance. I didn't see Hondo or Ren anywhere.

"Are we supposed to wait for the others?" I asked.

Brooks shrugged and fixed her gaze on the symbols carved into the lintel. "'The words before all words,'" she read aloud.

Trails of smoke curled from Rosie's nose as I peered into the shadowy doorway. Garbled whispers floated out on a cold draft.

"What are those voices?" I asked.

"Maybe library ghosts?"

"Maybe we shouldn't go in," I said. Rosie whined her agreement. For being such a huge, ferocious hellhound, she sometimes still had a scaredy-cat heart. Like me.

"Ghosts can't hurt you," Brooks argued.

"How do you know?"

"I don't." Brooks grabbed my arm and pulled me into the whispering darkness.

20

·

Dim lights flicked on overhead, casting shadows against the chipped blue stone walls.

The air smelled like old cigars and dark chocolate. Rosie stalked next to me, sniffing and leaving trails of smoke.

The whispers seemed to lessen with each step we took down the winding hall. A minute later, the space opened into a massive tri-level room with floor-to-ceiling bookshelves encased in glass.

The domed ceiling reminded me of a church, except this one's stained-glass windows were melded with shimmering gold. At the center of the room was a 3-D holographic orb, glowing blue as it spun in midair.

"This is amazing!" I walked past rows of roughly hewn wooden tables to get a better look.

"Kinda gives me the creeps." Brooks rubbed her arms vigorously. "All these books and pages and . . ." She paused before adding, "Dead writers."

"Did you have to put it that way?" I asked, still taking it all in. When I'd gone to regular school, the library was always my favorite place. It smelled good and had too many stories to count. But this library blew the doors off anything I'd ever seen. "It feels like a cathedral for books." My voice echoed across the chamber.

"Or a mausoleum," Hondo said as he entered from another doorway, a steaming paper cup in one hand and a small book in the other. He was sporting his regular jeans and a SHIHOM tee embroidered with his name: HORRENDOUS HONDO, STAFF.

Ren was right behind him, cupping what smelled like cocoa. "You guys, there's a hot chocolate machine back there," she said. "Actually, it's an anything chocolate machine. You just tell it what you want, and presto"—she snapped her fingers—"it spits it out. And it's the best-tasting chocolate you've ever had. I bet it's Ixkakaw's recipe."

Hondo bit back a laugh. "You can even try one of your own candy bars, Diablo."

Rosie licked her chops and whined like just the word *chocolate* made her crave a snake head or two.

Brooks said, "I could use a chocolate iced donut. Zane?"

I nodded as she called Rosie over and headed out of view.

"Dogs can't have chocolate!" I shouted.

"She's a hellhound!" Brooks hollered back. "She can have whatever she wants."

"And check this out." Ren pointed to the globe, hurrying over to it. She reached out a finger, and the second she touched it, the glowing blue orb zipped away to a corner of the library.

"I said no touching," a woman's voice said.

What the . . . ?

Ren said, "Sorry. I forgot. You're just so cool."

"Is that thing alive?" I asked.

"Did you call me a thing?!" the globe asked, spinning back to the center of the room.

"Not a thing," I said, trying to erase my mistake. I mean, who wants to get on the wrong side of a talking globe? "I meant..." I fumbled for the right words as I went over to get a better look *without* touching the orb.

"You meant that I am a highly advanced achievement," the globe said. "With access to more knowledge than your puny brain could ever hope to contain."

"*Exactly* what he meant, Saás," Hondo said, sipping his coffee like he was enjoying this exchange.

"Her name is Sauce?" I asked.

"S-A-A-S. Mayan for *light*," Brooks said, with a dropping tone on the last *a* as she came back with a pile of chocolate donuts. She tossed one into the air for Rosie to snatch up.

"Watch this." Ren's smile lit up her whole face as she leaned close to the orb. "Saás, what is Jupiter?"

"Why do you waste my talent with such simple-minded questions?"

A holographic image of the planet appeared above the globe along with a bunch of text about Jupiter being the fifth planet from the sun, how much it weighs, et cetera et cetera.

"Cool, we've got an Alexa globe," Brooks said, handing me a donut. "Now can we look for the information we came for?"

"My name is not Alexa," the globe said. "So insulting. Alexa wishes she were as erudite as I am. She is a mere knock-off. Of course, many of the Maya inventions were copied and our advancements were never...Oh, never mind."

Hondo held back a smile. "I've got a better question, Saás. Who is the greatest wrestler of all time?"

"I will not be tricked," Saás said in a more annoyed voice. "Which standards are we using to measure? Career highlights? Look? Marketability? In-ring ability?"

I munched on my donut. The chocolate icing was glossy and as smooth as velvet. But it was the way it melted on my tongue and the nutty dark sweet flavors burst in my mouth that stole a breath. Literally.

"Whoa! This is . . ."

"Crazy delicious?" Brooks said, polishing off hers and licking her fingers clean. "Now can we get back to why we're here?"

Hondo said, "The first thing we have to do is find out if one of Ix-tub-tun's stones is missing."

Ren nodded. "If it is, Adrik and Alana may have . . . may have *had* a stolen stone. Unless Ix-tub-tun gave it away."

"Which makes no sense if the twins' dad was, you know . . ." Brooks peered at us through dark curls that had fallen over her left eye. "If their dad was *with* Ixtab."

Hondo raised his eyebrows and nodded appreciatively. "Wow, Capitán. I love how your mind works. It reminds me of—" He stopped himself before he said *Quinn*. "Er, reminds me how smart and calculating you are and—"

"Hey, Saás," I said. "Where can we find information on Ix-tub-tun's stones?"

Saás sighed. "This again?"

"We already tried that." Ren sipped her cocoa. "She could only confirm that Ix-tub-tun spat out a lot of magic stones."

Right. Nudging my chin toward Saás, I mouthed, *Is she recording us?*

Hondo said, "That's what I want to know. She could be blasting our convo all over the galaxy."

"As if anyone would care," Saás said. "All of you are insignificant. Except, maybe, the dragon."

"Dragon?" I echoed.

"Only one with the power of the dragon can unlock the knowledge in this sacred place," Saás said.

I thought the globe was malfunctioning until I remembered something Itzamna had told me that night in Cabo: *All the writers I deem worthy have the power of the dragon.*

Saás sighed and added, "Zane Obispo, surely you know that Itzamna deemed you worthy many moons ago."

"Zane has the power of the dragon?" Brooks said in a tone that bordered on impressed.

"So cool," Ren uttered.

I screwed up my face and cocked my head. "No, I did *not* know. If he did . . . I didn't agree to it."

"You should be honored," Saás said. "It isn't every decade or even century that this power is bestowed, so get a better attitude."

I rubbed my right temple in slow circles. "What does it even mean?"

"The truth contained within this temple is highly valuable to our history, our origins. It cannot be seen by just anyone, not even the gods. Only those with the magic of the dragon can call up the words and share them with others. Those who came before you were much more appreciative of the honor."

Hondo, Ren, and Brooks stared at me expectantly. "Okay, fine," I said. "How do I do call up the words?"

"Just ask." Then Saás, with a sizzling *pop*, vanished in a single beam of light.

"W-wait!" I stammered.

"Technogics can be moody," Brooks said with a light shrug. "And before you ask, *technogics* is a combo of *magic* and *technology*." She looked around. "Hey, maybe you'll find a chapat here."

"Chapat?" Hondo asked.

After I told him and Ren about the Fire Keeper's message and the warning from Ixkik', Hondo stroked his chin like a professor, considering something super deep. "'Are your eyes wide open?'" he repeated. "That isn't creepy at all."

"Weird," Ren said as a small rabbit shadow-hopped around her. "I had a bad dream, too. An alien took me to a magical metal shop and asked which materials were best for a spaceship, because she had to get to a cave of teeth. Or was it crystals? It was definitely crystals." She shook her head. "The strangest part? The alien had my mom's voice."

Brooks said, "Maybe those tree houses mess with godborn brains."

That was a seriously disturbing thought. "Come on, let's stay focused on the stone." I looked around. There were no signs defining the sections. "There are thousands of books here, and categories. Where do we even begin?"

"*S* for *stone*?" Ren suggested. "Or *I* for *Ix-tub-tun*?"

"Or *Z* for *Zotz the loser*?" Hondo said with a sneer.

"Maybe there's a catalog of stones," Brooks said. "Look for a really, really fat book."

Yep. That definitely narrowed it down. As far as I could tell, all the books looked fatter than double-stuffed encyclopedias. But at least encyclopedias have numbers and letters on the spines. These books only had worn symbols that were hard to make out because the bindings were so old and tattered. Almost as ancient as the scrolls lodged in the cubbies that were scattered between shelves.

Brooks raised her eyebrows. "Well? Go ahead, Zane. Call up the words."

I felt stupid. Stupider than stupid. "Hey!" I brightened. "Maybe I can just summon the right book."

Hondo folded his arms over his chest. "Now would be good."

I leaned against Fuego, tracing the dragon head with my thumb. "Er..." I said to the air. "I'm looking for a book on a magical stone spat out by Ix-tub-tun. Are you here?"

Only the sounds of our breathing and Rosie's snorting could be heard.

Ren glanced around, then looked back at me. "Maybe just tell the words to appear for us?"

"Maybe Saás was wrong," I said, feeling flustered. "I mean, don't you think Itzamna would've told me, 'Hey, I gifted you the power of the dragon, which doesn't mean you can fly or do anything cool, but you'll be able to read the books in the library'?"

"Magic comes in many varieties," Brooks said. "And it's all about the specific variety you need in the moment. Right now, we need to be able to read these words."

Fine. Fine. Fine. But a flying kind of magic would have been cooler. "Words," I commanded, "show yourselves."

The three-story-high glass cases slid open with what sounded like a deep and eerie breath.

"Whoa!" Hondo said.

"Power of the dragon," Ren whispered. "Awesome."

"That's it?" I asked, disappointed. "No hand delivery of the right book? Pretty weak, Itzamna, if you ask me." I thought of all the searching we still had to do and groaned.

Brooks, Ren, and Rosie headed up the open staircase to the upper floors while Hondo and I stayed on the first level. We tugged book after book off the shelves and flipped through pages written in languages I had never seen before. Just when I was beginning to think this was hopeless, I opened a book wide and, to my amazement, the words floated an inch off the page. When the text settled back down on the spread, it was in English.

"Whoa! Did you see that?" I asked Hondo, skimming the words. "It's about a war...."

"Right," Hondo said, unimpressed. "But how can you trust words that just float off the page and change like that? Keep looking."

I set down the book and opened another. This one had illustrations of dragons, bloodlettings, and diagrams of weapons like blowguns and throwing stars. Fortunately, none of them came to life. "We must be in the battle-slash-murder section," I mumbled.

Hondo opened another libro, and incoherent whispers

came out. He slammed it shut and threw it on the ground, silencing the voice. "What the hell was that?"

"Maybe it's some kind of magical audiobook?"

Hondo stepped back with his hands in the air. "I am not opening those páginas otra vez. ¡No gracias! ¡Qué scary!"

The guy would jump into killer sludge for a magical stone, but he wouldn't touch a book that whispered?

Ren was talking to Rosie upstairs while Brooks stomped loudly on the third floor.

"Finding anything?" I yelled up to them.

"Early history of medicine," Ren called down from a balcony. "Astrophysics, poisonous plants . . . So far, nothing on a magical stone."

Brooks grunted. "Anyone want to read the same old boring creation myths in which the gods glorify themselves? Ooh, here's something!"

"WHAT?" we all shouted at the same time.

She leaned over a railing, peering down at us. "Sorry, I meant . . . it's not what we're looking for." Brooks held up a thick leather-bound book. "It's all about how to psych out your opponent—mind and spirit stuff. Hondo, you'd love this!" she said before she went back to the hunt.

Just then, there was a shuffling and a bump. I lifted Fuego, prepared to turn it into a spear, as Brooks turned into a hawk and swept down to the first floor in 0.3 seconds. Hondo and I turned to see Adrik and Alana enter. Dark circles bloomed beneath their brown eyes. There was a long moment of astonishment in which no one knew what to say or do. Like, should I ask about Ixtab? The stone? How they slept?

Brooks assumed her human shape. "Did you follow us?"

"I share a tree house with Ren," Alana said, tugging on her sunglass strap. "When I heard her get up—"

"Oh, sorry," Ren said, descending the staircase with Rosie. "I tried super hard to be quiet."

Adrik came over to me like a guy on a mission. "Next time you haul me into a dream, Zane, how about no classrooms," he said. "I mean, come on, man! That queen was wee-ee-ird."

Everyone's eyes zoomed in on me. "Uh, I... I didn't haul you into my dream. You were just there," I said. Then I added, "Which means you heard Ixkik', too?"

"Yeah, man," he said, shuddering dramatically.

Alana ran her hand along the edge of a table. "The Sparkstriker said Adrik's power is dream walking, but he's in big-time denial. He thinks it should be something cooler, like mind controlling or lightning throwing or something like that."

"Did I *say* that?" Adrik grunted. "I just have this feeling it's more, okay?"

"Lightning throwing?" Hondo sipped his coffee. "Is that a thing?"

Did that mean Adrik was the one who had gotten the dominant power?

"What are you doing in here?" Alana asked.

"Trying to find out more about your stone," said Brooks. She gestured at the three levels of bookshelves. "But it would be a lot easier if you just came clean."

"Yeah," I said. "How about you tell us what the stone does exactly?"

The twins exchanged glances.

Finally, Adrik said miserably, "What does it matter? It's gone now. We failed."

Alana touched her brother's arm. Her eyes flicked from face to face. "Okay, we'll tell you."

21

•

•

"It opens things," Alana said.

"Things?" I asked.

"Like it's a key?" Brooks tilted her head.

Adrik nodded. So that's how they had opened the laundromat door.

Alana spoke quietly. "But I don't see how that helps Zotz and Blood Moon."

"How did your dad even get the stone?" I asked.

"The goddess of the underworld," Alana said like I was slow on the uptake.

"You mean the amazing Ixtab!" Ren said excitedly.

Amazing Ixtab? I was about to argue but then picked up on what Ren was doing—she wanted the twins to feel good about their goddess mom, even though she ruled the land of the dead and was kind of sinister. Okay, a *lot* sinister.

Rosie threw back her head and howled at the sound of Ixtab's name. Jealousy thrummed in my bones. Why was my dog so loyal to the goddess? Because Ixtab had saved her life and made her a hellhound? Or did this have to do with the orb Ixtab had planted in Rosie's ear?

Brooks looked like she was trying to find a teaspoon of patience in this flood of chaos.

"The stone's from *Ixtab*?" Hondo's pacing came to a halt. "Not Ix-tub-tun?"

"We don't know where Ixtab got it," Adrik said. "We didn't even know she was..." He took a shaky breath. "Come on, man. Our dad didn't exactly say, 'Hey, your mom is the goddess of the underworld' like it was some bedtime story."

Alana added, "He just said that our mom gave it to him. That it was a way for him to see her in case of an emergency. But he didn't know how to use it, exactly. We thought we would come here and get answers, talk to someone in the know."

That made sense. Ixtab was all about emergency measures—like the gateway to the underworld she had created for me but never gave me instructions for.

Adrik's eyes went wide and he collapsed into a chair.

"What's wrong?" Alana rushed over.

"I...I had a dream last night," Adrik said.

"Are you being melodramatic again?" Alana narrowed her eyes, studying her brother.

"I thought we were talking about the stone?" Brooks whispered to me.

"I had forgotten the dream until now, when we started talking about Ixtab," Adrik said. "Then it just popped into my head."

"What happened in it?" Ren asked.

"It was right before Zane dragged me into his dream," Adrik went on. "I was on a huge lumpy sofa that practically swallowed me up, and this bird-size butterfly swooped in from nowhere. It started talking to me. . . . It might have been Ixtab." He shook his head.

"What did she say?" I asked.

"She wasn't super clear," he said. "I mean, she *was* a giant butterfly, and her voice was kind of far away, but I'm pretty sure she said that the stone has a name." Adrik looked up. "She called it an entry stone. It opens places . . . places protected by the greatest power and magic anywhere."

Ren's hand flew up to her mouth. "Of course! Ixkik' and Zotz want to break through the magic that surrounds SHIHOM!"

"To murder us while we sleep!" Brooks cried. "This place is protected, Zane! Like the island. If they got access . . ." Her voice trailed off as she pondered the horrors.

It seemed like an excellent guess, and even had high probability. But there was one problem: the fire deep inside me simmered, telling me that murdering us in our sleep wasn't part of the plan. There was something bigger—something we weren't seeing. But what?

"No," Hondo said, shaking his head. "Ixkik' definitely wants to murder us with our eyes wide open. She practically said so."

"Why didn't Dad warn us?" Alana looked stricken.

"Maybe he wasn't up to speed on everything," Adrik said.

I scratched Rosie's neck as I tried to wrap my head around everything, but she seemed agitated and kept ducking my hand.

Brooks said, "Maybe Ixtab gave the stone some other powers we don't even know about."

Alana rolled her eyes and snorted.

"What's wrong?" Ren asked.

"Sure," Alana said like she was talking to herself, "give a stone some powers, but forget about your daughter."

"No one forgot," Adrik said. "It's just dormant, is all."

"Dormant?" Brooks raised her eyebrows. "What does that mean?"

Alana scanned our faces. "It means..." Her mouth trembled, and I thought she might start crying, but she held it together. "If I have any power at all, it's hiding or sleeping or whatever."

Adrik said, "It's going to show up, Alana."

Alana twisted her mouth nervously. "The Sparkstriker said it might never show up, and now my vision has..."

"Has what?" I stepped closer, gripping Fuego tightly.

Alana tipped back her head. "It's gotten worse since the ceremony."

"Like more sensitive to light?" Ren asked.

"Like blurrier," she said.

"She even thought she had a brain tumor," Adrik said, snickering.

Alana shot him a glare that could kill.

"It's true," he muttered.

Just then the biblioteca walls began to tremble, and the domed ceiling split open with a thunderous crack.

We all whipped our heads up to look. Rosie lunged in front of us, baring fangs of fire.

A god with shiny black hair stood on the edge of the hole, wearing his signature aviator shades and sparkling blue robe.

"Itzamna!" I said. "What are you doing here?"

"Really, Zane. You *need* to pay more attention to the story unfolding right in front of you!"

22

•
••

Itzamna floated down from the ceiling, his robe billowing behind him. The guy really knew how to make an entrance.

Under her breath, Brooks told Adrik and Alana that Itzamna was the moon god, bringer of writing and culture, and father to the Bakabs, who hold up the sky.

And giver of dragon power, I thought, but this wasn't the time or place for that talk.

"He does sort of look like the moon," Alana whispered.

When Itzamna stood in front of me, his mirrored lenses reflected all of our stunned faces.

"What . . . what are you doing here?" I asked again.

Before he could answer, Rosie threw back her head and let out a mournful howl. Waves of fire blasted from her mouth toward the open roof.

"Rosie!" I tried to grab hold of her, but it was like she was possessed.

Itzamna placed a trembling hand on her head, immediately quieting my dog. "At least some of my power still works," he muttered. "Quite the hellhound, Zane. Good for you—all heroes need a partner. Makes for a richer story. Ah, but that's not why I'm here."

Like the first time I met him, his voice hit musical notes that were both relaxing and haunting. Slowly, he removed his glasses. His eyes and the circles underneath them were blacker than an underground tomb. "How do I look? You can be honest. Awful? On a scale of one to ten, one being a corpse."

Brooks half snorted/half grunted. I could only imagine what was going through her head. *This guy is so full of himself. And Rosie isn't Zane's only partner.*

"Maybe a five," Alana said. Adrik shook his head in disagreement, but I was glad he didn't say anything stupid to anger the god.

Ren smiled, practically bouncing in place. "You're the god who can see the whole universe, so that means you'd know if there is alien life, right?"

Hondo groaned, palm-smacking his forehead.

Itzamna studied Ren like she was an alien herself. "I do not divulge secrets of the universe. Certainly not to non-gods."

"Why not?" Ren asked, but Itzamna ignored her.

"I am here with news of the gods," he said. "Dreadful on the one hand, expected on the other. But the universe is master of her own destiny, and it is not my job to interfere or be attached." His chin quivered like he didn't believe his own words. What was his deal? "That's my most-often-used line. Is it believable?"

Ignoring his question, I argued, "But you *do* interfere. You got into my head in Hell's Kitchen. You helped me."

Itzamna nodded. "True. I did indeed assist you in not dying. We couldn't have the story end so soon, could we?"

I groaned inwardly. What was with this guy and cuentos?

"I am only here to give you a message loud enough to get your attention, because one"—he held up a single shimmering finger—"it will determine what you do next. Two, it will heighten the stakes. And three—and this is perhaps the most important . . ." His face contorted into a silent wail and he collapsed into a chair, gripping his chest and sucking in gulps of air. "I cannot . . . keep up . . . this facade . . . of strength."

Ren hurried over and fanned him with her hands. "Make fists," she said. "Deep breaths."

Alana jumped into first aid mode, too. "Count backward from one hundred. Breathe nice and slow. That's it. You're just having a panic attack. It will pass."

"Gods have panic attacks?" Hondo muttered to me. Then to the freaked-out god he said, "Hey, dude—you need some water or something?"

Itzamna inhaled through his nose and exhaled through his mouth, wiping his brow with his sleeve. "I do apologize for my inappropriate outburst—it's just that . . . well, the fourth thing is that I don't want to be worthless. I don't want to be forgotten." He dropped his head into his hands as Ren patted him on the back and Alana told him to keep breathing.

Rosie snorted and stomped her front paw like she couldn't believe the great god Itzamna was acting like a . . . human.

Brooks gripped my arm from behind. *This is so not going to be good.*

"What's your news?" I asked Itzamna, knowing I was going to hate the answer 100 percent. And knowing that if it sent the god further into a panic attack, we might all end up in a tailspin of terror.

At that exact moment, the walls grew hazy, then vanished altogether. We found ourselves standing on the shore of a crystal-clear lake. On the other side, a magnificent tree sparkled in the sun.

"Whoa!" Adrik said, his mouth hanging open. "That's sick! How'd you do that?"

"Is that the World Tree?" Ren asked, stepping closer to the water's edge.

"It's huge," Hondo said, craning his neck to see where the Tree stretched beyond a thin veil of pinkish-gray clouds.

"I tried to fly over there yesterday," Brooks admitted, "to get a better look, but I kept butting up against some kind of invisible wall."

"A protective measure," Itzamna said. "There is more magic surrounding that Tree of Life than there is in all the gods' blood."

"Wait," I said, my eyes still on the tree that looked like a painting. "The lights—they look dimmer than they did yesterday."

"Why are they flickering like that?" Alana asked.

Itzamna pushed his glasses up his long nose. "The lights are flickering because the Maya gods are gone."

"Yeah," Adrik said. "They left last night for their meeting."

"Not gone from *here*," Itzamna sputtered, starting to hyperventilate again. "Gone from awareness, wakefulness, consciousness. Zotz and Ixkik' have taken them."

"How?!" The heat inside me charged to the surface and small flames erupted across my knuckles. "What does that mean?"

Hondo drew closer, as if he needed a front-row seat to make sure he had heard the moon god right. The muscle in his jaw twitched as he spoke slowly. "Gone from *their* consciousness, or ours?"

An umbrella-like shadow appeared, hovering over Ren protectively. Thankfully, it didn't grow a face. Or fangs and claws. "Pacific's gone?" she whispered, twisting her gold watch in circles around her wrist.

Alana covered a gasp trying to exit her mouth.

"All the gods..." said Itzamna. "Except me, of course."

"Each light represents a god," I said, remembering what my dad had told me. I felt sick to my stomach. And not just because the gods were out of play, but because whatever Zotz and Blood Moon's plans were, they were winning. By a long shot.

"You're saying they're asleep somewhere? Were they, like, knocked out or something?" Brooks asked with a defiant tone. "No way could anyone do that to the mighty Kukuulkaan. No way."

"How the heck do you knock out a god?" Adrik muttered.

"Please do not waste time arguing a useless point," Itzamna said. "We must talk about *me*. How to save my legacy. My beloved tree!"

"Then find the gods," Adrik demanded. "Bring them back."

"I can't." Itzamna sighed. "I'm not the one who took them."

"Zotz and Ixkik' did it!" I said.

"They don't have the power to enslumber the gods," Itzamna said. *Enslumber?* Is that even a word?

My thoughts spiraled. Zotz and Ixkik' never did the

expected or obvious. Was this what the Red Queen had meant when she'd said that they were five steps ahead? Five. Steps. Ahead. Those three words rang out in my head on repeat.

Five. Zotz and Ixkik' killed Akan.

Steps. They are conniving plotters.

Ahead. Something so unexpected it will have your head spinning.

"Crap!" I shouted.

All eyes fixed on me. A low growl erupted from Rosie's throat as she pawed my shoulder, practically knocking me over.

"Akan's death was a setup!" I spoke forcefully. "They didn't kill him to raise an army—they did it to raise some Mexica god with the power to put the Maya gods to sleep." I hated to admit it, but the plan was ingenious.

Brooks paced as massive black wings sprouted from her back. "But what if it's even more than that?"

"What do you mean, more?" Alana asked.

"Zotz knew that if he killed Akan," Brooks said, "the gods would call an emergency meeting."

"Yes," Itzamna said matter-of-factly. "That *is* protocol."

"And Zotz was waiting," Ren added with a shudder.

"Surprise attack," Hondo said.

"It was an ambush," Adrik said.

"Plot twist!" Itzamna said as he stood and swept his robe behind him. "How did I not see this coming?" His brows creased together tightly, pushing his glasses down his nose. "I let myself get distracted with SHIHOM, with you god-borns, that's how."

A sudden hush fell over the room. Brooks's eyes glazed over as she whispered, "The time rope."

"No one can take it from Pacific," Itzamna said. "Even while she's in a deep slumber, her rope would go with her."

Rosie let out a small whimper, like she was just as relieved as the rest of us that the time rope was safely away from Zotz and Ixkik'.

"Are you sure?" I asked.

Itzamna nodded, but it was Ren who spoke first. "My mom told me that when the gods exiled her, they tried to take the rope, but it was impossible. No one, not even a god, can take what is a part of the time goddess. Not unless she gives it away."

Ren's umbrella shadow loomed even bigger as Itzamna began to pace. I was thankful that she had more control over her shadows than she used to.

"I do believe you all are beginning to give shape to this tale," the god said.

I heard Itzamna's words, but my brain could barely process them. How had we been so easily duped? How could not one stinking god have seen this?

"Ixkik' is trying to get into Xib'alb'a," Itzamna added, "to claim it for herself, which could give her access to the Tree's roots." He shook his head woefully. "Thankfully, she cannot penetrate the Tree's powerful magic."

We all shot glances at each other. "Unless she has an entry stone," I said.

The god's face collapsed inch by inch as we filled him in.

A terrifying idea bloomed in my head. "Are they planning to come back here to finish the job? Kill all the lights?"

"'Killing the lights,' as you put it, wouldn't kill the gods," Itzamna said. "They want in for another reason."

"We have to help the gods!" Ren cried.

"Including me," Itzamna moaned.

"We can call on the giants and other sobrenaturals," I said, trying to remain cool-headed.

"I tried that," Itzamna said. "But no one has answered. It's as if they're ignoring me. Or maybe I'm just not strong enough." His eyes flicked to the Tree.

Brooks gasped. "My sister would never ignore . . . They must be in danger, too."

"This is seriously messed up." Hondo's hands curled into tight fists.

My brain was definitely going to implode. "Or maybe no one heard Itzamna's calls," I argued. "We have to stay calm—"

"And deal only in facts," Ren said, turning to the god. "You can see everything from the top of your Tree. So where are the gods?"

"Where are Zotz and Ixkik'?" I pressed.

"What are they going to do next?" Alana asked.

Brooks added, "And who's the rotten sleep god they resurrected?"

Adrik finished with "How do you wake a sleeping god?"

"Such good questions." Itzamna massaged his temples. "Yes, I can see all of creation from the top of my Tree, but in case you haven't noticed, the Tree is not fully charged. Do you get my meaning?"

"The Tree isn't a cell phone." Hondo's voice was spiked with real fear. I hated the sound of it.

Itzamna pointed at my uncle. "Great analogy. Give this guy a prize!"

"This isn't a game," Brooks said, drawing her wings closer.

"Ah, but in a way, it is." Itzamna hiked his bushy brows. "All stories are games of great proportion. And, unfortunately for us, Zotz and Ixkik' are winning." He took a few more steps. "You must think like them. *Be* like them."

"We will never be like them," I ground out.

Rosie whined and nudged my shoulder with her nose. I patted her, but she kept at it.

Itzamna drew closer. "There isn't a lot of space between the hero and the villain," he said. "The villain thinks he or she is the hero of their own tale."

The thought of Zotz and Ixkik' and the wicked hero twins being cast as heroes made me sick.

"But you're a god," Adrik said. "Why can't *you* think like them?"

"Must I keep repeating myself?" Itzamna said with a pained expression, like the words themselves were daggers slicing open his heart. "I . . . I grow weaker with each passing moment. I need the gods' power to sustain my own. Don't you see? Zotz and Ixkik' have thought of everything. Soon, they will storm Xib'alb'a, and you are merely half gods. You cannot defeat them."

"Tell us how to fix this!" I growled.

Rosie's eyes erupted in red flames.

Wringing his hands, Itzamna said, "If they do have this so-called entry stone, then they have access to everywhere." He rubbed his forehead. "I can use my last reserve of magic to protect the Tree for a while. But it will only buy you two or three days at most." He blew out a long breath. "And even if you somehow succeeded in locating the gods," he added, "you would not have sufficient power to wake them."

I took a breath and leaned against Rosie, feeling her heart thudding beneath her thick chest. Her soft brown eyes looked up at me, filled with a message of some kind.

"What is it, girl?"

In answer, she reared on her hind legs, growled angrily, and bolted.

23

•
•••

"Rosie!" I ran out of the library after her, leaving the others behind.

I followed the hot tug in my gut that led me deep into the jungle, down a winding path. Above me, I heard scuttling sounds followed by howls of laughter. I stopped and looked up.

Three monkeys were perched on a branch, their golden eyes glaring down at me. The center one smiled, smacking its lips.

"Where did the dog go?"

The monkeys stood on their hind legs, gnashing their teeth angrily. Then, as if it felt bad for me, one of the critters pointed to the right. I followed its hairy little finger to a dead end. There was no path, only a thick wall of branches and vines.

Rosie's roar echoed from the other side. With Fuego, I began slashing through the foliage. Sharp branches cut my face and arms. I finally made my way through to a small clearing where Rosie was pacing while blowing little bursts of smoke from her nose. When she saw me, her eyes blazed and she raced ahead.

Where are you taking me? I wondered as I trailed her as closely as I could.

After a few more minutes, we came to what could only

be described as an orange glass house with a thatched roof. It was two levels, stacked one on top of the other with sharp angles that jutted out.

The surrounding trees and vines arched protectively over the place, providing shade from the sun.

"Why did you bring me to a Lego house in the middle of the jungle?" I asked.

Rosie nudged my back with her head, urging me toward the entrance. "What is your deal? You're the one who led us here," I argued. "And you want *me* to go first?"

She gave a quick nod.

"Fine," I muttered. "Big chicken."

There was no door to knock on—just an open entrance. "Hello?" I said.

Rosie whined as I stepped inside. The room was hot with thick, humid air that burned my nose and pressed in on me from all sides. There were rows and rows of tables where leafy green plants sprouted from pots. Pink-and-yellow-and-purple-flowering vines spilled over their containers' edges, dropping to the dirt floor.

"Do not step on the vines!" came a man's voice.

My eyes darted around and I saw the top of a bald head peek out from behind some plants. It headed my way.

I stepped back, looking over my shoulder for the exit, just in case. The entrance I'd come in was gone—as in no más!—replaced by another orange glass wall.

A man about the size of yesterday's air spirit rounded the table and came into full view. He had a dirty handkerchief in one hand and a trowel in the other. His eyes were the deepest brown I'd ever seen, and his skin was the color of wet sand. Wiping his tool on pants that for sure looked like they were made out of dried grass, he asked, "Who are you? What do you want? Didn't you see the No Trespassing signs?"

"Uh—no," I said, side-glaring at Rosie. No chicken necks for her for a year!

The little dude harrumphed. "Did Aapo send you?"

"Aapo?"

"Don't act all innocent," he said. "You look like the kind of spy my sister might hire—tall, young, and awkward. Well, guess what? Tell her she can't have it." He shook his head and said, more to himself than to me, "No, that won't do. I need to send a *powerful* message to her, to get through her thick skull." He flicked his eyes to mine. "I could take one of your fingers, send it to her in a box. She hates extremities."

My stomach bottomed out.

He wiggled his thinning brows like dismemberment was the best idea he'd had all day. "So, what'll it be? Thumb, or pointer?"

"I'm not a spy!" My heart began to punch its way out of my chest. "I'm sorry, sir, but my dog . . . she led me here."

Rosie sniffed the air and sat on her haunches all casual like, as if the guy hadn't just threatened to cut off one of my fingers. Some protector she was.

The guy's gaze fell on Rosie like he was noticing her for the first time.

"That's no dog," the guy said, rubbing his head while he stuck out his neck to get a better look. "Which means you can't be working for Aapo, because no hellhound would go near her." His shoulders seemed to relax. "Does your beast like snake heads? I have a tub of them in the back corner."

Of course you do.

My insides clenched, but Rosie's ears perked up and her mouth started to drool. She took off in the direction he'd pointed. She really needed a leash!

I just stood there, drumming Fuego on the ground. Was I supposed to make small talk? Smell the flowers? Beg to keep my fingers?

The guy sneezed, then wiped his reddish nose with the handkerchief. "Imagine an earth spirit having allergies! The universe has the worst sense of humor."

Earth spirit? Was this who the Red Queen had wanted me to find? It had to be! But then I remembered what the air spirit had said yesterday: *Can't trust earth or mountain spirits.* Maybe I could get to know him a little before I decided whom to trust. "I'm Zane. And you are?"

"I already told you, I'm an earth spirit."

Okay, next question. "So, you grow all this?"

"What do you mean *this*?" The guy flung his trowel away like he wanted to fight me or something. "I am sure you mean do I grow magical, amazing, out of the ordinary, mind-blowing creations like never seen before?"

He narrowed his eyes and drew closer. Then, with a sniff, he threw some pea-green dust into my face.

The foul-smelling stuff flew up my nose, sending me into a coughing and wheezing fit that lasted about ten seconds until I finally inhaled a clean breath.

Ah, oxygen. So underrated.

I gripped Fuego, ready to take on this earth spirit, but as soon as I exhaled, I started to giggle. Before I could stop myself, more giggles erupted, and pretty soon I had dropped my cane and was rolling on the floor laughing at absolutely nothing.

The earth spirit stood over me, rubbing his chin and frowning. "That's not the effect I was going for. Tell me, what are you feeling?"

Feeling? I was doubled up, roaring with laughter. I couldn't talk, could barely see, since my eyes were leaking like crazy. My sides were going to split open and all I could think of was how long it would take for my friends to find my dead body.

The laughter gripped me like an iron claw. It was torturous. Worse than tortuous.

The earth spirit said, "This is not the right effect. Not even close!"

I sucked in a breath in between uproarious hoots and managed to grunt, "Make . . . *ba-ha-ha* . . . it . . . *ba-ha-ha ga-ha-ha* stop."

The guy walked out of the periphery of my vision, and when he came back, he kneeled down and shoved a small red flower into my mouth. "Eat this."

The thing tasted like ground-up aspirin. Look, I didn't want to eat it, but I also didn't want to die from laughing hysterically. The second I swallowed the last morsel, the laughfest ceased. My ribs felt like they were going to snap in two if I so much as sneezed. Tears streamed down my face. I rolled onto all fours, catching my breath. "Why . . . did you do that?"

"It was supposed to make you speak only the truth," he said, sounding perplexed. Then he gasped, sneezed twice, and shouted, "That means you're not human!"

"I *am* human, but I'm also a godborn." I cleared my throat, grabbed Fuego, and stood up.

The guy remained on his knees and bowed his head down to the floor. "Oh, master, godborn, blood of the gods, forgive me," he wailed. "I had no idea. I'm old. I don't get many visitors. I have terrible allergies. I can't think clearly. I was mistaken. I should have known." He looked up at me. "I'm Kip, at your service."

I helped him to his feet. "It's fine. Really." I mean, it was totally *not* fine, but the guy looked so desperate and freaked, I couldn't watch him spiral downward another inch.

Rosie reappeared, licking her chops happily as if I hadn't almost just been murdered by laughter.

"The Red Queen," I said. "She told me about you. She told me to find or follow chapat."

"Chapat?" Kip brightened. "Why didn't you say so? I can show you the way."

"You can?" This was too easy for my comfort.

Kip headed toward the back of the greenhouse.

"I almost died," I muttered to Rosie, who gave me a wary *yeah-right* expression. "Fine," I said, seeing my hellhound's logic. "But it *felt* like I was going to die."

We followed the spirit out a doorway into a lush flowering garden in the middle of the dense jungle. At the center of the garden was an undulating path in the shape of a centipede.

Chapat is a labyrinth? I thought.

"This is chapat. A place to meditate away your worries," Kip offered as he wrung his hands.

Rosie howled and reared up on her hind legs, punching her front paws like a prizefighter.

"Meditate?" Seriously? The Fire Keeper wanted me to meditate? Was this some kind of joke?

Kip wiped his head with his handkerchief, flicked his eyes to Rosie, and said, "This is a special path. It will ease your worries, I promise."

If he only knew that my worries started with hijacked gods and ended with a ruined world.

Gesturing toward the path, Kip said, "Like me, the centipede is a very misunderstood creature, but this will clear your mind. I promise. And then you will have good memories of my home."

I drew closer to the labyrinth, holding my breath.

The Red Queen's voice rang out in my head. *Follow chapat.*

Just as I was about to step onto the trail, Kip gripped my arm. "I nearly forgot. You must consider your deepest worry as you walk. The path will do the rest."

"Got it."

"And you won't tell your godly mom or dad about the laughing fit, right?" He giggled anxiously.

So he hadn't heard about the missing gods yet. I stepped onto the path, promising I wouldn't rat him out.

One foot in front of the other. It took all of three seconds for my worries to bubble to the surface.

Enslumbered gods.

Step.

When you least expect it, you'll pay with your blood for this.

Step.

Are your eyes wide open?

Step.

Those were some pretty gargantuan worries, but the earth spirit was right. With each stride, my fears began to fall farther and farther away. They were still there—I could see them, but I couldn't really feel them, if that makes sense. Maybe Hondo was onto something with this meditation stuff.

My peripheral vision was reduced to nothing but shifting shadows. Then darkness closed in until all light had vanished. The air was still and cool.

Water drip-drip-dripped in the distance.

Peering through the blackness, I saw that I was in a tunnel with dirt walls and low, craggy ceilings. One by one, tiny torch flames flickered to life along the wall.

Was this some kind of hallucination?

"Hello?" My voice echoed across the chamber as I walked forward. Okay, maybe it squeaked, but yours would, too, if you went from light to underground dark in 0.2 seconds. Was this a trap? What if the earth spirit was some kind of baddie working for Zotz and Blood Moon?

No. No way would Rosie bring me somewhere dangerous.

One step.

"Hello?" My voice echoed across the dark.

Two steps.

Faint images began to appear on the wall. A deep tremble ran through me as I peered closer.

The picture rippled, almost as if it were being reflected off water.

Whoa! This wasn't an image—it was a memory. A memory of the day I'd met Pacific in the ocean, when she'd given me the jade tooth. She floated on her surfboard, wearing her spotted leopard cape as I shivered nearby in total freak-out mode. It was hard to believe that had happened only nine months ago.

I froze in mid-step, watching the memory play out. Pacific's voice was like surround sound—it echoed from every torch: *I am the* keeper *of time,* she said. *No longer the controller of it. Just as I keep but cannot control fate.*

The memory vanished. "Pacific?" I called out.

There was no answer. Only her words, which sounded again: *I am the keeper of time.*

I took another step, and a second memory appeared. I was standing in the Old World with Jazz, Brooks, and Hondo the night I was claimed and took down Ah-Puch. Something heavy surged up in my chest. I don't know—sadness, longing, some kind of wishing that I could go back. But to what?

Jazz was smiling as he pointed up at the pyramids and said, *This is how the marking of time came to be. It was invented in this place. Then someone, no one knows who, created time, and the world began. Or at least the third version of it. Man, I wish I had a camera!*

Brooks gazed up. *Some say the gods lost the time rope. It used to be wrapped around the earth, but it disappeared, and now they can't time-travel anymore.*

I reached out as if I could touch the memory, but it vanished just as Jazz's words echoed: *It was* invented *in this place.*

Heart pounding, I took another two steps. The next image flared to life. It was from just a few months ago, when I'd stood on that rooftop in Xib'alb'a with Quinn. She looked terrified—that was clear now, but I'm not so sure I saw it then. I peered closer, knowing the details mattered.

Quinn said, *The Sparkstriker saw something evil in her lightning pool, something that scared her. I've never seen her frightened. She said the seeds of this evil could only be discovered in the underworld.*

Again, the memory faded, and the words whispered across the tunnel: *The seeds of this evil could only be discovered in the underworld.*

I took another five steps into the tunnel. The flames hissed and groaned. Where were these memories taking me? Why did they matter?

As soon as the images disappeared, I fell against the wall, finding it hard to breathe, like the tunnel was losing air. "Come on, Fuego," I said with as much strength as I could muster. I had to know where these memories led. I had to follow them to the end.

The last memory gripped me hard, and I swear it was like going back to that awful day all over again. I had just become one with fire and was helping the godborns escape the junkyard prison Zotz had created.

I started for Brooks's and Hondo's cages, to set them free, when Ah-Puch grabbed hold of my arm. *Do not be fooled by anything you see here*, he said. *The twins' mother, Ixkik', is the master of deception.*

Master of deception.

Master of deception.

The memory exploded, forcing me to stumble back. Clutching Fuego, I blinked and saw that I had come to a dead end at a cave wall. A rocky ledge stuck out about waist-high, and it cradled a stone bowl. While I stood there, a blue flame erupted in the bowl, like a match had just been struck.

I ran my hand over the flame, trying to make sense of the memories that had appeared. Of all that I'd been through over the last year, why was I shown those particular moments? Why did they matter the most?

I had started to replay them in my mind, looking for any significance, *any* connection between them, when I heard:

"ZANE!"

Ah-Puch?

24

•

••••

I spun wildly, expecting to see the god of death,
but the cave was empty. "Where are you?"

"Literally?" His voice was small and distant. "Floating in
utter darkness. Again."

"Are you with the other gods? I don't know where you are,
or how to save you." I clenched Fuego with both hands. "How
are you even talking to me?"

"I am the god of death, remember? Hard to put me under
completely. And you and I are connected, in case you forgot."

"I didn't forget." How could I? Our minds were forever
linked the moment I saved his life with the jade stone.

"But that's not the point...." His voice trailed off, and I
didn't catch what he said next.

"Talk louder," I said. "I can barely hear you."

"Not surprising. I am in terrible shape. The lowest of the
low."

A plump orange-and-black-striped centipede climbed up
the rock wall near the bowl of flame until it was at my eye
level. Its skinny legs were twitching and 500 percent revolting.

I stared, trying not to get too close. "Wait. Is that you?
You're an insect? How—"

"This is no time to talk about forms and energy, Zane."

The centipede's head swayed ever so slightly. Did the thing even have eyes?

"Er...okay. What do you want me to do? How do I save you?" I prepared for the god of death to lay out a brilliant multi-point plan.

Instead, he said, "You can't save me. You can't save any of us."

"WHAT?! No! Why...why would you bother coming here if—"

"To say good-bye. To tell you that you really were one of my favorite enemies. And to ask you to give Ren a message from me. Gods don't feel attachment or love—not like you humans do—but my heart was bigger when she was around. Tell her that."

"NO! *You* can give her that message! I just had a bunch of memories about time and magic and evil, and I think they're connected....Just tell me where you are."

"No idea. But it's far. So far that it took everything I had to reach you. It's almost as if..."

"As if what?"

"It doesn't matter."

"It *does* matter! Zotz and Ixkik' can't get away with this!"

"Don't you see?" he said angrily. "They already have. We walked right into their trap. We are to blame for our stupidity."

"I have to try to help!"

"I knew you would feel that way. That's the other reason I came: to warn you. Do not risk your life for gods that are already gone. Your father would kill you."

"Yeah? Well, he's out of commission right now, so no one's

killing anyone." My voice had risen to full-throttle panic. "What do you mean, 'already gone'?"

"We are no longer here, Zane."

Anger throbbed in my chest. My eyes blazed. "Look, you know I am going to come for you! You know I can't just sit back and do nothing."

"Listen to me!" He growled like he was using his last ounce of strength. "That's exactly what Zotz and Ixkik' want. It will only send you down a dark and dangerous rabbit hole, and there will be no victory," he said. "I am . . . I *was* the god of death, darkness, and destruction. If I could see a way out, don't you think I would tell you? Don't you think I would love nothing more than to shred our enemies?"

"You never give up!" I said, knowing that I had to keep him here, keep him talking. I had to be more convincing. "You fought your way back from the inferno I trapped you in. Back from death! You know better than anyone that there's always a way out!" Maybe he wouldn't help me save the gods, but he might care if it meant saving Ren. "They have the entry stone—they're coming to SHIHOM to kill all of us. We need you!"

He was silent, so silent I was worried he had left. Then he finally said, "The devourer . . ." He spoke through what sounded like gritted teeth.

"Devourer?" And just like that, the memory of Ixtab telling me about the Mexica earth goddess who gives and devours life slammed into my brain. Ugh! Why couldn't I remember her name? "You mean the devouring goddess?" I blurted. "Is she the one they resurrected? She did this to you?"

"Yes," he groaned. I could tell he was barely holding on.

"Please give me more clues about where you are. Think of anything."

"Ren," he managed. "She is the only one..."

"The only one what?!"

The centipede shivered once, then began to crawl across the wall, and I knew Ah-Puch was gone.

"Ah-Puch!" I shouted. "Come back!"

The word *devourer* made me sick to my stomach. Were the gods being eaten alive by that Mexica goddess?

Fury, panic, and bone-deep fear scrambled all my thoughts. This. Was. So. Not. Happening.

In my mind's eye, I placed the memories side by side:

I am the keeper of time.

Time was invented in this place.

The seeds of this evil could only be discovered in the underworld.

Master of deception.

"What does it mean?" I said. The blue flame rose higher.

Time.

Evil.

Deception.

I set Fuego against the wall and thrust my hands into the blue blaze, as if I could will more memories to appear. I'd been led here, to this exact spot, for a reason. The crackling flames spat and hissed. I leaned in closer, plunging my face inside them as the same words echoed through me:

Time. Evil. Deception.

Time. Evil. Deception.

As the words repeated, a picture appeared in the fire. It was the same image Alana had drawn in the sand, except more detailed: three circles with glyphs and evenly spaced teeth and notches, like gears. The smallest circle, labeled with the Maya number system, was housed inside a medium-size one, and third was much bigger. I could tell that if one circle was turned, the other two would move as well. It looked like this:

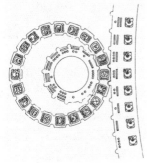

It's the three ancient Maya calendars, I thought.

Then *poof!* The calendars dissolved, and the flame went out. I staggered, trying to still my pounding pulse as I grabbed Fuego and leaned against it. That's when I noticed the centipede was still clinging to the wall. Its body pulsed once, twice.

Ah-Puch?

The insect started to lengthen. Then it plumped up like someone was filling it with air. As it grew longer and fatter, it whipped its neck and creepy antennae in my direction.

Right. Some peaceful labyrinth this was.

When the centipede had reached a length of about three feet, its mouth (which, by the way, had an evil-looking hook on each side) opened wide—wide enough to swallow a baseball.

"Gaaah!" So I screamed. Sue me. You would have, too,

especially if you knew that centipedes usually wrap their bodies around their prey and release a bunch of venom into them, i.e., give them a slow and painful death, before eating them.

¡No gracias!

"Intruder," the nasty centipede whispered.

I backed up slowly—you know, no sudden movements to freak out the bug. "I was just leaving," I grunt-laughed.

"K'iin," the centipede said, "can only be seen by the dead. You are not dead."

Keen?

The beast jumped onto my shoulders and wrapped itself around my neck, squeezing. My air was immediately cut off, and I felt razor-sharp legs piercing my skin.

I clutched its slimy body, trying to rip it off as I summoned the fire within me, but the thing held on and squeezed like a vise. I could feel its poison burning in my blood.

My vision started to fade. I fell to my knees, clawing and gasping.

Then, with one last effort, I willed Fuego into spear mode and thrust it into the centipede, ripping hard to the right.

Shkwert!

Warm bluish blood oozed down my shirt. I dropped to my knees, choking on the humid air as the bug's gutted body slipped off me and writhed on the ground. Noxious yellow gas spiraled from the corpse and filled the chamber, burning me so bad I could feel the hair on my head singeing right off.

Just as I was about to expel a flame to bring down the entire chamber, the darkness and gas disappeared.

25

•

—

I was back in the jungle, doubled over, sucking wind. My ears were ringing with the same three words: *Time. Evil. Deception.*

"Stop!" I shouted, covering my ears. My hands flew to my hair. "I have hair!"

Rosie and Kip hurried over.

"Are you making fun of me?" The spirit narrowed his eyes. "Being bald has its perks, you know."

I shook my head and sucked in more fresh air.

"What did you see?" Kip asked. "You were gone for quite a while. Why are you choking? Do you have allergies, too?"

The ear ringing faded when I tried to talk. "A centipede"— cough—"tried"—double cough—"to kill me." But when I looked down, there was no centipede blood on my hands, my shirt, or Fuego.

Rosie sniffed me ferociously, checking me out. Then she grunted once, like *Yeah, right.*

"Not possible," Kip said. "The labyrinth is a place of safety and peace. Of visions and answers to your problems. Tell me, what exactly did you see? Before the chapat."

I hesitated, standing upright. "Memories." I turned my

hands over, looking for any cuts or bites, but there were none. Had I dreamed the whole thing?

"Ah, the Hall of Memories," he said. "That's usually a nice walk."

"You mean hell walk," I said.

"'Your mind is a gift, a miraculous warehouse of answers,'" he said. "That's a direct quote from one of my old textbooks. I wasn't much of a student, but I remember that one in particular—"

Rosie growled, revealing her fangs.

"Welp," Kip squeaked, jumping back. "Ahem. Yes, okay. Whatever you saw had to be important. What else?"

No way was I going to tell him about Ah-Puch or the words that were still flickering inside me like a freshly lit flame. But maybe the spirit would know what the image of the calendars meant. I stood and said, "I saw three wheels with glyphs and numbers."

"Ah," he said. "So, you have a dance with time."

"Dance with time?" I echoed.

"Well, you must be preoccupied with it if you saw the calendar. Are you worried about growing old? Or running out of time? Or—"

"I heard a voice, too," I said. "The centipede said *K'iin.*" I knew that word. It meant *sun* or *day.*

His face went pale. He began to shoo me away. "Time for you to go. Ha! I meant to say you must go. I didn't say *time.* Okay, buh-bye."

"Wait! What's wrong?"

Rosie paced nervously, grunting trails of smoke. Was this why she had brought me here? To see an ancient calendar? To hear a voice whisper *sun* or *day*? Did she know Ah-Puch would come to tell me good-bye? There was no way she could have known that little peace walk would bring me face-to-face with a killer arthropod. Unless Ixtab's dumb orb had messed with my dog's brain somehow.

The spirit twisted his fingers. "Please. You really have to go now."

"What are you so afraid of?" I asked as a sick dread filled me. "K'iin? The calendar?"

"Would you quit saying that word?" He glanced over his shoulder. "We are not to speak of this."

"Why?"

"Because what you saw"—Kip looked around, then leaned closer—"it's sacrilege. Do you hear me? I could lose an ear or an eye if caught talking about it." He shuddered, grasping his lobes. "I like my ears and eyes."

"Look," I said angrily, "you're going to lose a lot more than that if..."

The guy's face was filled with terror. I took a breath. Getting mad at him wasn't going to give me the answers I needed, and blaming him wasn't going to make me feel better.

"Sorry," I said, more calmly this time. "I have to know. Please. I think this is why I was supposed to come here. For this message." A message *someone* didn't want me to receive.

He stared at me with wild eyes. "You must go!"

"I'm not leaving until you tell me."

Clenching his jaw, he turned away.

"I'll put in a good word for you with the gods..." I said in a last-ditch effort.

He snapped his attention back to me. "You'll ask the gods for a favor? For me? A new greenhouse, maybe? Bigger than my sister's?"

"Yes. I'd be happy to." Not that the gods ever listened to me. Or were even still around, but I made the silent vow anyway: *If I see them again, I'll make sure you get a new greenhouse.*

"And you promise never to come back here?"

I agreed immediately.

He rubbed his head as his eyes flitted everywhere. "K'iin is a calendar created by the time goddess at the beginning, before there was anything," he said quickly.

Fire sped through my body, carrying the memories of Pacific being the creator of time and Ah-Puch saying something about Ren. It was all connected. But how?

And then I remembered that night in the boat with Itzamna, and his claim. "I thought Itzamna created the calendar," I said, feeling more confused than ever.

"The human one, yes. But K'iin," he continued, "keeps time for the whole universe. Do you understand? Not the world—the *universe*! There are different strands of time—not that I understand any of that. It's all tied up in the goddess's magic rope, the one she is to carry for all eternity."

"How do you know all this?" I asked.

"Spirits talk," he said. "We're masters of gossip. Once, a rotten little mountain spirit tried to steal a story for his own and—"

"Back to K'iin?" I prompted.

He sneezed, then wiped his nose with the back of his hand. "Yes. Yes. When Pacific was exiled, she sealed the calendar and hid it so the gods would never be able to access its knowledge without her," he said. "The mountain spirits claim to know where she put K'iin, and so do the air spirits. Hmph. If anyone knows, it would be an earth spirit!" He squinted one eye. "But those who went looking for it—they never came back."

I suddenly felt like I was test-flying the world's fastest rocket and was about to get sucked into a black hole. "So, no one ever found it?"

Rosie drew closer, like she didn't want to miss the answer.

"Did you not hear me?" Kip shook his head. "Of course not. Who wants knowledge that could bring about their own death?"

"But what's so great about the calendar?" I asked. "I mean, even if someone found it, how could they use it?"

Kip rubbed his chest in small circles like he had a bad case of heartburn. "K'iin means *sun* or *day*, but it also means *T-I-M-E*." He spelled out the word. "Legend has it that if you find this calendar—which you won't, because the goddess is very good at hiding things—and you stand before it..." He stroked his chin. "No, maybe you sit before it, or... It doesn't matter. But you have to pay—"

"Pay?"

"You know what? You interrupt a lot," he said.

I tried to keep my cool, but I was ready to blow. "Please go on. You were saying something about payment?"

"It's no biggie—just an offering of some sort. You can't expect to get something for nothing, can you?"

It felt like I was having a heart attack. "Right, but there are good kinds of offerings, like cookies, and bad kinds, like blood, or my heart, or..." I shook away the thoughts. "And what would I get in return?"

A smile slowly spread across his face. "Ah, yes. You'd be able to see across all time and dimensions."

A calendar that could see across time and dimensions? My mind was officially blown. At the risk of having the guy threaten to cut off a finger again, I asked, "It sounds super cool and all, but why would someone want to *see* across time?"

"For knowledge. To find something lost. Or hidden," he whispered.

Like the stolen gods! Yes! Now we were getting somewhere.

"But that doesn't explain why the centipede would want to kill me."

Rosie's claws erupted from her three paws. Her shoulder muscles tensed. Now *she reacts?* I thought.

Kip raised a finger, "Ah. Because the dead cannot spill secrets."

"Well, I didn't die."

"Good point," he said. "No more questions." He sneezed three more times. "You're making my allergies worse."

"Just one thing," I said. "If someone wants to know the future, why not just visit a seer?"

He thought about it, then lowered his voice, "Seers have a limited view of the *human* experience in *this* world."

"And?"

"And K'iin describes the idea of the sun and its relationship to the universe. I really hope someone teaches you these facts. I mean, it's kind of embarrassing that you don't know this stuff already. We got it drilled into us.... Oh, never mind," he said. "Let me explain it the way it was taught to me. The sun...the big orange ball in the sky?"

"I know what the sun is!"

Rosie snorted once, then plopped onto her behind.

"Good," the spirit said. "The sun always rises from Xib'alb'a and travels across the sky, just so the west can devour it." He held his hands out pleadingly. "Don't you see? The sun sacrifices herself every day so things can begin anew. Even though she is consumed, she returns. K'iin is constant like the sun, and greedy beings are like the west, wanting to possess K'iin's power: the ability to see *all*."

I must have been giving him a blank expression, because he shook his head again. "It isn't for you to seek," he said. "The chapat's warning was proof of that. You were never meant to see that image. Do you hear me?"

Thunder boomed. Lightning flashed.

"We have angered the gods!" Kip cried. "Don't forget your promise." Then he disappeared into thin air. I whirled to find his greenhouse gone, the labyrinth vanished.

The sky split open and rain poured down on us in sheets.

And just as Rosie and I bolted into the jungle for cover, I heard a bloodcurdling scream.

26

⠸

As I followed Rosie toward the sound, the rain turned to snow, which must have really freaked out the trees. So much for a perfect seventy-four degrees, I thought as my godborn positioning system kicked in, a cold sensation tugging me to the right.

Angry voices flew toward us.

A girl shouted, "Hit him!"

Rosie and I stumbled through the whitening jungle until we came to a multiterraced courtyard filled with dining tables and chairs. From where we stood, on the uppermost level, I could see tables covered with plates of half-eaten breakfasts: bacon, eggs, fruit, donuts, and other items. On the lowest tier, a dozen or so godborns were gathered under a clump of trees. The rascal monkeys hovered in the branches above, clapping and chomping their teeth.

And in the center? Marco and some tall dude who definitely hadn't been on my godborn tour. Which meant he must've been part of the junkyard battle. The two of them had their fists up and were circling each other like careful wolves, waiting to see who would make the first move.

My eyes darted everywhere, but I didn't see any of my friends. Maybe they were still in the library? Louie stood off to the side, and even from this twenty-foot distance, I could tell he was trembling as he ate a Storm Runner candy bar.

Marco quickly wiped some snowflakes from his eyes. "Stop with the storm already, Louie!"

"I can't help it," Louie said. "I don't like fights."

Louie was causing the storm? His dad *was* Chaac, the god of rain, but Louie hadn't even been trained yet.

"Punch him already!" someone commanded.

A gust of wind swept across the courtyard along with a more frenzied flurry of snow.

Everyone looked up, blinking against the instant winter.

"Hey!" I shouted.

No one reacted—they were too engrossed in the fight.

"Go find everyone, Rosie," I said. "Bring them here."

She took off into the forest.

With Fuego's help, I hurried down to the fray, pushing through the small crowd that was munching on donuts, bagels, and burritos.

"Look!" someone called out. "It's Zane Obispo!"

I stepped between Marco and the tall dude just as a fist was thrown.

Bam!

The knuckles landed squarely on my jaw, driving me to my knees. White stars danced in my vision, blood filled my mouth, and my skull felt like it had been crushed with a hammer.

That's when everything descended into chaos. Bagels were flung. Then donuts, bacon, and fruit. Before I knew it, soggy food was showering down faster than the snow.

Feet shuffled; hollers and grunts sounded. People were shoving and tripping one another, ducking and dodging. Monkeys shrieked and swung from the trees as the snow thickened. It was total mayhem, and for what?

Wiping blood off my lip with the back of my hand, I managed to crouch-stagger away from the wayward fists and flying bananas. I really wanted to launch some flames, but we were too close to the trees. A powdered-sugar donut smacked my cheek just as an earsplitting roar sounded.

Everyone froze—except the monitos, who vanished into the trees.

Hondo stood at the edge of the pandemonium with a grim expression and Rosie at his side. "Who started this?"

It really was ironic. I mean, here was the guy who used to throw ragers and watch wrestling matches with his friends through clouds of cigar smoke. And now he was acting like some kind of . . . adult?

The tall dude, who had grape jelly smeared across his face, pointed at Marco. "This jerk. He threw the first punch."

At that moment, the thing I hated most about Marco was his *punch-now-ask-questions-later* attitude. It was his fist that had knocked me to the ground, and the guy didn't even look sorry.

"You guys want to fight?" Hondo said to the entire group. "You've got extra energy to spend? All godborns to the arena—now!"

"But training doesn't start until tomorrow," someone said.

"Yeah?" Hondo's jaw looked like it was set in stone. "Well, tomorrow came early."

Everyone hesitated, bits of food dripping from their faces. Then Rosie, with eyes blazing, roared so loud, godborn feet got moving rápido.

As everyone filed out, Marco spat a loogie on the littered ground and said to me, "Don't look at me! He totally deserved it, and you got in the way."

The tall godborn came at him, but he didn't connect before Hondo threw up an arm, blocking the guy's advance. "Dude! I won't ask again."

"What about him?" The guy pointed at Marco, who was wearing the kind of smirk everyone wants to wipe off with a double bleach wipe.

"Go!" Hondo warned, pushing his snow-covered hair back.

The guy muttered under his breath and took off while Marco clenched his jaw.

"You okay?" Hondo asked, noticing my fattening lip.

I nodded, opening and closing my jaw as he clapped me on the back. Then, with a snicker and raised fists, he teased, "Did you have to box it out with the miniature monkeys?"

"Ha! Funny," I said. "But we don't have time for this. I found chapat."

"What's chapat?" Marco asked.

Hondo exhaled and turned to Marco. "Why are you still here?"

Marco stepped closer, his chin turned up all defiant. "Something creepy happened," he said, looking around. "And since I don't see anyone in charge, I guess you guys should know about it."

Louie stepped out from behind a tree, a miniature monkey

on his shoulder. He was feeding it scraps of chocolate. For the first time, I noticed the snow had stopped.

"Marco was sticking up for me," he said, and the monkey nodded vigorously. "That guy was making fun of my dream about Chaac. I saw the rain god opening and closing his mouth like a fish." He mimicked the movement. "He was drowning in darkness."

Drowning in darkness... The words were eerily close to what Ah-Puch had said about floating in utter darkness.

"So you had a bad dream," Hondo said.

Marco snorted. "We *all* had the same dream. Or close enough."

"Who's *all*?" I asked, taking deep breaths to prevent my heart from flying out of my mouth.

Louie puffed up his cheeks and exhaled super dramatic like. "Me, Serena, Marco, and a few others that we talked to."

My pulse raced and blood pounded in my ears. I could sense how close we were to getting answers. "What was your dream, Marco?"

He shoved his fists into his pockets and said, "Darkness, all that same stuff, but my . . . but Nakon and I were skydiving. He couldn't open his chute and said he was trapped. And then he said some other stuff I didn't catch, except . . . 'not here.'"

A loud screech drew our attention to the trees above. Brooks flew down in normal hawk form, and just as her talons touched the ground, she shifted into a human. She had really gotten good at sticking her landings. Louie's monkey threw its hands into the air and screamed as it leaped into the nearest tree.

"You scared him away," Louie whined to Brooks.

Glancing around with a scrunched nose, Brooks shook a glob of donut off her shoe and said, "I've been tearing apart the jungle chasing miniature monkeys for the stuff they've been stealing, and you've been here having a food fight and making friends with the thieves?"

"They're not *all* thieves!" Louie cried.

Brooks's eyes flicked to my bloodied mouth.

"I'm fine," I said before telling her about the drowning-in-darkness nightmares.

She threw her attention to Louie and Marco. "You guys had the same dream?"

Louie shivered. "Something real bad is up."

"We bet you know what it is," Marco added, crossing his arms.

Hondo dragged a hand through his hair. "I better get to the arena, see if the other godborns dreamed about their godly parents. Maybe it all adds up to an answer. You good here?" he asked me.

Nodding, I steered Hondo away from the others and said in a low voice, "I need to tell you what I learned. I'll meet up with you in thirty."

After my uncle took off, I rejoined the two godborns. Louie said to me, "That lightning ceremony hurt, by the way. You could have warned us about that."

Marco had the same scowl he'd worn that day when he was imprisoned in the junkyard. "Did *you* dream about Hurakan, Zane?"

"No." *Only the Red Queen.* And then I wondered why

Hurakan *hadn't* tried to reach out to me. Probably because the Red Queen had taken up all my headspace.

"So the gods are trying to communicate with their kids through dreams," Brooks said, but it was more like she was talking to herself.

"Well, they're doing a pretty bad job of it," Marco said. "You'd think gods would be able to speak more clearly."

Louie took another bite of the bar and spoke around a mouthful of chocolate. "My dad talked real clear during my claiming."

"What do you mean?" Brooks asked.

"When I was pounded with lightning," he said, "he told me I was the son of the great rain god and didn't need any training. He said our powers were a force. . . . No, that wasn't the word. Maybe he said our powers were the greatest of all the gods. Yeah, something like that." He licked chocolate from the corner of his mouth.

Marco harrumphed, then his eyes widened. "Wait! Why would the gods need to talk to us in our dreams . . . ? Where are they?"

"At their mountain resort," Brooks said with so much sarcasm I thought her tongue would fall out of her mouth.

Alana emerged from the trees, followed by Adrik and Ren. "We just ran into Hondo. You found chapat?"

I nodded.

Marco's eyes flitted from face to face. "Come on, man. What are you guys not saying?"

Ren sidestepped a smashed pile of grapes and said, "All the Maya gods were taken by some Mexica sleep god, and Zotz and Ixkik' have an entry stone that gives them access to this place so they can get in and murder us."

Ah-Puch's unfinished words filled my head: *Ren is the only one.* The only one what?

"Well, that's one way to put it," Brooks muttered.

"Actually, I think it's the devouring earth goddess," I said. "Not a sleep god."

"Did you say 'devouring'?" Louie whined. "As in eating?" His eyes bugged out. "Is someone going to eat the gods?"

I spilled the beans to Marco and Louie about my Red Queen dream and the clues she gave me. After all, we were now in this together—I felt like keeping the truth from them would only make things worse.

Louie looked woozy as he sat on a nearby chair and unwrapped another chocolate bar.

Marco ran his thumb over the scar on his chin. "And this Itzamna dude is the only one not asleep? Pretty convenient, if you ask me." The way his brain went straight to corruption made me think he really was the god of war's kid.

Louie gave a short nod. "Yeah, Zane. How do we know the moon god isn't behind all this?"

"Nah," I said. "The guy was for sure freaked. Plus, his strength comes from the World Tree, which is powered by the gods. Anyway, we don't have much time before the underworld falls to Zotz and Ixkik'... and once that happens—"

"Adiós, gods," Marco said flatly.

"But they're already out of commission," Louie said. "Why kill them, too?"

"Maybe they aren't in a great hiding place?" I guessed.

"Maybe..." *Think like a villain,* I told myself. "Maybe hiding them isn't enough," I said, and as the words fell from my mouth, they felt truer than anything that had been said so far. "They can't risk the gods being found. They want to end them forever."

"We have to tell everyone the bat god is coming," Louie said.

"No!" Marco clenched his jaw. "That would only cause a panic."

"We can't keep this a secret," Brooks argued. "It's only a matter of time before the godborns start asking questions."

"We can make up an excuse," Adrik suggested.

Alana tugged on her hair, pacing slowly.

"We aren't going to lie to them," I said. I knew the damage lies can do, the mistrust they create, and that was no way to treat the other godborns. They deserved to know that their lives were in danger.

"I'll tell them," Louie volunteered, raising his hand. "I'd rather do that than go on any rescue quests or do anything dangerous."

"Who said anything about a rescue?" Marco said. "I don't even know Nakon."

Ren looked stricken. "So you don't care if Zotz and Ixkik' hurt your dad?"

"Nakon never cared about *me,*" he said, crossing his arms. But his mouth trembled, betraying the fact that *he* did care.

"Fair enough," Adrik said. Alana socked him in the chest and he rubbed the spot. "Ow!"

I know Marco sounded super harsh, but I kind of under-stood. I used to be all sorts of angry at my dad for not being around when I was growing up. Connecting the godborns to their parents would take time—time we didn't have.

I quickly told them about the labyrinth, K'iin, and Ah-Puch communicating with me, withholding the part about Ren. I needed to talk to her alone about that.

Ren's eyes filled with tears. "A.P. can't just give up!"

"Gross!" Louie gasped. "A giant centipede tried to eat you?"

"What did Ah-Puch mean by 'already gone'?" Brooks said.

"I don't know," I said, frustrated. "He just said 'We are no longer here.'" I turned my gaze to Marco. "Like Nakon said to you. But where is 'here'?"

Marco's expression hardened. "How should I know? Maybe you should ask the calendar."

"It's not a bad idea," Brooks said. "I mean, we're talking about a calendar that can see across time and dimensions."

"We're talking about a calendar that can find the gods," I said.

27

•

••

Maybe I should have softened the blow a little
bit. Revealed the details more gradually. I mean, it was a lot
for the godborns to absorb all at once. The Maya gods had
been taken, and we didn't know how to find or wake them.
There was a cosmic calendar that might help, but if it existed
at all, it was hidden, too. And everyone who had tried to find
it was dead. Meanwhile, Zotz and Ixkik', masterminds of
power and evil, were raising the stakes every minute. Not to
mention the devourer, a wicked Mexica goddess, being resurrected. Oh, and the World Tree was likely to fall in the next
couple of days, meaning none of us were safe.

Things were grim. So, no, I didn't sugarcoat it. I laid it all
out there.

No one spoke.

Marco shoved a table; its legs scraped across the stone
floor. "Find and unlock a thing that only the dead are allowed
to see? Do you have a death wish, man?"

"It's a threat," Ren said. "Don't you see? Pacific put security
in place to keep people from looking for her calendar."

"The centipede tried to choke him!" Marco argued. "That's
no threat."

My mind kept turning things over and over and over, trying to put all the pieces together.

Time. Evil. Deception.

"Why didn't the Red Queen just tell you about K'iin?" Louie asked. "Then you might not have gotten choked."

Brooks said, "Seeing the future isn't an exact science—sometimes it only comes in little pieces."

I stared at Ren, wondering what her role was in all this. Was she the time part? Or was I grasping at straws? I thought about her dream—if it was real, was Pacific trying to communicate with her?

"Ren," I said, "your mom mentioned a cave . . . ?"

"The Cave of Crystals."

"What if that's where K'iin is?" I asked. "Could she have been trying to tell you where to find it?"

"So we could *see* where she and the other gods are being kept!" Ren nearly shouted.

Marco shot me and Ren a glare. "Are you all listening to yourselves? Who cares about K'iin! Let's get out of here and save ourselves."

"If Zotz and Ixkik' are in control," I said, "there is no 'out of here.'"

I could tell Marco's wheels were turning. Prison, death, or quest? Quest, death, or prison? Finally, he grunted. "Fine. But can we at least be smarter than the bat and Ixkik'? We have to think like they do and try to anticipate their next move."

"How can we be smarter than a god?" Adrik asked.

"We all have gifts," Marco said.

I threw a side-glance at Alana. Her shades had dropped to the middle of her nose, and her eyes were glued to the ground.

"My dominant power is 'duplicity,'" Marco went on, making air quotes. "I guess I can change faces. So far all I get are different eyebrows or a different chin or nose. It's dumb."

"Cool," Ren said. "Can you show us?"

Marco scowled. "That would be a definite no."

"At least you don't have to be asleep to use your powers," Adrik grumbled.

"Seriously?" Alana kicked a half-eaten apple across the ground. "At least you guys *have* gifts! So stop complaining!"

Everyone got awkwardly quiet. Louie offered her a piece of chocolate. But Alana stormed off without another word.

"I'll go talk to her," Ren said.

"No, I'll do it." Adrik shook his head. "I'm her brother."

After he left, Ren faced Marco. "Okay, son of war. How do we anticipate Zotz and Blood Moon's next move?"

"What if they're out of moves?" Louie said. "What if *this* is it?"

"Jerks like that?" Marco raised his eyebrows. "They like power, but they like gloating over it even more. This is a game, and winning is no fun unless it's public."

"Whoa," Louie said. "You got all that because you're the god of war's kid?"

Marco cringed. "No," he said. "I play sports. But it's the same idea."

The hairs on my arms stood at attention. Marco was right. Zotz loved an audience. But not Ixkik'. She liked to slink around in the shadows like a thieving rat that only comes out at night. And until we knew for certain which one of them was in charge, there was no way we could guess their next play.

"As fascinating as all this is," Brooks said, "shouldn't we be asking how to find that cave?"

Silence fell over us like a thick cloud.

Marco rubbed his thumb over his scar. "*If* you can find K'iin, and it shows you where the gods are, and *if* you survive, you need to figure out how to wake them up."

"And rescue them without getting eaten," Louie said.

"First things first," I said, feeling overwhelmed.

Ren nodded. "We need to go to the Cave of Crystals."

"You mean *you* need to go," Marco said. "I'll stay here and..." He didn't finish, but his eyes said it all. They were a mix of anger and defiance, and I understood. He didn't want to sit around doing nothing, helplessly waiting to go down.

"Okay. You get ready to defend SHIHOM and the World Tree," I said, "if it comes to that."

Louie covered his face with his hands and moaned.

"We'll take the twins with us," I said.

Brooks ran a hand through her hair. I could tell she was frustrated and not used to so many voices brewing in the quest pot. "Zane..." she said in a warning tone.

"What? We can't do this alone," I told her. "We'll need the godborns' help."

Ren kicked a lump of melting snow with the toe of her boot, fixing her eyes on Marco. "Find out all the godborns' gifts. Make a list of which will be the most useful."

"But don't tell them anything," Brooks put in. "Not yet."

"Fine," Marco said. "But about this quest... Where's the

element of surprise? Zotz and Ixkik' know you're going to try a rescue mission. They'll be waiting."

Ren twisted her watch anxiously.

Ah-Puch's words echoed through my head: *Ren is the one...*

And then, finally, the revelation hit me like a two-ton wrecking ball. The idea was bold and brilliant and unexpected. Even old Zotz and faceless Ixkik' wouldn't anticipate this move, not in a million years. My mouth spread into a full-on grin as hope filled my chest. "You're right," I said to Marco. "They're expecting us to storm the castle."

Brooks followed my gaze to Ren's watch and caught on. "Because that's what we've done before," she said slowly. She went over to Ren. "But for *this* quest, we have a secret weapon."

Ren's eyes met mine, then she glanced at Brooks. I saw understanding bloom in her eyes. She nodded slowly and whispered, "We're going to stop time."

28

•
•••

Mission Don't Get Devoured had officially
started.

Rosie and I met up with Hondo, and I told him the plan.
He hated it. Every single detail of it. But that didn't stop him
from telling me, "I'm going with you."

"No, you've got to stay here. The godborns need training,"
I said. "And someone has to be in charge in case Zotz and
Ixkik'..." My voice trailed off, but Hondo got my meaning.
He was already frowning and nodding.

Deep down, I was hoping really hard that our enemies
would never make it to Xib'alb'a. That they would never reach
the Tree's roots. Yeah, I know. It was wishful thinking.

Hondo squeezed my shoulder. "If you don't haul butt back
here right after your dance with time, I will hunt you down."

"Haul butt," I repeated. "Got it. And you'll be okay?
You'll...?" I hesitated, practically choking on the words. I
didn't know what else to say. *You'll keep everyone safe? Stop
Zotz and Ixkik' from invading?* It was too tall an order even for
a ride-or-die uncle with a magical warrior mask and a tough
nawal at his side.

"I got this," he said. He released his grip, and we continued walking toward the temple. "How will you find this Cave of Crystals?"

"We're going to ask Saás."

By the time we arrived at the library, Brooks, Ren, Marco, and Louie were already there. Louie was sitting cross-legged on top of a table, reading a thick book entitled *Things You Didn't Know Could Kill You but Can*.

Alana and Adrik came in behind us. Alana clapped to get our attention and announced, "I have something to tell you guys."

"As long as it isn't more bad news," Marco grumbled.

"Remember when I said I was seeing blurry spots?" Alana asked.

We all nodded. Rosie's ears perked up.

"Well, I kind of walked into one of them."

"Walked into one?" Marco snorted.

"The blurry areas are gateways!" Adrik practically shouted.

I thought about what Ik had told me back in Hell's Kitchen. *They're all around us.* I twisted my hands around Fuego. "You can see all the gateways?"

"I don't know about *all*." Alana's eyes darted from face to face before landing back on mine. "They look like blurry pockets of air. There's one in this room."

"Where?" Hondo asked.

She pointed to the center of the room, near where Saás slowly revolved.

"Whoa!" Ren breathed. "That's amazing. *You're* amazing."

Alana's face flushed with pleasure and she said, "Shadows and time are way cooler."

"But how do you know where the gateway goes?" I asked, more concerned with the logistics.

"Yeah," Brooks said. "We could end up in—"

"Saigon or Turku," Louie cut in.

Turku?

Marco traced a swirl in the table's wood with his finger as he eyed the room suspiciously. "I don't see anything."

"Doesn't mean it isn't there." Adrik's words rushed out. "Tell them the rest, Alana."

"Do I need to sit down for this?" Hondo asked.

Twisting her pinkie, Alana went on. "I sort of wasn't paying attention, because I was mad, and, well, I walked into one of these blurry spots. I ended up"—she took a breath—"on the other side of SHIHOM, near a lake. At first, every portal I found took me somewhere here on the grounds. Then I went through one that led somewhere else."

I thought about what Ik had told me back in Hell's Kitchen—how you can't just fall into a gateway. Everything has to align just right. Something about angles, rising planets, and I think it was unflossed teeth. "How?" I asked. "Where?"

"After I went through a few, I got used to it," Alana said almost shyly. "I tried again, this time thinking of home."

"I went with her to our house," Adrik said. "It was *wild!*" He let out a controlled breath. "Wicked Witch was downstairs humming a tune like she didn't give a lick that we were gone. I messed up her bed and tossed some of her stuff around so she'd think she was being haunted. Ha! It was sick!"

"Witch?" Louie slammed his book closed. A few snow

flurries tumbled down from the open roof. "Sorry," he said, stopping the flakes immediately.

Brooks drew closer to Alana. "But how did you guys get back here?"

"We just came back the way we went," Alana said like she was telling us how to ride a bike.

"But gateways always close after you use them," Ren said.

"Mine stay open, I guess," Alana said with a shrug.

My thoughts came to a stuttering halt. "Hang on," I said. "Are you telling me—"

"She can *control* gateways," Adrik said, before turning to his sister. "See? You never believe me! I told you your gift would show up." He held his hand out, palm up. "You owe me some dinero! Twenty bucks."

"Define *control*." Hondo looked suspicious.

Rosie wagged her nub tail and panted like she was saying *Let's go, let's go!*

Had I been wrong? Was Alana the one with the greater powers? Controlling gateways sure seemed bigger and better than dream walking. . . . A ball of heat expanded in my chest, making it hard to breathe.

"You're like a walking Google Maps?" Marco scratched at his scar. "You can just tell the gateway where you want to go?"

Alana shrugged again.

It made perfect sense that she would get this gift from Ixtab, who had once escorted the dead to the afterlife and so needed lots of gateways.

Brooks's eyes met mine, and in that second, I knew the

question she was about to ask. "You said you can control gateways, but can you actually—"

"Conjure them?" Ren finished. "Because that would be so cool. We could conjure one to shove all the Maya gods through." She threw her hands out to illustrate.

As if anything were that simple.

"Unless they've already been devoured," Marco muttered, still tracing his finger across the wood table. I swear he was Brooks's long-lost fatalistic hermano.

"Don't even say that!" Ren warned.

"Alana is still figuring out how to use the gateways," Adrik said, "so don't expect too much." He leaned toward her. "Right?"

Hondo clapped three times. "Focus, godborns. Right now, some of us need to get to K'iin." He glanced at Alana. "You think you can open a doorway to this Cave of Crystals from Ren's alien dream?"

"Crystal alien what?" I could tell Marco was on the verge of mad-scientist laughter. Like one more word about magic or other unexplainable events was going to make him snap.

"I don't know..." Alana said nervously. "I don't know where that is."

"That's what we're here to ask Saás." I pointed to the globe.

Ren asked the glowing orb to tell us the exact location of the cave.

And you know what Saás said? Actually, I can't repeat it. Whoever programmed her either had their head in the gutter or was in a super-bad mood at the time.

I bet it was Ixtab.

Anyhow, I had to pull the dragon power card again. (Hey, access to knowledge in the temple meant *all* knowledge, including Saás's.) When I insisted that she answer, the globe finally said in a bitter tone, "What you seek cannot be accessed."

29

•
••••

"What do you mean?" My voice echoed across the chamber.

"I wasn't done!" Saás snapped. "La Cueva de los Cristales is part of a hostile environment in Chihuahua, Mexico. It's a horseshoe-shaped cavity connected to the Naica Mine. Without proper protection, one can only last ten minutes and thirty-two seconds there. Godborns might last an extra two minutes."

"What do you mean, 'protection'?" Brooks asked.

"The cave is a magma chamber," Saás said. "That's an oven to you. Its air temperature can reach one hundred and thirty-six degrees with ninety to ninety-nine percent humidity. But there is a greater problem."

"Greater than being cooked to death?" Marco snorted.

"The cave is currently flooded," Saás said. "A watery world of ninety-nine percent certain death."

My heart sank. I felt like every step forward jerked us two hundred steps back.

"There has to be another way in," Alana said. "A back door?"

"No back door," Saás said. "But there is an air pocket—an

area precisely seven feet two inches by eight feet three inches. Should I begin writing your obituaries?"

Marco picked up Louie's book, white-knuckling it like he might launch it at the globe.

"Hold up!" I said. "Are you saying we have to nail the landing exactly?"

"That is correct, if you are stupid enough to go there. Would you like me to compute your chances of success?"

Alana's face drained of all color. Adrik put his arm around her shoulder and squeezed.

"We *have* to go there," Ren said to Saás, frowning. "Give us the exact coordinates." Sometimes I forgot that in Ren's previous life she ran a blog for alien sightings and spent most of her time mapping clues and trying to prove aliens were real. She was well versed in the impossible.

Saás rattled off the coordinates. "There. I've practically drawn you a map! Good-bye."

"Wait!" Brooks hollered, but Saás had already shut down.

We all stood in silence. If our minds could've talked aloud, the library would've been buzzing with chaotic, terrified noise.

"Hey, Louie," I said as an idea slowly took root.

"Why are you looking at me like that?" He started backing up.

"You think you can create another snowstorm?"

He hesitated before the full meaning of my words hit him. Then he shook his head vigorously. "No. I am *not* going cave-diving only to be cooked to death! I do not do quests. I already told you."

Brooks inched closer to him and said, in the gentlest voice I'd ever heard her use, "We need you to be brave, Louie. Please. You're the only godborn who can help us survive the cave. You wouldn't want any of us to die of heatstroke, would you?"

"It's just a calendar," Hondo added. "What's it going to do? Paper-cut you to death?"

"A calendar that wants blood!" Louie argued. He rubbed his cheek. "That bat god really freaked me out last time."

"He's more likely to come *here*," Itzamna said.

We all spun to see the moon god standing behind us.

No one had a chance to ask the awful question *How do you know?* before Itzamna dropped the devastating bomb: "Our enemies have infiltrated the underworld. More than half of Ixtab's army has joined Camazotz—the other half are being held for execution. Demons are climbing up the roots of the World Tree as we speak."

Louie collapsed into a chair and let his head drop onto his folded arms. Snow began to fall more heavily.

"Traitors," Ren hissed.

Alana and Adrik scowled, and I wasn't sure if they were confused, scared, or angry that their mom's world was now under attack.

Itzamna shook his head sadly, staring down at the sunglasses in his grasp. "We have three days, tops."

"We'll help!" I cried before I'd even had the chance to weigh our options. Did we even have any? Stay and fight a battle we were sure to lose, or try to find K'iin in a watery death trap.

Brooks's dark wings emerged, extending at least seven feet. We all ducked as she began to pace frantically.

Marco said, "We need to split up. Zane—you, Ren, Alana, and Louie go find the calendar."

Louie's eyes bugged out and his face went sickly green.

Marco continued. "Hondo, Brooks, and I will stay and—"

"No one is staying!" Itzamna's voice hit a low baritone note that made the walls tremble. "Everyone must evacuate. We cannot risk the godborns."

"Evacuate?" Hondo balled his fists. "So, basically, you want us to run?"

"No," the god said. "I want you to protect the power of the godborns, while I try to protect my home. End of story."

In that moment, I saw that Itzamna had changed. He was no longer the lighthearted *give-me-a-great-story* god. But I guess fear can make you do and say things you normally never would.

Ren shook her head, pressing her lips together. I could tell she was trying to think of a way out of this.

Itzamna said, "I also received a message from the Sparkstriker."

More messages? *Please, please, please let this one be good,* I thought.

"The enemy took one of the Sparkstriker's top spies." The god's eyes flicked to Brooks. "They have Quinn."

Brooks sucked in a sharp breath. "No! How?"

Hondo's eyes flashed with hot anger, and I thought he might clock the god just for delivering the awful news.

"What do we do?" Brooks cried, flapping her wings. "I can't let her get hurt . . ." Then her voice trailed off as her eyes popped wide. "The hero twins," she whispered.

"What about those jerks?" Hondo spat.

"Don't you see?" Brooks said. "Jordan would never hurt Quinn." Her words flew out like they were trying to keep pace with her racing thoughts. "And he wouldn't let his mom do it, either. They're just trying to bait us." She paced faster. "Quinn trained me to be smart and anticipate the enemy's next moves. If they had wanted to kill Quinn, they would have done it already. They haven't killed the gods yet, either, and that tells me..." Her hands went up to her mouth.

"What?" I asked.

Brooks paused for a heartbeat. "They don't have access to the gods," she whispered.

"How could they not have access to their own prisoners?" Marco asked.

"You think they hid them so good they can't find them anymore?" Louie scratched his head anxiously.

"Or you're wrong and they *did* kill them," Adrik said.

Alana socked him in the arm. He rubbed the spot tenderly as Itzamna said, "The Tree's lights would have gone dark if the gods were dead."

"Then we stick to the plan," I said. "Figure out what K'iin can tell us."

At the same moment, the ground shook violently and the stone floor split down the middle with an earsplitting *craccckkk!*

Horrible howls and wails rose up from below.

Fire erupted in my gut, telling me we had to leave, and we had to leave *now.*

"The demons are getting closer," Itzamna cried. "The scent

of godborn blood is feeding their frenzy. If you leave, it will slow them down. And buy me time."

Hondo clenched his jaw and stared at me like he was looking for an answer or approval. "Go," I said. "Take the godborns—"

"To Montana," Adrik cut in.

"It's a hideaway our dad made," Alana explained. "The godborns will be safe there, at least for a while. You can tell them it's part of their training so no one freaks out." Her eyes searched mine, and I found myself nodding as the fire inside me calmed, telling me to trust her.

Ren took hold of my arm and said telepathically, *Zane, we can do this. But we have to hurry.*

The remains of the ceiling trembled dangerously, like one breath could make it fall.

There was no time to ask any more questions. "Hondo, Brooks, Rosie, and Marco, start rounding up the rest of the godborns. Get them to"—I glanced at Adrik, hoping I could rely on him—"Montana."

Rosie shifted her legs like she was ready to bolt.

"I'll open the gateway as soon as you have collected everyone," Itzamna said to Brooks. "But you will have mere seconds to get through before the demons sense there's an opening."

"Stay safe, Diablo," my uncle said to me.

Brooks only nodded. Her eyes met mine and held my gaze for an eternity of two seconds that seemed to say *You better not die.* Then she was gone along with the others.

The demons' howling erupted from the cracked floor again, and man, I wanted to torch the place. But it wouldn't do us any good. The monsters would come through, and we wouldn't be any closer to K'iin.

Itzamna placed his sunglasses in my hands. "Use these to communicate with me. Find K'iin. Get the answers we need, and do it soon!"

I took the shades, figuring he was too weak to communicate by any other method.

Itzamna added, "Alana, I can only open a gateway for one group, I'm afraid, which means you will have to go with Zane and the others. We need your magic to get them to the cave. But you must be fast. Do you understand?"

The twins exchanged glances, and then Alana nodded. "I got this," she said before she walked up to the "blurry spot" none of the rest of us could see. Despite her confident words, she looked unsure, sick, or terrified. I wasn't sure which.

I hung the sunglasses on my collar as Ren, Louie, and I followed Alana.

She extended her hands, cleared her throat, closed her eyes, and pinched her eyebrows together in concentration as Ren repeated the coordinates. Nothing happened.

Louie chewed on his thumbnail. "Think cold," he said. "It might help me make a storm. And whatever you do, don't think of monsters."

Alana whirled on him. "Gahh! Now I'm going to think it!"

"Ren," I whispered, "do you remember the cliff in Mexico with Ah-Puch?"

"When we combined our powers?" She pursed her lips together, nodding. "But that only works if you've been where you're trying to go. And also, Ah-Puch said it was a secret."

A secret tied to a threat: *If you ever tell anyone I showed it to you*, Ah-Puch had said to us, *I will rip out your spines and send you spiraling into the darkest depths of Xib'alb'a.*

"Yeah," I said to Ren. "Except this is an extreme emergency, and we...uh...don't have to tell him."

"What are you guys talking about?" Alana said. "And *why* are you talking?"

"We're going to jump-start you, but you have to swear never to tell anyone we did this," I said. After the others promised not to betray my confidence, I placed my hand on Alana's shoulder, and Ren did the same on the other side. Louie followed our lead and took Ren's hand. Like before, a deep buzzing began in my feet. It snaked up my legs, spreading into my torso.

"Focus, Alana," I whispered.

I feel something, she said telepathically.

Connect to it, Ren said to Alana. *Don't be afraid.*

The magnetic pull was getting stronger. And stronger.

An iridescent doorway formed in front of us. Beyond it was a blackness even I couldn't see through. Shrieks sounded in the distance.

That can't be good, Louie said.

And just as we stepped into the screaming void, I glanced over my shoulder at Itzamna. He was no longer in god mode. He was now a massive blue dragon soaring through the open ceiling and into the sky.

Unlike all the other times I'd marched, fallen, or been tossed into a shimmering gateway to tumble like a sock in the dryer, *this* portal was gentle. There were no bone-chilling gusts or vicious whispers. No sharp projectiles or body slams.

We left the library behind us with two steps and were zipped into a darkness blacker than Zotz's wings on a moonless night.

"Where are we?" Alana spoke between quickened breaths.

"Zane?" Ren said. "Can you see anything?"

"Nothing."

A distant moan/growl came next.

Louie made an *eep* sound.

And then we emerged in what looked like a backlit ice cave. Except it wasn't cold, and I heard the sound of wheels on a track, like a train. The place felt more like a theater stage than the real deal.

"Where the heck—" I began, but my question was swallowed up by a bobsled/car thingy zipping past on the rails a few yards in front of us. Shrieks and laughter filled the air.

"Oh no!" Alana cried. "I brought us to the Matterhorn."

"At Disneyland?" Ren's knees nearly buckled before I righted her.

"Those coordinates were for Disneyland?!" A gran sonrisa lit up Louie's face.

The ride had a tangy metallic smell. Another bobsled zipped by. Okay, I don't know about you, but when you visit Disneyland for the very first time, you don't expect it to be through a magical portal when the universe is on the brink of a bat god takeover.

"How did we end up here?" Ren asked. "Did I read the coordinates wrong?"

"Louie said to think *cold*," Alana said with a sigh, "and *monsters*, and . . . I guess this place sort of popped into my mind, with the abominable snowman, and . . . Sorry. I got nervous."

"He said to *not* think of monsters," I reminded her.

"This isn't *my* fault," Louie argued. "But super-good choice. Like, way better than meeting up with a dumb calendar."

Alana's eyes frantically swept the space. "I blew it. We can go back the way we came, or . . . Wait! I think"—she started climbing over the rails toward another alcove—"there's another gateway over here."

Perfect! Forget getting killed by an evil god. I was going to get crushed by a racing bobsled.

"Hurry." Ren tugged on my arm. "Before we get arrested by Disney policía!"

"Disneyland has cops?" Louie asked as we hopped the rails. "You think they wear Mickey ears?"

"You're not helping," I said.

"Think hot cave this time, with a seven-foot landing," Louie said. "And don't think about—"

Alana shot him a glare. "I got this, Louie."

We joined hands, waiting for Alana to take the first step. When she did and we plunged into the gateway, all I could think was *Please, Alana, don't throw us into an avalanche of knives.*

We hurtled through the air for 2.3 seconds. Yes, I counted them.

"AAAAHHHHHH!" That was Louie.

In a fierce gust of wind, we were whooshed out of the

portal and dropped onto the floor of a cave. The air was thick and hot, barely tolerable. I peered across the dark watery world.

Alana gripped my hand tighter. "Are we...?"

I sucked in a sharp breath. "You aren't going to believe this."

30

I raised Fuego over my head. Its blue light cast an eerie glow across the cave.

"Whoa!" my friends said on a long breath.

We stood on a barely there ledge mere inches away from a steaming pool where thick, towering white crystals grew in every direction. They poked out of the water like giant icicles or massive iridescent tree trunks that had fallen all slanted and skewed.

"They look like shimmering dinosaur bones," Ren said, rotating her arm like she had a kink in a muscle.

Louie said, "This reminds me of Superman's Fortress of Solitude. Did you ever see the movie where—"

"Louie," Alana wheezed, "just turn down the heat!"

Pressing his mouth into a tight line, Louie rolled up his sleeves. "I kinda need inspiration."

"Like what?" I asked, already feeling light-headed from the 99 percent humidity.

"BOO!" Alana leaped at Louie, who startled so bad he would've gone over the edge if I hadn't grabbed his arm.

"Not cool, Alana!" he said with a scowl.

Snowflakes began descending from the cave ceiling.

"But *you* are, Louie!" Alana said, side-hugging him.

He grunted in surprise.

I nodded my agreement, totally grateful that we weren't going to get cooked. The snow fell thicker and faster, and the temperature plummeted. The water below us froze with a *crackkksss shppplitzzz*.

"Seriously, that's so, so amazing, Louie," Ren said, blinking snow off her lashes. Then she turned to me. "You should use the sunglasses, Zane. You never know when a god's help could come in handy."

I'd almost forgotten about them between Disneyland and Venus turned North Pole.

As soon as I put them on, the world tilted. I saw purple and silver flashes, like a strobe light. An image of Itzamna burst out of one of the sparks, and it was like he was standing right in front of me. Well, more like his face was floating right in front of me. The image looked like a selfie, with the god's hair blowing in the wind as he smiled wide for the camera. When I lifted the glasses off my nose, no Itzamna.

"Are we going to FaceTime or not?" Itzamna said with a voice as clear as if he was standing right next to me.

"I can hear him!" Louie said. Ren and Alana nodded that they could, too.

"FaceTime?" I asked. Gods did FaceTime?

"Move your head to the right," the god said. "I can only see what you can. Ah, yes. I remember this cave—I think I held a New Year's party there back in 300. Or was it 400?"

"Itzamna!" I said. "Why didn't you tell me you could turn into a dragon?"

"I did! Haven't you heard anything I've said? Dragon is my most powerful incarnation."

"But I thought you didn't have much power left," I argued.

"Are things okay at SHIHOM?" Ren butted in.

"No demons yet. The magic is holding for now."

"Why don't you sound worried?" Alana asked. "Like before?"

"Oh, let me explain," he said. "I am a segment of Itzamna's consciousness—not the god in his glorious totality. Do you understand?"

"Uh-huh," I muttered. The gods were pros at splitting themselves into pieces so they could be in more than one place at a time. It was pretty weird. But we didn't have time for chit-chat. "What should we do next?" I asked, wondering if I was going to have to look at his floating face for the entire quest.

"How should I know?"

I was about to argue that he was an all-seeing god when Ren's left arm jerked up over her head in a spastic sort of way.

"Do you have a question?" Louie asked. "Like, how do I make it snow?"

"I didn't raise my hand," Ren said, her eyes wide as her arm continued to waggle over her head like she was a marionette whose strings had been pulled. A bright light pulsed from the watch on her left wrist as a single strand of gold, no longer than four inches, peeled away from the band and hovered in midair.

"Uh, Ren?" I said, staring at the suspended strand.

She followed my gaze and gasped, struggling in vain to bring her arm back to her side. "It's a piece of the time rope," she said. "But why is it loose?" She grabbed the end closest to her with her upraised hand, and it stuck fast to her palm.

"It isn't loose now," said Louie. "I think it likes you."

Ren still couldn't lower her arm, and the string started pulling her forward.

"It's leading us somewhere," Alana said, pointing.

"Probably to our deaths." Louie groaned.

We all stared in awe as the gold string stretched longer and longer, floating across the ice, weaving between the crystal towers.

"Follow the gold!" Itzamna commanded.

"Right," I grumbled. "Great idea."

We stepped onto the ice and trailed the gold thread as it zigged and zagged, snaking up some of the massive quartz formations like it was sniffing them out before dropping down in front of us again.

"It's looking for K'iin," Ren whispered.

"No," Itzamna said in a hushed voice. "They're looking for each other."

"How do you know?" Louie asked.

"Because the watch was made with pieces of the time rope," the god said. "And K'iin is made of the same threads. They're like magnets trying to connect." He sighed appreciatively. "I must hand it to Pacific—she's quite ingenious."

Ren's expression brightened.

White puffs streamed from our mouths as we stalked the now nearly ten-foot-long gold thread. It stopped and hovered over the ice before it slipped out of Ren's grasp. It formed a hoop that floated down to the surface we were standing on.

With a sizzle and a flash, the golden circle sank into the ice. We stood around the five-foot-wide hole it had left behind.

Ren squatted to investigate. "It's a tunnel. We should take it."

"I'll wait here," Louie said. "Keep everything frosty."

"We stay together," I argued. "Unless you want to risk never getting home."

"Like I said," Louie added, "I'm totally following you guys."

Ren dangled her boots over the hole's edge. "It's so dark in there," she said. "Zane, can you see anything?"

I got down on all fours and poked my head inside. It was like looking down the steepest tube slide at the water park. "I can't see past the bump. But that could be a serious drop, Ren. Maybe we should find another way...."

Ren nodded, then said, "I have to follow it." And she pushed past me and slid into the tunnel.

"Ren!" I plopped down onto my butt, turned Fuego into a tattoo, and went in after her. My first thought was *I'm going to kill Ren*. My second thought was *This is what an iced pinball must feel like*. I rocketed down a near-vertical drop that forced my stomach into my throat.

I was certain Alana and Louie were right behind me, because their howls and screams echoed so loudly I thought they might crack the ice.

"Looks dreadfully cold," Itzamna said, faking a shiver sound. "And dangerous."

I continued to plummet in the darkness, racing at what felt like fifty miles per hour, twisting and turning, looping upside down three times. I may have even lost gravity for a second before the god's glasses flew off and I was hurled into open air. There was no time to think or panic or do much of anything but close my eyes as I plunged into a steaming lake, feetfirst.

The water folded around me, peaceful and calm. *I could easily stay suspended here forever,* I thought. *It's so warm. So easy. So quiet.* I slowly opened my eyes. Red-and-orange starfish clung to underwater cliffs. A giant black stingray glided by. Shimmering pink and yellow plants swayed gently above a silvery-green reef.

This was underwater heaven.

All my thoughts and fears melted away as I floated weightless, worriless. *Who needs air when you've got a view like this?*

And then a face appeared. To be specific, a boy's pale face. I didn't recognize him. He was maybe ten years old, with dark, buggy eyes. Kind of ghostish-looking. But nothing could scare me out of this haze, this trance the water had me in.

Then the boy's arms wrapped around me—his skin cold compared to the warm water. He pulled me to the surface as I struggled against his Herculean strength. He had puny limbs, so how could he just overpower me like that?

I had no concept of how long I'd been underwater. I was feeling so serene, I'd forgotten about everything else. The second I hit the surface, reality washed over me. I gasped for air as I treaded water. I was under a gray sky and facing a black-sand beach lined with massive trees. Their branches were so heavy they bowed to the water's edge.

"Zane!" Ren stood on the shore, waving one hand over her head.

I coughed up water and swam over to her while the ghost

boy drifted back under. I looked down to see him staring up at me, unblinking.

The air had cleared my head, and instantly all my worries and fears rushed right back in. I dragged myself onto the sand and shook off on all fours like a dog, thinking the water had to be drugged or magic or cursed.

"Are you okay?" Ren asked, seemingly more concerned about my cough than the fact that a ghost kid had hauled my butt to the surface. "You might have trouble focusing for a few minutes until the water's effects wear off."

"Where are we?" I asked, peering around the empty beach. Beyond the thick trees a massive bluish-green mountain loomed, looking like a gigantic pile of moss.

"The rope led us here. Isn't it amazing?" She sounded happy, but when I looked up at her, Ren was grimacing. That's when I noticed the hand over her head was once again gripping the time thread, which seemed to be struggling to get free.

"You need help with that?" I asked, getting up and reaching for it.

"NO!" Ren shoved me back with her free hand.

"What the heck?"

"Sorry, Zane, but it will fry you—as in instant electrocution—if you touch it."

"Yeah, that would be bad." I willed Fuego into my grasp, but nothing happened. Huh. I thought maybe my cane was waterlogged or something.

"It's only safe for me to hold the thread," said Ren.

"Gotcha," I said as my scrambled mind veered off in

another direction. "Did you see that kid?" I coughed a couple more times. "Did he look kinda see-through to you?"

Just then, the ghost kid's head popped out of the water and tossed Itzamna's glasses at my feet before disappearing back under the surface.

"Thanks!" Ren called out to him like they were long-lost friends.

"You know him?" I snatched up the glasses and started to pace. It felt odd without Fuego keeping me balanced.

"Just met him."

"Did I already ask where we are? And what's taking Alana and Louie so long? You look like you need help with that thread."

Shaking her head and sighing, Ren said, "Yes, you asked, and I really hope they get here soon, and no, I already told you that you can't help with the thread." She took a breath and added, "I thought *you'd* never get here! You took forever in the time tunnel, and you're not going to believe—"

I held up my hand, feeling light-headed. "Did you say 'time tunnel'?"

She nodded excitedly. "I should wait until you're fully recovered to tell you, but it's just too increíble." She rambled on. "The time thread created the passage, and I guess everyone travels through time tunnels at different speeds. I've been here for like thirty minutes. Waiting. Waiting. Waiting."

"I saw starfish and a stingray," I said, rubbing my head. "Those are sea creatures, not lake creatures. Right?"

"It's not a lake—it's part of the sea," Ren said, looking at the ice tube suspended over the water. "I really wish Alana and Louie would hurry up."

My mind was slow to accept whatever she told me, like it was on lag time. Okay...ghost boy, sea creatures in a lake, time thread...A second later, my brain revolted.

"Thirty minutes?!" I shouted. "I jumped in right after you."

I glanced up at the time tunnel. The thing looked like it had grown out of the sky itself. Any second now, Louie and Alana would shoot out of the twenty-foot drop.

"Zane?"

Any second.

"Yeah?"

Ren took my hand in hers. *I have something to tell you, and it can't wait.*

I switched my gaze to the water, searching for that ghost boy...you know, to make sure he didn't try anything fishy when Alana and Louie showed up. *Did the water make me see that ghost?* I asked Ren.

That's what I have to tell you.

Even telepathically Ren's voice sounded weird. I turned to face her.

"The ghost is real," she said. "They're all real."

"All?"

At that moment, the air near the tree line shimmered once...twice.

A group of boys materialized. Scratch that. A group of *ghosts* appeared.

And one really big giant.

31

$$\dot{=}$$

When you're slung down a twisty time tunnel and end up in a ghost sea/lake that messes with your head, you think your day can't get any weirder. Ha! This day was definitely about to take a turn. A *big* turn.

Ren just stood there all calm and dry, clutching the thread like it was her lifeline.

The ghost boys ran around, hooting and tossing a football, slamming into each other. And the ten-foot-tall teen giant? Yes, teen! He had a couple of zits on his chin and looked like he hadn't washed his shoulder-length dark hair for two weeks. But unlike any teenager I knew, the guy had boulder-size arms folded over his massive chest.

"Zane, this is Sipacna," Ren said breathlessly. "Sipacna, this is Zane Obispo, son of Hurakan."

"Everyone calls me Zip." The giant reached out to shake my hand, but I backed away. My mind had returned in full force, enough for the realization of this guy's identity to knock me over.

"Sipacna?!" I blurted. "The evil mountain giant who killed—" I swallowed the words before they had a chance to escape. I knew all about this dude. First, my giant friend Jazz hated the guy. Second, Sipacna had killed four hundred boys at once. AT ONCE! Just because they'd interrupted his nap or something.

But the tale, like all Maya stories, doesn't end there. The "hero twins"—yeah, you know the ones—stuck their big noses where they didn't belong and decided they should seek revenge for the boys. Using a giant crab as bait, the brothers lured Sipacna to a canyon, where they crushed him under a mountain.

Pretty tragic tale, but if it was true, then Sipacna should have been dead. So how did he get *here*?

"Did you say *evil*?" he asked with a growl.

"Yeah," I insisted. "I'd say a giant who kills a few hundred kids for trying to build a hut is pretty wicked."

"Guys!" Ren tried to get between us, but I sidestepped her.

"What?! I offered to build the hut *for* them!" Sipacna argued.

"And made fun of their weakness the whole time," I said. "Can you say 'bully'?"

A football whizzed overhead.

"So, it's okay for them to try to kill *me*?" His jaw twitched. "They were plotting my death!"

"They were?" I asked. "Well, that's definitely not cool... but neither is you crushing them under the hut."

Sipacna seemed to chew on this morsel. Then he put his gargantuan fists on his hips and asked, "And you believe everything history tells you?"

Ren chuckled nervously. "Zip, it's just hard to know what's a lie and what's the truth sometimes."

"You're supposed to be an old alligator with fangs," I said, remembering the illustration in my book.

Zip grunted. "Whoever told you that is an idiot and doesn't know fact from fiction. And let me guess . . . in your version of the story, the twins come out as heroes."

Yeah, that should have been my first clue that the truth had been shaded. Ren quickly filled me in on the real story, which was that Sipacna's brother, Kab'raqan (aka Earthquake), flew into a rage one night and split the earth open, and the boys were "accidentally" swallowed.

"Like my brother, I used to have a terrible temper," Zip admitted. "It's a giant thing."

The ghost boys shouted and whooped as they tackled each other on the beach.

"Anyhow," Ren said, frowning, "Jordan and Bird lied—big sorpresa—and told everyone Zip had killed the boys."

"The twins also killed my dad, Seven Macaw." Zip's face reddened, and I thought the giant might cry. But he held it together.

Fury rose up in me. Was there anything the twins *hadn't* lied about? Is history really so messed up that you have to question every word? I recalled the message I'd seen on that wall in Venice Beach: HISTORY IS MYTH. Maybe those were the truest words ever written.

"Everyone hated me after that," Zip said sadly. "But I couldn't rat out my own brother. So the gods came after me, wanted to make an example of me. Offered glory to anyone who could take me down."

"I know the drill," I said, suddenly feeling like me and this Sipacna dude were compadres.

Ren said, "My mom felt super bad for him, so she faked his death, which the twins totally took credit for. Then she brought him to this in-between place she created to keep him safe."

"And she asked me to keep watch over K'iin," the giant added, smirking like someone who had just scored the winning goal.

I glanced over at the ghosts as my brain put the puzzle pieces together. "And these are some of the four hundred boys?"

Zip nodded. "The rest are around the mountain somewhere, but yeah, they sort of busted out of Xib'alb'a. I guess there's a no-playing-ball rule in the underworld, so they wanted out pretty bad." He gave a light shrug. "The kids were only trying to kill me because the gods told them to, so they felt used. Anyhow, Pacific and some others helped them escape."

Others, as in Ixtab?

"The gods would for sure miss four hundred boys . . ." Ren said.

"Ixtab told the jerks the boys had turned into stars," Zip added. "The Pleiades constellation. Great hiding place, right? The stars? I wish I could think like that."

Ren said, "It should totally be named the Four Hundred, but whatever."

I took a second so I could register everything in my spinning head.

Another hero twins myth that was a lie. Check.

Giant who escaped the gods and now guarded K'iin. Check.

Four hundred ghost boys who were supposed to be stars. Check.

Now that I had all that straight, we needed to get back to the reason we were here. People were counting on us. Itzamna was trying to hold off bloodthirsty demons, and our family and friends were hiding out in Montana. And the time thread? It looked like it was going to jump out of Ren's grasp again any second.

I clutched Itzamna's sunglasses, wondering if I should bring the god in on all of this.

Zip shook out his hand and blew on it. That's when I saw a wicked red slash across his palm.

"Is it getting better?" Ren asked.

Zip winced and said to me, "I made the mistake of touching her time thread. Sent me ten feet into the air, man. That's some wicked energy right there."

"It must be some kind of security measure," I said. "Maybe that's why no one can take the time rope from Pacific—it'll deep-fry their brains."

"Guess so," Ren said with a hint of pride in her voice.

"So, can you take us to K'iin?" I asked Sipacna, my hope rising.

"Not exactly," Ren said.

"I'm sorry again for trying to kill you," Zip said to Ren gently.

"He tried to kill you?!" I almost tried to summon my Fuego spear before Ren said:

"That was before he knew who I was, Zane!"

"Actually," Zip said, "that was before she saved my life by ripping the thread out of my grasp."

"He made a promise to guard K'iin," Ren argued. "He's just doing his job."

"But you're Pacific's daughter. He and she go way back!" I turned from Ren to glare up at the giant. "And we're trying to defeat the rotten twins who killed your dad—who ruined your life! Doesn't that count for something?"

Zip gave me a curious look, then said, "My life is better now than it ever was. I like it here." He watched the ghost boys fondly as they continued to roughhouse in the sand.

"But if we don't find K'iin, you'll lose everything," I argued. "And so will we."

His face fell, and I felt sorry for the guy. "I took an oath. That means something to me."

Ren nodded in understanding, and my hope was extinguished. We'd come here for nothing.

Then the giant took a deep breath and added, "I can't tell you where K'iin is," he said, "but if you can find it, I won't stand in your way."

"Incoming!" one of the ghosts shouted.

Alana rocketed out of the time tunnel, followed by a screaming Louie.

Ka-splash!

A couple of ghosts jumped into the water to haul them out.

"Get ready to freeze," I warned, looking up at the sky for the first sign of snow.

Ren shook her head. "None of our godborn powers work here."

"It's a precaution," Zip said, stroking his chin. "Keeps the scales balanced in my favor."

"Good thing Pacific's do," Ren added with a small smile. She tugged on the still-aggressive thread.

Three things happened at that exact moment:

1. Louie and Alana swam frantically to the shore.

2. A ghost yelled, "Touchdown!"

3. And the golden thread jerked Ren off her feet.

That's when I knew it had found what it was looking for.

32

∴

The thread dragged Ren across the sand.

Zip groaned. "I got you, time girl." He scooped her up and lifted her onto his shoulders, taking huge strides to keep up with the flying golden strand.

"Come on!" I shouted to Alana and Louie. "We can't lose them." I spun and did my best to lope after the giant without Fuego.

"Zane!" Alana quickly caught up to me. "Where are we?"

"Who are those kids?" Louie cried.

"Just hurry!" I called out. "I'll explain later."

We rushed into the trees, climbing over fallen limbs and ducking under bowed branches as we headed into deeper and darker shadows. The sky had all but disappeared.

A few minutes later, we came to a black rock wall that stretched into the clouds.

Zip and Ren stood there, him panting, her still on his shoulders and clutching one end of the time thread as it rammed its other end against the wall.

"Zane!" Ren cried as we arrived. "It wants to go inside the rock."

"Or to climb up it, and we can't follow if it does," Louie said.

"Give it more slack," I said. "Let's see what it does."

"For the record," Zip said, "I didn't bring her here. The rope did. I just kept her head from getting split open."

Zip lowered Ren as she released more of the strand inch by inch. Once she saw that it was trying to make a shape in the rock, she let go completely. The thread immediately spiraled into a tight coil and pressed itself into the wall, vanishing. With a pale green flash, the wall started rippling like water.

"The gold thread—it's not coming back, is it?" Ren said.

Zip nodded. "There's only so much time magic to go around. Guard the strands you have left," he said, pointing at her watch.

Louie swayed. "I feel dizzy."

I grabbed hold of him as Zip inched back from a circular shape in the wall, which was swelling and pulsing. "Looks like you need to step into that thing," he said. "So this is where we say good-bye."

Ren threw her arms around his knees and said, "Thank you for everything."

"It's a doorway," Alana said. She reached her hand into the wall like it was nothing more than smoke. "We should go now. I don't think this is going to last."

She slipped inside, followed by Ren and a disoriented Louie. Just as I was about to step in, I turned to the giant. I had so much I wanted to say to him, but the only words I could come up with were "I'll make things right."

He smiled and gave me a thumbs-up. "I hope you find what you're looking for."

I entered a chamber no wider than the Red Queen's tomb, but with a high ceiling.

The floor was covered in fine white sand, and the walls looked like the inside of an abalone shell: iridescent swirls of intense pinks, greens, blues, and purples on a silvery back-drop. Each swirl cast enough light to illuminate the room, and my friends turned in circles as they took it all in.

I stuck Itzamna's shades back on, hoping the god's magic would work here, like Pacific's.

His face immediately appeared and he said, "I'm glad to hear Zip is doing well."

"You knew he was alive?" I asked.

"I will not even dignify that with an answer." Then: "*Of course* I knew!"

"Yeah, yeah. You see everything." Seems to me he could have given us a heads-up. . . .

Ren didn't leave our friends in the dark. She briefly explained to Alana and Louie what had happened when they were in the time tunnel.

Alana took it like a champ, whispering stuff like "Whoa" and "Bomb dot com" while Louie got even paler.

"You okay?" Ren asked him. "I know it's a lot to take in."

His nostrils flared. "I . . . I rocketed down a time tunnel?" We all nodded.

"And into a lake with some kids?" he went on.

"*Ghost* kids," Ren corrected.

Louie's eyes grew wider. "And I chased a giant through a creepy forest?" His words hung on an *I-can't-believe-it* breath.

His mouth fell open, and as he looked up, his face bloomed into this huge goofy smile. "I'm a freaking ninja!"

Alana swept a wet strand of hair off her forehead and chuckled as I clapped the guy on his back.

A distant groan sounded. Everything went creepily silent and still—the kind of silence that cramps your insides and makes you worry about lurking ghosts and hidden snakes.

Then, one by one, the walls' colors peeled themselves off in glowing pink, green, blue, and purple ribbons. Tiny threads hung from the end of each six-inch-wide strip.

"What are those?" Louie whispered.

The spectral strips swayed left, right, and back again like kite tails blowing in the wind. Then, one by one, they floated above each of our heads. Pink followed Alana. Purple drifted over Ren, green hovered over Louie, and I got a shimmery blue.

"Why are they following us?" Louie said, reaching toward his band.

Itzamna gasped. "No one move!"

My heart leaped into my throat. "Why?!"

"Those ribbons—" he began.

"Are they going to choke us to death?" Louie asked in a trembling voice as he quickly withdrew his hand.

"Those are your destiny strands," Itzamna said. "One tug of the thread and your future is gone, changed, morphed, ruined."

I glanced up. Each of our "destiny strands" was frayed at the bottom.

"My destiny is a ribbon?" Alana asked, ducking to avoid hers.

"No," Itzamna offered. "Your destiny is *written on* the ribbon."

"I don't see any words or symbols," Ren said.

"Only a god or K'iin can read it," Itzamna whispered.

"Why are our destinies *here*?" I asked.

"It's complicated," the god said. "But all destinies are connected to time and space, and K'iin *is* time and space, which tells me the calendar is close. Your essences attracted your destiny strands. Got it? Good. I really hate repeating myself. Just keep your hands to yourselves."

Everyone stood staring in silence, as if each of us were waiting for the other to ask Itzamna to read what was written on the ribbons. Believe me, I considered it, but I didn't ask. Not because I didn't want to know my future—I just didn't want to know my *entire* future.

A loud grinding sound drew our attention.

"Uh, guys," Ren said, pointing to the middle of the floor. "What are *those*?"

A row of six stone statues rose up from the sand. They were massive, like twenty feet tall, and had their backs to us.

"Are they alive?" Louie wheezed, craning his neck to see. The rest of us hurried over to check out the fronts.

"They look like . . . some of the gods," I said. I quickly identified them in order: Nakon, Chaac, Ixkakaw, Kukuulkaan, my dad, and Ixtab.

"Ixkakaw's nose is much more refined than *that*," Itzamna critiqued. "And Chaac has much buggier eyes!"

Seeing my dad's face, even in stone, made my insides cave. Had he, Ah-Puch, and the other gods already been devoured? No. I couldn't ... *wouldn't* think about that now.

"Why would my mom make statues of gods who exiled her?" Ren frowned. She glanced up at me. "Not your dad and Kukuulkaan, of course."

"Are they holding blue *eggs*?" Louie stalked closer.

Each statue held a basketball-size blue orb in its cupped palms.

"K'iin must be inside one of those," Itzamna said.

"The calendar is in an egg?" Louie said.

"They aren't eggs," I told him.

"They sure look like it," he muttered.

"But which one has it?" Alana said.

Shaking her head, Ren said, "It has to be Kukuulkaan or Hurakan, right? My mom wouldn't trust K'iin to any of the other gods."

"Unless she's like my aunt and wanted to be ironic," Alana said with a huff.

"It's too obvious, Ren," I said. I'd learned a long time ago that when it came to Maya gods, expect the unexpected.

"Just try them all," Louie said, "so we can get out of here. This place is giving me the heebie-jeebies."

"Except to get to the orbs we have to climb the gods," Alana said. "And in case you haven't noticed, Louie, we don't have a ladder or wings."

Brooks would have really come in handy about then. I thought about summoning and throwing Fuego before I remembered I couldn't use its magic in that place. Besides, with my luck, my spear would shatter the orbs, destroy the calendar, and stop time, which would totally suck.

"Got any ideas, Itzamna?" Ren said, ducking away from her destiny ribbon.

"How good a climber are you?"

"I thought you were supposed to be helpful," I growled.

"I *am* being helpful," the god argued.

Louie stepped back, looking up as he pointed to the orbs. "Wait! I think the eggs have something written on them. Look."

The spheres were rotating slowly. I walked down the row of gods, and as the orbs came full circle, I saw that there was a single Mayan word etched into each. Then, like in the SHIHOM library, the words floated up in the air and came back down in English. "'Choose. The. Right. Fate. Wisely. Trespasser,'" I read aloud.

Alana scooted away, shaking her head. "Something is so wrong."

"What makes you say that?" Louie said. "Just because we're inside a creepy chamber with our destinies hanging over our heads and there are statues holding spinning eggs with warning labels?"

I thought about something else he'd failed to mention: people had died seeking K'iin. But I kept that to myself.

"We just have to think smarter," Ren said. "Hurakan's word is *wisely,* and Kukuulkaan's is *fate.* Do you think those are clues?"

"I just want to know why *I* didn't get a statue," Itzamna said. "I am the great moon god, after all."

Louie rubbed his forehead, never taking his eyes off the figures. "What do you think would happen if we picked the wrong egg?"

"Buh-bye, destiny," Alana muttered.

I stood right under the stone gods with their cold, menacing eyes. A chill ran through me. "Louie's right," I said, inching back. "Pacific wouldn't entrust K'iin to *any* of the gods," I added, thinking out loud. Yeah, I know she and Kukuulkaan have a thing going now, but she didn't seem like the type to trust her boyfriend with her greatest treasure. "I don't think K'iin is in any of those spheres. I think they're a decoy."

"Zane," Itzamna said, "turn a few degrees to the left."

"Why?"

"Just do it," he said.

The instant I did, the moon god gasped. "Oh. My. Stars. I wasn't expecting that."

33

"Did he just say 'Oh my stars'?" Alana asked.

"There!" Itzamna shouted. "Do you see it?"

"Where? I don't see anything," I said, frustrated that the god was stuck in my lenses. I mean, it would have been super helpful if the guy could point in 3-D.

"Take another step." His voice trembled with excitement.

"Fine, but..." As I followed his instruction, the toe of my sneaker hit a bump under the sand and I nearly tripped. I squatted, and as I brushed away the thin layer of grit with my hand, my heart beat faster. "Guys? There's something on the floor." I stared down at the discovery. "Maybe a painting?"

"I told you I was helpful!" Itzamna said. "Oh, I feel so alive. I haven't had an adventure of this magnitude in a millennium."

Ren and Alana rushed over, and we went to work sweeping the sand to the corners of the room.

"I thought we weren't supposed to touch anything," Louie said. "You guys could get sucked into a void or dropped inside a trapdoor. Just saying..."

Once the floor was cleared, we stood back to get a better view. The image was of the night sky, including all the planets and a bunch of constellations, like Orion and Scorpius and others I couldn't name.

"Whoa!" Louie joined us. "It looks like the genu-INE article. Check out how the stars sparkle. You think there's lights under the floor?"

Ren's eyes searched the length of the very real-looking galaxy. "Zane, you're right. My mom wouldn't trust the *gods* with K'iin," she finally whispered. "But she *would* trust it to the *universe*."

Alana studied the floor with a doubtful look. "I don't see any calendar...."

"Do you know where it is?" I asked Itzamna.

"I can't do everything for you godborns," he complained.

"So you don't know," Alana guessed.

The god didn't answer.

Ren had a look of pure astonishment on her face.

"What's wrong?" I asked her.

"I was just thinking how the stars—the constellations—are the same ones the ancient Maya gazed at thousands of years ago and that...that somehow connects us to them."

"I don't want to be connected to no ghosts," Louie said.

Ren looked like she was going to argue or call blasphemy, but instead she said, "Look for something out of place."

"Like a missing planet?" Louie asked. But he wasn't helping to look. His eyes were glued to his destiny thread bobbing a foot or so above him.

I shook my head. "That would be too obvious." Pacific had stayed hidden for hundreds of years without the gods even knowing she was alive. She for sure knew a thing or two about playing hide-and-seek. Like, she'd stashed four hundred boys in a constellation....

"That's it!" I shouted.

Everyone turned to me.

"K'iin is hidden in the stars!"

"I was going to say that," Itzamna offered.

Ren got down on her knees and traced her fingers over the universe. She gasped, pointing. "Zane, you're right. Look! There—at the bottom of Orion.... It's supposed to have a triangle of stars, but there's only two!"

"You seriously know stuff like that?" Louie said.

"She has a blog about aliens," Alana said, peering closer at the star chart.

"The Maya called Orion *Ak 'Ek*, the Turtle Star," Ren said, churning out the words so fast I had to focus to catch them. Her expression was nothing but tight concentration. She was puzzling it all out, and to be honest, it was amazing to watch her brain in action. If anyone knew the planets and constellations and all things astronomical, it was Ren.

"So what does Orion's missing star have to do with K'iin?" Alana asked.

"For the ancient Maya," Ren said, never taking her eyes off the night sky, "a turtle shell was a symbol for Earth." She took a shaky breath. "They believed that time began with the planting of three stones on the tortuga's back." She held up three fingers, smiling. "The stones are the stars. Right, Itzamna?"

He hesitated, then said, "Yes, that's correct. I told you to look more to the left, Zane!"

"Seriously?" Louie said. "The world was made on a turtle's back?"

"Exactly!" Ren said. Her blue destiny thread hung a mere

two feet over her head, swaying to the left like it was trying to peek over her shoulder.

"Louie," I said breathlessly, "what did you just say?"

"The world was made on a turtle's back?"

My heart did a little jig. Okay, maybe a big one, as Louie's words reminded me of someone else's. They rocketed out of my mouth. "'The world was born on the back of a story,'" I said. "'And the world might be saved—'"

Everyone threw sharp *say-what?* glances my way.

"Itzamna!" I said, pointing to the constellation. "Was that the part you didn't finish that night in the boat? Were you going to say *the world might be saved on the back of a story*?"

"Affirmative. Very poetic, isn't it, Zane."

"But—" My mind was spinning. "How did you know? Did you foresee all this?"

"Of course not," he said. "I believe *everything* is story—story is the greatest magic and power in the universe. It can paint something good or evil, beautiful or ugly. It can create believers and liars and murderers and kings. If I saw all this coming, don't you think I would have warned the gods?"

"Excellent point," Louie said, ducking away from his destiny string.

It felt like a million-volt electrical current was running through me.

Ren pressed her finger into the spot where the third star should have been.

We waited.

And waited.

Nothing happened.

"Try the watch," Alana said like she'd just been holding her breath.

Ren closed her eyes, inhaled deeply, and pressed her wrist against Orion. The second the watch met the floor, that section shook, then opened with a wide, grinding yawn.

A bright light poured out, as if the moon itself was rising.

Louie jumped back. "What's down there?"

I blinked and whispered, "I think we found K'iin."

34

In a single blink, the iridescent walls around us flipped to reveal new ones made of intersecting mirror shards.

The piercing light coming up from the floor bounced off the shards and skewed our reflections, like fun-house mirrors that give you a giant football-shaped head or stunted elephant legs. Alana put her sunglasses on as we all stepped back and watched the beam dance around the room.

A woman's soft voice echoed across the chamber. "Seekers."

We all looked at each other like *Who/what the heck?*

"Yes. We are seeking K'iin," Ren said with so much confidence I was kind of in awe.

"The calendar," Alana added.

"I am very familiar with K'iin," the voice said.

"Where is it?" Louie asked.

There was silence and then the voice said, "You are inside it."

"You're K'iin?" I practically shouted.

It was a big moment—I mean huge. We had been looking for a magical object that could see across time and dimensions. I'd been imagining a toy model of the calendar. But we were inside the artifact. *Inside!*

"Yes," she said. "And I do not like trespassers."

Itzamna's voice dropped to a tiny whisper. "Take off the shades. Hurry."

"Why are you whispering?" I asked quietly.

"Just do it!"

I figured the god had to have a good reason for wanting to hide, so I removed the shades as slyly as I could, hung them on my waistband, and covered them with the bottom of my T-shirt.

Ren blew out a long breath, standing taller. "It's nice to meet you . . . er . . . We're so glad to be here, and we're not trespassers."

"We kind of are," Louie whispered.

"You were not invited," the voice said. "Which makes you trespassers."

My brain was on overload, and I felt a little woozy. I wiped my forehead, wishing I had Fuego to lean on. Then I took a couple of calming breaths like Hondo had taught me. They totally didn't work, by the way.

"We're here to ask a question," I said, recalling what the earth spirit had told me. "Isn't that how this works? If we stand before you . . ."

I didn't get to finish my sentence before the mirrored walls rippled and the light dimmed a few watts. "I see who you are," K'iin said. "Godborns on a mission. A futile mission to save what cannot be saved, to reverse a fate that was set eons ago."

My chest tightened.

"We haven't even asked the question yet," Ren said, frowning. "How do you know our mission is futile?"

"Such limited thinkers."

"What did you say about fate?" I drew in a sharp breath. "Are you saying the gods *knew* they would be devoured?"

"Not all fates are revealed, son of fire."

Our destiny ribbons floated a few inches closer to each of us—so close to our faces that we had to step back.

Louie nudged my arm. "She knows who you are. That can't be good."

"I know who *you* are, too, son of Chaac," she said. "And you, Alana, daughter of Ixtab. I see all."

"Eep," Louie chirped.

If she could see all, why hadn't she detected Itzamna? And why didn't he want her to see him?

Ren lifted her chin and said, "Then you know my mom is Pacific, the great goddess of time and fate. The one who hid you here."

"Ah, yes. You look like your mother—in the eyes. Maybe the cheekbones, too. But you are here to ask a question, to discover what you cannot see on your own. And I am growing weary. So, let's get on with it, shall we?"

We all nodded. I had just started to open my mouth, when K'iin said, "And before you speak, I must make you aware of the fine print. Knowledge is expensive. Your question will cost you. Nothing is free. And sacrifice is the price for all things worthy. Do you understand?"

"Yes," Ren said even before K'iin's question mark hung in the air.

I jerked a Storm Runner chocolate bar out of my pocket, and the second I held it out, I knew I'd made a mistake.

"That will not do," K'iin said. "Do you wish to proceed, or shall I carve you an exit?"

The four of us shared a worried glance. Everyone nodded, except Louie. He kept his head down and whispered to me, "Can I have the chocolate?"

"We want to proceed," I said as my gut clenched.

"I will choose who asks the question," K'iin said. "And who will pay for the answer."

Ren snapped her hand up, careful to avoid her destiny ribbon. "It should be me. My mom is Pacific and—"

"Yes, we have established your bloodline."

"I'm the one who saw your image in the labyrinth," I said. "I should pay."

Silence. A long silence. Like a *something-is-broken* silence.

"Hello?" Alana's voice echoed across the chamber.

The mirrors shimmered pink, purple, green, and blue. "I'm processing. Looking across time, weighing consequences," K'iin shot back. "Ah, yes. I have chosen."

I held my breath.

"Renata Santiago," K'iin said, "I choose you to ask the question."

Ren's expression was total shock at first, but then she managed a small triumphant smile.

"Wait!" I started to argue, when K'iin added:

"And you, Zane Obispo, will pay the price."

"What?!" Ren cried, her smile gone. "No! That isn't fair."

My legs almost liquefied right onto old Orion/Turtle Star.

K'iin was silent for a couple of heartbeats and then said,

"Nothing in this life is fair. Only death. Now get on with it. You are wasting my energy."

Ren's blue eyes met mine. They were filled with regret or sadness or maybe just an apology that I was the one who would have to sacrifice something. I was praying super hard it wouldn't be a body's worth of blood.

"Hang on," I said. "Shouldn't we know what it's going to cost first?"

K'iin said, "I must know the question before I can determine the value of the answer."

I couldn't argue with that. I gave Ren the go-ahead with a curt nod.

She shook out her hands, took a couple of deep breaths, and closed her eyes. "O Great K'iin, where are the Maya gods?"

Again there was silence. I figured K'iin was looking across dimensions, or thinking, or both. The mirrors glimmered. "Well," she finally said, "the answer to your question is of incredible value."

My heart pounded with the force of a charging bull. "How much?"

"The blood of a godborn is very powerful," K'iin said.

I felt so queasy I gripped my stomach. "How much blood?" I asked again.

"All of it."

The ground dropped away, and I felt like I was plummeting into a dark chasm.

"I have something better than blood!" Ren shrieked. She held up the watch with a trembling hand.

The air went still. Our destiny strands stopped moving.

"Why would I want your watch?" K'iin asked.

"It is made of the same time strands you're made of," Ren said, looking offended.

"Ren," I said, grabbing hold of her arm so I could talk to her telepathically. *We need that to stop time when we rescue the gods!*

I will only give her a single strand, she said. *That will leave us enough.*

We all held our breath.

Alana's eyes flicked in my direction. "What if—"

"What-ifs are wasted energy," K'iin said. "I have made my decision, and the answer is no."

Louie looked like someone had just slugged his dog in the jaw. "No?" he echoed.

Both my legs threatened to give out.

"But I'm not going to take the blood, either," K'iin said. "I am going to give you what you seek for the sole purpose of entertainment."

What was she, Itzamna's long-lost twin? No way could it be that easy.

"And also a promise," she went on, "that you will repay me with a favor someday, Renata Santiago."

Boom! *There* was the fine print.

Ren nodded before I could warn her not to trust the ancient calendar.

K'iin went on to say, "You will only receive a single answer. Is this your final question?"

Why did I feel like a contestant on a really bad game show?

Just then, I wiped more sweat off my forehead with the back of my hand, and in doing so my fingers accidentally hooked my destiny thread. When I tried to pull them free, they got more entangled in it.

"Don't tug!" Ren shouted.

"What do I do?" The words just barely got past the gran lump in my throat. If I moved my hand, I might mess up my destiny. But I couldn't stand like that forever. . . .

I wondered why I wasn't feeling heat in my veins, and then I remembered that I had no fire power in this place. It was for the best. If it came out, I could've accidentally sent my future up in flames.

"Can you let go slowly?" Ren suggested.

Gingerly, I reached out with my other hand, which was quivering like mad, and unwound the single thread that had ensnared two of my fingers.

Everyone exhaled with relief.

But when I tried to let go of the thread, it stayed glued to my fingertips. As I struggled to get it off, the thread pulled the destiny ribbon, squinching it in the middle. Finally, the string separated from my skin, but when it did, it snapped back to the ribbon and made a knot the size of a cherry seed.

I bent over, completely winded.

"At least the ribbon didn't unravel," Alana said. "That's good, right?"

At that, I straightened a little, and Ren's eyes caught mine. She was clearly worried, but her words were confident. "Knots are always good. They probably keep out the bad stuff."

"Actually, they cause congestion," K'iin said. "Knots represent—"

"Wh-what was—" I stammered.

"Your future has been altered significantly," K'iin said. "I cannot tell you how or when."

"That's so mean!" Ren cried. "Why would you dangle that in front of him?"

"Sooo mean," Louie agreed.

K'iin said, "The moment was meant to be, godborns."

"Guys," I said in a voice that sounded too far away, "it's okay. It's done."

"Then you *did* make him pay after all," Ren said angrily. "Now give us our answer."

The mirror shards spun and turned, seeking their puzzle partners, until we were looking at a perfectly smooth surface. Slowly, an image appeared in it. There was no mistaking what I was looking at—the same place where Hondo, Brooks, and I had gone to find the hero twins, and where I had met Jazz, the giant, and Antonio, the Fire Keeper. "It's Venice Beach," I whispered. "Again."

"Why would the gods be in California?" Ren asked suspiciously.

She was right to wonder. It seemed like the worst place to hide the gods—unless Zotz and Ixkik' wanted them to be found.

"We need something more specific." Alana threw her head back defiantly.

Louie nodded. "Like an address."

"Oh, I can give you an address, but it won't help you,"

K'iin said in a gleeful tone that made me wish I could launch a fireball into the mirror.

"What do you mean?" Alana asked.

K'iin told us the exact location. "But if you go to that address, you will not find the gods."

"Zane just paid with his destiny, and you made me give you an IOU!" Ren spluttered. "Why would we do that for nothing?"

"You didn't ask me *how* to get to the gods," K'iin said, "only where they were."

"You're talking in circles," I spat.

"Why won't we find the gods?" Louie asked. "You just told us the address."

The mirror began to crack and split. The image of Venice Beach shattered into a thousand pieces.

"Because," K'iin said, "the gods are trapped in 1987."

35

•

≡

1987.

1987.

1987.

Did I mention 1987? The gods were trapped in time more than thirty years ago? As soon as those mind-blowing, impossible words were spoken, our destiny strands vanished. Dust and debris drifted down from the ceiling. The stars on the floor started flashing brightly.

Alana shielded her eyes, scrambling for her shades. "I don't see any gateways in here."

"I don't want to die in an ancient clock!" Louie cried.

"K'iin?" Ren said. "Are you there?"

The hole in the floor went dark. The walls began to close in on us at a rapid pace—so fast we would go splat in a matter of seconds. Four feet. Three.

"Zane!" Alana cried.

We pressed our hands and feet against the encroaching walls, trying to stop them. "K'iin!" I screamed.

"I can't do you a favor if I'm dead!" Ren shouted.

A beam shot out of the floor again. "Just testing your resolve," K'iin said. "Ready, set, go!"

The room turned upside down. The ground—or was it the

ceiling?—disappeared under our feet, and we tumbled into a dark abyss. We finally stopped, one on top of another in a pile of limbs, and I thought we might be stuck there forever. But then I opened my eyes to see that we were jammed at the end of the time tunnel. We had fallen *up*! Alana and Ren were ahead of Louie, and I was dead last, clinging to his ankle to keep from sliding back down.

Louie kicked, nearly smashing my nose. "Hey!" I shouted.

Alana was close enough to the top that she could climb out, then help the rest of us.

As we clambered out into the ice cave, no one spoke. No one said *What the hell?*, *K'iin's bonkers*, or *You should never trust an ancient calendar.* Maybe we were all in shock. K'iin's cost was too high, because the answer equaled a no-way solution.

And then Ah-Puch's words flew into my brain: *We are no longer here, Zane.*

So he knew. He *knew* he was lost in time and he hadn't told me, because he thought he was protecting Ren, protecting *all* of us from attempting an impossible quest. But here's the thing about gods—yeah, they're strategic and cunning and powerful and sometimes super smart, but they lack something that matters even more. They don't have the stubbornness of a human heart. Not by a long shot.

Alana led us to an invisible gateway that she was hoping would get us to Montana. We needed to bring our comrades up to speed, and it wasn't like we had anyplace else to go.

"How will we ever save the gods now?" Alana whispered, staring at Ren's watch. "Do you think you could...?"

Ren caught Alana's meaning. "I can only stop time for five minutes. That isn't the same thing as traveling through it."

Zotz and Ixkik' were bigger geniuses than I'd given them credit for. They had managed to hide the gods in a place no one could ever reach. Well, unless you lived in the '80s. So Brooks had been right. Our enemies no longer had access to the gods.

"If we don't save them," I said, "does that mean none of us were ever born?"

Ren thought for a second, then shook her head. "Not unless they also wipe out the gods in 1987," she said. "Right?"

"How should I know?" I groaned. "You're the time goddess's daughter!"

Alana paced. "Ren's right. If the gods are in 1987, they'll still meet our moms or dads. So we get to live."

"For now," Louie snarled sarcastically.

For now was good enough for me.

This was the part when I would typically say to my friends *We'll find a way.* But to be honest, I was all out of optimism, and that's saying a lot, because I practically stockpiled the stuff. How could we ever save the gods now? There *was* no *We'll find a way,* no Ixtab to go to, no Hurakan to lean on, no Fire Keeper to give me answers. All we had were each other and a weakening moon god.

I didn't even have the heart to put the sunglasses back on and give Itzamna the terrible news.

Alana inched back. Her eyes flashed midnight blue as she turned her head to the right and said, "Oh my gods! Are you okay?"

"Not really," Louie said, gesticulating. "I think we got taken. I think that K'iin thing is a con artist."

Alana batted his hand down and said, "Not you, Louie! It's Adrik. He fell off his horse."

Horse?

"You can talk to Adrik from this far away?" I asked. I knew they had a super-killer twin connection that didn't even require physical contact, but this? It was over-the-top epic!

"Did everyone get to Montana safely?" Ren's words rushed out in a flood of worry.

Alana nodded. "He says everyone is fine, but he hit his head hard and got knocked out. Then he went into a dream world where he almost connected with a god, but he isn't sure which one."

"Tell him to try again!" I cried.

Alana frowned condescendingly at me. "Zane, he is not going to get a concussion on purpose just to talk to gods who wouldn't be of any help anyway." Her eyes drifted away as she nodded. Then she looked up again and said to us, "Adrik says he hit his head so hard that maybe his for-real gift got knocked into place. He's laughing, but I don't think it's funny. No, it's not, Adrik! None of this is funny."

"What does 'for-real gift' mean?" Louie asked.

"He says he'll show us when we get there," Alana said, rolling her eyes.

"I'm just glad everyone is okay," Ren said.

A sudden fire raced up my spine, pulsing in waves of heat like it was trying to tell me something. I was relieved to feel it again but pretty sure I didn't want to know what it was warning me about. My mind riffled through all the possibilities. Or impossibilities. I knew there was no place on Earth where Zotz and Blood Moon wouldn't be able to find us. But I didn't say anything. I didn't want everyone to freak out.

And then the fire bloomed in my chest so hot I gasped. A disastrous realization came to me. Holbox! If the entry stone was powerful enough to grant our enemies access to the World Tree, it could also break through Ixtab's magic border around the island. Crap! Why hadn't I thought of that before?

The threat Ixkik' had previously launched now hit me right between the eyes: *Oh, how those you love will pay, Zane Obispo. I promise you they will pay.*

"I have to go home!" I shouted. "My mom—she's not safe. Ixkik' said she would come for her."

Ren covered a gasp, then said to me, "I'll go with you!"

Alana swept her hair off her face and with her eyes averted said, "Right. Okay."

"Are you still talking to Adrik?" Louie asked.

She held up her hand to silence any more questions. Leaning against the icy wall, she nodded. What was Adrik telling her? Finally, she looked up at me with an almost smile. "Your mom is on her way to the ranch. Hondo sent for her."

I thought my chest was going to collapse into my stomach. Relief cooled the fire in my veins as I thought about how much I loved my strategic-genius uncle in that moment.

"On her way how?" I asked. "How do we know she wasn't followed?"

Louie said, "Yeah, like a decoy, and she'll lead the baddies right to us."

Alana hesitated. Her eyes shifted back to their natural gray. "We, um . . . we know people, and she's not alone."

Know people? Who was she, some kind of mafia kid?

"What do you mean, 'not alone'?" I pressed. "She's a human, not a sobrenatural. A bunch of demons could snatch her on her way to the Cancún airport, or at the gate, or . . ." I admit it—my brain was in high-alert panic mode. And why did Alana look so calm? It was muy annoying.

Then four words spilled from her mouth that took my panic down a notch. "Rosie is with her."

Rosie. My perfect, beautiful, faithful hellhound, who could travel like mist. When I saw her again, she for sure was going to get a lifetime supply of snake heads or any other gross thing she wanted.

"Plus," Alana went on, "your mom didn't have to go to Cancún. A helicopter picked her up and took her to a landing strip. She's now in flight. . . ." She squirmed like she didn't want to talk about this but knew she didn't have a choice. "On my dad's jet. They're only an hour from Montana."

Jet. Servants. Mansion. Right. Alana and Adrik acted so chill and down-to-earth I forgot they were rich.

"You have a private plane?" Louie's eyes bugged out. "Like, a real one?"

Alana's cheeks brightened. "It's my dad's."

"Can you get us to the ranch *your* way? Through the portal?" Ren asked Alana, changing the subject *and* the focus.

Alana smiled gratefully. "If you guys help me," she said. "Like in the library."

We all joined hands. Louie squeezed himself in between me and Ren as Alana said, "Think Montana. I'll do the rest."

The rest ended up being a side trip to a pizza place. We landed in the kitchen supply closet and all Louie could say was "I tried to think Montana, but I'm hungry and pizza sounded really good."

"You can eat whatever you want at the ranch. Now focus!" Alana commanded.

The promise of food was enough to get Louie on the same page, because the next thing I knew, we had rolled out of the gateway and smack-dab into a steaming pile of manure.

The good news was we hadn't landed face*down* in the stuff. We all got up and inspected our dirty clothes. The bad news? When we looked around, we saw we were in a cattle pen, facing a thousand-pound-plus bull that looked like he wanted nothing more than to split our guts wide open.

36

I summoned Fuego to my hand just as Alana said, "Nobody move," with not a single tremor in her voice. Maybe she was used to bulls? Maybe this was her pet and, like Rosie, he just *looked* ferocious?

The muscular beast was about ten feet away—too close for comfort. He pawed the dirt and started to rumble and grunt.

Rrrummph. Rrrummph.

"*Eek!*" Louie squealed.

"Nice bull-y," Ren purred.

I gripped my cane as we stood frozen in the fenced pasture not sure what to do. I know what you're thinking: *You've got amazing Fuego! You're the son of fire!* But I couldn't just gore the innocent animal or turn him to steak.

The bull glared at us, tossing his head. I quickly threw up a wall of smoke, hoping it would be enough to at least slow him down if he decided to charge.

He decided to charge. And guess what? The smoke only gave us a ten-step lead at best, and the corral's gate was a good thirty feet away.

"AAAAH!" we screamed, and ran. Have you ever tried to sprint through mud and manure? It's worse than wet sand. And a whole lot smellier.

"Do something!" Louie screamed.

"Ren, shadow!" I hollered.

Suddenly, the world went still. No sound, no movement, no breeze around us. Just my crashing heart and wheezing breaths.

I came to a stop in my poop-covered shoes, held my side, and turned to Ren. Her watch was glowing.

"Thanks . . . for . . . stopping . . . time," I said between gasps.

"No way could I sic a monster shadow on the poor thing," she said, a small smile playing on her lips. "But sometimes you just have to take the bull by the horns."

"Ha!" Louie muttered, nearly tripping as he slowed down.

"I thought we'd be skewered for sure." Alana fell against Ren, laughing between gasps of air. "Old Smalls is faster than I remember."

"Smalls is bigger than a tow truck." Louie was panting and sweating like he'd run a marathon in the Sahara Desert.

We all spun to see the bull suspended in the air mere steps behind us. He was in mid-stride, openmouthed, and wearing a glare so deep it looked etched on his face. And those long spiky horns that could double as demon fangs, size extra-large? Practically in my back pocket. Okay, I didn't have a back pocket, but you get the point.

But something was missing. The last time Ren had stopped time was at SHIHOM, and she had used a shadow to protect those of us she didn't want frozen. So where was the shadow now? When I asked, she just shrugged and said, "It was all instinct. Maybe I'm getting more precise?"

As we headed to the gate, I took in the amazing scenery. All trees, mountains, and a dozen shades of green that folded in on us as if to say *Welcome*. The daylight was fading, and it was hard to tell where the horizon ended and the sky began.

"Can we eat now?" Louie said as he exited the corral.

We hosed ourselves off near the cows' water trough, and I steam-dried everyone's clothes as best as I could by waving handfuls of fire over them. Then we walked about a quarter mile. The land rose and fell until we emerged on a wide grassy plain that smelled like pine and wet wood. In the distance was a log mansion complete with a wraparound porch and at least six stone chimneys. Behind the house was a gran white barn, a field of grazing horses, and three other houses—we'll call them mini mansions, because they were way bigger than a normal house but not quite supersize.

"Whoa!" Louie said. "*This* is the hideaway?"

Alana nodded and sighed as we approached the wide porch of the main house. Lights shimmered behind the big windows.

Hondo bolted out of the front door, slamming the screen behind him. "Adrik said you found K'iin?"

I nodded.

"So where are the gods?"

"Where is everyone else?" I said, wishing I didn't have to give him an answer.

"They're doing a training exercise over by the barn," he said. "Don't deflect, Diablo."

"How are the godborns?" Ren asked. "Do they know anything?"

Hondo eyed us suspiciously. "They know nothing. Now how about you tell me what *you* know."

Alana walked up the porch steps and said, "I have to find Adrik." Probably to check on his head bump. And then she was gone, followed by Louie, who was no doubt looking for the kitchen.

Hondo's eyes found mine and held my gaze. I saw the questions rising, so I cut to the chase. Not wanting to repeat myself, I put on Itzamna's shades.

"Zane!" the god cried. "You left me alone for so long I thought K'iin had thrown you into a time loop. Those are the worst—imagine living the same moment over and over and over for all eternity."

"We're fine," I said before I explained the shades to Hondo. He just rubbed the back of his neck, shaking his head. "Wait a second," I said to Itzamna. "How come you didn't want K'iin to know you were there?"

"We have a bad history, and that's all I'm going to say on the matter."

Yeah, probably some dumb calendar war, I thought.

"If she's so all-seeing," I asked, "how come she didn't see *you*?"

"She wasn't looking."

"Zane," my uncle said impatiently, "give it up, man."

"The gods are lost. . . ." Being the bearer of bad news sucks. Big-time. "They're in a place we can't get to," I said, and even as the words left my mouth, I didn't want to believe them.

"Of course we can get there," Brooks said as she came around the side of the house. "Just tell me where. I'll fly around the world if I have to."

I loved that Brooks thought that scheming and planning and outsmarting your opponent would always win the day. And I really wanted her to believe that for a little longer, but there *was* no longer. There was no way to prepare her or Hondo for what I had to say next. "They're in 1987."

Brooks shook her head. She staggered back like someone had punched her in the chest. "WHAT?! How? No...Why?" Her brain was in full-throttle denial mode. "Did you say *1987*...as in the year?"

I nodded slowly.

A terrible silence pressed against us, against our breath and hope and confidence.

My uncle ran a hand over his long hair. "We have to stop them."

"We will," Ren said, touching his arm gently.

"How?" Hondo asked.

"Nothing is impossible," Brooks said. "If we can pool the godborns' powers and work together, we can fix this. Right, Zane?"

Her determined amber eyes softened as she looked my way, and I found myself nodding, making a silent promise I wasn't sure I could keep.

"Can any of the godborns travel through time?" I asked hopefully.

Hondo quickly told us about the godborn gifts. They ranged from being able to talk to animals and bending like a rubber band to walking through solid surfaces and having supersonic hearing. "No time traveling," he said.

Brooks twisted a strand of hair around her pinkie. "But Marco has off-the-charts super strength." She said it with so much admiration I felt a stab in my chest. I know, I know, bad time to be feeling jealous. But give me a break—he couldn't be *that* strong.

"And Adrik," she went on, "he . . . uh, got a new skill when he hit his head."

"Alana said something about that," I said. "What is it?"

But I didn't get an answer, because Itzamna gasped so loud I thought it was his last breath. "That's it!" he shouted.

"What's it?" Ren said.

Itzamna posed a question none of us had thought to ask: "How could Zotz and Ixkik' lock the gods in time?" He paused, like he was waiting for one of us to say what he already knew. "The time rope!"

Ren practically jumped out of her skin. "But I thought no one could take the rope from Pacific!"

"They would only need a single strand for a one-way ticket," he said. "Zotz and Ixkik' must have found a way to steal it before the devouring, and they used it to send the gods back to 1987."

My mind buzzed with one part hope and another part horror. "But how could they send them across time all at once? There's, like, a couple hundred of them."

"Do I have to do everything on this quest?" Itzamna sighed. "I don't know where the enemy would get that kind of power."

"Power isn't always what you think it's going to be," Marco said as he waltzed onto the scene with a scowl and a puffy black eye. I didn't bother asking. His eyes darted from face to face. "What? Did I say something wrong? Who wants to fill me in?"

Ren grabbed his arm and must have told him everything telepathically, because his eyes (even the puffy, half-closed one) went wide.

"Man," Marco said, rubbing his chin. "1987? A hiding spot your enemy can never get to? Wish I'd thought of that. But why *that* year? Seems kind of random."

"Perhaps it was as far as they could go with so many gods all at once," the moon god said.

"Itzamna," Ren said, drawing closer to me, "you said that Zotz and Ixkik' only needed a strand of my mom's rope to trap the gods in time."

And then Ren's logic seemed to hit all of us at the same time.

"The watch!" someone said.

"The watch," Brooks echoed.

"Ren!" Hondo lifted her off her feet, spun her, and set her back down. "You're my favorite bruja godborn, you know that?"

In the labyrinth, Ah-Puch had told me Ren was the key. This must have been what he meant!

"We can go back in time, too!" Brooks said.

Marco grunted and muttered something under his breath I didn't catch.

"How many strands will we need, Itzamna?" Ren was breathless.

"To make a rope strong enough for a round trip?" he said. "At least two."

Ren gave a half-hearted smile. "I already lost one thread, and Zip said there's only so much time magic to go around. I don't know how many more are in the watch." Ren held her wrist up to my glasses for Itzamna to see. "Do you?"

"Does it matter?" Hondo said, pacing. "We just have to make it work with however much we have."

Itzamna took a shuddering breath. "Even under the best circumstances, time travel is not easy. It's not like going through a gateway. It requires precision. Perfectly executed precision. And failure can spell disaster."

"I'm in!" Hondo said with renewed energy.

Everyone else nodded and raised their hands—everyone except Marco, whose shifty eyes told me he was weighing the risks and rewards. "Wait," he said. "Any chance I—*we* could get stuck in 1987?"

"A very good chance," Itzamna said. "But that isn't the only risk. You could get devoured. But even worse, you could disrupt the time continuum. You could do something in 1987 that would have consequences today. Dire consequences."

"Like what?" Ren asked.

"No idea," the god said. "Just avoid all people."

Marco stuffed his fists into his pockets. "Even if we could get there, how do you plan to rescue the gods and get them back across thirty-plus years without anyone noticing?"

"One step at a time," I said, not wanting to lose the momentum and hope we were building. "What do we have to do?" I asked Itzamna.

The god said, "To ensure the most precise landing, you will need to return to where time began."

"The Old World," Hondo, Brooks, and I said at the same time.

The images I'd seen in the labyrinth flew at me. Were they clues?

Time. Evil. Deception.

"We can totally do this, guys," Ren said, nodding vigorously.

"No human has ever done it successfully," Itzamna said.

"Well, no human ever succeeded in finding K'iin, either," I reminded the god.

"You're a godborn," Itzamna retorted.

"Exactly," I said with a smile.

Marco continued to scowl. "Time travel. You guys are serious."

Ignoring him, Itzamna said, "Someone on the 1987 crew will need to stay connected to the present at all times. ALL times. Losing the connection will result in you being imprisoned in the past."

"And . . . ?" Brooks asked like she knew there was more, because there is *always* more.

"How do we stay connected?" Hondo asked.

"That's the darker, more terrible piece that must be put into place," Itzamna said.

"Yeah," Marco said. "How to get the gods back!"

I braced myself. "Tell us, Itzamna."

"You'll need a shadow crosser."

37

Shadow crosser.

I heard those two words and knew instantly they couldn't equal anything good.

"The shadow crosser is the anchor," Itzamna went on. "Someone powerful enough to hold the time thread to ensure the travelers come back."

"I'll do it," Hondo said without hesitation. In that moment, I swear my uncle looked like he was made of only grit and granite.

"You are merely human," Itzamna said flatly. "You possess neither the physical nor the mental strength that this will require."

Hondo didn't even flinch. "I can do it. I won't let you guys down." I knew he was planning to use the warrior mask Quinn had given him.

Brooks's face fell as she grabbed Hondo's hand and looked him in the eye. "I know how brave you are, Hondo, and you always have our backs, but maybe this time . . ." She hesitated. "Maybe Marco should be the anchor."

"Except I didn't volunteer," Marco said, looking insulted.

I could tell Brooks's words hurt my uncle, but she didn't

know about his secret weapon or how much he loved Quinn. And you can't buy that kind of reliability.

"Hondo can do it," I said. "There's no one else I trust to bring us back."

"Uh, no offense, dude," Marco said to me, "but I'm the strongest one here. Not that I want the job or anything."

Itzamna said, "It isn't a matter of just holding the time thread—it's a matter of crossing into the shadows between this time and the next. It is a perilous place filled with anger and fear and darkness. No one, not even a god, would want to travel there."

"Then how did *you* guys time-travel?" I asked.

"We employed shadow crossers—usually magicians," Itzamna said, like it was no big deal. "But they knew the risks. They understood that their minds would never be the same afterward."

"Why would they do it?" Brooks said, looking horrified.

"Riches. Fame. Glory for their legacies and families," Itzamna said. "They always believed they would be the exception and not the rule."

"That's awful!" Ren scowled. "How could the gods be so mean?"

"How can *humans* be so mean?" Itzamna said. "In our world, there is both light and dark, good and evil in everyone."

"I'm not evil," Ren argued.

"You haven't yet had to be," the god said quietly.

Hondo came closer. "Listen, I fought through the twins' poison. That was dark and worse than any nightmare," he said. "I don't talk about it, because why give power to the memory, but it's what led me to meditation and mindfulness. Maybe it was also training for this exact moment."

Marco nodded slowly and stared at my uncle with total respect.

"It will feel like your skin is slowly being picked off your bones," Itzamna said, dragging out each word dramatically. "Your body, mind, and spirit will be tormented in ways you cannot imagine."

Hondo crossed his arms over his chest, indicating his decision was final.

"I'll be your wingman," Marco said to Hondo, and for the first time, I liked the guy. For once, he wasn't trying to protect himself or get out of doing anything. He saw how important it was to my uncle to do this part of the quest, and Marco had faith in him, without even knowing him. That counted for a lot.

"How do we know how many threads are left in the watch?" Ren asked Itzamna.

"You must draw them out," he said. "But it will take more than your own strength."

Ren twisted her mouth, thinking. "We'll use the godborn connection," she said. "It will generate more power."

Just then, a black SUV with tinted windows came down the gravel road that led to the house.

"That must be your mom," Hondo said to me as the car pulled into the driveway. I tugged off Itzamna's shades and, with Fuego's help, hurried over. Mom jumped out of the car and threw her arms around me, clinging so tight I thought she might snap my ribs. Rosie leaped out after her, her tongue hanging out the side of her mouth. I patted my dog's neck with one hand while I hugged my mom with the other. We stayed like that for a few more seconds—a few more seconds in which the sky was a beautiful blue, the world was turning as it should, and nothing could touch us. Not even the truth of what had already happened and what still lay ahead.

Mom pulled back first, keeping a tight grip on my arms. "Zane, you're okay. Everything is okay." She repeated those last words a few more times, like just saying them could make them true.

Rosie whined and pushed her head against my shoulder. "How's my girl?" I rubbed her between the eyes before she lowered her head and started sniffing my ankles and legs like she could smell where I had been.

By this time, Alana had made her way over and was talking to the driver, who was still behind the wheel, nodding at whatever she was telling him.

"Mom," I started, "we ... we have to ..." I didn't even know what I was trying to say, but she did. Moms always know stuff like that.

"I know about the gods being trapped," she said.

But you don't know they're in 1987.

"And I know I can't talk you out of whatever you're planning to do. And I'm sorry and angry that you've been put in this position, and ..." She took a deep breath and added, "If anyone can do this, Zane, it's you and Rosie and Hondo." Her eyes darted toward the group by the front porch. "You *all* can do this."

I wondered if she would say the same thing if she knew we had to travel back in time. Or if she knew that Hondo was going to have to go through worse than hell, again.

But before 1987 and hell, we needed food and sleep.

And we were in the right place for both. Apparently, Alana and Adrik's log mansion also came with a chef, and the guy was a master at grilling a killer burger. My plan had been to spill the truth to the godborns before dinner, but Hondo and Brooks thought that was a bad idea.

"We need to keep them calm," Hondo said.

"Why freak them out?" Brooks added.

"I can't keep all this secret anymore," I argued. "They deserve to know."

Brooks sighed and said, "At least wait until after they've eaten."

Hondo chuckled. "Yeah, frenzy is much better on a full stomach."

After I cleaned myself up in one of the guesthouses, I made my way back outside. The smell of smoked beef and sizzling bacon filled the air. Normally that would be enough to start me drooling, but right then, it made my stomach turn. And as I rounded the corner of the house, I froze. Dozens of tiki torches cast long shadows across the cluster of picnic tables where the godborns sat laughing, talking, and chowing down.

The white barn loomed behind them, and I headed for it, suddenly needing to clear my head. Yeah, I know what you're thinking: *You've fought gods and faced demons!* But in the moment, all that seemed a whole lot easier than delivering bad news to a crowd that had no idea what was about to hit them.

Back in New Mexico, whenever I had frayed nerves, Rosie and I would hike my volcano, the Beast. Since I was minus the Beast, I took off into the forest, hoping the right words would come to me there. As the trees closed in all around me, everyone's voices trailed off.

Except one. "Zane?"

Gripping Fuego, I spun to see Brooks step from the shadowed trees.

"We need to talk," she said.

"What's up with the sneak attack?" I asked, forgetting how eerily quiet she could be.

She came over and stood right in front of me. "I'm just going to say it. I know you've got a thing for me." She kept her eyes on the wedge of night sky between the trees.

Whoa! I wasn't ready for that. I felt like I'd been mowed down by an eighteen-wheeler. Was I supposed to agree? Tell her she had bad timing? Say nothing? "Can we...uh, talk about this later?"

She shook her head and turned so I couldn't see her face. "It's not going to work out. I needed to tell you, since, you know, one of us could die in 1987."

I take it back. I felt like I had been mowed down by an eighteen-wheeler *twice*. As my mind and heart and every cell in my body struggled to find the right words, Brooks busted up laughing, clutching her gut. Then I saw her morph right before my eyes. She wasn't Brooks—she was Marco!

"Dude!" he cried, still splitting a gut. "You should have seen your face."

A tornado of fire whirled in my chest. It would have taken 0.2 seconds for me to incinerate his stupid smile—and believe me, I wanted to—but I had to restrain myself. I couldn't blaze the guy for a practical joke.

Remember what I said about liking the guy? All that went up in smoke. Literally.

I reached for the best Hondoism I could come up with in the humiliating moment: *Keep it frontal. Don't go limbic.* In other words, I couldn't let the limbic part of my brain go berserk, because I'd lose control and power.

I gripped Fuego and was muy glad for the dark. "I guess you graduated past busting noses."

"I told you I would get stronger," he said with a smirk. "Just took some practice."

I felt smoke drift from my eyes, and I walked away quickly so Marco wouldn't see it. I started back toward the barbecue area.

Marco kept pace. "Dude, it was just a joke. Everyone knows you've got it bad for her—you could read it between every line of those books."

I stopped in my tracks and turned to face him. Flecks of moonlight sifted through the trees. "Great. While you're obsessing over me and Brooks, I have to go tell the godborns that Zotz has pretty much won," I said. "That we're about to do something no human has ever lived through, and if we don't make it back, their lives are going to—"

"Why would you do something so stupid?" Marco asked, suddenly serious.

"It's rotten to keep lying to them."

"Rotten?" He bit back a laugh. "Dude, that's the worst strategy I've ever heard. Wait—you're serious?" He shook his head. "They'll freak, and you know what happens when a big group of people freak? They do stupid things. They feed off one another's worst fears and do anything to survive."

I jammed Fuego into the soft earth. "I told them they'd be safe at SHIHOM, and now I'm supposed to lie to them? They need to know so they can be prepared."

"No one is safe *anywhere*," Marco argued. "Especially not godborns. So yeah, lie to them. Let them think this is still part of their training."

For half of a second, I considered taking Marco's advice. I mean, he was a pretty awesome strategist. But as the son of war, he was also a master manipulator who was probably trying to manipulate me right now.

Fire rushed through me in waves, but I couldn't tell if it was directing me to listen to Marco or stay on my own path.

"That was a really good impersonation of Brooks," I said as I took off for the barn, using Fuego to create a quick distance between us.

Marco called after me, "Zane, you don't know what you're doing!"

38

When I got to the barn, Hondo took me aside
and asked, "Are you sure about this?"

I nodded, and he leaped onto an empty picnic table to
announce that I had news. Everyone went quiet. Then a few
whispers floated across the meadow:

"It's Zane."

"What's he going to say?"

"Is this part of our training?"

Brooks and Ren looked at me, and for half a second,
Brooks's eyes blazed, which I knew was her way of telling
me *Good luck* or maybe *You're a bonehead for telling them the
truth.*

Adrik and Alana stood nearby, their faces obscured by
shadow. I looked around for my mom, but she was nowhere
to be seen. Rosie stalked the perimeter, her gaze glued to me.

I climbed onto the table and gripped Fuego with sweaty
palms. My blood rushed through my veins like hot lava and
my pulse roared in my ears. Seeing all those eyes on me,
waiting, expecting me to say something, was worse than terrifying. It reminded me of the days when I was the last kid to
get on the school bus and everyone stared at me, judging me
solely on my limp.

"Uh..." Yes, that *is* how I began my impressive speech. "We're, uh...I mean, this isn't a training exercise. The gods... they've been abducted, Zotz and Ixkik' have taken over Xib'alb'a, and demons are crawling up the World Tree."

Murmurs broke out.

"You lied to us!" someone accused.

Ren shouted, "We're trying to protect you, to—"

"By keeping us in the dark," said a short guy with blond hair. I recognized him from my godborn search and rescue in Washington State. He'd been a runner.

"No," I said. "I mean, we were trying to figure stuff out. Trying to—"

"Are all the gods gone?" some girl called out.

I nodded. "Except Itzamna."

"And the bat god and Ixkik'," someone said.

"Only three gods are left?" the guy who had fought with Marco said.

"I know," I said. "It's terrible."

That prompted a bunch of *yeah*s and other stuff I probably shouldn't repeat. And then a girl—the redhead who'd been in the cage next to mine in the junkyard—stood and said, "We don't need the gods. We're getting stronger. We can kill the last three gods and take over." I think spit flew from her mouth at that point, but I was so shocked I can't be sure. "*We* can control everything!"

I waited for her to say she was kidding, to start laughing or something, but her expression was so hard and stony, I knew without a doubt she was serious. I felt sick.

This wasn't how things were supposed to go!

"It's a sign . . . like it's meant to be," she said, a smile tugging at her lips.

Serena stood up next to her, nodding. Her new black hair made her face look pale and waxy. As her dark eyes swept the grassy yard, a moonbeam illuminated the space like a huge spotlight, which made sense—she was the daughter of Ixchel, the moon goddess. Back in the junkyard, when we were still in Zotz's clutches, Serena hadn't cared how dangerous facing the gods was. Her words had been like venom: *Did you see what we've been through? Caged, tormented by that . . . that bat god.*

There was no doubt about it: she still wanted revenge.

As she walked toward me, the moonbeam lit a path for her. She stopped a few feet away and said, "We never asked for this, Zane. The gods are the ones who abandoned us, never cared about us in the first place. They wanted us dead! Why should we care about them now?"

Brooks climbed up onto the table next to me and held out her hand. "Because we all belong to a Maya legacy that is bigger—"

"*We* are the Maya future!" some guy yelled.

"And you're just a nawal!" someone else said.

Brooks's massive wings appeared and she looked like she was about to take off and pummel whoever had launched those words, but I took her hand. "Not now," I said. "It's not worth it."

Her eyes blazed fiercely. She squeezed my hand like I was the anchor keeping her in place. "It might be worth it," she muttered.

"Brooks . . ."

"Fine."

I couldn't believe what I was hearing. I mean, the godborns sort of had a point about the gods, but it was a terrible one. Marco slipped into the shadows, his eyes darting from godborn to godborn before landing on me with a knowing look I hated. He'd been right. I had underestimated the godborns' fear and anger. And obvious lust for power.

"Really?" I asked, my voice louder now. "You'd rather live in a world where Zotz and Ixkik' control everything?"

"You didn't hear me," the redheaded girl said. "*We* will control everything. Let Zotz and Ixkik' *think* they've won, and when they're not looking—"

"Bam!" someone shouted. "We blindside the old losers."

Brooks leaned closer, still squeezing my hand. *This is a revolt,* she said. *I've seen it before. Or at least heard about it. Tell them what they want to hear and do it now.*

My eyes searched Hondo's and Ren's faces. They looked as stunned as I felt. "Okay," I said, digging deep, because pretending to go along with the godborns' plan was going to require an Oscar-worthy performance. "You guys are right. The gods are jerks. They probably don't deserve saving." The words tasted sour in my mouth. "But we need to plan, to figure out a way to take out Zotz and Ixkik'—"

"And the hero twins!" A bolt of lightning ripped the sky. I searched the godborns' faces, wondering who had caused it. Some looked terrified in the torches' flickering light, others looked unsure, and at least half a dozen appeared ready to riot.

"And the hero twins," Brooks echoed as her eyes continued to burn. "They'll go down, too."

Ren's attention was fixed on the crowd. She was forcing a hard stare, one that hid the horror I knew she was feeling. A large dragon-like shadow rose beside her as she said, "It's time for the godborns to reveal their powers."

Marco stepped into the moonlight and walked toward me, talking while all eyes were on him. "We will keep training, getting stronger, and once we find the bat god, the twins, their mom, and *all* our enemies," he said, his expression tight, "we will attack, and take what belongs to us."

The crowd got to their feet, chanting, "Godborn power! Godborn power!"

Brooks gripped my hand like an iron vise. *Zane, what have we done?*

Marco's eyes fixed on mine. I didn't know him well enough to be able to read his expression, but one thing was certain: there would be no truth tonight.

Only more secrets and lies.

39

It was hours before the godborns chilled out and finally caught some z's. But even in the peaceful setting of the Montana mountains, with everyone else deep in their dreams, I was haunted by the memory of that terrible chant: *Godborn power!*

How could they have turned so quickly? If they were that hungry for power and control, then they were just like the gods. Maybe Itzamna was right—everyone had good and bad, dark and light in them. I was glad I hadn't been wearing Itzamna's sunglasses. I couldn't imagine how he would feel knowing the godborns were rebelling when he was doing all he could to save SHIHOM and the World Tree.

By midnight, we had a plan. *We* included Hondo, Brooks, Ren, Alana, Adrik, Rosie, and, yes, Marco.

I was skeptical of including Marco, but he had a valid argument. "Don't hate me because I'm such a great actor," he practically sang. "I said those things so the godborns would think we're are all on the same team. Come on, man, put on your strategic hat!"

"Aren't we?" Ren asked. "On the same team?"

Brooks nodded. "We have to bring the godborns back

around," she said. "There were some who were *not* on Team Takeover. I saw it on their horrified faces."

"We can't bring *anyone* around," I said, "until we bring the gods back from 1987."

We met behind the barn at dawn to kick off our quest. Here's how things were going to go down: Hondo would be the shadow crosser. Marco would be the 1987 thread's connection to the present. He didn't seem too excited about the job. "You mean I have to carry around a gold rope the whole time?"

"You *are* the strongest," I reminded him, which only made him grunt.

Brooks, Ren, Rosie, and I would find and rescue the gods while Alana stayed in Montana to hold down the fort/ranch (and hoped no one mutinied).

Itzamna told us he could communicate with us in the Old World, but not in 1987—that would be too far back.

Mom popped into the barn with Louie in tow. "And where do you think you're going?"

Rosie wagged her tail and ran over to greet her.

"I told her everything, including the godborn treachery," Louie said.

I groaned and steeled myself for an argument. I wanted to strangle Louie. We really didn't have time for this. . . .

Mom patted Rosie absentmindedly, then marched over to me. "1987? Really?"

"Don't try and stop me—"

"Would you listen if I did?"

"No."

Rosie let out a small whine like she was sticking up for me.

Mom rubbed Rosie's chest and added, "Then I'll help out here."

Whoa, that was unexpected. I let out a sigh of relief.

"I'm good at keeping kids in line," she said. "Well, except you, Zane."

"I'm not," Louie said. "But I can freeze anyone who tries to bounce."

Alana smiled at my mom. "We could definitely use the help."

Adrik stretched his long arms over his head and yawned. "I wish I could go with you guys. 1987 was so cool. Such a sick year for music."

"Please," Mom said, batting her hand in the air. "1987 was enough the first time."

"Think of the souvenirs I could bring back," Adrik argued.

"This is serious," Brooks said. "And we can't have any weak links."

"I'm no weak link," Adrik said dramatically. "I've got Spidey senses!"

"He can steal memories," Alana said snidely, "so he thinks he's some kind of superhero now."

Adrik snorted. "I can talk for myself, Alana." He faced me. "I can steal memories."

"Like clear someone's mind?" I asked, part-impressed, part-horrified.

"Nah," he said. "Just one at a time. But it's complicated. You see"—he held up his hands like he was gripping a basketball—"first I have to use the dream world to find the memory."

"Unless he's *in* the memory," Hondo added.

Rosie nodded like she was following the convo while Mom's expression was one of total awe.

"How do you know you can do this?" Ren asked.

Adrik's eyes shifted from face to face like he was deciding whether he wanted to tell us the truth or not. "Um...when I got pounded with lightning, I was transported to this really cool beach, and I heard a voice in the wind, calling me a memory thief." He shook his head. "At first, I wasn't too psyched about that...I mean, who wants to be called a thief, right?"

"So he didn't want to tell us," Alana added.

"Not true, Alana!" he argued. "Well, it kinda is, but the Sparkstriker had said I was a dream walker, so I figured someone got it wrong. I asked that globe lady—the one in the temple—and she gave me all kinds of info." Adrik rubbed the back of his neck. "I practically had to beg her for it, but at least now I know."

"Globe lady?" Mom asked.

"I'll explain later," I said.

"Did you steal someone's memory already?" Brooks asked Adrik.

"Mine!" Alana scowled.

"Gimme a break," Adrik said. "It was a dumb memory of a time I hid one of her roller skates. I didn't think that memory was a big deal, and I had to practice on someone...."

Alana stuck out her tongue at him.

"Can you give the memories back?" I asked.

"Not that I know of," he said.

Marco rubbed his scar. "So how do you do it?"

With half a shrug, Adrik said, "How do you change your face?"

"I just think it."

"Same."

"Adrik could be useful on your quest," Itzamna said in my sunglasses.

"How?" Ren asked.

"Memory thieves can be quite cunning, and if you run into someone you know—someone from the present day—he could erase any knowledge you don't want them to keep."

Adrik elbowed his sister's arm. "Did you hear that? *Cunning.*"

I hadn't even thought about running into someone we knew. Were Jordan and Bird in Venice Beach in 1987? My stomach turned.

Alana pointed and said, "There's a gateway in that field— we can use it to get to the Old World. Then I'll come back here, and"—she hesitated for a moment—"Adrik can stay with you, since he's so *cunning.*"

"Awesome!" Adrik said with a big grin. Then he got serious. "You sure, sis?"

"I'm sure. It'll be like a vacation for me," she joked, but I could tell she was trying to hide her concern for his safety.

Mom asked, "Are you all positive you're ready for this?"

Rosie yelped and bolted in the direction Alana had pointed, across a grassy meadow where yellow and purple flowers bloomed.

I turned to say good-bye to Mom. She blinked back tears, made the sign of the cross on my forehead with a trembling hand, and said, "You're my favorite son."

"I'm your only son."

"So you'd better come home," she said before hugging me and giving everyone else blessings.

Louie stood back and added, "If you see any cool souvenirs, bring me some."

"We aren't going to be shopping," Brooks huffed.

"But vintage Madonna..." Alana whispered as she joined hands with me and Ren, who connected with Marco.

Adrik placed his hand on his sister's shoulder. Brooks, Hondo, and Rosie stood behind us, so close I could feel their hot breath on my neck.

"Okay, those who have been to the Old World," Alana said, "visualize it. The rest of you, think of how Zane described it in the book."

A second later, we plunged through biting darkness that circled around us like frenzied hands, reaching for, clawing at, and generally trying to rip us open.

Thankfully, it only lasted a few seconds. We landed with a *thunk, oof,* and *"My back!"*

I sat up and looked around. We were definitely in the Old World, right in the center of a semicircle of five pyramids. Rosie ran around sniffing the ground like she was happy to be back in the place where I'd first seen her in hellhound form.

As everyone got to their feet, oohing and aahing all over the place, I took a deep breath. Man, the place was just as creepy and amazing as the last time I'd been there. Cobwebs hanging from the silvery trees, a split sky that looked ready to collapse. I half expected to see the Sparkstriker, but she must have been busy cleaning her lightning pool or polishing her ax.

I pushed Itzamna's shades up the bridge of my nose. "The Old World could really use an overhaul," he said.

Brooks came over with the others. "How are things going at the World Tree, Itzamna?" she asked tentatively, like she was afraid of the answer.

"We've seen better days, but so far even my diminished powers have kept the enemy at bay, and—"

"Tell us how to do this, Itzamna," Ren interrupted. "There's no time to waste."

Rosie grunted, smoke curling from her nose as she sat on her haunches like a statue. She was ready and willing, like always.

Within five minutes of hearing Itzamna's instructions, we had linked our powers to draw two time threads from Ren's watch. Everyone released the collective breath we'd been holding.

"That's enough, right?" Ren said, searching my face as if I had the answers, but really she was asking Itzamna.

"Three would've been better, or four," Itzamna said, "but if this is all you have, then it'll have to do. You will need to fuse the two strands to create a rope strong enough to support time travel. Then you will give one end to Hondo. Ren, you take the other end. Once you get to 1987, you will hand it off to Marco."

"Won't people notice them carrying a big ole gold strand?" Adrik asked.

"No," Itzamna said. "Mere mortals won't be able to see or touch it. And it will always remain straight no matter how many turns you take—although it's best to remain as stationary as possible." He took a breath and went on, "The thread will do all it can to return to the present. It will lie to you, Marco, try to trick you. You mustn't fall for it."

"The thing talks?" Marco moaned.

"After twenty-four hours in 1987, the time rope will vanish," Itzamna said. "Once that happens, you will be stuck there. Hmph—maybe that's a good thing. There might not be much to come back to."

"You didn't tell us we had a *deadline*!" My voice rose a few notches.

"You only have two threads," the god said. "That's why I said three or four would be better."

"Okay." Brooks exhaled a long breath. "How do we get to 1987?"

"Just tell the rope that's where you want to go—but please, for the love of stardust, make sure you say Venice Beach, *California*. Otherwise you could end up in Florida or Italy. Time threads have wicked senses of humor, and you must always be literal and specific. Got it?"

"And how do we get back?" Marco looked like he wasn't sure *any* of this was a good idea.

"It will know the way to the Old World," Itzamna said. "Just make sure you are together and physically connected in some way—holding hands, looped arms, whatever. May fortune smile upon you all!"

We said good-bye to Itzamna and Alana. Adrik even gave his sister a hug, saying, "Don't visit the Witch again while I'm gone. I don't want to miss out on the fun."

I didn't think it was a good idea to leave Hondo out in the

open while he clung to a time thread that held our lives in the balance, so we headed deep into the jungle. Finally, we found a perfect place: a small clearing in the middle of a thicket of trees.

"Ready?" I asked my uncle.

He gave a solemn nod.

Ren joined the two time threads. There was a flash of light not unlike lightning that forced us all to recoil for a couple of seconds. The golden glow illuminated the jungle and bounced off the metallic trees.

Hondo reached into his pack and pulled out the warrior mask.

Brooks's face registered all sorts of emotions. "Where did you get that?"

He didn't hesitate or try to lie. "Quinn gave it to me."

Brooks searched his face, and I could see the puzzle coming together in her mind. "You and Quinn? But..." Her eyes softened and she gave a slight nod. "Okay, Hondo. Okay."

I hugged my uncle tight. "You got this."

He nodded and pulled away. "Just come back in one piece, Diablo."

Ren said to Hondo, "Remember your meditations." She carefully handed one end of the rope to him, and I half expected him to yowl like a dying sheep. But he took the cord like it was nothing. So Zip had been right. As long as Ren gave it willingly, there was no risk of her incinerating someone's flesh.

With the other end of the glowing rope in her hand, Ren walked away from Hondo. The strand grew longer and longer, just like it had at Zip's place. Brooks, Adrik, Marco, Rosie, and I stood next to her and looked back at Hondo. The great pyramids loomed above the trees like stone ghosts.

Hondo clenched his jaw, then placed the mask over his face. My heart plummeted.

"Let's get in and get out," I said, knowing that every second we spent in 1987 was a second Hondo would be forced to spend in the shadows of torment.

We stood in a row like train cars, each gripping the shoulder of the person in front of us. I placed my hand on Rosie's shoulder.

From the back of the line, Ren said, "Venice Beach, California, 1987," over and over until the edges of the world began to bleed, colors faded, and a tunnel of utter blackness swallowed us.

The ground beneath our feet started moving forward like we were on some kind of conveyor belt, slow at first, then faster and faster. Ren's voice was on repeat as music echoed and car engines roared. As the words floated over us, I could only hear "1987."

Voices rose. Dishes clanked. "1987."

Birds chirped. Waves crashed. "1987."

A bright light filled the tunnel, and the next thing I knew, a volleyball slammed into my head.

40

"Sorry, dude," said some guy with crazy curly hair and rainbow trunks as he retrieved his ball from the beach. He took a look at the six of us and tried to hide the laugh I could tell was ready to split his face. "Uh, nice sweats."

Obnoxious electric-guitar music blared from somewhere down the shore. The smells of salt water and burned hot dogs floated through the air.

Marco pitched a fake laugh. And then, in the span of a single breath, he shifted his face to look exactly like the dude's and said, "We're with the CIA."

"Marco!" I warned.

The guy dropped the ball faster than his mouth fell open.

Thankfully, Marco shed the guy's face just as quickly, but the damage had been done. I thought the guy was going to take off screaming, but instead he said, "You just made yourself look like me!"

"It was a magic trick," I said, nearly vomiting while Marco snickered. Brooks shot him an angry glare.

"I know what I saw!" the guy insisted. Rosie sniffed his feet, then staggered back like she didn't like what she smelled.

Adrik said, "You're confused," as he extended his palm and blew across its surface.

The dude blinked twice, gave us a *who-the-heck-are-you?* glance, and took off.

I spun to face Adrik. "Did you just . . . ?"

"Snag that last memory?" Adrik said, swiping his hands together dramatically. "Yup."

"Super cool," Ren said.

"You better never try that on me," Brooks warned.

"Pretty sus if you ask me," Marco said.

Brooks socked him in the arm. "We're supposed to blend in, not stand out!"

"Yeah, well, we should have raided a costume shop, then," Marco said, rubbing his bicep.

Marco was right. No one had thought about dressing in whatever people wore in 1987, which, by the looks of it, was colorful trunks, bikinis, and big hair.

"And we can't even go shopping!" Ren groaned.

"No shopping?" Adrik asked. "That's why I came." He threw out his hands before anyone could smack him. "Kidding. Kidding."

"Our money was printed long after 1987," I said, realizing we should have thought of that, too. I stroked Rosie, who had her eyes closed and head tilted toward the bright sun like she didn't have a worry in the world.

Adrik said, "I brought some green from my aunt's secret stash, and yeah, it's old. I checked the dates on the bills. Good thing *someone* is thinking."

Marco clapped the guy on the back and said, "Just track down the gods. I don't want to hold on to that time rope forever, and"—his eyes darted around—"I already don't like 1987, so I don't plan on sticking around."

Brooks asked, "What's the address K'iin gave, Ren?"

Ren fumbled in her pocket for the scrap of paper she'd written it on and held it up for us to see.

Brooks shook her head and blinked. "I should have known!"

"What's wrong?" I asked Brooks.

"That's . . . that's Jordan and Bird's old address," she sputtered. "Of *course* their mom would send the gods to the only people she trusted."

My stomach dropped.

"The bad dudes?" Adrik asked. "They lived in Venice back then? I mean, now . . . er . . ."

Brooks nodded, her expression going from shock to total dread in less than two seconds. "Yeah, they did their magic stealing in that place for a long time." Her eyes shifted to me. "Before they moved up to Beverly Hills, that is."

"But if they know in 1987 that they're hiding the gods . . ." My mind ricocheted off my skull. "Does that change the future?"

"Unless they don't *know* they're hiding them," Marco offered.

"What do you mean?" I asked.

Marco explained that, like Ah-Puch had been, the gods could be imprisoned in an object—concealed somehow—and the twins might not even realize they had them in their possession. "Maybe it was like a UPS delivery," he said, "with a note saying *Guard this with your life. You'll understand in thirtysomething years.*"

Brooks was nodding. "Right. If Itzamna is correct and Zotz and Ixkik' only had a one-way ticket, then they would've had to send a message to the twins, because no way would they risk themselves getting trapped here."

"Unless they used a shadow crosser, too," I said.

"But if two threads gives us twenty-four hours, then they would have had even less," Marco said.

Brooks looked around. "Even if they only had twelve hours, it would be plenty of time to deliver the goods and get back."

Logistically, it was possible. But I didn't think Zotz or Blood Moon would take the chance.

"So what do we do?" Ren shielded her eyes from the midday sun as seagulls squawked overhead. "We can't just show up at the twins' front door and ask if they've had any mysterious messages or deliveries lately."

"Guys," Adrik said, "people are kinda staring at us. You think it's the matching black threads?"

"Let's keep moving," said Marco.

We headed toward the boardwalk, weaving between beach towels and umbrellas. Cigarette smoke drifted through the air as people whizzed by on bikes and roller skates. One guy tried to pet Rosie until Brooks said, "She bites."

The place was a sea of miniskirts, short shorts, and lots of tanned skin all oiled up. "Is that dude wearing clown pants?" Adrik asked.

"I think they're called parachute pants," Ren said. "My dad used to have some in his closet."

"So weird not to see a single phone," Marco said, looking around. "Like, people are actually talking to each other."

Rosie yawned and licked her chops as we headed for a shaded bench. Marco plopped down with a grunt. Ren handed him the time rope, which ran along the beach to the spot where we had first arrived and disappeared into the sand. Itzamna was right—no one noticed it.

"What if I get hungry?" Marco said.

"Just don't go far," Ren said. "The less the time rope moves around in 1987, the better."

"And remember," I added, "Hondo is on the other end, going through hell, so no games."

Marco grunted. "Yeah, I know all about hell. Just hurry back."

Brooks walked over to Marco. "Please," she said, kneeling in front of him. My heart twisted like a used dishrag. "Don't let go of the rope. No matter what."

"But you heard Itzamna. It's going to try to trick me. Man, it better not start talking."

"Good thing you're the son of war," Ren said, patting his shoulder. "If anyone can do it, you can."

"Don't forget I'm also the strongest." He glanced my way with a smirk that I knew was meant to get under my skin. It didn't. Okay, it totally did. But he was holding our destiny in his hands, so I had to be chill. For now.

Brooks stood and took a deep breath as she stared down the boardwalk. Uh-oh. I knew that look. It always equaled *change of plans.*

"What are you thinking?" I asked.

She gave me a sly grin. "We can't just show up at Jordan and Bird's. So we're making a pit stop first."

"A pit stop?" Adrik moaned. "Why?"

Without saying more, Brooks took off, heading north. We all rushed to keep up with her.

"Brooks!" I met her stride. "What's the deal? Shouldn't we talk about this?"

"You know I do nothing without a plan, Obispo," she said. "We're going to see an old friend."

"Who?" Ren's boots clicked along the walkway.

"Jazz."

"Jazz?" I shouted as we passed—fittingly enough—a record store. I had the fleeting thought to run in and tell everyone to hold on to their albums because they might become valuable one day. "Was he even alive back then?" I asked, practically tripping to keep up with her, even with Fuego.

Brooks blew a curl off her face. "Giants age super slowly, but yeah, he was—*is* around, and I bet he can help us." She explained that he'd known the hero twins since he was a kid, when his older brothers ran security for them, before Jazz got the job. She'd seen a picture of him from back then and would for sure recognize him.

Rosie snorted, zigzagging between groups of people who couldn't see her for what she truly was. All they saw was a black three-legged dog.

Brooks turned down a side path, then took a hard left. The street was lined with old-style cars parked in front of flat-roofed houses with short-walled patios. Palm trees and other greenery grew over the peach, gray, and white walls.

"This isn't the way to Jazz's shop," I said.

"He didn't have the shop as a kid, Zane," she said, walking faster now.

"Then how do you know where he lives?" Ren asked.

Brooks smiled and pointed at the street sign: BROOKS AVE. "It was the first thing he told me when we met: 'When I was a kid, I used to live on a street with your name,'" she said, trying to do her best Jazz impression. "Sometimes he would take me here and show me the house he grew up in, just to get me out of the twins' lair for a little while when I lived there with Quinn."

"But if we go see him," Ren said, hop-skipping to keep up, "won't he remember you in the future?"

Brooks threw a side-glance in Adrik's direction. "That's where you come in."

"You want me to drain a giant's memory?" Adrik was already shaking his head.

It felt wrong on so many levels, yet I knew Brooks was right. We couldn't give Jazz a memory of us when he was going to meet us in the future. Who knew what kind of time rule that would break?

Brooks stopped in front of a white house with bright turquoise trim. "This is it," she said. There was a small round hatchback parked out front and a sign on the gate that read: TRESPASSERS WILL BE EATEN.

Yep, we were in the right place.

With a deep breath, Brooks reached over the gate and unlatched it from the inside.

"Uh," Adrik said, "maybe we should knock or call first?"

"No time for that," Brooks said as we all piled onto the little patio, where a dozen potted plants drooped, near death. The sounds of rock music and rolling wheels drew our attention. We followed them to the back of the house, where we ducked behind a hedge. Before us was a huge skateboard ramp in the shape of a giant U.

A blond boy, maybe eleven or twelve years old, glided up the incline and spun in midair before looping back down. His two friends cheered. "That was the baddest!" one shouted.

The other guy shook his head. "My turn!"

The blond kid kicked the end of his board, popping it up into his hand. "We need to put rockets on these things so we can go faster."

"That's him," Brooks whispered with a huge smile.

I did a double take. I'd expected to see Jazz the giant—a huge bald, burly dude with an eye patch and tattoos. But this kid? He had shoulder-length hair, zero eye patch, and looked totally human.

"He's no giant," Adrik said.

"He has hair," Ren said.

"Giants don't get big until around age thirteen," Brooks said.

Rosie groaned, drawing Jazz's attention to the bushes. I threw my hand up to shush her, but it was too late. Jazz tugged something out of his waistband and rushed over. "We got company, guys," he said to his friends.

And then he zapped me.

41

∴

I woke up on a lumpy green couch with springs
poking my spine and white stars dancing in my vision.

Jazz stood over me along with Brooks and Ren.

"He's alive," Jazz said. "That's good. My laser worked like
a pro. I should tweak the output a little, though."

I sat up, feeling a lot of déjà vu and a little disoriented.
"You really didn't have to zap me."

"You could have been an ancient sea monster or evil magician," he said casually.

"Do I *look* like a monster?"

"So you *are* a magician!"

"I already told you," Brooks said. "They're *all* magicians."

Oh boy. Round two. The first time I'd met Jazz, Brooks
had tried to pass me off as a magician, since no one knew
godborns existed. I only hoped we could pull off the lie better this time.

"Maybe I wanted to hear it from him," Jazz said to Brooks.
"Don't have a cow."

Ren sat next to me and offered me some of her Pepsi,
which I waved away. "No thanks."

"You okay?" she said. "You went down fast. Good thing
Rosie slowed the fall."

"Where is she?" I glanced around. I was in some kind of living room with high ceilings, probs to accommodate the giant family members I was super glad weren't here. The windows were framed by green drapes the same color as the lumpy couch.

"You mean the hellhound?" Jazz said. "Out back, chowing on some hamburger meat. I've never heard of a hellhound traveling with magicians and a nawal."

"Like I told you," Brooks said, "we're here on a secret mission to take back something the twins stole from the gods."

"Yeah," Jazz said, nodding. "I heard you. And I really don't want to know. As long as I get paid, and as long as you guys leave before my brothers get home tomorrow, I don't really care." He pushed a lock of blond hair off his forehead, and I wondered how much Brooks had agreed to give the guy. "But you'll never get through the twins' security," he said, "even if they aren't going to be home."

"But I bet *you* could get through their security," Ren said.

"Maybe," Jazz said. "Probably. I've been working on this new—"

"Why aren't they going to be home?" Brooks perked up.

"Another yacht party." Jazz yawned. "They have them practically every night. I think Prince is supposed to be performing tonight. Barf. They totally should have gotten Guns N' Roses. Now *that* would have been gnarly!"

Why did I have the feeling Hondo would love this kid?

A hot flame sparked inside me at the mention of the party, as I remembered what had happened at the last one I attended: Hondo had been poisoned. I hated that we had to wait until tonight to try our rescue—when the clock was ticking and Hondo was suffering and Marco was probably arguing with the time rope that, to be honest, I didn't trust to stay put.

"Prince?" Adrik walked in with Rosie just then. "As in *Purple Rain*, and *Diamonds and Pearls*? That's sick!"

"It *is* kinda sickening," Jazz said, misinterpreting Adrik. "*Diamonds and Pearls*? Never heard of it."

"Right," Adrik said, letting out a light laugh. "It doesn't come out until—"

Ren pretend-tripped and spilled her soda all over Adrik's shirt. Rosie settled onto her belly and groaned.

"Not on the rug!" Jazz hollered as he took off into the kitchen, probably for a towel.

As soon as he was gone, I whispered, "I think the twins might have the gods on the yacht."

Brooks nodded, keeping her voice low. "It makes sense, since water throws off the gods' ability to track anyone. And they would still have to hide our gods from the 1980s versions."

And then it hit me. "The 1980s gods!" I nearly yelped. "We can ask *them* for help!"

"You guys want some brownies?" Jazz called from the kitchen. "They're special—made with Maya chocolate. If I were you, I'd definitely want some chocolate before I died."

"No one's going to die!" Ren hollered.

Brooks shook her head, processing my suggestion. "First we'd have to find the gods, and then we'd have to explain everything. I'm sure they would totally listen—right before they cut off our heads."

My mind caught up with hers a second later. "Yeah, you're right. Telling them about the godborns would for sure equal no godborns in the future."

Adrik took a swig of Ren's soda before mopping up the spill with the towel Jazz brought him.

Ren folded her arms across her chest. "So, Jazz, can you tell us more about this party?"

"Yeah," Jazz said. "If you're not on the invite list, no chance you can get in."

"How do you know all this?" I asked.

"My hermanos head up security for them."

"And you're willing to help us crash the party anyway?"

"And beat the *we-know-better-than-you* jerks at their own game?" Jazz said, grinning. "Heck yeah."

Brooks paced, avoiding the sticky soda spill. "Do you have a boat?"

Jazz smirked. "Do I have a boat? Are you kidding? Of course I do," he said. "It's not a yacht or anything, but it's got this really souped-up engine and—"

"Can we use it?" I asked.

"No way," Jazz said. "No one drives *Betty* but me. But that'll cost you extra. Especially since you're asking me to undermine my bros."

"You just said they're jerks," I reminded him.

"So?" He pushed his hair off his face and gave us the elevator gaze. "And if you're going to try to fit in, you'll need something better to wear."

"Like what?" Ren asked.

"I heard it's a Star Wars party," Jazz said. "You can go as

any character except Luke or Han. Those are reserved for the twins."

Adrik took off with Jazz to get us Star Wars outfits. Apparently Jazz "knew" some guy who ran a warehouse.... Sounded sketch, if you ask me, but as long as we got the costumes—preferably ones that hid our faces—I was cool with it.

By the time they got back a couple of hours later, the sun had set, and Ren, Brooks, and I had a plan. We'd head out to the yacht, climb aboard, blend in with the other Star Wars characters, and do some serious sleuthing. We'd have to make sure the twins never saw me or Brooks, since that would definitely mess up the future.

Rosie would help us sniff out the gods. That meant we had to conceal her, too, which is where Ren's shadows would come in. If the twins saw a hellhound cruising around their boat, they'd sound the alarm for sure.

Jazz blew into the house and tossed the costumes on the sofa. "May the Force be with you!"

Adrik shook his head as he came in behind him. "I wanted to be a stormtrooper and have a blaster," he grumbled, "but this is all the guy had left—stupid brown robes with hoods."

"Stupid?" Jazz said, a vein popping out of his forehead. "Obi-Wan is the best character," he argued. "Smartest. Toughest. No one messes with Obi!"

I'd seen the original Star Wars trilogy, and Obi-Wan was pretty cool. I mean, not as cool as Han Solo, but what did I care? I just wanted to get off that yacht *with* the gods and *without* anyone seeing us.

We had a quick bite of canned pork and beans and soggy fish sticks. Gross, I know, but Jazz said he only knew how to heat up food, not cook it.

After dinner, I changed into the white shirt and brown robe, then met up with Adrik and Ren in the living room. Rosie was lying on her side with her eyes rolling back as Adrik scratched her belly.

"Where's Brooks?" I asked.

"She flew off to take Marco some food and make sure he was okay," Ren said. "I hope the time rope isn't messing with him."

Oh. Right.

"I'll go find her," I said, frustrated that she would leave us when every second mattered.

Jazz came in and leaped over the back of the sofa, landing with a thump. "We better hurry. Once Prince arrives, no one else will be getting on that boat. I heard he brings his own security."

"Brooks and I will meet up with you guys," I said. "Where do you keep your boat, Jazz?"

"*Betty's* parked at the Marina del Rey docks," Jazz said. "About two miles south. Just be quick. I gotta be at the arcade."

A few minutes later, I arrived at the bench where we had left Marco. But no Marco. Seriously? I was going to incinerate the guy! All he had to do was sit there and keep hold of our ride home. The crowds had thinned to a few stragglers cruising down the boardwalk and beach. I scanned the area and didn't spot him *or* Brooks.

Where could they have gone? As I hooked a right down an alley, I collided with someone.

"Zane?" Brooks said. "What are you doing here?"

"Me?" I said, trying to hold my annoyance in check. I mean, who cared that she wanted to feed the son of war and thought he was the strongest? I couldn't think about that right now. Time was running out.

"Where the heck's Marco?"

"I found him on the beach," she said, like it was totally okay that he had left his post. "He's up to his ears in sand."

"What do you mean?" Was he building a sandcastle or something?

"He said the rope was messing with his head, trying to make deals with him, so he buried himself so he wouldn't have to listen anymore."

"Do you think we can count on him to stay put?" I said, handing her the Obi-Wan costume.

"He won't let us down," she said.

Those five dumb words made my stomach twist into a million knots.

"Come on, Obispo," said Brooks as she changed into a hawk. "Let's go find some gods."

42

::
::

We touched down on the dock in Marina del
Rey, instantly spotting our crew, which wasn't hard to do,
since they were all dressed like Obi-Wan Kenobi. Even Jazz
was playing the part, and he had what looked like a real
lightsaber—or maybe it was just another one of his zapping
tools.

Betty was a small navy-blue motorboat with bench seating behind the wheel. Jazz seemed to know his way around
the controls, because a minute after we boarded, he zipped
into the open water. The sea looked like black glass, shiny in
the half moonlight. No one said anything. We all just kept
our eyes on the water as if pretending that we weren't about
to do what we were about to do. Rosie propped her front paw
on the gunwale and let the wind hit her face like she used to
back in New Mexico, when she rode in Hondo's truck. For half
a second, I could see her as the dog she used to be.

Jazz said, "Check it out," as he flicked a switch and the
motor went silent. But we were still cruising.

Adrik got to his feet. "How did you do that?"

Looking over his shoulder, Jazz wiggled his eyebrows.
"I told you she was souped-up. Like the *Millennium Falcon*.

Maybe someday I'll figure out how to make her jump to light speed."

"Wow," Ren said. "You're really smart. I mean, I know you're an inventor—" She stopped herself, throwing me an *oops* look. I couldn't even be mad. I mean, it was hard to forget everything we knew about Jazz's future and who he would grow up to become.

"I like that," Jazz said, nodding. "Inventor." A minute later, he brought the boat to a stop and faced us. "I need some insurance."

"Huh?" we all said at the same moment.

"You say you're magicians," he said. "Prove it. Show me some magic."

Ren shifted in her seat before drawing a long black shape out of the water. "Shadow magician," she said.

Jazz seemed impressed. Then he turned to me and Adrik. I flashed some fire. Adrik? He just said, "Sorry, dude. My magic is in the dream realm."

Jazz folded his arms across his chest. "All magicians can do at least one trick."

"We really have to hurry," Brooks said.

Adrik sighed and said to Jazz, "I can tell you your future. You will open your own shop. You're going to invent a flashlight that can kill demons, and you're going to help save the world."

Jazz beamed. "Like a lightsaber?"

"I just said you'd help save the world," Adrik said, "and *that's* what you focus on?"

Jazz went back to the wheel, still smiling. "A demon-killing flashlight is so much better!"

Rosie paced restlessly. The cool sea air seemed to be getting colder. I half wished that the 1987 version of Pacific or Mat would show up and offer us a hand, but I knew that was impossible.

"We'll sneak up on the yacht's stern," Jazz said. "Check things out from a distance so you guys can decide how you're going to get on."

About ten minutes later, we had traveled so far across the ocean I could barely see the shore's twinkling lights. A few hundred feet away, a massive yacht—as in mini cruise ship status—came into view. Someone waved orange batons from its deck as we heard a helicopter approach. Soon the copter hovered directly over the twins' vessel.

"That must be Prince!" Jazz yelled over the sound of the whirring blades. "He'll create a good diversion for you."

Adrik craned his neck as if he could catch sight of the rock star and then started flapping his arms in the air and jumping up and down.

"Adrik!" Brooks scolded.

He scowled and sat back down. "Seriously? *Prince* is up there!" he said, pointing. "Like . . . you do know who that is, right?"

Rosie panted excitedly as Jazz slipped the boat into *hold-on-for-dear-life* gear. We raced over the water so fast my cheeks jiggled. I thought we would catch air, but Jazz had mad boating skills. Within two minutes, he had pulled *Betty* up to the yacht, just as the copter was touching down on the front helipad. Yeah, the yacht was *that* big.

Jazz was right. Everyone had rushed to the bow to meet Prince, so there was no security at the stern. No *anyone*.

"I'll wait here," he said. "You don't have much time to sneak around. Just try and blend in like Luke and Solo did when they dressed as Stormtroopers aboard the Death Star."

We pulled up our hoods and climbed up the ladder to the first deck. Rosie? She just turned to mist and reappeared up there.

"Guys," Brooks said from beneath her hood, "avoid anyone who looks like Han or Skywalker."

Everyone nodded.

"I've got a bad feeling about this," Adrik said.

Just then, the crowd erupted in cheers and screams. Prince must have disembarked. Adrik started in that direction until Ren pulled him back. "Hey," she said. "We're not here for that."

I could see Adrik struggling with the choice of seeing his rock idol or finishing the god rescue mission.

"At least you'll get to hear him," Ren offered.

I turned to Rosie, who was now cloaked in one of Ren's shadows. "Okay, girl. Find those gods."

Rosie took off down the narrow deck and ducked into a cabin. No, *cabin* isn't right. It was more like a mini ballroom with two huge chandeliers, shiny marble floors, and a dozen tables topped with shimmery gold tablecloths. We breezed through, passing a few more rooms that were just as impressive until we came to a set of double doors. Inside was some kind of art gallery. The room was dimly lit and had framed artwork evenly spaced on the walls. Music reverberated from the bow, literally rocking the boat as the crowd screamed. Adrik looked miserable as he glanced toward the sound.

Rosie sniffed the room. Little waves of smoke curled from her nose and eyes. Small breathy grunts told us she was getting close. Then she stopped at the far wall, where a floor-to-ceiling canvas painted entirely in turquoise was hung.

"The gods are in a painting?" Brooks whispered.

Ren's eyes searched the place, freezing on something over my shoulder. "Uh-oh," she murmured as four round shadows rose from her hands and flew toward the security cameras in each of the room's corners.

"Crap!" I said.

"They had cameras back then?" Adrik said.

"Let's just hurry," Brooks said, rolling her eyes.

I stepped closer to the painting, willing Fuego into light mode. I used my spear to scan the canvas's surface. "Are you sure, Rosie?" I said, searching for any clue as to how the gods could be locked in a painting.

Brooks was at my side, tracing her fingers lightly over the canvas. Rosie stood at attention like one of those pointer hunting dogs—she didn't even look like she was breathing. Her eyes glowed white as blue smoke flowed out of them.

"Rosie?" I asked, thinking she seemed kind of possessed.

Footsteps sounded on the deck outside.

"Those must be the Stormtroopers," Adrik moaned.

"We have to hurry," Ren said, twisting the dial on her

watch. "I'll stop time for a few—" Her face fell. "It's not working!"

"Why?" Brooks said.

Ren shook her head, her eyes dancing across the floor like she was searching for the answer. She looked up. "I think it's because we used all the time threads." Before that could even sink in, she danced her fingers in the air and a wall of shadows rose up, blocking the doorway.

My heart was in triple-beat mode as I waited helplessly, wondering what Rosie was up to and hoping Ren's shadow was strong enough to keep out whoever was on the other side of those doors.

The blue smoke from the hellhound's eyes washed over the canvas like a storm cloud, covering it from edge to edge. The paint began to melt, dripping down the wall and onto the floor with a sizzling sound. The smell of burning hair filled the room.

Voices shouted on the other side of Ren's shadow wall.

"They're here!" Adrik cried.

The smoke cleared.

The painting was gone. We all inched back, mouths open, as we stared through a window where the artwork used to be.

"What is *that*?" Ren whispered.

43

••
•••

Beyond the window was a creature no bigger than an orangutan, floating in a huge aquarium. Glaring blue lights illuminated the sleeping beast, which looked like a squatting toad with a gaping mouth, green crocodile skin, and massive claws that hung off tiny T. rex arms.

"It has to be the devourer," I said barely above a whisper.

The aquarium seemed to go on forever, disappearing into darkness.

"Open up and we won't kill you!" someone shouted from the other side of the shadow wall. Then: "Let's get Xb'alamkej."

Footsteps ran off in the opposite direction, looking for Xb'alamkej, aka Jordan.

My mind couldn't think fast enough. But I knew one thing: the hero twins had enough magic to break through Ren's shadow, and if the guards got the brothers, the twins would want to kill us not only for crashing their party and interrupting "Purple Rain," but also for stealing a precious commodity.

"Why is the devourer in water?" Ren whispered. "Isn't she an earth goddess?"

"Maybe water's like her kryptonite," Adrik said.

The creature's eyes flicked open. They were a sickly white with gray flecks in the center. The devourer raced toward the glass, slamming herself into it with so much force I thought it might crack open.

We all jumped back.

But instead of looking hungry or angry, she looked petrified. That's when I noticed that her legs were locked in chains that stretched into the dark deep.

"Why chain her up?" Brooks asked. "Isn't she working *with* Zotz and Ixkik'?"

"You think all the gods are in her stomach?" Adrik said, looking greenish.

"You know, I think you may be exactly right," I said, putting the pieces together. "That's how they sent all the gods back in time at once."

"Then they're all . . . ?" Ren couldn't finish.

"No," I said, remembering the message from Ah-Puch. "They're just stuck in darkness." At least, I *hoped* so.

An alarm sounded. A burning tug started in my gut. "The twins are getting close," I warned.

"How do we get her out of there?" Adrik asked. "Preferably without getting killed?"

The devourer swam away, so far she disappeared into the murky water, only to reappear in front of us a moment later.

"She's trying to tell us something." Ren pressed her face to the glass.

Whining, Rosie pawed the aquarium.

"There must be an exit . . ." I said, trying to hide the desperation in my voice.

"Like through there?" Ren pointed to a door on the opposite side of the room, leading to the starboard deck.

Brooks got closer to the glass and craned her neck to look up. "The tank is open at the top. We can access it from above, but we'll have to rip through the net."

"You're going to go *in* there?!" Adrik's voice was in freak-out mode. "What if she eats you, too?"

"There's no other way to release her," Brooks said. "And if I know the twins, those chains are laced with magic—a magic so thick nothing is going to open them except more magic."

I wished we still had Alana and Adrik's stone. I would just have to try to reason with the beast.

"Ren," I said, "hold off the twins with more shadows. Adrik, stay close to her."

Rosie let out a growl that shook me to my bones. "You too, girl," I said, before vanishing Fuego and turning to Brooks. "Let's go."

We threw off our heavy Obi-Wan robes, cracked open the starboard-side door, and checked for guards. This deck was clear and shrouded in darkness—all the lights were on the concert. Brooks shifted into a hawk and flew me up to a feeding platform that stretched partway over the tank. A net hovered about a foot above the water. Brooks quickly clawed a hole wide enough for one of us to squeeze through.

The devourer tried to rise up to meet us, but the chains kept her down.

"I'll go in and try to break the chains," I said.

Brooks nodded and I dove in.

The devourer immediately lunged at me, her mouth open wide. I reared back, but not before she put a claw on my shoulder and . . .

Talked to me?

She blinked at me as she said telepathically, *Hurakan said I could trust you.*

My dad knows I'm here?! Then I asked the dreaded question: *Did you eat the gods?*

They are alive. We must hurry.

How do I know you won't run away when I release you?

Look! She clung to me, and in that moment, an image formed in my mind's eye. There were no details of place, only fuzzy edges and Blood Moon's haunting voice.

Follow the time rope, the goddess told the devourer. *I'll wait for you here.*

The devourer did as commanded, and it looked like she was trailing a demon. The scene disappeared and was replaced with one of Jordan and Bird. Ixkik' said to them, *It is done.* Then a pair of bony hands cut the time thread with scissors.

The vision faded, and I flutter-kicked back to the surface. So that's how Blood Moon had sent the gods to 1987—she'd used a disposable demon as bait! But could I trust what I'd seen?

As soon as my head was above water, I told Brooks, "She was tricked." I glanced at the door to the gallery, hoping Ren's shadow wall was holding.

There was no time to consider options. I willed Fuego into my grasp and launched the spear into the water. It hit the chains down below, and they broke open with a burst of light. The devourer remained motionless for a moment, and just when I thought she might scuttle farther into the dark depths, she rose to meet me and Brooks.

We tried to lift her out of the tank and onto the platform, but she was too heavy.

Use the ocean exit, the creature said telepathically, gripping my arm with her claw. *At the bottom of the tank.*

"How far down is it?" I asked.

A few hundred feet. But I am weak. She grimaced. *I need help.*

Releasing the devourer, I repeated her words for Brooks, then said, "That's too deep for me to dive."

"Someone has to make sure she gets to Jazz's boat," Brooks insisted.

The devourer sank beneath the water. Her skin glowed a sickly yellowish green.

Brooks tucked her hair behind her ears and took a deep breath, leaning closer to the water.

"Brooks, what are you doing?!"

Not taking her eyes off the murky depths, she said, "I'll get her there. I can do this."

"No way!" I argued. "It's too dangerous."

She took my hand, looking me in the eyes. "I'm a water nawal, Zane. Remember? We're not going to blow this whole mission because of some dumb ocean."

"That dumb ocean could kill you!"

A loud bang drew my attention away from Brooks. I heard Rosie bark.

Just then, Brooks grabbed the collar of my T-shirt. She spun me to face her. I wobbled, nearly falling into the water. She jerked me close.

And then she kissed me.

That's right.

She. Kissed. Me.

As if it were easy and natural, as if she wasn't about to take a death dive. She pulled back and stared at me. For a minute, we were frozen, unable to break eye contact. I stopped breathing. Her cheeks flushed. I opened my mouth to speak, but nothing came out. She took another deep breath.

"See you at the boat." Brooks slipped into the water, diving into the dark so fast I lost sight of her within three seconds.

"Brooks!"

I spun in time to see the gallery's starboard door bust open. Jordan (Skywalker) and Bird (Solo) burst through. Aside from their dumb costumes, they looked just as they had the first time I met them: arrogant and cruel.

I leaped off the platform onto the deck, using Fuego to break my landing. I drop-rolled as the twins came at me. Electrical sparks shot out of their hands. I threw up a wall of smoke as Rosie shot streams of fire from behind them. "Rosie, no!" I shouted. As much as I wanted to make these guys pay, killing them in 1987 would ruin the future.

The twins spun around to find themselves facing a shadow grizzly bear. Ren and Adrik emerged from the gallery door and snuck past it, running toward the stern. Rosie galloped after them.

To get the twins off their tails, I cut through a passage to the port side and went the wrong direction, toward the concert. "Hey, fellas!" I taunted. "You're missing the best song!"

A group of Stormtroopers turned their attention from the music. "Stop!" they shouted.

Jordan and Bird burst out of a door behind me. I was trapped.

Suddenly, the deck behind the twins exploded in flames. Rosie had doubled back and was trying to barbecue them. As much as I wanted to get away from Jordan and Bird, I for sure didn't want Prince and all the innocent people on board to get hurt.

That's when I saw a row of sprinklers lining the overhang. I hurled a wave of smoke to activate them, and the twins recoiled from the spraying water.

I flew past them, toward the stern and my friends.

As I did, Jordan yelled, "You'll die on this boat!"

He hit me with an electrical current so strong it ran through my veins at blinding speed and threw me off my feet. I spun in midair and crash-landed on my back. Out of pure instinct, I willed Fuego into spear mode and aimed it at the twins. The moment the weapon left my hand, regret pounded its fists against my bones.

Rosie had me by the collar, dragging me away as Fuego slammed into Jordan's chest. The twin fell to his knees, blood trickling from his mouth.

His eyes met mine, and I could tell my face was imprinting on his brain.

44

..
....

No! You can't die!

If Jordan died now, Quinn would never get mixed up with him, and Brooks wouldn't come to my school to tell me about the prophecy I was a part of. It would mess up the future for sure!

Bird drew some kind of light around his brother and helped him to his feet. Did that mean he was going to be okay?

The next thing I knew, Rosie had leaped off the side of the boat with me in tow. As we soared through the air, I saw Prince on the bow, gazing up at the stars as if he was clueless about the chaos that had erupted all around him.

Rosie and I splashed into the cold sea. The water gripped me hard as Fuego circled back into my grasp. Jazz pulled *Betty* alongside us and hauled me up while Rosie scrambled into the boat. The others were already there—Ren shivering under a blanket, and Adrik standing at the stern, hollering up at Prince, "*Diamonds and Pearls* forever!"

"They had security cameras!" I shouted at Jazz.

He nodded. "I totally took care of that. Scrambled their feed."

Heart pounding, I took a quick look around. "Where's Brooks?"

"Not here, and we can't wait any longer," Jazz said. "The twins are already getting into their speedboat."

I grabbed his shirt. "We can't leave her. She's got the devourer."

"The what?" Jazz raised his eyebrows in confusion.

Just then, Brooks burst out of the water in hawk form with the devourer clinging to her back. She let out a piercing cry of triumph right before she blended into the inky sky.

"Never mind," I said to Jazz.

We sped away across the water, reaching airborne speeds, but it wasn't fast enough. Within two minutes, the hero twins were racing behind us. It was as if Fuego hadn't done any damage to Jordan at all. Electrical bolts flew at us like bullets.

I created a wall of smoke, obscuring their view.

"They saw me," I told Ren and Adrik, careful not to let Jazz overhear.

"Maybe they won't remember you later," Ren said.

"Maybe they will."

Adrik leaned in as the wind whipped all around. "They're too far away for me to steal a memory. You need to let them catch up."

"We'll get fried!" Ren said.

Rosie roared with the ferocity of five lions. She shook her head and flashed her fangs.

"How close do you need to be?" I asked Adrik.

"I have no idea," he said, shrugging. "Maybe fifteen, twenty feet?"

I waved my arms above my head, hoping Brooks was paying attention.

"What are you doing?" Ren shouted.

A few seconds later, Brooks landed on board. She was so well camouflaged against the night sky, I hadn't even seen her descend. The devourer slipped off the hawk's back, unconscious. Ren squatted and cradled the toadlike head in her lap.

Jazz glanced over his shoulder with wide eyes. "Great costume! That looks just like Jabba the Hutt!"

Brooks shifted back to human form and man, I wanted to hug her for being so brave. But there wasn't time. "Can you get Adrik and me close to the twins so he can do his thing?"

"Seriously?"

"We can't risk them remembering me in the future," I said, still trying to catch my breath. "Ren, you and Rosie keep Jazz on course for the beach. We'll meet you there."

With a sigh, Brooks turned around. Adrik and I gripped her shoulders, and she shifted into a hawk beneath our hands. She launched herself into the darkness with the two of us hunched over her back, trying to remain undetected by Jordan and Bird, whose focus was still on Jazz's boat.

We soared across the sky, keeping our eyes on the enemy below.

Brooks glided lower and lower. She was in serious stealth mode.

My heart rammed up my throat. We would have one shot at this—a single shot to save the future.

I watched as *Betty* broke through the waves, Jordan and Bird a mere fifty-ish yards behind.

"They're still too far away," Adrik said.

Brooks's wings flapped silently as we sailed closer and closer to the twins.

Just as Jazz's boat skidded onto the beach, I whisper-shouted, "Now!"

Adrik lifted a hand to blow a breath and lost his balance. As he began to slip off Brooks, he cried out. I grabbed him by the waistband of his drawstring pants, gripping it so hard I thought my wrist was going to snap. Adrik made a choking sound, which I could only assume meant I was giving him the worst wedgie of his life.

Jordan looked up. His eyes searched the sky and zeroed in on us.

White bolts came flying at us, some slamming into Brooks's ribs. She screeched and rotated too far to the left, nearly tossing me and Adrik.

Brooks! I yelled telepathically.

I'm okay, she said with a shaky voice. *Just hurry.*

I felt helpless. I couldn't put up a smoke screen because it would block Adrik's view, and I couldn't scorch or spear the evil jerks, either.

Then an idea occurred to me. Carefully, I created a thin stream of smoke and directed it toward the twins. It was enough to blind them, but not so wide it obscured Adrik's line of sight. We swept by, slowing down and getting so close I could reach out and touch the brothers. Adrik blew a breath across his palms.

The motor of their speedboat cut out. Jordan and Bird looked at each other and shook their heads like they were disoriented.

We did it! Adrik shouted telepathically as Brooks rocketed toward the shore, where the time rope awaited. A thrill wave washed over me. Had we really done it? Had we really traveled back in time and stolen the gods out from under the twins' noses?

You okay? I asked Brooks.

Just a little shocked, she said.

Ha, ha.

Right?

As soon as Brooks set us down on the sand, I saw Ren, Rosie, and the now-awake devourer. Ren came running over. "He's gone. Marco's gone."

45

••

—

"Gone?" Fire erupted across my knuckles. "How can he be gone?"

"We checked the bench!" Ren cried. "He's not there."

I was flooded with relief. "He moved," I said as Brooks changed into her human form. I was glad there were only a few loiterers on the beach, far away and not looking in our direction.

"He's buried!" Brooks shouted as she ran across the sand. "Over here."

We all followed as she made her way to Marco. His face still poked out of the sand, and his eyes were closed. When we approached, he opened them, and they went wide. With one mighty heave, he launched himself out of his makeshift grave. Then he danced around us, fists up. Thankfully, the time rope was still gripped in his hand.

"You can't have it!" he shouted with crazed eyes.

"What's the dude's deal?" Jazz asked.

The devourer studied Marco's face. Her scaly skin looked slick in the moonlight. "He's in shock," she said with a voice as soft as velvet. It wasn't the sound I expected from the Mexica goddess, who did kind of resemble Jabba the Hutt.

I wished she could expel the gods right then and there, but we had agreed that they should be released in the future they came from.

With her hands out in front of her, Ren approached Marco slowly, carefully. While Marco's attention was on Ren, Rosie came up from behind and began licking the back of his neck.

I thought Marco would scream or try to fight, but instead he collapsed to his knees. After a few seconds of catching his breath, he looked up at us with calmer eyes. "You guys took too long."

"Are you okay?" Brooks asked.

"Okay?" Marco repeated. "This stupid rope has a mind of its own and..." His gaze landed on Jazz. "Can we just go home?"

Jazz started to say something, when Adrik closed the distance.

"Wait!" Brooks said, stepping between them. She whispered to Adrik, "Can you let him keep one memory? Of when you told him about his future?"

Adrik shrugged. "I can try."

"Thanks for everything, Jazz," I told my future giant friend. "You're a real hero."

He beamed and stood three feet taller. "Will I see you guys again?"

"You can count on it," Brooks said with a knowing grin.

We all hooked arms. I kept one hand on Rosie. Adrik turned to Jazz, blew a breath toward the boy, and said, "Remember the demon-burning flashlight, Mr. Inventor."

And just as his words landed, the rope tugged us back to the present.

We stepped into the Old World, keeping a strong hold on one another. Sharp branches stabbed at our arms, necks, and faces as we weaved through a tight path toward the place where we had left Hondo.

He wasn't alone.

The Sparkstriker stood over his slumped form.

"Hurry!" the Sparkstriker said. That's when I saw she was carrying Itzamna's sunglasses.

Hondo, shivering and moaning, still held tight to the thread. I rushed over and jerked it out of his hands. The rope burned my palm as I tossed it away. It ricocheted off the metallic trees with a loud snap and burned itself into the sand.

"Hondo!" I pried off the warrior mask, and it turned to ash. Beneath it was the face of an old man—wrinkled and hollow, sunken and sickly. His eyes stared off into space like his mind was gone.

Everything inside me turned to mush.

Brooks was instantly at my side. Rosie was right behind her, and she immediately began licking Hondo, trying to heal him. But he stayed the same zoned-out old man.

"Why isn't it working?" I choked out.

Panic dug its stupid claws into me as Ren ran up. Waves of fear and pity washed over her face as she stooped in front of Hondo and gripped his hand. Tears sprang to her eyes. "Come back to us," she whispered.

"I waited here with him," the Sparkstriker said, "to make sure he didn't let go."

"He'd never let go," Brooks whispered, wiping her eyes with both hands.

The Sparkstriker said, "We've run out of time. I talked to Itzamna." She held up his glasses. "The enemy has landed in SHIHOM."

Gasps rose up around me, followed by *"How?" "When?" "No!"*

Marco said, "How 'bout the devourer gives us back the gods before we go storming SHIHOM?"

The goddess was hunched over, gripping her stomach like she was going to hurl.

"I'm trying," she moaned. "It's not working."

"Maybe it's like having a baby," Ren said, "and you just have to let it happen on its own time."

Adrik's mouth fell open. "Please say that was just a joke."

"We must get to SHIHOM *now!*" the Sparkstriker yelled. She dashed toward a metallic tree and slammed her ax into it. The reverberation rang so hard my spine and skull trembled. Itzamna's glasses dropped from her grasp.

"What are you doing?" I shouted.

"Summoning my warriors," the Sparkstriker said.

As if once wasn't enough, she banged her ax against another tree and another until I was sure all my bones were shattered and the world had broken into a million tiny pieces.

I tugged Hondo into a protective hug as the trees vibrated violently. The Old World became a colossal blur as brutal winds raged against us.

The ground quaked. My friends clung to me. The warriors arrived, their capes fluttering. Rosie howled fire. Waves of flame rolled across the sky, making it burn red.

Yeah, it pretty much felt like the apocalypse. But I didn't yet know how bad the apocalypse could look.

46

After a dizzying few minutes, we found ourselves inside a tree house. Everyone had made it except the Sparkstriker's warriors—I guessed she had sent them somewhere on the ground.

It was daytime, but the air was thick with ash and the smell of smoke. Gray light spilled into the large room where we stood. A thin white trunk poked up through the floor and extended all the way through an opening in the ceiling. Above us, plump green leaves drooped from bowing branches. The space was decked floor to ceiling with books and furnished with modern sofas and chrome tables.

Before I could ask where we were exactly, the Sparkstriker said, "This is Hurakan's place. Hidden from any eyes below. We will be safe here."

"Safe?" The word came out in a long shuddering breath as I laid down my uncle on one of the couches. I didn't think we would ever be *safe* again.

"No such thing as safe," Marco muttered, looking around.

"Gods have tree houses?" Adrik asked.

A lump formed in my throat. "Hurakan?" My eyes landed on the open book set facedown on the coffee table: *The Book of Questions* by Pablo Neruda. I thought two things: *My dad reads?* And: *He has questions?*

That didn't exactly inspire confidence.

I glanced at the devourer goddess asleep on the rug. "What's she waiting for?"

"I bet it takes a lot of time and energy to throw up that many people," Adrik said.

"She's not going to vomit them." Marco's expression twisted into one of disgust. "Is she?"

The Sparkstriker said, "I don't know how one releases a bunch of gods stuck inside. They didn't cover that in my training." Her eyes diverted to Hondo. "And I've never seen anyone in his condition, either."

"But my uncle's going to be okay, right?" I asked, by which I meant *not old*. And *not dead*.

"We just have to wait and see," the Sparkstriker said like we were waiting for a stupid steak to thaw.

Brooks muttered something under her breath as she went over and parted the window curtains. "Guys?" she choked out.

My gaze trailed beyond the drapes and the glass entryway, past the huge balcony. Gray ash clung to hundreds of blackened trees. Pillars of smoke rose into the sky.

"Ohmigod!" Ren breathed.

In that moment, I swear it felt like the Earth's atmosphere had been sucked into space.

"They're burning the jungle to the ground," Marco growled.

The Sparkstriker cursed a few times under her breath. "We need the gods *now!*"

Ren glanced over her shoulder at the devourer. "We have to help her release them."

Rosie, who was standing protectively next to Hondo, groaned. She turned and gently pawed the toadish-looking monster, but the devourer didn't respond.

"The World Tree!" I blurted. It wasn't a question, but everyone seemed to get my meaning: *Is it still standing?*

The Sparkstriker rushed onto the circular balcony outside. We followed, careful to avoid the wide hole where leafy vines and branches reached up through a thick layer of mist.

The Sparkstriker tapped her ax along a vine that was growing across the deck. At once, the World Tree came into view at the far end of the jungle. Its bark was scorched, and its leaves had withered or fallen off. The lights on its trunk flickered so faintly my heart stopped.

Brooks sucked in a gulp of air. Ren cried out, "It's dying!"

Fire raced through me, pulsing hot in the center of my chest, spreading down my arms and out my fingertips. A strange thrumming began in my ears like a distant drumbeat. And then there was a terrible primal cry like nothing I had ever heard.

The bells in the Sparkstriker's hair rang. She gasped, then removed Itzamna's broken shades from her pocket.

"What's wrong?" I asked.

She set the glasses on the deck and tapped them with her ax. An image immediately formed before us like a hologram.

It was the Red Temple. A huge bonfire blazed in front of it. Dozens of demons were carrying books and scrolls out of the library and throwing them onto the burning heap. Bits of ash floated into the air, but strangely, there was no smoke.

Then I saw Itzamna. He was in dragon form, but this time no bigger than a cat. He flew above the fire, flapping what looked like injured wings as he dashed into the flames and tugged out a libro with his mouth. But it was too late. The book was smoldering.

He was circling very low. *Get out of there!* I thought. And just as he came in for another pass, a lurking demon plucked him out of the air.

"No!" I shouted as the image vanished.

The Sparkstriker snarled, revealing some very yellow teeth. "We must act quickly."

"They're trying to erase history," Ren said shakily. "Like they did with my mom—like..." Her voice trailed off, or maybe we just got distracted by the brilliant light that suddenly illuminated the balcony.

I spun to see the devourer standing in the tree house doorway. She was on her knees with her head thrown back. A thick shaft of white light flooded from her mouth. It stretched into the sky and broke into dozens of glowing pieces, falling back to the earth like shooting stars.

"The gods!" Ren shouted.

Could it be? I watched in awe as the comet-like shapes zipped into the charred jungle. A couple of them hit our deck, bounced off the wood, and fell down the hole. Two landed on the deck itself.

"We're saved!" Adrik threw his arms into the air dramatically.

The bells in the Sparkstriker's hair began to ring like crazy. "No!" she cried.

"You mean yes!" Adrik said with an unsure grin.

Everything was happening so fast, I didn't know if I should be focused on the blobs of light or the Sparkstriker's *no*. She slammed her ax into a vine, causing it to instantly twist around other vines and form a small platform. She stepped onto it and vanished into thin air.

Rosie let out a mournful wail, and when I whipped around to face her, her eyes burned with red flames. Then she too disappeared in a curtain of mist. "Rosie!"

"Uh, Zane," Brooks said, bent over the two shapes that had landed on the deck. "You're going to want to check this out."

"I think this hole is some kind of portal," Marco said, peering into it.

While Ren cooed encouragingly at the devourer, I joined Brooks. Adrik and Marco followed. There were two sprawled figures—one male, one female. Their eyes were closed, but thank the saints, they were breathing.

We all stared at them in shock. Not because they had survived being devoured or had dropped out of the sky as balls of light. Nope.

"They don't look like gods," Marco said, tilting his head to the side like he was studying pinned cockroaches. "More like your average twelve-year-old."

"Did we get duped?" Adrik asked.

I turned to the devourer, who was still on her knees. Ren was rubbing her back.

"These aren't the gods," I growled.

With claws firmly planted on the deck, the devourer took long deep breaths. "Th-they are," she sputtered.

My head pounded. "Why are they—"

"Not adults?" Adrik finished.

"Dude," Marco said, "I don't care how old they are. They need to wake up now!"

Ren touched the devourer's shoulder and said, "That's right, just breathe. It must've been hard to carry so many gods. That was a lot of power to hold inside!"

The goddess forced herself to rise to her full height, which was only about five feet. "I don't know why they are children," she said weakly. "A side effect of time travel, perhaps?"

"Well, fix them!" I shouted. We needed their full strength if we wanted to save Itzamna and oust Ixkik' and Zotz.

"If the gods are back," Brooks asked, staring into the distance, "why isn't the Tree lit up?"

We all looked over and froze. Except the devourer, who grimaced and clutched her stomach.

"Maybe because they're knocked out?" Marco held his chin, pressing a thumb into his scar.

Ren came over and gently shook the unconscious gods, but nothing happened.

"I bet that's why the Sparkstriker left so fast," Brooks said.

Marco nodded like he'd had the same idea but sooner. "She was afraid Zotz and Ixkik' saw that little light show."

"And now they know the gods are alive," Adrik said.

"Which means the element of surprise went kaboom." Marco made an explosion gesture with his hands.

Ren looked panicked. "Guys!" she cried. "If the gods are all asleep out there in the jungle, they're sitting ducks."

Hurakan!

"We have to find them," I said, gripping Fuego. "*All* of them."

Brooks walked over to the devourer, looming several inches over her. "Are you the devourer and giver of life," she said to the goddess. But there was no inflection, no question mark. She wasn't asking—she was telling. Or reminding. But where was she going with this?

The goddess nodded slowly.

"And you said you were tricked," Brooks said.

Another nod.

"Then prove you're on our side, be the giver of life, and *undo* the damage you've done."

The devourer's eyes were black and sunken. "The water..." she said. "I am an earth goddess. I don't like the water—it weakens me. I...I need my powers...."

"To do what?" Marco said. "Devour all of us?" His eyes drilled into mine. "What if this is a trick?"

The devourer sucked in a sharp breath and collapsed to her knees. Adrik reached out and broke her fall. "Dude, is she going to die on us?"

Terror filled every inch of me, and for some reason, Ixtab popped into my head. I hoped Rosie had taken off to find her. It wouldn't matter what the goddess looked like, either—my hellhound would know her in any form. Yeah, Rosie needed to track down the goddess and wake her up, because if anyone is awesome in *the-world-is-ending* mode, it's Ixtab.

"We can't just stand around here," Brooks cried. "I'll fly down there and find some of the more useful gods—"

"What if they're like these guys?" Adrik cut in, gesturing to the sleepers. "And what if they won't wake up?"

"What if you get caught?" Marco paced the deck, teetering too close to the edge of the hole.

Ren nodded. "I can use shadows to keep us hidden, Brooks."

"Hang on," I said. "I'm going, too."

"Me four," Marco added.

Brooks said to Marco, "I'll be faster if I'm only carrying Ren." Then to me, "You need to stay with Hondo."

A terrible battle raged inside me. Deep down, I knew I shouldn't leave Hondo alone when he was in such bad shape. But I also knew I needed to help find the gods.

"Zane," Brooks said, grabbing my arm, "Ren and I can do this."

"Just get Hondo back into fighting shape," Ren said, clearing her throat like that might hide the catch in her voice.

They were right. I couldn't leave my uncle. Not now.

"Just don't take any chances," I said. "Ixkik' and Zotz will know who freed the gods—they'll be waiting."

"We got this," Ren said, creating a shadow around her and Brooks. The sombra was so thick I couldn't see either of them, only a dark form that departed with a rush of air.

We hurried past the devourer to Hondo, who was still on the couch. His breaths were raspy and short. I felt like I had walked into the worst day of my life complete with dead ends, wasted chances, and lives hanging in the balance.

"Let me help," the devourer said, shuffling over. "I believe I can restore him."

"You just told us you're too weak," I argued.

"We can all do it together. The blood of the gods runs through your veins," she said to Adrik, Marco, and me. "That blood is power."

"You're not getting any of *my* blood," Adrik said, shaking his head and stepping away. "Nope."

"Not blood," she corrected. *"Power."*

Marco backed up, too. "Nuh-uh. No way. Not falling for it."

I glanced at my uncle. He was still—too still. "Hondo's going to die," I growled at Marco. "So unless you have a better idea . . ."

Adrik looked around nervously, wringing his hands like he wasn't sure what to do. "As long as it doesn't involve actual bleeding, I'll help," he finally said. "But maybe you should point Fuego at her throat just in case."

"I like the way you think," Marco said to Adrik. "Okay, I'll pitch in, too," he told me. "And if I do end up dying, at least I'll die a kick-butt hero, right?"

Unless Jordan and Bird tell your story, I thought, remembering their lies about Ah-Puch and Sipacna.

"No one's going to die," I said, wishing I could keep that promise.

We took Hondo out to the deck, mostly because I wasn't super confident that our godborn power experiment wouldn't accidentally start a fire and burn down my dad's tree house.

I turned Fuego into a tattoo. Then Marco, Adrik, and I

piled our hands on top of one another's like we were about to start a football cheer. "Call everything you've got to the surface," I told them. "All of it."

The devourer took a deep breath and stretched her small scaly arms out in front of her. A leafy vine crawled up her leg and torso and began wrapping around her wrist.

"What's the vine for?" Marco asked suspiciously.

The devourer said, "Earth magic. Combined with godborn power, it will heal me, and then I can heal him." She gestured toward Hondo, stretched out on the deck.

A little hesitantly, still not sure we could trust her and repulsed by her yellow-green crocodile hide, we placed our hands on the goddess. I focused on the fire that lived and breathed inside me, and I knew my friends were concentrating, too, because our fingers started to tremble. A couple of seconds later, our skin glowed a pinkish red, like someone was pressing a flashlight against our palms.

Heat pulsed in my veins.

An electrical energy buzzed through me and zipped out of my fingertips right into the goddess's body. A wicked wind rushed the deck, swirling all around us. The vine on the devourer's wrist glowed with a pale green light as it wound up her arm and around her throat. She let out a blood-curdling scream, threw her head back, and released a dark shadow from her mouth.

"What is *that*?" Adrik stumbled backward.

The form rose up, its wings spread wide. I gasped.

It was the bat god.

47

••
••

All I could think was *NO! We did NOT just use our powers to release our enemy!*

But hang on—it gets weirder. Or maybe more awful, depending on whether you're a glass-half-empty person or a glass-half-full person.

Like the other gods, Zotz was not in his usual form. He was a teenager. As his eyes settled on me, confusion swept across his young face and he tugged his shivering black wings close to his thin body. I kind of felt sorry for the guy, this weak and puny version of our once-formidable foe.

"Ixkik'," he snarled. "Trap—" With that, he collapsed next to the other zonked-out gods.

Willing Fuego into my grasp, I inched closer for a better look. Yep. He was out for the count. At least for now.

The full weight of Ah-Puch's words hit me in that moment: *Camazotz is a natural-born killer. He is cunning and smart, but he's not this smart. He's working with someone.*

Zotz had been duped by Ixkik'!

Marco nodded as Adrik's mouth fell open. "Is . . . is that . . . ?"

"Adrik, meet the mighty bat god." Marco's voice was filled with hate. "How about we roll him off the deck? Or skewer him with your spear."

I gave Marco a *don't-even-think-about-it* glare. We would need to interrogate Zotz about Ixkik' as soon as he woke up. I turned to the devourer to ask what the holy Xib'alb'a had just happened, but the words got stuck in my throat. The goddess was bent over Hondo, and she was no longer in the form of Jabba's twin. She was an older lady with white-streaked dark hair that hung down her small back. Placing her gnarled hands on my uncle's shoulders, she chanted some words I didn't recognize. A white aura surrounded Hondo, flecks of sparkling dust floating in the light.

I held my breath.

Please work. Please. Please.

We heard a moan and hurried over. At first, the aura was so bright I couldn't see if he was still the dried-up wrinkled dude. Gradually the glow faded and I saw . . .

Hondo was Hondo!

Relief flooded every cell in my body.

My uncle shifted, struggled to open his eyes.

"I have fulfilled my debt," the toad/monster/goddess said. The leafy vine she was wearing expanded and twisted around her until she looked like a shrub. In an instant, the leaves blew up, leaving nothing behind except dust.

"Whoa!" Adrik said.

Hondo's eyes flew open the second the last bit of dust settled.

"Are you okay?" I asked. My voice came out way more panicked than I wanted it to.

He grabbed his side, wincing as I helped him to his feet. "I saw awful things, Zane. Dark and terrible."

I pulled him into a hug, and he muttered incoherently. Had the shadows stolen his mind?

He jerked free, keeping a tight grip on my shoulder. "The shadows hold the secrets, Zane. I saw everything. I saw Blood Moon's plot. She tricked them all—even the devourer and Zotz!"

"I know," I said, searching his eyes.

He stepped back, took some deep breaths, and ran a hand over his face.

Marco nodded appreciatively. "We made it back from 1987 because of you," he said.

"Yeah, man," Adrik said. "Thanks. That was some seriously brave (*bleep*) right there."

Hondo looked around. "Where the hell are we?"

We quickly explained as Marco kept an eye on the sleeping forms of Zotz and the other two mystery gods. Hondo collapsed back onto the deck, folded himself over his knees, and took another deep breath. "I could really use some Flamin' Hot Cheetos," he whispered. "With salsa." His eyes flicked to the bat god. "Why would Ixkik' turn on *him*?"

Marco's eyes narrowed. "To make way for her rotten sons." He said it with so much assurance, I knew he was right.

"She wants to make Jordan king," Hondo said.

"King of what?" Adrik asked.

"The sobrenaturals," I said, but something didn't add up. Ixkik' wouldn't go to all this trouble just to crown one of her brats. "She has to be up to something else—something bigger."

Hondo's eyes darkened. "Whatever it is, we have to stop her."

48

"Are you sure you're strong enough to do this?"
I asked Hondo as we prepared to go down to the half-burned
jungle.

"We have to strike now," he said. "We might not get a
second chance."

"Uh, guys?" Adrik said, gesturing to Zotz and the other
two unconscious gods. "Someone needs to keep an eye on the
baddie, right?"

"I am not hanging out here alone with that dude!" Marco
argued.

"You'd rather go up against the creepy goddess?" Adrik
asked.

Just then, the branches beneath the deck trembled. A low
growl climbed up the trunk. I'd know that growl anywhere.
I peered into the hole.

"Rosie?"

A paw emerged from the mist followed by the rest of my
hellhound. Forget using a ladder—she had clawed her way
up the tree like a powerful jaguar with Ren and a fifteen-ish
Pacific on her back. I knew it was the time goddess, because
who else wears leopard-spotted capes and carries a golden
time rope, which, by the way, was trailing behind my dog.

"Ren!" Adrik hollered.

"Rosie can wake the gods!" Ren cried out as soon as she saw us. "Isn't that awesome?"

"*Freaking* awesome!" Hondo said, kissing the tips of his fingers and throwing them toward the sky.

My heart hammered in my chest to the rhythm of a single word: *hope-hope, hope-hope.* If Rosie could wake the gods, it would be like a couple hundred to one. They could pummel Ixkik'!

When the trio had fully emerged from the hole, Ren's gaze landed on my uncle and she grinned so wide I thought it might split her face. "Hondo!" She leaped into his arms. "I knew you'd be okay." He hugged her, spinning her off her feet. Even Pacific smiled.

I rubbed Rosie's neck. Her soft brown eyes held mine like she already knew what I was going to ask of her. She needed to rouse more gods.

Find as many as you can, I told her telepathically. *Find Hurakan ... and Ixtab.*

With a barely perceptible nod, she vanished in a stream of mist.

"Does this mean we're saved?" Adrik said.

Pacific tugged on her hood and sighed. "We have no powers ... yet."

We? I wondered who else was awake.

"What do you mean, 'no powers'?" I squeezed the dragon head of my cane.

Marco groaned as he pressed his knuckles into his eyes. Yeah, I knew the feeling—the highs and lows of Maya madness. The forever dangling carrot, promising a treasure but delivering a sucker punch to the gut.

"Well, that sucks," Adrik said.

"It doesn't matter," I insisted. "We have to go down there. We have to—" I suddenly realized that Ren hadn't returned with Brooks. "Where's Brooks?" I asked, hoping the hawk would appear any second.

"She's scoping out some stuff," Ren said. "When we found Pacific, Brooks and I decided I needed to get her back here safely."

"You left Brooks alone?!" I didn't mean for my voice to rise to over-the-top freak-out, but this was Blood Moon we were dealing with, the same one who had Quinn. That fact might have impaired Brooks's judgment. Brooks was the world's best planner until her heart got involved.

"I have to find her." I rushed to the deck's hole, careful not to touch the time rope that was still hanging over the edge.

Pacific took my arm gently, stopping me. "The nawal promised to be careful. Let the hawk hunt, Zane."

Hunt? Hunt what? Ixkik'? Demons? Jordan and Bird? It felt like acid was burning a hole in my stomach. I looked down through the deck's opening . . . and saw the time rope quiver.

Ren gasped. "I almost forgot!" She brushed past me, dropped to her knees, and leaned over the opening, pulling on the rope. "You still down there, A.P.? You need help?"

"I'm a god," he grunted.

"Ah-Puch is here?!" I nearly blew flames out of my nostrils.

"Okay, maybe a little tug," the god said.

"You made the dude climb?" Marco shook his head like it was the world's greatest tragedy.

"Is there any other way to get up a tree?" the god of death grumbled from below.

Pacific yanked the rope, and a second later, Ah-Puch's hands emerged through the hole. They were followed by a familiar head of dark hair . . . but a not-so-familiar face. He clung to the edge.

I grabbed his skinny hand and hauled him up as the time rope unwound from his waist, snapping into Pacific's grasp. "I think the branches would have held you," I said.

"Now you tell me."

Even if Ren hadn't outed Ah-Puch, I would have known it was him. The fourteen-year-old-looking dude had the same dark suit (now a few sizes too big), the same arrogant stance, and the same *I'm-better-than-you* expression. Except now it was grim and tight. And instead of a *Thank you for traveling back in time and risking your lives to save us,* he said, "That was truly dreadful." I had some words for the god of death about how he had given up back in the labyrinth, but now wasn't the time.

His dark eyes fell on Zotz, and for the second time I quickly explained everything that had happened.

Ren's mouth formed a small O like she wasn't at all surprised by Blood Moon's deceit.

Ah-Puch looked at the sacked-out gods and snorted.

"Do you know who they are?" I asked.

"Other than the bat loser?" he said with a snarl. "I think that's Ixkakaw, and the other one? Some minor god."

"Louie will be happy," Adrik said, then added, "The goddess of chocolate survived the trip."

"This is terrible," Pacific said, tightening her grip on the rope.

"Terrible is right." Ah-Puch shook his head somberly. "First, I am a glorious death god, then a withered old man, and now *this*? What has the universe come to?"

"Probs destruction," Adrik muttered.

"Guys," Marco said, gesturing toward the World Tree, "shouldn't we figure out our next play before the whole place goes up in smoke?"

"We need to crush Ixkik'," Ah-Puch said. He waggled his thick eyebrows and added, "But *I* get dibs on the twins!"

Was that a zit on his chin?

Hondo harrumphed like the god of death was going to have to arm-wrestle him for the honors.

"No offense," Marco said, "but you're probably not going to crush anyone without your godly powers."

Ah-Puch looked like he might lunge for the guy's throat, but Ren patted his arm and he stood down.

She said, "The gods still have brilliant minds. They can help us strategize."

"This is why you're my favorite," Ah-Puch said with a smile. "But I'd rather kill."

Ren gave him a hard stare.

"They totally deserve it," the god of death said defensively.

Pacific began to pace. "We will not win in open battle."

I considered what moves we had left. I knew my friends would fight even if it meant losing, and I couldn't let that happen. "Ixkik' already knows we're here," I said.

"So what do you do when your enemy is waiting for you to make the next move?" Adrik asked.

Marco dragged a thumb over his jaw. "You make it."

The sky darkened and the air trembled.

Everyone froze.

At the same moment, a familiar voice twisted up through the clouds, gentle and quiet like a slithering snake. "Welcome back to SHIHOM, Zane," Ixkik' said. "Did you really think you could hide from me?"

"We were hoping," Adrik mumbled.

"My son Xb'alamkej is now king over all magic, over all the sobrenaturales," Ixkik' went on. "And he has a new queen." She laughed lightly. "Finally, the mighty nawal is his bride, as it was always meant to be."

Always meant to be? Just because some really bad matchmaker once put Jordan and Quinn together? Didn't he remember that she joined a spy network just to get away from him?

Hondo sucked in a sharp breath. He looked like he might punch a second hole in the deck, but he just shook his head and whispered, "She's lying."

Ren patted his shoulder as my eyes darted around, searching for the source of the voice that seemed to be coming from all sides.

"We will have a new reign," Ixkik' went on. "A new era in

which the ruthless gods will exist no more. You may choose to run or hide, but we *will* find you. Or you can meet my terms, and no one has to die."

Everyone looked stricken. My throat closed up, making it hard to breathe. "We'll never hide!" I shouted.

"She cannot hear you," Pacific said. "Not here."

Ah-Puch was uncharacteristically quiet as Ixkik' released a purring laugh that sent chills down my legs. "You may have freed the gods, but they are still asleep. And my demons are hunting them down at this very moment and awaiting my signal to destroy them. So it looks like I am the victor."

All I could think about was my dad, helpless at the murderous claws of some random demon.

"You're a coward!" Hondo yelled with so much ferocity I thought, *She must have heard that.*

My chest blazed hotter than Chak Ek' and I had a terrible urge to barbecue the cruel goddess, but I couldn't let emotion rule my mind. That was exactly what she wanted. What she was counting on.

Ah-Puch grinned, and before I could ask what he *possibly* had to smile about, he said, "She doesn't know *some* of the gods are already awake."

"How do you know?" My chest felt like it was collapsing under the weight of a hundred skies.

"She speaks with too much confidence," Ah-Puch said.

Okay, so as bad as things were, we had at least one tiny element of surprise. But what good would it do us? Pacific and Ah-Puch were as young as the godborns but with no powers.

The rest of the gods were asleep, the demons were hunting them down, and the World Tree was dying.

"So you choose silence," Ixkik' said. "It does not matter, because I know you can hear me. Now heed this: I want you, Zane Obispo, alone at the Tree."

49

"And there it is," Marco muttered. "There's the next move."

"But why does she want you so bad?" Adrik asked me.

"To finish what we started at the Pyramid of the Magician," I said. She wanted to make good on her promise: *Someday, when you least expect it, you'll pay with your blood for this. My sons will show no mercy. Nor will I.*

I turned to Pacific. "Is there a way I can talk to her . . . from here?"

Pacific opened her mouth, probably to tell me no, when a look of revelation swept across her face. "The vines," she said. "The entire jungle is one organism. Each stone, tree, and animal is linked. Touch one of the vines and speak. Wherever she is, she will hear you."

I squatted, placing my hand on a nearby vine. "If I come," I said, "then I get something, too."

There was a long and painful silence. Finally the voice said, "I don't strike deals."

"Then I won't show," I bluffed, my stomach twisting into a million tiny knots. And before she could respond, I added, "We both want something."

Ah-Puch snorted and said, "Aren't you glad you have

experience with this sort of thing from negotiating with me for your life?" His eyes swiveled to the others. "I taught him everything he knows."

"What are your terms, godborn?" Ixkik' said.

"No way," Hondo said, clenching his jaw. "If you go, Zane, she'll kill you."

Marco shook his head. "She's definitely baiting him for something bigger than death."

"What's bigger than death?" Adrik asked, shuddering a little too dramatically.

"That kid is right," Ah-Puch said, pointing to Marco.

"The name's Marco," the son of war said, trying to get Ah-Puch's attention.

But the god of death ignored him. "Ixkik' is playing games. She wants Zane for more than a quick—or even a slow—kill."

"Slow?" Ren's eyes went wide with terror.

I thought about my terms, knowing that if I asked for too much, I could blow the whole deal. She would never let the gods go, but maybe...

"My terms are that you don't kill the gods," I told the goddess. I was about to demand that she let my friends go, too, but I didn't want to give away the fact that they were here.

"The rest of us could bolt," Adrik said. "Go back to Montana."

I took my hand off the vine and said, "Nowhere is safe. Besides, we can't just leave the gods and Brooks and—"

"Quinn," Hondo put in.

Man, I felt for the guy. If Quinn really *had* been married off, there was nothing he or any of us could do to change it. Brooks had once told me that, in the sobrenatural world, arranged marriages meant forever, like, *your-souls-are-bound-together* kind of stuff. So why would Quinn agree to it?

"We need to find as many of the gods as we can," Ren said. "Bring them here and then regroup. Figure out what to do next."

I loved Ren for trying to come up with a nonviolent plan, but deep down I knew I had to take down Ixkik'. And the only way to do that was to face her.

Ixkik' spoke softly, but her words were biting. "You must come and negotiate with me in person."

Ren shoved me aside and placed her hand on the vine. "So you can kill him?"

"Ah," Ixkik' said. "I see you brought your godborn friends. Well, don't count on their help. I want you and you alone."

I didn't even have to throw a glare Ren's way. I could tell by her expression she realized her mistake. "I'm sorry," she whispered, releasing the vine like it had burned her palm.

"Listen well, Zane," Ixkik' said. "I know how fast you can move when you want to. So I will give you ten minutes to reach the Tree. For every minute you are late, I will kill a god."

"Wait," I told Ixkik'. "I—"

Marco cut me off. "There has to be a way to trick her. Let her think she's won and then—"

"We go in for the kill," Ah-Puch interjected.

At the same moment, Adrik cried, "Look!" He inched back, his face drained of all color.

Our gazes followed his trembling finger to the World Tree in the distance.

Two god lights on the trunk sputtered haphazardly before winking out.

"NO!" I screamed. What if one of those lights had belonged to Hurakan?

A grunt of shock flew from Pacific's mouth.

"I just want to make sure you understand what's at stake," Ixkik' said. "To ensure you do not question my intentions and power. Don't try to run away, and don't resort to any tricks. Any plan you think you have is a foolish one, I can assure you."

"I understand," I said, the words choking my windpipe. "Just let me . . . let me think for a minute."

"If she wants you this bad"—Ah-Puch paced the deck—"it means you are of great value to her. There is still a part of her plot that hasn't been completed, and it won't be until—"

"She has Zane," Pacific added.

"You're the ace in the hole," Marco said like I had won some kind of trophy.

"Rosie and Brooks will find the gods," Hondo suggested. "And we can . . . we can split up. We can look, too."

"Even if we could," Ah-Puch said, rubbing his chin, "we wouldn't be able to reach them all in time. Demons are excellent hunters."

"We have to try!" Ren cried.

This wasn't happening.

This. Was. Not. Happening.

I felt like my legs had been swept out from under me. I took my hand off the vine. "I have to go to her," I said. Because what choice did I have?

But then I remembered how her mist had extinguished my fire skills at the Pyramid of the Magician, how it had held Brooks in place. How could I go up against a goddess with that kind of power? A goddess I had never even seen in the flesh.

"And then?" Adrik asked, rubbing his forehead anxiously.

I didn't have an *and then*. I didn't have anything but my determination to keep the gods and my friends alive, and right now the clock was winding down on both.

"Look," I said, "we didn't go all the way to 1987 to give up now."

Ren gripped my hand and squeezed. "Zane, no. There has to be another way."

"There is none," Marco said. "Blood Moon knows she's calling the plays."

Ixkik' added, "I have eyes everywhere, and I will know if you are not alone. And if you betray me? More gods will die. The choice is yours. Are you ready?"

"She is a vile creature," Pacific said, white-knuckling her rope.

"Can't you just stop time?" Adrik asked the goddess.

"I already tried," Pacific said. "It's tied to my power, which isn't working."

Ah-Puch stroked his chin, avoiding the zit. I knew that look. He was plotting, and when the god of death plots, it definitely means *Run for your life*. "Let us do ground control, Zane," he said. "We'll find as many gods as we can and bring them back here."

"But the demons," I said. "You have no power to go up against them."

A looming clawlike shadow grew above Ren's head. "We have our godborn powers, Zane."

I grabbed the vine again and said, "I'm ready."

"Because I am fair and just," Ixkik' continued, "I will start a clock to time your journey."

A loud sound filled the forest, grating on the last of my nerves.

Tick. Tick. Tick.

Marco gripped my shoulder. "There's no more time to huddle, Zane, so...so...uh, call a great play when you get there."

"Right." *He means well*, I thought. *But he's about as useful as a single chopstick.*

"We'll find as many gods as we can," Pacific said, tugging up her hood.

"Remember," Ah-Puch said, "Ixkik' doesn't want to kill you. Well, at least not yet. So try to learn all you can about her plan, why she wants *you* so bad."

"Okay, but when you find the gods," I said, "promise me you'll get them out of here."

Look, I didn't have some sudden affection for the gods (at least most of them), but there is an order and a balance to the universe and they're part of it whether I like it or not.

"We won't let you down," Ren said as I stepped into the hole, hugging the trunk.

"Zane," Hondo said. Our eyes met. "Be careful out there."

Nodding, I stepped onto a platform below and summoned my cane. The platform unfolded into a kind of moving escalator, and a cool mist wrapped its arms around me. Someone seemed to be rolling out the red carpet for me. With Fuego's help, I ran down the steps and burst into the jungle.

At the same moment, a brilliant golden light flashed above.

It was so sudden I shrank back, shielding my eyes.

But just as quickly, the light vanished.

I kept heading for the Tree.

50

••
══

Tick. Tick. Tick.

The sound was even louder on the ground. I picked up my pace, weaving between the foliage. A rustling sound drew my attention upward. A few miniature monkeys crisscrossed the trees. I felt their eyes following my every move as they swept across the branches like ghosts.

"Thanks a lot," I grumbled. "Everything is getting ready to blow up and you're still looking for something to steal. . . ." My words trailed off as I realized I was chewing out a bunch of primates that had just lost half their home.

I rushed through the jungle, letting the fire inside me guide me to the World Tree. What was I was going to find there? More dead gods? A goddess I wouldn't even recognize? A death trap? All I knew was that I had to buy my friends enough time to find as many of the gods as possible. But somehow even that plan felt like a defeat.

Tick.

Terror settled into my gut.

Tick. Tick.

Sombras pressed in on me from all sides.

Tick. Tick. Tick.

I came to the edge of the field and stopped, taking a few deep breaths. My eyes skimmed the silent meadow and landed on the World Tree.

The árbol was a contorted black monster with thick shiny webs choking its branches. Its god lights barely flickered.

I tried to keep a firm grip on my cane, but my palms were slick. Then came the familiar cold tug in my gut that made me nauseous. Two tall figures emerged from the tree line on my right, about twenty yards away.

Jordan and Bird.

And all I could think was *These guys again?*

They weren't in their hairy bat guises. They were in their six-foot-five, athletic human forms, muscles bulging under their identical black tracksuits. But they didn't impress me. I preferred monsters who looked like monsters.

"Zane Obispo," Bird said, dragging a thick rusted chain. *Clink. Clank.*

My eyes followed the shackle until I saw...it was connected to a dragon's throat.

Itzamna!

My heart slammed into my spine. "Let him go!"

The dragon was cat-size and pale gray, his withered skin nearly translucent. His eyes were hollow, his cheeks gaunt, and his mouth sagged as he lumbered behind the twins with his head hanging low.

"But he makes such a good pet," Bird said with a sneer.

My anger pulsed hotter than lava, and I wanted to launch a million rivers of fire at these jerks. But I had to stay cool. I had to find out what Ixkik' had planned.

Half a dozen blue-skinned demons emerged from the trees behind the twins, their reptilian eyes unblinking as they all drilled their gazes into me.

Instinctively, a ball of fire ignited in the palm of my hand.

Jordan snorted, but he stopped a good fifteen feet away from me. I could see dark circles under his eyes. Was he sick and tired of being manipulated by his mother? "Relax," he said. "No need for pyrotechnics."

"Unless you want more gods to die," Bird said.

"Oh, I get it," I said, still feeling waves of acid in my gut. "Ixkik' sent you to do her dirty work. Too scared to come out herself?"

Itzamna lifted his gaze. He blinked slowly as he sent out his weak telepathic voice across the field. *Zane, it's over. Run. Save yourself.*

"Shut up, old man," Bird said to the dragon, jerking the chain. Jordan and Bird cut up like they had missed their favorite brand of entertainment: cruel and twisted.

"Leave him alone!" I shouted.

A sudden movement caught my attention. I glanced at the Tree to see a sliver of mist wind up the massive trunk like a snake.

Ixkik'.

"Sorry you couldn't make it to the wedding," Jordan said, adjusting the collar of his jacket.

"You mean the one where you forced Quinn to marry you?" I said, trying to keep my anger in check.

Jordan laughed. "Forced? No one *forced* her to do anything."

Bird said, "We gave Quinn a choice. She chose to be queen.

Much better than being a lowly nawal spy working for some has-been Sparkstriker who's going to be dead anyway."

So the Sparkstriker wasn't dead yet. See? That's what happens when you let your enemy do all the talking. They throw you nibbles of information that eventually add up to a whole meal.

"Pretty sure Quinn would never choose you," I said. "She ran away before, remember?"

Jordan's face hardened, and he began to lunge at me. Bird threw up an arm to block his brother. "We should try to get along," he said to Jordan. Then he cast his gaze on me. "Considering our mother's plan for you."

Get along?

I hated these guys. I thought about all the lies they had told, all the stories they had rewritten, and wondered how many other falsehoods had been tucked into the corners of history without anyone's knowledge.

"And what plan is that?" I ground out.

"Surrender, of course." Blood Moon's voice sliced the warm air. "You bind yourself to me and I will allow the gods to live."

"Why would you let the gods live when you worked so hard to get rid of them?" I asked, closing my fist around the flame in my palm.

She hesitated. "The gods have no powers left. The devouring and time travel ravaged them. *Tsk, tsk.* How sad to be reduced to useless children. Ah—I couldn't have planned it better myself, Zane."

I dug Fuego into the soft earth. No way was I going to throw up the white flag for nada. I mean, let's not forget this was the mastermind behind my dad's near execution. This was the master of deception who always seemed to be a few steps ahead. Ah-Puch was right. If she wanted me alive so bad, it was for a really big reason. "I'm not negotiating with mist," I finally said.

"Who said anything about negotiations?" Ixkik' said.

Bird shook his head. "Just let us torture him."

"Yes, it would be quite satisfying," Ixkik' said, "but let's not forget he has value to our long-term plans."

There was that word again. *Plans.*

"But I'm king," Jordan argued with Ixkik'. "Shouldn't *I* get to decide?" Instantly, a brilliant green-feathered headdress appeared on his head.

Was that his crown?

"Kings must sacrifice their heart's desire and rule with their minds!" Ixkik' growled. Her tone was a big fat warning: *Don't make me rip that crown off your head.*

But a monkey beat her to it. The little guy swept in out of nowhere, snatched the headdress off Jordan, and vanished in a fit of squeals before the jerk could react.

"Under my rule," Jordan yelled with a raised fist, "primates will be reduced to kitchen help!"

I couldn't help but snicker. "So, if he's king," I said to Bird, pointing at Jordan, "what does that make you? A second-class prince?"

Bird snarled, and before he could speak, Jordan cut in. "I'm the oldest. Oldest gets to be king."

"By fifty-eight lousy seconds," Bird spat.

"Boys!" Ixkik' warned, instantly silencing them. Then:

"Do you surrender, Zane? Because I have already captured so many gods—more every second—and my demons are eagerly awaiting my command to strangle the life from their pathetic throats."

Another god light flickered in the tree trunk like it was being smothered.

"STOP!" I screamed. Smoke trailed from my mouth and nose. My heart wanted to fight, but my mind told a different story. I had learned a few things about godly negotiations and how to use your one ace in the hole to get as much as possible.

"If I surrender," I said, "you'll let the gods go?"

"I'll let the pathetic creatures *live.*"

"Which means they'll be in prison," I said.

"A roomy prison," Bird offered as he rolled up his sleeves like he didn't expect this to end without a brawl.

I was curious what Blood Moon's final play was going to be. If I could anticipate it, I might be able to find a way out. "Why do you want *me* so bad?"

Jordan and Bird shared a glance. I thought they might bust up laughing, but they managed to keep it together. So Mom's plan was that nasty, eh?

"Enough talk," Ixkik' said. "Do you surrender in exchange for the gods' lives?"

It was an impossible choice. How could I agree to the gods being locked up forever? Shouldn't they get a say? And what about my friends? They were outmatched and outnumbered. *Unless,* I thought, *unless I can get Ixkik' alone and end her.* That would take the queen off the board. It would throw the demons into a tailspin and enrage the twins so much they wouldn't be able to see clearly enough to win a battle against a bunch of kick-butt godborns.

"How about we smoke out your friends," Ixkik' said, "and ask them what they think you should do?"

With the flick of Jordan's wrist, a few demons took off into the jungle. Before I could blink, a fire erupted beyond the trees. Billows of black smoke rose into the sky.

Itzamna released a pathetic cry.

"No!" I screamed, trying with all my strength to pull the fire into me, but it was growing too big too fast. Monkey shrieks carried through the jungle. "STOP!" I shouted.

"Choose!"

"I'll do it!"

The flames died as a thin stream of mist floated across the meadow along with Blood Moon's voice: "A deal with a god is binding," she said as the mist took the shape of a bony hand reaching toward me.

"On one condition," I said angrily. "You have to spare the gods—"

"We've established that," Ixkik' said in an annoyed tone.

"And you have to let my friends go. They have to leave here unharmed."

"Done!" Ixkik' said. "You will serve me for as long as I decide in exchange for your friends' freedom and the pathetic gods' lives."

Wait. Why had she agreed so quickly?

The phantom hand lingered in front of me, waiting. My gaze swept across the field, landing on the dragon. Itzamna's eyes were vacant, absent of any answers.

"I want collateral," I said, swinging my attention back to the mist that was Ixkik'. "Proof you will keep your word."

Bird sneered. "Like what?"

"I want to see Quinn."

Jordan and Bird shared a surprised glance.

"And I want you to let her escort my friends home." I knew that the godborns, Hondo, and Brooks would never leave here without a fight, and I thought that maybe, just maybe, Quinn could talk some sense into them. And if she couldn't, she had an army of demons that could force them to go.

Jordan rubbed his forehead, clenching his jaw so tight I thought he'd grind his teeth to powder.

"You can have ten seconds with her," Ixkik' said.

Jordan glowered at the Tree.

A few seconds later, a crow descended from the sky and landed right in front of me, shifting into Quinn. Her hair was dull and hung loosely around her face. She wore a long, simple black frock and a defeated expression.

"Zane," she said. Tears flooded her eyes, but they didn't fall. "I will take your friends to safety, and then I will return to . . ." She faltered. "To my husband. You have my word."

Jordan's expression was a combination of relief and suspicion.

Quinn began to back away, and as she did, she mouthed to me, *Don't be fooled.*

In that moment, every ounce of me hurt, like I had been pummeled in the wrestling ring for days. Fire erupted across the unburned parts of the jungle.

The phantom mist hand drew closer. "Shake!" Ixkik' shouted. "Or I burn it all down!"

"NO!" Quinn spun wildly. Enormous black wings sprouted from her back. Claws erupted from her fingers. "You promised my sister would go free!"

Ixkik' laughed. "I didn't promise anyone *else* would."

51

Quinn fully shifted back into a massive crow, shrieking like La Llorona as she took off into the darkening sky. But just as she got about twenty feet off the ground, a chain made of mist grabbed hold of her leg and held her in place. She struggled uselessly.

I reached for all the power in my storm runner leg, calling any bit of fire to me that would listen. Sweat trickled down my neck and back as the heat burned through my veins.

The ghost hand hung there, waiting.

"You can end all this with a simple handshake," Ixkik' hissed.

It's my fault she wants you, Itzamna managed. *I should have seen it.*

What are you talking about?

The power of the dragon.

What did that have to do with *any* of this?

Itzamna's voice was choked off by a hard tug and Jordan's laughter.

Bird's gaze landed behind me. A look of bewilderment swept across the twin's ugly mug. And then I heard a familiar voice outside. Mine!

"Guys," my voice said, "looks like you're making deals with the wrong Zane. How embarrassing."

I spun to find me—standing behind me! Marco? The dude even had Fuego—okay, it was a cheap imitation, but only I would know that.

The twins shared a *what-the-heck?* glance.

Marco stood at my side, smiling, waving the cane in the air like it was some kind of wand.

"Do you *want* more gods to die?" Bird said.

"If one more god light disappears from that tree," I said, jumping into action, "you'll never get the real Zane."

Ixkik' hissed angrily.

Jordan rubbed his chin. "Oh, I think we already have the real Zane. Unless you," he said, directing the question to Marco, "can shoot fire the way he can?"

Crap! I hated to admit it, but that was a really good next move.

Marco shrugged and held out his palm like he was waiting for a gold coin to be dropped into it.

Instantly, I created a cone of fire around Marco and me, wide enough so as not to scorch him and high enough that the twins couldn't see through it. "You have to get out of here!" I told him. "She's burning down the jungle!"

He smirked. "We have this brilliant plan. Adrik called Alana—telepathically, I mean—and . . ." He fanned his face. "Could you turn down the heat?"

"Alana's here?" I needed godborns to be leaving, not coming!

"No, she—"

Just then, another teenager's voice reached into my mind. *Get Blood Moon out in the open, Zane.*

Okay, I didn't recognize the voice, but I for sure recognized the tone. *Dad?* Rosie must have found him and woken him up!

A blast of thick mist killed the flames, leaving me and Marco visible again.

"Enough games!" Ixkik' growled. "Two godborns are even better than one. Get them, boys!"

Jordan and Bird flew toward us. Marco lifted his fake spear, and just as I raised my hands to release a torrent of fire, thunder rumbled. Lightning flashed. Everyone, even the demons, froze and looked up.

The sky split open with a crack and a boom. Hail pummeled the earth, followed by sheets of rain that doused the flames burning the jungle.

"Take that!" Marco shouted.

The water-hating demons shrieked and ran for cover.

"Come back, you fools!" Ixkik' yelled.

The field flooded so fast, I barely had time to process where the rain had come from. As if he could read my mind, Marco shrugged and grinned. "Louie was bored in Montana."

That's when all Xib'alb'a broke loose.

There was a bone-rattling shriek as I felt the rush of Brooks's wings overhead, and I thought I heard Hondo's voice somewhere in the commotion. I couldn't see Blood Moon's mist anymore. Quinn's chain vanished, and she flew off into the jungle. Jordan and Bird instantly shed their human forms, opting for their monstrous bat selves instead. They unfolded their leathery black wings, and their eyes glowed red as they took off into the stormy sky. To get Quinn, I guessed.

Marco's face changed back into his own, and he flashed a sinister grin. He moved like lightning, racing after the demons that had taken cover under the trees. Dragon-shaped shadows rose up from the soaked earth, their wings so massive they blocked out most of the daylight.

Ren!

"Kill the gods!" Blood Moon commanded, but I had no idea where she was or who she was talking to. Were there really demons holding the gods, just waiting for her cue?

Zane, Hurakan called telepathically. *Make her show her true face. Only then can you defeat her. Do you understand?*

I wanted to ask my dad what the heck he was talking about, but at the same moment, a sliver of fog lifted off the Tree's trunk and zipped into the jungle. Using Fuego, I ran after it.

I rushed into the dark web of half-burned forest. The mist snaked between the trees, faster and farther. Rain slammed against the earth, limiting my vision. I turned up the speed, bounding over fallen branches and twisted vines. Voices shouted in the distance. Thunder crashed.

And then the trail stopped. I was at a dead end. Heart pounding, I stopped and looked in every shadowed direction, but the mist was gone.

"Come out, Ixkik'!" I shouted, wiping my eyes.

In answer, a purplish-gray fog—so dense I couldn't see my own feet—wrapped around me. All sound vanished like I was underwater.

My brain raced in a thousand directions at once, never arriving at a solution that would (a) get me out of this and (b) get me out of this alive. Waves of nausea rolled through me, combined with anger that I had been so stupidly bold that I ran right into this trap.

Shivers gripped my body, and I clung to Fuego to calm them. "You wanted me.... Well, here I am!" I increased the heat under my skin to stop my teeth from chattering, because no way did I want Ixkik' to see how scared I was.

"Yes, here you are," she said slowly, quietly. "I knew the real Zane would follow me."

"Why don't you quit hiding behind your mist and face me?"

Ignoring my request, the goddess said, "I thought you were smart, godborn. Haven't you figured out my genius plan yet? Aren't you dying to know it?"

"It's not so genius if your demons are on the run and the gods are alive."

"That's of no consequence," she purred. "I'm sure your friends have run into my entire army by now, and the gods are weak and worthless."

My friends knew what they were doing. They wouldn't walk into some dumb demon trap...would they? As for the gods..."They'll get their powers back," I said. "And they'll come for you."

"Perhaps," Ixkik' said nonchalantly. "But it will be too late, and I have you to thank for that."

I tried to move forward, but the mist was like a blanket wound tightly around my legs. It swirled up my torso, sending an icy chill up my spine. The fact that Blood Moon was talking to me meant she wasn't ready to kill me. Not yet, anyway. "Me? I'll never help you, so I guess you'll have to find someone else."

"Oh, but there *is* no one else. You are Itzamna's chosen scribe."

"So?"

"The fool gave you—*you*—the power of the dragon."

Yeah, and a lot of good that was doing me now. "How does that help you?"

She didn't even hesitate. She couldn't wait to impress me with her plot. "The dragon represents both power and magic. And that means that you and you alone have the power to rewrite all I have destroyed."

Rewrite? *That* was her endgame? I pushed back my sopping hair, trying to put the pieces together. She had needed the stone to get into SHIHOM and the library, a place that Saás had said the gods couldn't access. Then Ixkik' had proceeded to burn the history books, but why?

"Pretty sure people will know fact from fiction," I said, wishing I wasn't glued in place.

"You are so simpleminded," she said. "No one will ever know, and I am done talking. It's time for us to begin."

I knew better than to believe that. She was dying to show me how smart she was, to dangle her power in my face. "So how does it work, exactly? You think I'm going to use some magic dragon power to write a bogus story while you keep me imprisoned? The truth paper won't let me." I took a deep breath and pushed my luck just one more inch. "Seems like you haven't thought this out very well."

The goddess laughed. "There is no such paper anymore. When I burned history, I burned truth itself!"

Gripping Fuego, I leaned forward. "What do you mean, 'truth itself'?"

"Those books . . . those words were more than history. When I destroyed them, a gap was created in the sobrenaturales' imaginations and memories."

A gap? I shook my head. "I still remember, and so do my friends." I didn't know if that last part was true, but I was pretty sure that if I could recall Maya history, they could, too.

Ixkik' exhaled dismissively. "Oh, the forgetting will come once I fill the gap. When *you* write a new history in which Jordan is king. All the sobrenaturales will know him as their only ruler, and they will hate the gods and godborns even more than they do now." She let out another exaggerated sigh. "It won't hurt too badly, Zane. You won't remember the past. You, too, will fall under the spell of your own words. Isn't that magnificent?"

I felt sick. Worse than sick. Of all the possible plans that had run through my head, this for sure wasn't one of them. She was going to make herself a hero and the rest of us villains.

"No way," I whispered, wriggling uselessly in the mist. "I won't do it."

"Oh, but you will, because I have a new pawn on the board."

The rain slowed to a fine sprinkle as the silvery-purplish

mist parted and slowly vanished into the air. I found myself in a dilapidated stone structure that looked like it had been bombed once or twice. Its arches and steps were battered and weather-beaten. Its walls and roof were half-gone.

Now that I was no longer wrapped, I could take a couple of steps forward. Flames erupted behind my eyes, coloring everything an angry red.

A woman materialized near the broken steps about fifteen feet away. She had her back to me, and thick silver hair cascaded to her waist. She wore a fitted green metallic dress that looked like it was made of lizard skin.

Make her show you her true face, Hurakan had said. *Only then can you defeat her.* I held back my fire. Waiting. Heart pounding.

Slowly, Ixkik' turned. Shock and terror gripped me so hard I fell back. My gasp ricocheted across the stone. I blinked, sure it was a trick of the shadows and light. But this was no trick.

The goddess had no face.

52

Did you get that? The goddess had NO FACE!

No eyes. No mouth. No anything! Where her face *should* have been, there was only a waxy-looking surface. Kind of like a bare Mr. Potato Head but way grosser.

Note to Hurakan: WHAT FACE?

"Do I look familiar, Fire Boy?" she cooed. "You've seen me before."

Fire Boy? Every inch of me froze. Where had I heard that before?

"Pretty sure I'd remember that," I said. Flames erupted under my skin. Man, did I want to launch a few at her, but I couldn't shake Hurakan's warning. What if I incinerated her too soon and ruined something?

"I was there at the twins' party in Beverly Hills," she went on. "The butterfly mask? You looked right at me. What a terrible night that was, the night you ruined my sons' destinies and all I could do was stand by and watch."

I stretched my memory to that night Brooks and Hondo and I had crashed the twins' fiesta. Brooks had pointed out the masked people. *That butterfly girl over there? She probably wants to be a model.*

Crap! Blood Moon had been there? Watching us? The idea of it sent chills down my spine.

"No?" she said. "Well, I'm quite certain you will remember this." She tipped her head down. I held my breath. She lifted her face. Bye-bye, Mr. Potato Head.

Hello . . . "Iktan?" I staggered back as shock waves rolled through me. Please, please, please tell me I hadn't spent three months with the enemy! "You . . . I . . . you . . . pretended to be a demon all this time?"

"I *am* a demon, Zane." Her blue skin stretched thin when she smiled.

"You're a . . . a . . . goddess," I argued.

"Of the waning moon," she clarified.

The *faceless* moon, I thought. "So you're what, like, part demon, part goddess?" What did that make the twins? Godborns *and* demons? Where was a chair (or better yet, a demon-burning flashlight) when I needed one?

Crappity crap crap!

That's why her poison had felt so powerful back in New York. It was god/demon poison! And that's how she had found us on our way to SHIHOM. She was there when Hondo and Ren called to tell me the claiming ceremony had been moved up. She knew we would be leaving early. "Not much of a power player among the gods, are you?" I spat out angrily.

"But look how the power has shifted."

Power. Shifted. Right. My senses flew back to me. This was my chance. But I had to be sure. "So, uh . . . is this . . . how you look for real? Just like any other demon? I would have thought, as a moon goddess, you'd be more special."

"Oh, but I am. The moon has many phases," she said. Her features melted like hot wax, dripping down her neck until I could see what was underneath. A paler-than-bone face, pockmarked and filled with spidery blue veins. She had no eyebrows, the same narrow eyes, a large round nose, and a wide mouth—probably to fit all those fangs.

Fire burned so hot inside me I didn't have to question the message. Yup, this was her true face.

Instantly, a flame erupted in my free hand, and I flung it at the goddess/demon/monster. Ixkik' batted it out of the air like it was nothing more than an empty soda can.

"Didn't the great Hurakan ever teach you to learn your enemy's strengths before you try to annihilate them?"

Was she immune to fire? I willed Fuego into spear mode and hauled my arm back faster than a flash of light. My spear ripped through the thick air only to smash into a wall of mist, which froze it in mid-flight.

Ixkik' laughed, flashing a mouthful of crooked fangs. Man, she could really use some orthodontics.

I watched as Fuego pulsed blue, struggling to break free of the goddess's magic. If my best weapons couldn't be used against her, how was I ever going to beat her? Hurakan might have been a powerless teen god, but I sure could have used his strategic mind at that moment.

"You said something about another pawn." Why did I have a sick, sinking, can-barely-take-a-breath feeling I was going to hate her next play?

"We'll get to that," she said. "But first, I want to make sure you paint me in the best possible light." Her dress shimmered as she came down the steps, drawing closer. She still reeked.

"And how's that?" I asked. "Evil?"

"See? There's the problem. Demons are always being demonized." She blinked her reptilian eyes. "My father was a great demon lord of Xib'alb'a," she said. "The demons followed and glorified him in ways the pathetic gods never would. I much preferred my demon brethren to the selfish, arrogant gods." She slowed down for this last part like she really wanted me to hang on to her every word. "And now I can finally let the demons rise to their appropriate status. I can reinstate my sons' greatness, which you stole from them. And *you* will help me by rewriting that history."

"I'm not going to steal people's memories and feed them lies!"

"Sounds like you could use some motivation," she said way too cheerily. "Ready to meet the pawn?"

Just then, I saw a shadow in the doorway. . . . But of what? Who?

Jordan (back in human form) walked into the crumbling structure.

He was carrying my mom by the throat.

53

Silence seemed to roll off the ruined walls in waves. Mom's eyes were fixed on me like she was trying to tell me something, but that jerk had his hand around her throat so tight she couldn't speak.

"Let her go!" I shouted.

Jordan smiled. "First tell me how brilliant we are."

Ixkik' looked at her son adoringly, like he wasn't the worst kind of monster.

"You want me to tell you your plan is brilliant?" I said. "Fine. It's brilliant."

"Not the *plan*," Bird said as he walked in. "My brother said to tell him how brilliant *we* are."

What were the twins doing here? I thought they had gone after Quinn. Had they already caught and imprisoned her? And what about Brooks? My insides collapsed.

Jordan squeezed my mom's throat tighter. Her eyelids began to flutter.

"You're brilliant!" I blurted. The blackest of smoke streamed out of my nose. The world smelled and tasted like ash. A few minutes earlier, all I had wanted to do was end Ixkik'. Now I only wanted one thing: my mom to be safe.

Ixkik' drew closer to my mom.

"I'll do it!" I was screaming now.

Why was Ixkik' getting so close to her? She ran a claw across my mom's chin. "What a pretty face," she said.

I couldn't hear much besides the *boom-boom* of my heart, which was about to shatter. "I just said I would do it! I'll shake your hand!"

Tears rolled down my mom's cheeks. She shook her head frantically.

"That's good, Zane," Ixkik' said. She extended her left arm across the fifteen-foot span to me like a Stretch Armstrong doll. Her veiny hand hung there, waiting.

"You'll let my mom and my friends go if I agree," I said, "and the gods will live."

Ixkik' bowed her head and blinked slowly. "You have my word."

I shook the demon goddess's cold, lifeless hand. Her arm retreated back to her side, but her right hand was still on my mom.

"Still, I need a backup plan," she said, "and believe it or not, I want you to be as comfortable as possible, since you'll be staying with us for a while."

"Yeah," Jordan added. "You should feel like you're surrounded by family."

Ixkik' swiveled her neck toward me, never removing her claw from my mom's chin. "Her face will look so good on me, don't you think? A snip here, a cut there, and voilà . . . all mine."

I gagged, then blurted out, "You said you'd let her go!"

"And I will," Ixkik' growled. "But you stole my sons'

futures. That deserves payback, so now I shall steal your mother's face."

Fire raced up my spine, ignited in my bones, and exploded in my head. I knew I only had one shot. I was a bomb detonating in three, two...

With one hand, I flung a massive fireball against the wall to the right, creating a distraction. While the enemies' attention was diverted, I blasted a stream of blue fire at the mist holding Fuego. Using the flames as if they were my own hands, I hurled my spear at Jordan faster than the speed of light. Unfortunately, it only grazed the side of his head. But it was enough to blind the jerk with a blast of dazzling light and force him to let go of my mom.

"Run!" I shouted as I threw a huge circle of black smoke around her. It wouldn't last long, but it would buy her a little head start. Bird took off after her as Fuego flew back into my hands.

Ixkik' released a guttural cry, spinning swirls of mist from her fingertips. I drop-rolled, avoiding her magic only by inches. The broken stone floor sliced my arms. Blood seeped out as I jumped to my feet, creating an inferno of fire all around me to block Jordan's advances. But it couldn't keep out Ixkik'.

The demon goddess's mist swept around me like a hurricane, dousing my flames. I launched Fuego at Jordan, who was coming at me with a ferocious look uglier than any demon. My spear ripped through his chest, but the guy kept coming.

Fuego circled back to me just as a swirl of fog wrapped its

poisonous arms around me. Invisible hands choked the air from my lungs.

"Stop!" Jordan shouted to his mom. "We need him!"

The goddess's mouth peeled back in a vicious snarl. The smell of sulfur and dead things spun through the air as I collapsed to my knees, gripping my throat, trying to break free.

Blood Moon's hate-filled eyes were glued to me. "You are bound to me now."

I gasped for air. Panic shredded my insides.

She squatted in front of me, so close I could count the veins pulsing in her forehead. She barely lifted one claw and the mist's grip loosened a little...enough for me to steal a breath.

"I need you for a while longer, godborn," she said, seething.

At the same moment, a thick shadow loomed behind Ixkik' and Jordan. Ren stepped out of it, as stealthy as a ninja. She held one finger to her lips as she twirled the time rope over her head like some kind of lasso queen. And that's when I knew what she was going to do—try to drop-kick Ixkik' into some kind of time warp.

YES!

One end of the rope snapped across the air like a sizzle of electricity. Ixkik' spun around. The mist choking me retracted and zipped across the space, stopping the rope in midair. Ren held the other end tight.

"How did you get this?" Ixkik' gasped as she inspected the golden cord, careful not to touch it.

Speechless for once, Jordan drew closer to the rope, too,

like it had some kind of hypnotic power. A golden light pulsed across the dim space.

"Let my rope go, Ixkik'," Ren growled as she tugged on her end.

The goddess, keeping her reptilian eyes fixed to the time magic, murmured, "It can be mine."

"I'll never give it to you!" Ren said.

With Fuego's help, I managed to stumble to my feet just as Brooks zoomed in as a hawk, ripped the rope away from the mist, and pitched it to her closest ally—me. The magic seared my hand worse than any acid, forcing an agonizing scream.

Dropping Fuego, I threw myself into the air and landed with a hard thud at the goddess's feet, close enough to try and throw the cord around her and Jordan's ankles. But they swept out of range so fast I missed, dropping the rope.

Ixkik' came at me, all claws and teeth, while Jordan lunged at Ren. Spiderlike shadows closed in on the twin. Thick legs surrounded him, and then a shadow web blasted out of their bulbous bellies, trapping him in place. I spun out of the goddess demon's grasp and swept myself up into a tunnel of flames.

"Your fire can't save you!" she yelled.

I looked up just as Brooks came in low, but this time she had a passenger that looked a whole heck of a lot like me. Dad? He rolled off her back and snatched up the loose end of the time rope. Agony swept across his face, but he didn't let go. He rushed Ixkik' from behind, wrapping the rope around her waist, barely keeping hold of the slack. The goddess demon wailed.

"Now, Ren!" I shouted.

Why wasn't she throwing Blood Moon into a time loop? Then I saw that Ren was struggling to hold on to her end as Ixkik' pulled at the rope, trying to break free. As powerful as Ren was, she couldn't give life to shadows and fight Ixkik' at the same time. Half a second later, the spider shadows holding Jordan vanished.

He flew at his mom, grasping for the cord.

"Free me!" she screamed.

For a split second, I was terrified that Ixkik' would just turn to mist and disappear, but then I realized this was why my dad had told me to make her show her face. Once she was trapped by the time rope, the demon goddess *couldn't* change forms.

Bird reappeared then, without my mom. Had she gotten away?

With an ear-piercing cry, Brooks zoomed in, grabbed Bird by the back of his collar, and carried him up into the night sky.

"Zane!" Ren shouted.

I spun to see Jordan knock Hurakan to the ground and grab a section of the rope. The jerk screamed as his skin sizzled. I lunged. We got tangled up, a wrestling blur of two godborns, struggling for the same prize. The cord scorched and burned every inch of skin it touched. I reached for the fire inside me but found nothing. The time rope was a power sucker.

Hurakan's voice raced toward me telepathically. *Get the rope around him, Zane!*

Jordan broke free and bolted toward his mother, who

was still trying to rip off the cord. Hurakan dove for him but missed by a long shot, landing with a double thud to his head that knocked him out.

"Zane!" Ren shouted. "I can't hold on much longer."

Jordan was unraveling the blistering rope around the demon goddess. I launched myself onto his back, seized the slack, and wrapped it around his throat. He wailed and shuddered.

"Get out of there, Zane!" Ren yelled. There was a burst of blinding light as I jumped back, but Ixkik' got her hands on my arm, gripping me so tight I couldn't distance myself. She put a loop around my wrist, searing my skin.

I tore at the rope, but its magic wouldn't release me. I summoned Fuego, and my spear zoomed over and began sawing the cord. Hot white sparks blinded me.

Everything spun violently. I was falling into space. Voices vanished. Darkness closed in.

Just when I thought I was gone, I felt strong hands grip me from behind. Tugging, twisting, breaking me free.

There was another flash of light so bright it was like a thousand suns were exploding. The earth shook once... twice. Then everything went still.

And I looked up at my rescuer.

54

"Mom?"

She fell to her knees and pulled me into a fierce hug, saying incomprehensible words broken up by her heaves and sobs.

"I'm okay," I reassured her. "See?" I pulled back and gave her a relieved but trembling smile. "All in one piece." Well, sort of, unless you counted all the gashes and burns the time rope had left on my arms, hands, and cheek, and the sheer terror still coursing through my veins. "Don't worry—Rosie'll fix me up."

"I could have lost you," she cried, her eyes wide with fear.

"But you didn't," I said. "You saved me. But how? How could you—"

"How could I, a mere mortal, save you?" she asked, a smile creeping onto her face. "Desperate moms have superpowers, didn't you know that?"

This time I was the one who pulled her into a hug.

"Zane!" Ren hurried over and threw her arms around both me and my mom, muttering, "That was too close," over and over and pretty much smothering us.

Hurakan groaned and turned onto his side. My mom's eyes fixed on him, and her expression froze when she saw the resemblance to me.

"Dad?" I helped him to his feet. It was muy cool that I was taller than him (by at least three inches). He rubbed the back of his head, grimacing. "This non-godly power stuff is dreadful."

Ren tapped his shoulder gently. "But it's not forever. I mean, you'll get your godliness back, right?"

He gazed at my mom, then looked away. "I imagine we will. Someday."

Someday was good enough for me, because it wasn't *never*.

"So Ixkik' and Jordan—" I began.

Ren cut in, "Are stuck in a time loop with no chance for parole. I wasn't sure I could even do it."

"You're sure they won't be coming back?" Mom asked. Her voice was still shaky.

Ren snapped the time rope, retracting it to the size of a ruler. "Positive."

"How . . . how . . . did you get the rope?" I asked, still dazed. "I thought only Pacific could use it."

She shook her head and sucked in a sharp breath. "Pacific knew the time rope was our only chance to get rid of Ixkik' for good." She hesitated, as if she couldn't believe she had possession of something so magical, so powerful. "It didn't work for her anymore, and after you left to face off with Blood Moon, we knew we had to do something drastic. That's when Marco came up with the plan to be you and throw Ixkik' off-balance."

Hurakan opened and closed his jaw like he had been clocked. Which he had. "Your mother sacrificed everything by giving that to you, Ren."

"Ren can't give it back?" I asked.

Hurakan shook his head, and Ren pressed her lips together. "It's definitely mine now," she said, "and I have a lot to learn. It almost slipped from my hands."

I tried not to imagine what would have happened in that event.

"Why didn't you just stop time?" I asked. Seemed like that would have saved us a lot of pounding.

"I tried," Ren said. "My watch doesn't work anymore, and even if it had—"

"You couldn't have also thrown them into a time loop," Hurakan put in. "Not simultaneously."

"Bird!" I shouted, remembering that Brooks had gone after him, which meant he was still a threat. "He's still free!"

"Bird's in a cage." Hondo's voice reached us before he walked in, hoisting an ax over his shoulder. His eyes darted everywhere before he let out a huge whoop. "I don't see the rest of the wicked familia around, so does that mean the plan actually worked?"

Actually? I wasn't about to ask how many time-loop practice runs Ren had been through. Probs none. I shuddered thinking how poorly all this could have turned out.

For the next couple of minutes, everyone talked over each other, telling me what had happened after I left Hurakan's tree house.

Ren said, "Rosie found your dad, and he told us that the only way to trap Ixkik' was to make her show her face, and that led us to figure out how to trap her, which led to Pacific giving up the time rope—"

Hondo cut in, "And Adrik was a boss. He took control, called his sister telepathically, because, man, we needed our friends to round up all the gods."

"And when I found out you were in trouble," Mom said, "I knew I had to come, too."

Just then, a loud roar from above caught all of our attention. We looked up to see a massive dragon, blue and shimmering, flying our way.

"Itzamna!" Ren shouted.

He had a teen passenger, and from the blazing eyes and murderous expression, I knew it was Ixtab.

The dragon perched on the remains of the roof, claws extended, and threw his head back to release a wave of fire that looked like it could incinerate the entire universe.

Hurakan said to me, "He wants to talk to you alone."

"You speak Dragon?"

"You don't?" Hurakan asked, and I couldn't tell if he was kidding or not.

Almost everyone took off toward the jungle. Mom, who'd been clinging to me, stretched my shirt as she left. My dad hung back.

"I thought he wanted to talk to me alone," I said.

"Who cares what he wants," Hurakan said. "I'm sticking around."

With a fiery snort, Itzamna floated down and shifted into his godly form. Teen Ixtab stormed over, glaring. "Zane Obispo! You are impossible to communicate with."

Whoa. Seeing the goddess of the underworld as a kid was weird. I felt like I shouldn't look directly at her, in case I laughed or something. But I didn't have a choice, because she was only inches from my face.

"Didn't you see I was inside Rosie?" she growled. "Can't you read hellhound signals? Howls? Fire colors in the pupils?"

"The orb," I whispered.

"Yes, the orb, you fool!" Steam practically rolled off Ixtab's head and I was super glad she didn't have her goddess powers right then. "I used the hellhound to keep an eye on things here, not knowing she would be my very lifeline, but getting you to listen to me was harder than turning a demon vegan!"

Hurakan said, "Zane rescued you."

Ixtab's eyes flicked to my dad, then back to me. "By the skin of his teeth."

"But you *were* rescued," Itzamna reminded the goddess. "We all were." Then, turning his attention to me, he added, "There's someone else we need to thank. Your uncle is the greatest shadow crosser I have ever seen. He truly saved us all."

A huge balloon of pride expanded in my chest. *The greatest shadow crosser ever.* Knowing Hondo, he was definitely going to have that printed on new business cards.

Itzamna went on. "This is a glorious day. Let's not ruin it with what might have happened and how close we were to annihilation, both literally and in the history books."

"Easy for you to say, Itzamna," Ixtab complained. "You aren't..." She glanced down at herself and groaned. "You aren't an adolescent!"

"You weren't in such great shape earlier," I said to the moon god, remembering his sickly gray self. "How'd you get better?"

"The gods might be in a weakened state," Itzamna said, "but with so many of them awake now, the Tree has been powered up, and me as well."

That gave me hope that everyone else would return to normal, too. I never thought I would say this, but I wanted that to happen soon, because hanging around with a bunch of angry teen gods might be worse than being with the angry old gods. "How long will...?" My eyes darted between Ixtab and Hurakan.

"We be like *this*?" Ixtab hissed. "It better not be long! I have an underworld to run, a spy network to oversee, demons to punish."

"There is no way to tell," Itzamna said, throwing a *chill-out* glance Ixtab's way. "But we are facing a bigger problem."

I clung to Fuego, wishing I never had to hear the word *problem* again. "What?"

"Our written history—the truth—has been completely destroyed."

Nodding, I said, "Ixkik' was going to make me rewrite it, to change sobrenaturals' memories, all because—"

"You are my chosen scribe with the power of the dragon," Itzamna said.

"Dragon this or that," Ixtab said, flipping her hair over her shoulder. "Who cares? Someone just needs to reconstruct what was lost. Looks like that's you, *godborn*."

All six god eyes were on me. "You want *me* to write the history? What do I know about it? Nothing! There...there has to be someone else."

"You're the only one who can," Itzamna said. "Well, technically, *I* could do it, but I am in serious need of a vacation and a float through some healing stardust." With one finger, he pulled on the lower lid of his left eye. "Look at these eyes. Puffy and bloodshot!"

"*You* need a vacation?" Ixtab growled. "I haven't had one in three centuries!"

As annoying as the gods were, and as tedious as it sounded to have to record centuries of history, seeing all those books go up in flames and knowing the truth could be stolen made me want to bring it back. "Okay, okay. I'll do it. But I'm going to need some help...."

"That's my boy," Hurakan said, which sounded really weird coming from a guy my age. "In the meantime, we will continue what we started at SHIHOM. But the godborn training will be incomplete without the truth, and our history will be in danger until we replenish it."

"There are other dangers," Itzamna said.

I rubbed my eyes and wished I was back on Isla Holbox, where I could toss all these problems and dangers to the bottom of the sea.

"Don't tell him all the horrors at once," Ixtab said, grinning.

I looked at the moon god expectantly.

He sighed and said, "Well, it does make for a more exciting ending to this tale."

I felt a pounding headache coming on. "Just tell me."

"Some of the godborns took off from Montana. We don't know where they went."

I was totally unsurprised. After all, Serena and a few of the others had publicly declared that they wanted to take down the gods, steal all the power and magic for themselves. But where had they gone? Did they really think they could hide from the gods? Okay, maybe they could at the moment, but that moment wouldn't last forever. "How many?" I asked.

Ixtab scowled, holding up five fingers. "I cannot wait to find the traitors and give them a long cruise down Blood River."

"You're offering cruises in the underworld now?" Ah-Puch popped out from behind a wall. He eyed Ixtab and covered his mouth like he might start laughing.

"Another word," she said, "and I will rip out your spine one vertebra at a time."

Ah-Puch held up his hands in surrender, a corner of his mouth curled up in a sly smile. "I was just going to say it's time for a serious party!"

Turns out the god of death meant it when he said *serious party*. It took two weeks to organize. The good news was that Itzamna postponed his vacation in order to attend, and in the meantime, he healed the scorched jungle. The bad news was that Ah-Puch was constantly hollering at the air spirits, whose "party standards were appalling at best." But once he told me he hadn't been invited to a fiesta in over a thousand years, I kind of understood why it was such a big deal for the guy.

When Ah-Puch wasn't party-planning, he and Hondo were prison-planning for Bird and Zotz. Let's just say they made a deal with Sipacna and the Four Hundred Boys. Yeah, the giant and ghosts were more than happy to take the villains off our hands, and something told me it was going to be pretty hellish for Bird and the teen bat god.

The godborns returned from Montana, except the rogue bunch that I really hoped someone else found waaay before Ixtab did. Blood River is pretty creepy—take it from someone who knows. Anyhow, they made us tell them the story of how we rescued the gods so many times I decided to write it all down. It only took a single night, thanks to magic paper and my having the power of the dragon. Ixkik' had lied about the paper being destroyed. At first, we couldn't find it, but then Itzamna discovered that the monkeys had stolen the stash during all the chaos. I felt kind of bad for the rascals when he reclaimed it, so I let them keep a few sheets. Sorry, Itzamna.

I also began rewriting true history, which should have taken a thousand years, but with the aid of Itzamna's magic, I would be done in a year, tops. To be honest, it wasn't half bad.

I had collected all the ashes from the bonfire and stuck them in a dozen huge stone vases. Whenever I sat down to write, the ashes would float into the air and whisper their stories to me. Rosie lazed about the biblioteca while I worked, perking her ears over every whisper. I guess hellhounds don't like ghosts too much.

The day of the party, Rosie seemed more restless than usual. She sniffed around all the library's corners and then lay down next to me with a sigh. She turned over and kicked her legs in the air, demanding a belly rub.

"I'm almost done," I said, writing the last sentence from

the ash whisper: *and the great land formed from the belly of the sea, glittering with gold.* I set down my pen and scratched my dog as her eyes rolled back with pleasure.

"She's a fine hellhound," Ixtab said as she walked into the temple.

I blinked. "You're . . . you're you again!" I said excitedly. "Are all the gods back to normal?"

With a groan, Rosie jumped to her feet and went over to Ixtab, nudging the goddess with her nose.

"Only a few of us," Ixtab said, patting Rosie's chest.

"Is my dad—"

"No," she said. "He's still an annoying teen, as is Ah-Puch. I really hope they return to godly status soon, because I'm tired of looking at a bunch of kids."

Rosie pawed Ixtab gently like she was trying to tell her something. My heart sank. What if she wanted to go back to Xib'alb'a with Ixtab? The goddess nodded at my dog, then zeroed in on me. "Are you going to the fiesta dressed like that?"

I glanced down at my SHIHOM uniform. "Isn't everyone?"

"Didn't you get the memo?" Ixtab said. "The air spirits are giving everyone a makeover. Well, as much as they can, given that you all are disgustingly part human."

"I'm good with how I look."

Ixtab smirked. "I came to say good-bye."

"You're not coming to the party?"

"I have an underworld to repair and demons to punish," she said. "And then there are the sobrenaturales who never got Itzamna's message. So I'm the only one capable of improving emergency response systems." She shook her head regretfully.

"But Adrik and Alana—"

"Will be just fine without me," she said, shifting her gold bracelets up and down her arm. "Besides, I already spoke to them, not that it's any of your business. They told me how brave you were, how . . . Well, it doesn't matter. You were there for them. So I have a parting gift for you."

"A gift?"

Just then, a circle of light surrounded Rosie—pink and gold with flecks of deep green. Oh no. What was Ixtab doing to her this time?

In a flash, Rosie was transformed.

My heart leaped into my throat.

It was my dog! My boxmatian!

"Rosie?" My voice squeaked, but I didn't care. I dropped to my knees as my dog bounded toward me, tongue hanging out of her mouth. I had missed that sweet face, that medium-size wiggly body. She sat down on her haunches and licked my face and neck excitedly, pawing my chest with her one front paw.

Tears filled my eyes. I looked up at Ixtab. "Thank you."

"She's still a hellhound," she said coldly. "Can change whenever she needs to. I couldn't risk her being defenseless, now, could I?"

I didn't care what Ixtab's reasoning was—or whether it was a thank-you to me, to Rosie, or the whole universe. I had my dog back. I had Rosie!

55

Dance music boomed across the jungle as Rosie and I made our way to the party. She leaped and loped like she had missed her old dog self, too.

Green and blue lights twinkled in the trees to the precise beat of the music. Monkeys leaped from branch to branch above me, smacking their lips and jabbering.

We came to the edge of the clearing, and I blinked in surprise. I didn't know the god of death had it in him, but man, the place looked awesome. New thatched-roof huts lined the borders, each lit up with torches and filled with tables of food and drink. The first two shacks were full of godborns. At least I *thought* they were godborns—it was hard to tell them apart from the teen gods.

At the center of the clearing was a glass dance floor with flashing blue, pink, and green lights. No one was dancing, but some kids were eyeing the space like they might take the risk. To my right was a waterfall, tumbling in slow motion so you could see winged golden fish leaping out of it in a coordinated dance.

Rosie startled as teen Pacific came up behind me. "Aren't you going to join the party?"

I patted my dog's head, hardly believing she was mine

again. "Aren't you?" I asked as I leaned against Fuego and took it all in, thinking how differently things could have turned out. It led to thoughts about snags in destinies, and how I might have ruined mine when I was inside of K'iin. Before I knew it, I was spilling my worries to Pacific about getting snagged in my destiny thread.

"Ah," she said. "And you didn't want to see?"

I shook my head. "Not if I couldn't change it."

"What if it was a *good* snag?" she asked. "A twist in the road that leads you to something you might have never found otherwise."

A *good* snag? "Oh . . . I just assumed . . ."

Rosie settled onto her side and began licking her paws. Have I mentioned how beautiful she is?

"Maybe you should stop assuming."

It felt like a huge weight had been lifted from my shoulders, and I turned my gaze back to the party with a totally different outlook. *Good snag.* I liked the sound of that.

"And what about Ren?" I asked. "The favor she owes K'iin."

"She made an honest deal, so that will be up to K'iin to collect when the time comes," she said casually. "But perhaps I can help alleviate the weight of the favor."

"That's good," I said. I mean, who wants to owe a mighty all-seeing calendar *anything*?

Ixchel and Ah-Puch were barking orders at the earth and air spirits, who had given up their strike when the gods gave them a raise and more vacation time. But clearly the spirits hadn't earned any more respect.

Speaking of spirits, I kept my promise to Kip and asked the

gods to give him a bigger greenhouse. Hopefully it wouldn't come with bigger centipedes, too....

My mom and dad were sitting at a table, sipping some gran blue drinks out of straws. They were talking and laughing like they hadn't seen each other in a millennium, and maybe this sounds corny, but I was happier in that moment than I think I had ever been.

Quinn and Hondo made their way to the dance floor, and let me just tell you that Hondo can't dance. Like at all. He jerks his arms and legs around like a badly strung puppet. But Quinn didn't seem to mind. Maybe because Itzamna had told them Jordan's date with a time loop meant she was no longer married to him. Plus, the moon god was going to bend the law about humans and sobrenaturals mixing, since Hondo had shown "sobrenatural bravery."

Ren, Marco, Adrik, and Alana headed to the floor next, jumping up and down to the beat. Louie joined them, doing a moonwalk with a monkey on his shoulder. I realized then that we were a family, and it had taken everyone's talents to beat our enemy: Louie's snow, Alana's gateways, Adrik's memory stealing, Marco's cloning, and Ren's time rope.

And Brooks's water powers. Without her, we never could have gotten the devourer out of that tank. I scanned the crowd until I spotted her on the far end of the clearing, glancing around like she was looking for someone.

Rosie whined. Her ears perked sharply as her eyes landed on Brooks, too. Brooks was wearing a white tank-top dress and she had her hair in a loose ponytail draped to one side like she couldn't decide if she wanted to let her hair down or not. Pacific must have seen me watching her.

"Did you ever wonder why you connected with her so quickly when you first met?" the time goddess asked.

Her question threw me off guard. My cheeks flared. How did she know that? Was *anything* secret from the gods?

"Nah," I said, shrugging it off. "She had a drawing of a demon on her folder."

But it was more than that. I knew it then, and I knew it now. Brooks got me, like, really got me, even though I annoyed her half the time. We always had each other's backs. And no matter how much time we spent apart, our link only grew stronger. As soon as she walked (or flew) onto the scene, I felt like everything would turn out okay no matter what. Even when monsters and gods were trying to crush us.

"Maybe there was a connection because you had already met her," Pacific said in a way that told me she already knew the answer.

"Huh?"

"I couldn't figure it out at first," she said, tapping her chin. "But then you went to 1987, and it made me wonder: Did something happen there?" she asked. "Something strong enough to create a bond with Brooks way before the two of you were born?"

Rosie let out a little groan.

Something? Like a kiss? Oh, crap! Had Brooks and I somehow changed the future?

Brooks's eyes locked with mine, and she started to walk over, which I guess Pacific took as her cue to leave.

I met Brooks halfway, ducking a monkey that was trying to swipe Fuego.

Brooks laughed as the monkey ran off, shrieking in frustration. Then her eyes landed on Rosie, and she fell to her knees to welcome my dog. "Rosie?" she squealed. "I can't believe it!"

The boxmatian ate up every stroke, scratch, and hug that Brooks gave her while I explained what Ixtab had told me. Rosie sniffed the air and took off toward whatever scent she had caught.

"So what now?" Brooks asked. "I mean, the world isn't ending, and there aren't any castles to storm."

"We could be normal?" I said, thinking that sounded perfect.

"A normal godborn and a normal shape-shifter," she said, nodding as she tapped her feet to the music.

"And a normal dog," I said, still wearing a goofy grin.

Brooks frowned. "Well, one thing isn't normal. I mean . . . I think we messed up."

"What? How?"

She hesitated. Her eyes flicked to the fiesta. "We kissed."

My heart flopped like a fish out of water. I thought she was going to pretend that never happened—let it stay in 1987.

Crap. Say something, Zane. Say something really smooth.

"Is that bad?"

NOT SMOOTH.

Shrugging, she said, "Don't know. It was in 1987, which means..."

"What?"

She glanced up at me. "I don't think it counted."

Uh, yeah, I didn't know what she meant by *counted*, but it happened, and what did it matter when it happened?

Before I could stick my foot in my mouth with more dumb words, Brooks said, "I mean...unless..."

"Unless what?"

"Unless you think it was real...I mean, like, technically, it wasn't, right?"

"Uh..." I gripped Fuego to keep from falling over. Yup, I was really good at this pouring-out-your-heart stuff. But then it was like my mouth got way ahead of my brain. "Yeah," I said, nodding. "I mean yes, it didn't count...I mean..."

Tell her what you mean, Zane!

Brooks tucked a stray curl behind her ear. "So we haven't had a first kiss, then, I guess."

Oh. OH!

And before I said another dumb thing, I leaned over and kissed her. Not a rushed kiss, or a life-or-death kiss, or even a good-bye one. Just a regular kiss. Between a normal godborn and a normal shape-shifter.

The music blared. My heart raced.

Brooks looked up at me, smiling. "I love this song!" Then she bounced toward the party.

"Where are you going?" I called after her, thinking I might start floating.

"Come on," she said over her shoulder. "Let's dance."

I didn't know what my destiny strand had in store for me the next month, or year, or five years. I didn't know what was going to happen to the gods or the rogue godborns. But maybe I didn't need to know. Maybe that was the best part of life: figuring out the now.

And right now, I was going to dance.

EL FIN

GLOSSARY

Dear Reader:

This glossary is meant to provide some context for Zane's story. It in no way represents the *many* Maya mythologies, cultures, languages, pronunciations, and geographies. That would take an entire library. Instead, this offers a snapshot of how *I* understand the myths and terms, and what *I* learned during my research for this book. Simply put, myths are stories handed down from one generation to the next. While growing up near the Tijuana border, I was fascinated by the Maya (as well as the Aztec) mythologies, and I was absolutely *sure* that my ancestors were related to the gods. Each time I've visited the Maya pyramids in Yucatán, I've listened for whispers in the breeze (and I just might've heard them). My grandmother used to speak of spirits, brujos, gods, and the magic of ancient civilizations, further igniting my curiosity for and love of myth and magic. I hope this is the beginning (or continuation) of your own curiosity and journey.

Ah-Puch (*ah-POOCH*) god of death, darkness, and destruction. Sometimes he's called the Stinking One or Flatulent One (Oy!). He is often depicted as a skeleton wearing a collar of dangling eyeballs of those he's killed. No wonder he doesn't have any friends.

Akan (*ah-KAHN*) god of wine

Ak'Ek (*AHK EHKH*) the Mayan name for the constellation Orion, meaning *the Turtle Star*

Aztec (*AZ-tek*) the term often used now for **Mexica**, one of the peoples indigenous to Mexico before the Spanish conquest of the sixteenth century. The word means *coming from Aztlán*, their legendary place of origin. The Mexica did not refer to themselves as Aztecs.

Bakab (*bah-KAHB*) four divine brothers who hold up the four corners of world, and all without complaining about having tired arms

Camazotz (*KAH-mah-sots*) a Maya bat god who, before he was exiled, lived in the House of Bats in Xib'alb'a, where his job was to bite off travelers' heads

Ceiba Tree (*SAY-bah*) the World Tree or Tree of Life. Its roots begin in the underworld, grow up through the earth, and continue into paradise.

Chaac (*CHAHK*) the Maya rain god

Chak Ek' (*CHAHK EHKH*) Mayan name for the planet Venus

chapat (*chah-PAHT*) Mayan for *centipede*

Hurakan (*hoor-ah-KAHN*) god of wind, storm, and fire. Also known as Heart of the Sky and One Leg. Hurakan is one of the gods who helped create humans four different times. Some believe he is responsible for giving humans the gift of fire.

Itzamna (*IT-sahm-na*) a Maya creator god associated with writing

Ixkakaw (*eesh-ka-KOW*) goddess of the cacao tree and chocolate

Ixkik' (*sh-KEEK*) mother of the hero twins, Jun'ajpu' and Xb'alamkej; also known as the Blood Moon goddess and Blood Maiden. She is the daughter of one of the lords of the underworld.

Ixtab (*eesh-TAHB*) goddess (and often caretaker) of people who were sacrificed or died a violent death

Ix-tub-tun (*eesh-toob-TOON*) a stone-spitting goddess

Jun'ajpu' (*HOON-ah-POO*) one of the hero twins; his brother is Xb'alamkej. These brothers were the second generation of hero twins. They were raised by their mother (Ixkik') and grandmother. They were really good ballplayers, and one day they played so loudly, the lords of the underworld got annoyed and asked them to come down to Xib'alb'a for a visit (no thanks!). They accepted the invitation and had to face a series of tests and trials. Luckily for them, they were clever and passed each test, eventually avenging their father and uncle, whom the lords of the underworld had killed.

Kab'raqan (*kahb-rah-KAHN*) Mayan for *earthquake*; a giant and brother to Sipacna

k'iin (*KEEN*) Mayan for *sun* or *day*

K'ukumatz (*koo-koo-MATS*) (also known as Kukuulkaan) one of the creator gods. He is said to have come from the sea to teach humans his knowledge. Then he went back to the ocean, promising to return one day. As Kukuulkaan, he is known as the Feathered Serpent. According to legend, he slithers down the steps of the great pyramid El Castillo at Chichén Itzá in Yucatán, México, on the spring and autumn equinoxes; festivals are held in his honor there to this day. El Castillo is definitely a cool—but also hair-raising and bone-chilling—place to visit.

Kukuulkaan (*koo-kool-KAHN*) see Kʼukumatz

Mexica (*meh-SHEE-ka*) a Nahuatl-speaking group of people indigenous to Mexico before the Spanish conquest of the sixteenth century. Now commonly referred to as Aztecs.

Nakon (*nah-CONE*) god of war

nawal (*nah-WAHL*) a human with the ability to change into an animal, sometimes called a shape-shifter

saás (*sah-AHS*) Mayan for *light*

Saqikʼoxol (*sock-ee-kh-oh-SHOLE*) the White Sparkstriker, a being who lives in the woods, wears a red mask, and dresses entirely in red. The Sparkstriker pounded lightning into the first daykeepers (diviners).

Sipacna (*see-pahk-NAH*) an arrogant giant who was killed by the second-generation hero twins when they dropped a mountain on him; according to Maya legend, he killed four hundred boys at once

Tlaltecuhtli (*tlah-tek-OOT-lee*) the Mexica earth goddess, whose name means *the one who gives and devours life*

Xbʼalamkej (*sh-bah-lam-KEH*) one of the hero twins; see Junʼajpuʼ

Xibʼalbʼa (*shee-bahl-BAH*) the Maya underworld, a land of darkness and fear where the soul has to travel before reaching paradise. If the soul fails, it must stay in the underworld and hang out with demons. Yikes!